Truly Yours

Barbara Metzger

D1009183

SIGNET ECLIPSE
Published by New American Library, a division of
Penguin Group (USA) Inc., 375 Hudson Street,
New York, New York 10014, USA
Penguin Group (Canada), 90 Eglinton Avenue East, Suite 700, Toronto,
Ontario M4P 2Y3, Canada (a division of Pearson Penguin Canada Inc.)
Penguin Books Ltd., 80 Strand, London WC2R 0RL, England
Penguin Ireland, 25 St. Stephen's Green, Dublin 2,
Ireland (a division of Penguin Books Ltd.)
Penguin Group (Australia), 250 Camberwell Road, Camberwell, Victoria 3124,
Australia (a division of Pearson Australia Group Pty. Ltd.)
Penguin Books India Pvt. Ltd., 11 Community Centre, Panchsheel Park,
New Delhi - 110 017, India
Penguin Group (NZ), 67 Apollo Drive, Rosedale, North Shore 0745,
Auckland, New Zealand (a division of Pearson New Zealand Ltd.)
Penguin Books (South Africa) (Pty.) Ltd., 24 Sturdee Avenue,
Rosebank, Johannesburg 2196, South Africa

Penguin Books Ltd., Registered Offices:
80 Strand, London WC2R 0RL, England

First published by Signet Eclipse, an imprint of New American Library,
a division of Penguin Group (USA) Inc.

First Printing, September 2007
10 9 8 7 6 5 4 3 2 1

PUBLISHER'S NOTE
This is a work of fiction. Names, characters, places, and incidents either are the
product of the author's imagination or are used fictitiously, and any resemblance
to actual persons, living or dead, business establishments, events, or
locales is entirely coincidental.
    The publisher does not have any control over and does not assume any respon-
sibility for author or third-party Web sites or their content.

For Valentino, my new best friend

Chapter One

1793

"Why do people tell lies, Papa?"

Lord Royce wiped the blood from his little boy's nose. "Because they can, son. Just because they can."

"But you told me to tell the truth. Always."

The earl sighed. "And I am certain most fathers tell their sons the same thing. But children do not always listen. Is that what the fight was about?"

The child nodded. "Timmy Burdock said it was Cousin Daniel's dumb old idea to steal the apples from Widow Flood's orchard. I called Timmy a liar and he hit me, so I hit him back."

"Why didn't Daniel hit him?"

"Because Daniel is so much bigger. That wouldn't have been fair, would it?"

Lord Royce dipped his handkerchief in a basin of water his manservant brought, admiring the boys' code of honor, but wishing his slightly built son would not feel duty bound to defend his bigger cousin. Seeing blood drip from his precious child's nose tore at his heart, even if the cause was a boyish squabble. "So what happened then, and how did you get so wet?"

"Widow Flood threw a bucket of water on us. And she's going to tell the vicar." He shivered, but not with the chill of his damp clothes. "She says Vicar will cane all of us. Will he, Papa?" The six-year-old raised his blue eyes to the earl—the same black-rimmed, heavily lashed sapphire eyes all the Royce males possessed.

Lord Royce could not lie to the boy. He never had, and would not start now. "For lying and fighting, and for stealing the apples? He just might."

"Daniel, too? It wasn't his idea, and he didn't hit anyone."

If the notion to trespass on the crotchety old widow's property was not Timmy Burdock's, and not Daniel's, the earl had a good idea whose idea it might have been. "Perhaps if you confess, and offer to help stack Mrs. Flood's wood for her after lessons at the vicarage, then Daniel might get off with a scold, although he did eat some of the apples, I'd wager. No one should ever take anything from another—not his good name, not even a mere apple. Do you understand?"

Young Rex, as Jordan, Viscount Rexford, was called, hung his head. "Yes, Papa. But Timmy should not have lied, either."

For a moment the earl was afraid— But no, of course Rex knew who had plotted the orchard theft, since Rex himself was the culprit. Then his boy said, "But how did Widow Flood not know Timmy was lying?"

The handkerchief fell to the floor at the earl's side. "How should she know, son?" he asked, holding his breath for the answer he knew was coming, the one he'd been dreading for years, ever since the boy's birth.

Rex's dark brows knitted in confusion. "Can't everyone tell the difference between a lie and the truth?"

"Can you, Rex?"

The boy smiled, showing a gap where a tooth was missing. "That's silly. Of course I can."

The earl knelt to his son's level and stared into those eyes, so much like his own. "What if I said I bought you a real horse for your next birthday, not another pony?"

The child threw his arms around his father and kissed him noisily on the cheek. "Oh, Papa! That's capital! That's what Daniel says, you know."

Lord Royce slipped out of his son's enthusiastic embrace, sweet though it was, despite the dampness. He could feel beads of sweat breaking out on his own skin. "What if I said the mare's name is Cowslip?"

"Why, that's a clanker, Papa. What is her name?"

"Molly Mischief?"

Rex shook his head no, now smiling at the game.

The earl studied the boy's face for a sign that he was guessing. Rex looked as certain as if his father had said the sun would rise tomorrow. "Very well. Your new horse's name is Angel."

"No, it isn't."

"Midnight?"

Rex jumped up and down. "Oh, Papa, does that mean she is a black? That's just what I wanted, you know."

He knew. But how did Rex know that name was the correct one? The earl lifted his son to sit on his lap in the worn leather armchair, glad he could still cuddle with this boy he loved so much, and wanted so much to protect. His son would grow past kisses and confidences soon enough. Why, he was in long dresses just yesterday, it seemed. Now he wore short pants and skinned knees, bloodied noses instead of diapers. The earl sighed and said, "Tell me, Rex, can you always tell when someone is lying? Not just a guess, and not just when you know the truth?"

"Like when Cook says there are no more macaroons, because she is saving some for her own supper, or when Nanny says she is visiting her sister on her afternoons off?"

The earl vowed to find out exactly where the nursemaid was going on her free time, and why Cook would lie to the boy, but not now. "Like that. How do you know? How do you know I did not eat the rest of the macaroons, or that Nanny is not going where she says?"

Rex frowned and hunched his shoulders. "I just do. Don't you know, Papa?"

Lord Royce brushed back his son's dark curls and kissed his forehead. "Yes, I do. I was hoping you did not."

"I don't understand, Papa."

"No, I do not suppose you do. I will do my best to explain, but I fear I cannot understand all of it myself."

Rex nodded solemnly. "That's true."

"I always tell you the truth. Except when we are playing games, like before." When the boy just stared up at him expectantly, the earl cleared his throat and went on: "Not everyone can tell a lie from the truth. Only a lucky few."

"You mean I can tell Vicar that Timmy wanted to steal the apples, and Mr. Anselm will believe me?"

"No, that is not what I mean. Not at all. You must not lie, ever, not even if you will not be found out. You have a gift, and must treat it honorably."

"Like my horse?"

"Yes. Just as you must care for the mare and never mistreat her, you must also show respect for this other gift."

"I do not know if I want this one, Papa."

"I am afraid you have no choice. Men in the Royce family have had the truth-seeing back through the ages. Now, it seems, you do, too."

Rex considered that for a moment. "And no one else does?"

"No, and you must never tell anyone of this gift, for they will think you . . . odd." Just how odd, the earl did not want to tell his son; how the talent for truth-seeing was frightening to some, horrifying to others—including Lord Royce's own wife, Rex's mother. But he had to make the boy understand. "One of our ancestors, Sir Royston, was hanged as a wizard."

Rex's dark blue eyes grew round as he thought of Merlin and magic and all the creatures in his fairy stories. "You mean I can change Timmy Burdock into a toad?"

"No. I mean Sir Royston's ability to recognize the truth was so uncanny, so different from what other people knew, that they thought he was sent by the Devil. He was not, of course. Such a gift"—if a gift it was, and the earl was never sure—"could only come from heaven. His son, and all of the Royce sons who came after, were more careful. They became magistrates and ambassadors and advisors to the Crown, all positions where knowing the truth was valuable, but they never let on about the talent." They'd become wealthy through knowledgeable investments, well titled for service to the country, and well respected for their sense of honor. "People admired them as wise men."

"Like you, Papa. Daniel's mother says you are the bestest, fairest judge in all of England."

The earl laughed. "Daniel's mother is my own sister. You must not put credit in her boasting."

Rex shook his head. "No, it's true. I can tell, remember."

"And if I say you are the best son in the entire world, would you believe me?"

With a gap-toothed grin the boy replied, "Of course, it is true-blue," which earned him another hug.

"Soon you must learn to be a bit more discriminating between truth-saying," the earl said, "and when someone believes what they say; when it is true to them. Of course your aunt Cora believes I am wise beyond measure. That does not necessarily make it true."

"It is true," Rex insisted.

"Thank you, my lad. But other judges' families must also consider their relative the wisest, just as every patriot believes his country the finest, and every believer feels his religion is the only path to heaven. The truth is not always black and white, you see."

"Of course not. It is blue."

"Pardon? The truth is blue?"

Now the boy looked uncertain. "That's what I said. Don't you know it, Papa? Can you not see it?"

"Do you mean the truth is . . . a color to you?"

"Of course. When someone lies, that's red. When they *think* they are telling the truth, like you just said, then it's yellow. Vicar Anselm talks yellow a lot. Except when he tells Mrs. Anselm's mother she is welcome to come visit. That's a big fat red lie. And sometimes people say things that are like rainbows, because they don't know, but hope so, I guess. And sometimes their words are all mud-colored—when they are confused, I think. Don't you see the colors when people talk?"

"No, I don't. I hear the truth in their words, like the purest note. A lie jangles, like when the pianoforte is out of tune, or when a church bell is cracked. My father said he always got a headache when a lie was told, and his father could smell the truth. One of our ancestors grew hot or cold, and another felt a buzzing in his ear. You see, the gift appears to everyone differently. No Royce ever saw colors, not that I ever heard of, so your gift is special, lucky boy."

The earl was not sure his son was so lucky after all, and now that he knew the boy could sense his uncertainty, he explained: "Sometimes even the most wonderful of gifts has disadvantages. What if Midnight bolts at thunderstorms or gnaws on the paddock gates? What if your old pony grows sad when you ride Midnight instead? Just so, knowing the truth is not always comfortable."

"Like?"

"Like when I say I will punish you for stealing Widow Flood's apples if Mr. Anselm does not. You know it is true, but you might wish it otherwise. Or when your friends tell fibs rather than hurt your feelings. White lies, they are called."

"Like when Nanny says I look handsome, even with my tooth missing? I know she is telling a Banbury tale."

"Or when we went into the village yesterday, and the apothecary told Mrs. Aldershot what a pretty baby she had, and told Lady Crowley her bonnet was charming. Such sour notes I heard! But just think if they knew he was lying. Their feelings would be hurt."

Rex giggled. "Not as much as if he said the baby

looked like a monkey and the hat looked like a coal scuttle."

The earl ruffled his son's curls. "Those are polite lies, and you will have to get used to them if you want to go out in the world."

"Will I have to tell them?"

"Of course not. You can be polite without speaking a falsehood. You can tell Mrs. Aldershot how amazingly small her infant's hands are, and tell Lady Crowley that her new hat suits her. Or you can say nothing at all. Just tip your hat and smile."

"The way you did, Papa?"

"Precisely. But there is a worse disadvantage to our gift than knowing false compliments for Spanish coin. Sometimes people will fear you. They cannot understand how you know they lie, and so they are afraid you can read their thoughts. Then you lose their trust, or else they are wary of saying anything at all."

"Is that what happened with Mama?"

"No, she—" He could not lie, not to his own son. "Yes. Partly. There were other reasons she left, reasons that had nothing to do with truth or lies."

They were both silent, thinking of the countess so far away in London. They were both wondering what they could have done or said to change her mind and make her stay. They were both missing her. The earl was drinking to dull his pain; the boy was fighting to relieve his anger. They both had tears now in their similar, startling blue eyes.

After a bit, Rex used the bloodied handkerchief to blow his nose. "Do you think she is coming back?"

"What did she tell you?" Lord Royce asked, hope tiptoeing through his heart.

"She said she would."

"And . . . ?"

The boy understood the unspoken question. "And it was all muddy."

And that was why people lied.

Chapter Two

1813

Twenty years later, Viscount Rexford was once more in his father's library, once more wounded, confused, and in despair.

Lord Royce wished with all his heart that he could hold the boy, kiss away his hurt, make everything better with the promise of a new horse. But his little boy was a soldier, and war was not something a father could make disappear. Rex's leg might heal, the scar on his cheek might fade, but those wounds to his soul, Lord Royce feared, were something Rex would carry for the rest of his life.

At least he had come home. Too many fathers' sons had not. Timmy Burdock would not bedevil the neighborhood ever again, and Daniel, the earl's nephew, was in London, by all reports drinking himself to death, trying to accomplish what the French had not. The three had joined up, for England and for the adventure, despite their families' anguish. Timmy had gone as a common foot soldier, but the earl had bought colors for his son and nephew when he could not convince them to stay safely in England. For that matter, they had been getting into too much trouble in Town, Rex's hidden talent causing whispers of cheating and bribery and unfair advantages. Where Rex went, Daniel had to follow, as usual.

No one was about to allow the only heir to an earldom to face the enemy, so Lord Royce used his remaining influence—and a shadowy connection at the War Office called the Aide—to have them assigned to a noncombat division. The Aide was one of a handful of people who knew about the family's truth-seeing, and he saw a great need for Rex's gift. With the viscount's unique talent and his cousin Daniel's intimidating size, the two had risen through the ranks, attached to the Intelligence Service. They had become known, and widely feared by both French and British troops, as the Inquisitors, Wellesley's most valued team of interrogators. Their methods were kept blessedly hushed, but they seldom failed to provide necessary, infallibly accurate information from captured prisoners, enabling the generals to plan their strategies and protect their own forces. Lauded by the commanders, the cousins were distrusted by their fellow officers. Spies were already considered less than honorable, and whispers of torture or Dr. Mesmer's new hypnotism or outright sorcery contributed to the stigma of the fact-gathering department. The Inquisitors never had to resort to barbarous tactics, of course, but the commanders found it expeditious to fan the rumors. The other young officers were glad to have the Inquisitors' findings, but they steered clear of the cousins. Captain Lord Rexford's piercing blue gaze saw into a man's very soul, and Lieutenant Daniel Stamfield's huge hands were always clenching, as if itching to choke the life out of his next unfortunate victim.

Then Daniel had to sell out when his father passed away. Rex was grievously wounded shortly afterward, perhaps because he did not have his stalwart companion defending his back. Daniel believed that, anyway, according to his mother, and was submerging his grief and guilt in a sea of Blue Ruin.

Now Rex was home, too, for what that was worth, and for all the earl saw of him. The young man had found his own way to cope with a crippled leg, an empty future, a world of nightmarish memories. Rex could not tramp across the countryside, but he could ride endlessly, and he could sail toward the horizon, not having to speak to anyone, not having to see their pity—or their fear. His only company was an enormous mongrel he'd rescued on his wanderings, an ungainly mastiff bitch who was utterly devoted to him. Rex named her Verity, because she alone among all females never lied to him. When he rode too far or too fast, Verity sprawled across the front door of Royce Hall, waiting. When he took his boat out on days fit for neither man nor beast, the big mastiff lay on the dock, waiting. She never ate while he was gone, never barked, and never let anyone touch her. Sometimes the earl would sit beside the dog, waiting too, worrying that he might still lose his only child—not to war, but to a reckless, nameless grief.

What could a father do? The earl pulled the blanket closer around his knees. He was not old, but he was not strong either, with a stubborn, debilitating cough that came every winter, and took longer to leave with each passing spring. More than that, he was a near recluse himself, seldom leaving the Hall, rarely entertaining company. He read his law books and occasionally contributed an article to a legal journal, but he was no longer one of the highest-ranking judges in the land, not since the scandal. Now Lord Royce was a rural justice of the peace, adjudicating disputes between his neighbors: straying cows, unpaid bills, verbal contracts gone awry. Rarely, when a prisoner of the assizes courts was desperate, Lord Royce might be called on to lend his legal expertise. Other times, if a case interested him, he might do some investigating on his own, when he had the energy to visit the prisons, to see for himself if the accused were truly guilty.

He had thought Rex would help him when the boy got home. Rescuing the innocent from a harsh justice system seemed a worthy crusade for a retired young warrior, especially one who could tell in an instant when the witnesses were lying, when the prosecutors were supplying false evidence. Rex had not been interested, preferring his bone-numbing, brooding excursions.

Such solitude was not good for the lad, Lord Royce knew. How could the earl not know, having spent almost half of his own life alone? Such loneliness sapped a man's strength and sometimes even made him wish for an end to the aching sorrow. Lord Royce brushed a bit of traitorous dampness from his cheek as he remembered the empty space in his own life, the empty rooms attached to his where his countess should have slept. He quickly replaced those memories, as always, with the image of the beautiful little blue-eyed sprite who used to laugh and giggle and bounce on his lap. It was too late for him, but the earl could not let his heir, his beloved boy, dwindle into a broken, bitter old man like himself. No, he *would* not, not while he had breath in his body.

The earl reached for the letter on the table by his side

and smoothed out the creases. Maybe this piece of paper held the answer.

This could not be happening to her.

How many hundreds of prisoners had cried out the same thing? Two or ten thousand, Amanda did not care. This simply could not be happening, not to her. God have mercy, for she had not done anything wrong!

Well, she had, if one could call stupidity a crime. And she had, indeed, argued with Sir Frederick Hawley. Of course she had; he was a bounder of the blackest sort. Amanda and her stepfather had argued frequently since her mother's death five years ago. How else was Amanda to see that the servants were paid, that his own young son and daughter were properly cared for, that their house did not fall down around their ears? Sir Frederick was a miser, a mean, dirty-tempered, dirt-in-his-pores dastard. And he was dead.

He'd been all too alive that morning when they had fought over Amanda's latest suitor. The heir to a barony was going to call to ask for her hand in marriage—and Sir Frederick said he was going to refuse, again. It was not that Amanda loved Mr. Charles Ashway, but he was a pleasant gentleman who would have made a decent husband, and a husband was her only chance of escaping Sir Frederick's clutches. At twenty-two years of age, she had long since given up on girlish dreams of finding true love and was ready to settle on a kind, caring man. She respected and admired Mr. Ashway, who seemed to offer her respect and admiration in return, two things sadly lacking since Amanda's mother had wed Sir Frederick ten years ago.

Her mother had been lonely, two years a widow.

Amanda could well understand that. She could understand, too, how her mother could feel sorry for Sir Frederick's motherless children, Edwin and Elaine. What she could not understand was how her mother could not see Sir Frederick for what he was.

Not three months after the wedding, he had dismissed Amanda's beloved governess, claiming that since his spinster sister was well educated enough to teach his own children, she would be adequate for Amanda. Amanda's nursemaid went next. She was too old, he claimed. And what need for Amanda's pony, in the city?

Then, when Sir Frederick realized that instead of his being elevated to his wife's social position, the former Lady Alissa Carville was demoted to the fringes of the polite world that he inhabited, she became nothing but a burden to him. Amanda's mother was a frail burden, moreover, too sickly for his baser needs. Worse, her widow's annuity ended at her marriage, and the bulk of her wealth was in trust for Amanda.

Sir Frederick should have looked a little harder before he leaped, too. It was a bad bargain all around, with Amanda the loser. She lost her mother to despair, having to watch her pretty parent fade into a fearful shadow that disappeared altogether after five years of drunken tirades and ungoverned rages.

Amanda vowed not to make the same mistakes, and vowed to escape Sir Frederick as soon as she was out of mourning and her stepsister was older. That was three years ago. Sir Frederick had other ideas. Having himself declared her guardian, her stepfather rejected any number of suitors, claiming they were fortune hunters or philanderers, when he actually had no intention of parting with her dowry, her trust fund, or the interest they brought.

No matter that Mr. Charles Ashway was above reproach. Sir Frederick was going to turn away his offer for Amanda's hand. Further, the baronet had shouted that fateful morning, he intended to refuse any other suitors she managed to bring up to scratch. By the time she reached five-and-twenty, he swore, he intended to see her fortune dissipated to a pittance.

"Bad investments, don't you know."

She would be a penniless spinster with no hope for a home or a family of her own. The servants, no, the whole neighborhood, could hear her opinion of that. They all saw the red mark on her cheek from where Sir Frederick had struck her, threatening worse if she went to the solicitor or the bank.

She went to Almack's that night anyway, certain to find Mr. Ashway there. Surely such a worthy gentleman as Mr. Ashway would understand Amanda's plight, would be willing to wed her in Gretna if need be, then fight in the courts for her inheritance.

Mr. Ashway turned his back on her.

She boldly placed her gloved hand on his sleeve. "But sir, we were to have this first dance, recall? We spoke of it yesterday."

Mr. Ashway looked down at her hand, then toward his mother and sisters, who sat on the sidelines of the assembly rooms. He adjusted his neckcloth, then led her toward the room set aside for refreshments.

"I take it you have spoken to my stepfather?"

Mr. Ashway swallowed his lemonade and made a grimace, whether for the insipid drink or the distasteful Sir Frederick, Amanda did not know. "You must not pay heed to whatever my stepfather said. We can circumvent his control; I know we can."

"The same way you circumvented the rules of polite society? I think not. After all, I have my sisters' reputation to consider, and my family name."

Amanda was confused. "What do you mean? What could he have said?"

Her onetime suitor put his glass back on the table. "He said he could not let a fellow gentleman marry soiled goods. Need I be more specific, madam?" He turned without offering her escort back into the ballroom, where Amanda's stepsister and Sir Frederick's sister, their chaperone, waited.

Amanda did not seek them out. She called for her wrap and went home in a hackney, too furious to think clearly beyond telling the doorman that she was ill. She had to let herself into the house, since the servants were not expecting them back until much later. She was not sure what she could do, yet she could not simply do nothing. Her good name was being destroyed, her dowry being siphoned off to her stepfather's account. Soon she would have nothing left, and less hope.

A light gleamed under Sir Frederick's library door, and she was so angry she went in to confront the fiend with this latest crime. If nothing else, she would make him see how blackening her reputation would reflect poorly on his seventeen-year-old daughter, Elaine, whom he had hopes of marrying off to a wealthy peer.

He was not in the library. The fool had left an uncovered candle burning, though. Amanda went to extinguish it, but she tripped over something that should not have been lying on the Aubusson carpet.

A gun? Had Sir Frederick become so dangerous then,

or so drunk, that he was threatening the servants with loaded pistols? Suddenly realizing her own vulnerability, Amanda was glad he was not home after all. She picked the pistol up carefully in case it was loaded, to put it back in the drawer.

She screamed. What else could she do, finding Sir Frederick there behind the desk, with blood and gore and one sightless eye staring up at her? She screamed and Sir Frederick's butler came, buttoning his coat, his wig askew.

"The master always said you were no good."

Then she put down the gun.

Too late. Oh, so much too late.

The servants were shouting or crying. The Watch pushed them all aside. Elaine and her aunt rushed in. Elaine fainted, but Miss Hermione Hawley started shrieking and kept at it until the physician came, and the sheriff's men.

They dragged her off, Amanda Carville, granddaughter of an earl, hands bound, in a wagon, to a dark-paneled, crowded chamber. The room was filled with poorly dressed people and the stink of unwashed bodies. A rough-handed guard shoved her forward, her wrists still bound, to face a bewigged gentleman who never looked up from his papers. She could barely comprehend his words when he spoke to her captors, so numb was she, seeing nothing but her stepfather's face—what there was of it. She never got a chance to speak before her guard led her away. She did hold onto enough of her wits to hand the guard her earbobs, in exchange for his promise to get one message to the family's solicitor, another to an address in Grosvenor Square.

"There will be a better reward for you if you keep

your word. My godmother is wealthy and generous. She will untangle this mess."

Amanda had no idea if the guard delivered her messages or simply kept her earrings. He left her in a tiny room, a closet, perhaps, without a candle or a crust of bread. The next morning a different, larger guard, this one with missing teeth, pulled her out, back onto a wagon with other manacled prisoners, all crying and shouting their innocence. Amanda was shoved into a fenced yard with scores of ragged women, women she would have tossed a coin to if she saw them on the street. They grabbed for the cape she still had on, her gold ring, the lace off her gown, her gloves, even her silk stockings.

"No," she screamed, "I did not do anything."

They laughed at her.

"'At's what we all say," one old hag told her through broken, blackened teeth as she snatched at the hairpins holding Amanda's blond hair in its fashionable topknot. "You won't be needin' these where you're goin'."

Someone tossed her a scrap of wool. The blanket was tattered, filthy, and likely infested with vermin, but Amanda huddled under it, away from the coughing, wheezing women who were fighting over her belongings or trading them to the guards for bottles of gin or chunks of cheese. She spent a night and another day there, with no food and no one to listen to her protests or pleas.

On the third day she was hauled up from her corner and taken to a hearing in front of a high bench. Someone must have received her messages, she thought thankfully, for a dignified barrister stood beside her in elegant black robes. At last someone would listen to her.

"Thank you," she began, only to be glared at and told to be silent.

"But I—"

Her own defense walked away from her. A gavel pounded and she was dragged off again. This time she was cuffed on the ear for demanding to be heard.

Dizzy, she was taken back to the prison, but pushed into a different room, a windowless cell with nothing but a straw pallet on the ground and one thin blanket.

"No, you do not understand—"

The matron slapped her. "It's you what don't understand, me fine lady. Someone paid for private lodgings, but you're agoin' to be tried for murder and then hanged afore the month is over, and that's the end of it." She smacked Amanda again for good measure, before shoving her so hard that Amanda fell to the damp, cold stone floor.

Amanda had no money, no friends, no influential connections. Sir Frederick had seen to that with his boorish behavior. The only reason she and Elaine still had vouchers to the exclusive assembly rooms was through the kindness of Amanda's titled godmother. The only reason Sir Frederick permitted them to attend was for Elaine's sake, so she could make a profitable match. Young Elaine could not help Amanda now, and heaven knew where Sir Frederick's son Edwin was, or if he considered her a murderess. Her mother's people were all deceased and her father's uncaring family lived in Yorkshire, days away from London. Too late, Amanda recalled that her godmother was in Bath taking the waters. Surely the countess's servants would send for her. Surely . . .

No one came the next day, or the next. Amanda was alone. No one was coming, because no one believed her innocent. She stopped counting the days by the bowls of gruel pushed through the slot at the bottom of her door;

she stopped shouting when she heard keys jangle in the corridor. She stopped hoping when the cough came, and the fevers and chills.

But no, this could not be happening to her. She would not let it. She would simply . . . not let it.

When she was a girl, Amanda had discovered that if she curled up very small and stayed still as a mouse, sometimes no one would notice her. That's what she had done when her father lay dying after the carriage accident, when everyone was rushing about, crying. She had learned to stay in the shadows when her mother wed Sir Frederick, not letting herself hear her mother's weeping afterward, when there was nothing she could do. She got better at retreating into her own world after Lady Alissa's death, not listening to Elaine's aunt Hermione carping at her to stop daydreaming.

She could go anywhere in her mind—to a place no one could find her, no one could hurt her. So Amanda curled up there on the prison floor and dreamed of blue skies and picnics with her parents—while she waited to die.

"Oh, no, you don't. No one cheats Jack Ketch in my gaol." The warden kicked at her, and then two other prisoners held her while they poured gruel down her throat. She brought it back up, and they slapped her and punched her some more, but she did not feel the blows, did not see the tormentors; not where she was.

"What, ya think playin' the queer nabs will save you? You ain't seen no Bedlam then, have you? You'd be beggin' for the noose, you would."

They left her alone, and she crawled deeper into her own self, as far from this living hell as she could go while still living.

She did not even hear or take notice when the guards

bid on who would have her first, when the warden had
his day off. She only heard her father calling her back
from the lake edge. "Come to Papa, poppet. Come now."
    She was halfway there.

Chapter Three

"No," Rex said. "I will not do it." He had not bothered to sit down, showing his disdain for his father's summons and his intention to be off as soon as the earl said his piece. Instead, he leaned against the mantel, taking the weight off his injured leg. His shirt was open at the collar, with no neckcloth. His breeches were ripped and stained, his too-long hair curling into his shadowed eyes. He needed a shave and he smelled worse than the dog at his feet.

Lord Royce wrinkled his nose, but did not criticize his son's appearance. That Rex had appeared at all was boon enough. "Not even as a favor to a friend?"

Rex raised his glass of brandy. "It is your friend, your favor."

"As a favor to me, then?"

"What, go to London where I am always half-blinded by the swirls of insincerity? Why, I doubt if there is one person in the entire city whose tongue isn't warped with lying. If they are not dealing in falsehoods, they are spewing slander at each other."

The earl could only nod. Being out in society made his

own teeth ache with the cacophony of lies that constantly bombarded his senses.

"And now it will be worse," Rex went on. "They will all offer regrets about my leg—when not one of the bastards means it. They'd rather I had not come home, a reminder that war is about gore and guts, not parade marches and pretty uniforms. Everyone will look at my imperfect face and pretend the scar is not there. And, recall, I was an embarrassment to the army, an unspoken blot on the corps. An officer who did not fight, a lord who did not act with honor. A spy. Do you think the whispers have not reached Town, that Daniel and I were monstrous savages, as far from gentlemen as one could fall?"

"You were wounded in the service of your country and commended any number of times. They will remember that!"

"They will remember that I tortured prisoners of war until they gave up their secrets, contrary to every code of decency. Or should I confess that I was merely listening for the truth?"

The earl sipped at his wine, looking away.

Rex lifted his own glass in a mock salute. "The way you did, Father?"

Lord Royce had not been able to defend himself against charges of corruption in the high court. What could he say? That he knew the prisoner in the dock was innocent—because the man had said so in the pure, chiming tones of truth? He'd be laughed off the bench. Instead he was accused of taking bribes. After all, what other reason could he have for freeing that poor thief instead of hanging him? All the evidence and witnesses pointed toward a guilty verdict, a successful prosecution by the Crown's barrister, who happened to be an ambitious toad.

Instead the felon had gone free—on a seeming whim. If Lord Royce were not accepting money, Sir Nigel had declared, then he was insane, irrational, unfit for the duties of the high court. Hearing the truth in a tone of voice? Humbug.

The truth would have been worse, if anyone could believe it, dredging up those old tales of witchcraft and sorcery. What, the judge could read minds? England was as comfortable with such eeriness now as it was in ancient Sir Royston's time. They might not hang a peer, but they would label him a lunatic and lock him away. Worst of all, the truth would have condemned young Rex to the life of a freak, like the two-headed cow in the traveling circus. Lord Royce had retired from the bench instead, claiming ill health. He could have taken his seat in the House of Lords, listening to the discordant notes of pettifoggery and being subjected to stares and innuendos. He could have become an idle aristocrat, drinking and gaming away his days and nights, if anyone would play at cards with one who was suspected of dastardly acts. Rumors were rekindled about why Lady Royce lived apart. Surely he hid heinous secrets. Lord Royce did not refute any of the charges or make explanations. He chose to live in the country instead, raising his boy.

"I would go to Town myself if I could," he said now, plucking at the blanket covering his legs. "But . . ."

Signs of his father's infirmity always distressed Rex. He swallowed his brandy and said, "Deuce take it, what is so important about this girl that one of us must travel to London? I read the newspapers. They made much of it— the murder of a baronet. Everyone knew Miss—what is her name?—was known to despise her stepfather, and the scandal sheets reported rumors that she was sneaking out at night to meet with her lover. She was holding the pistol, for heaven's sake!"

"My correspondent does not believe Amanda—Miss Carville—killed the devil." The earl rustled the letter in his hand. "If she is guilty, then justice will be done, and should be done. But what if the young woman is innocent? Not only would she hang for a crime she did not commit, but a cold-blooded killer would be free to strike again. You should be the last one on earth to judge her without hearing her words for yourself."

"No, you should be, dash it. The law is your preserve, recall, not mine."

The earl started coughing then. Rex hurried to his side and poured a drink of cordial. "You are not faking this spell, are you, damn it, just to manipulate me into doing your bidding?"

Still coughing, the earl shook his head no.

"Say it, by Jupiter. Say you are truly too weak to go to London yourself."

"I . . . I am too weak in body . . . and in courage. Truly."

"Truly," Rex echoed, defeated.

Then the earl threw back his son's words. "Bravery is your preserve, recall? Although no one would know it by the way you are acting."

Rex limped back to the mantel. "You think I am a coward for not taking up a life of indolence and indulgence?"

"I think you are hiding here, yes. But I am not asking you to become a wastrel, nor to set yourself up as a Bow Street investigator. I merely ask you, on behalf of an old friend, to speak to the young lady, to listen and discover if she actually is guilty. That is all."

"Unless she is innocent, in which case I will have to

stay in London long enough to destroy the Crown's case against her."

"You said yourself she is likely guilty. Sir Frederick Hawley was a blackguard by all accounts, and it was a mere matter of time before someone took his measure."

"Someone took his life, dash it." Rex ran his hand over the scar on his cheek. "Send funds for a competent barrister, then, who can argue that Miss—what did you say she was called?—acted in self-defense."

"I cannot. My . . . friend asked me to see to it personally."

Rex knew that deuced few of his father's friends had stood by him. "Who the devil is this old friend, anyway, that you cannot simply say no?"

"Miss Carville's godparent. Your mother."

Rex threw his glass, the handblown, hand-etched crystal, into the fireplace.

Hell, London. Rex sat back against the seat of his father's carriage, trying to ease the blinding pain that was already holding his head in a vise grip, and he was not halfway there. Every innkeeper, every livery stable owner, every serving girl along the way had lied to him. Every purveyor of foodstuffs or cattle or sex was trying to sell him inferior quality at superior prices because of the crest on his father's coach. Even the offers from the tavern wenches were lies, for he could read the disgust in their eyes when they noticed his limp and his scar. Oh, they would still take his coin for a hasty tumble, and another if they promised not to speak, but the welcoming smile was a lie. So he kept his coins—including the ones he had learned to offer doxies to keep them from feigning orgasm, so his own pleasure was not ruined by that particular, inconveniently timed falsehood. Why, if half those lusty fellows who considered themselves such great lovers—aye, and half the married men, too—could only know the truth, their ballocks would burn in shame.

So Rex did not accept the offers of companionship, although a brief interlude of mindless pleasure would have given his thoughts a needed rest. Hell, he did not need company; he had Murchison. His father's valet caught Rex's glance and silently handed over a clay jug of ale, mixed with a headache powder. Of course he was silent, for Murchison never spoke. He wrote notes when he had to, or used hand gestures. He did not hear, either, the earl insisted, although Rex had always misdoubted the small, bald man's disabilities, for Murchison was too knowing for a supposedly deaf man, always providing precisely what was needed, which was why his father had insisted Rex take the valet along.

"You cannot go about the way you look now," Lord Royce had declared, curling his lip at Rex's disarray.

"I have absolutely no intention of going about, as you say." The last thing Rex was prepared to do was reenter society.

"You will be calling on a lady, even if she is in prison. She deserves your respect."

"Perhaps you want me to wear satin knee breeches to call on your murderess at Newgate? Or my dress uniform?" Officially, Rex was still on sick leave, but he intended to sell his commission soon. He was not going back to the army, in any capacity. He had fulfilled his duty six times over.

His father had not answered, and Murchison had packed what Murchison deemed necessary. He had eased Rex's way at some of the inns, silently but effectively ensuring the meals were hot and well prepared, the linens clean and aired. And there was no doubt that Murchison made a quiet, undemanding companion, unlike Verity, who insisted on frequent carriage stops, regular meals, and not letting the viscount out of her sight. The dog would have pined for him, the earl had pointed out—if she did not follow the coach all the way to London.

Of course Rex remembered, too late, why he never took Verity aboard his sailboat despite her pleading eyes. The mastiff got seasick, and carriage sick too, it seemed. Which caused Murchison to speak for the first time in Rex's hearing, in profane, creative French, which explained why the man pretended to be deaf and dumb. A Frenchman at Royce Hall near the Dover coast would be shot before he could say Jacques Rabbit.

"Does my father know?" Then Rex answered his own question. "Of course he does. He knows everything."

The valet shrugged, said "He saved my life" in English, and did not speak again for the rest of the trip to London, not even to tell his real name.

"Montclaire?" Rex guessed. "Marceau?"

Verity's groan of discomfort was his only answer.

Once they neared Town, Rex found an inn that would accept the massive dog and the mute valet. The accommodations were simple and the food simpler, but the ale was good and the stables better. He could have found a bunk in the army barracks if he were on his own, but not with a Frenchman in tow. He might have slept on Daniel's sofa once he fished his cousin out of whatever sewer he was frequenting these days. Perhaps the inn was better after all, for he had no more desire to see his cousin than Daniel had to see him, he assumed, not after the way they had parted in Spain. Hell, he supposed he owed Daniel an apology now, too. But how else was he to get the big lummox to go home to his mother's aid, except by telling him that he was in the way, that Rex was tired of having an ugly oaf looking over his shoulder, that he was weary of Daniel the giant nursemaid?

Hell, indeed.

First the girl, Rex decided, gratefully mounting his rented horse instead of suffering another mile in the closed coach. How long could it take to ask Miss—he still could not remember her blasted name, likely because he did not want to know her—his two questions: Did she kill her stepfather? Was it in self-defense? He had to hear her answers; then he would know what kind of lawyer to hire for her. His father still had some influence among the legal gentlemen who cared about seeing justice done. The earl had more than enough blunt to hire some eloquent bloodsucker of a barrister who did not care if his client were caught red-handed beside a dead body.

After dealing with the girl, Rex could try to shake some sense into dense-headed Daniel. He'd make his apology, then make the fool go home to manage his estate. With any luck, Rex could be on his own way back toward Dover and Royce Hall in the morning, to his riding and sailing. His injured leg was as strong as it was going to get, he supposed, but the strenuous activity let him sleep at night. He thought he ought to take his own advice and start riding along with his father's steward, to learn about the lands that would someday be his. He had never envisioned himself as a farmer, though. He was a soldier, by Jupiter, with a dangerous reputation and a diabolic knack.

The alleged murderess was lucky; he had only two questions for her. Damn, Rex's whole life was a question.

*   *   *

"Bloody hell," Rex cursed when they opened the cell door. "What the devil happened to her?"

"That would of been the scuffle in the yard, afore some bleedin' heart gentry mort sent funds for a private cell."

"That bleeding heart lady is my mother, by Zeus, and she would have sent enough blunt for better treatment."

The guard shrugged. "Resistin', she was."

Rex looked at the brawny warder, then at the small scrap of a woman asleep or unconscious on the floor. Her gown hung in torn and bloodied shreds, her feet were bare, and her hair was so filthy he could not tell the color. Someone had lopped off the rest, likely to sell to the wig makers. "She must have put up quite a fight."

The guard counted his keys, not coming into the rancid-smelling cell.

Rex had to. "Miss Carville?"

"She don't talk. Don't do nothin'. That's resistin'."

Rex knelt, grimacing in disgust, at the guard's reasoning, his stiff leg, and the dirt that would get on the fresh uniform that Murchison insisted he wear. He touched the girl's gaunt shoulder to awaken her. By light of the guard's candle he could see cuts and bruises, discolorations and swellings. Even through his gloves he could feel the heat of her fevered body. She did not stir. "Bloody hell," he swore again.

As a boy, he had once come upon a wounded deer, trembling, yet too weak to run away. He'd dispatched the poor creature and never hunted again, but the image had stayed with him. Miss Amanda Carville was like an injured helpless fawn. Something about her stirred protective instincts he never knew he had. There was no way in Hades he could leave her here to die in this filth. Only an ogre, he told himself, could look at her and not feel pity. Rex looked at her and felt rage. He turned and had the guard by the neck before the bigger man could call out for help. In a flash, out of nowhere, Rex's knife was pressed against the man's jugular vein. "Was she raped, besides? Tell me now, and tell me the truth, for, by Heaven, I will know if you lie."

The guard looked into Rex's eyes and knew he was inches away from death for the wrong answer. Captain Lord Rexford's reputation had preceded him. "N-no. Not yet. Tonight . . ."

Rex slipped the knife back up his sleeve. "Tonight the lady will be out of here. See to it." He tossed the man a leather pouch filled with coins.

"But there ain't no bail for capital offenses," the guard complained, tucking the purse under his filthy shirt anyway.

Rex was already unbuttoning his coat to wrap around the woman. "Then see that she is released for medical reasons. And you'd better pray she recovers or I'll have your hide, and every other warder here. The woman is a lady, by Jupiter."

"She be a murderess, Cap'n."

"She is not convicted yet—only *charged*. With Lord Royce as her legal counsel, she will be free before the case comes to trial."

His father's name still held sway in the prison, but the guard scratched his head. "I don't know 'bout releasin' her, not even to your custody, pardon, milord. Sir Nigel won't be happy none."

"Sir Nigel . . . ?"

"Aye, the chief prosecutor for the Crown. Sir Nigel

Turlowe. He wanted to see the mort hang particular-like, her shootin' a titled swell and all."

Nigel Turlowe, before he was knighted, was the man who had orchestrated Rex's father's downfall and disgrace. That made getting Miss Carville out of prison sweet, besides necessary. "You can tell Sir Nigel for me that the charges must be dropped for insufficient evidence."

The man's jaw gaped open. "But there was witnesses, and the gun."

"The witnesses lied." They always did. "Tell him. And tell him we will bring suit for the mistreatment of the prisoner. We shall start with him, name the warden and the matrons and every blasted guard in this benighted place. If the suit does not work, I will see what my superiors at Whitehall can do. Have you ever heard of a gentleman called the Aide?"

He could tell by the guard's suddenly shaking hands that the Aide's reputation was worse than his own. "If all else fails, I will personally pay a visit to every last one of you bastards. Do you understand?" The knife back in his hand again made his meaning fairly obvious. The guard nodded.

Rex glanced toward the bulge of the leather purse at the man's waist. "I am taking her. Make it right, make it legal, or make peace with your god."

No one stopped Rex as he limped through the halls of the prison carrying his slight burden. Then he was out in the fresh air, headed for his . . . horse.

Damn. If ever he needed Murchison and his father's coach, this was it. They were an hour outside of London, though. Two hackney drivers sped away, rather than take up a sickly passenger from Newgate.

"Now what?" Rex asked. The woman did not answer. She was so quiet he would have wondered if she still breathed, but he could feel her chest rise and fall even under his uniform jacket, which enfolded her. For how long? He knew he could not stand outside the prison gates waiting for a messenger to fetch Murchison and the carriage. Miss Carville needed help, now, and his bad leg could not support her for so long. So he draped her limp body over his horse's neck until he mounted and gathered her up again, silently apologizing to both the woman and the horse for such rough treatment.

Then he cursed again, turning the horse in a wide circle while he thought. What the devil was he going to do with Miss Amanda Carville now that he had her? He could not take her to the house, where she had—perhaps—shot the owner. If Sir Frederick's household had cared about the chit, she would not have been in such mean accommodations in prison. She'd had no visitors, the guard had said, confirming their belief in her guilt. Rex could not take her to his inn, not with the riffraff there, or the lack of a physician or an apothecary or a decent woman. He could try a hotel in Town, but Lud, he'd be laughed at for trying to bring his filthy, fetid burden into a respectable place. Daniel's lodgings were out of the question, even if he know the location. The girl needed tending, not likely to be found at whatever rough bachelor digs Rex's cousin had claimed. No, Rex had one choice. One blasted, blighted choice: Royce House. Where his mother lived.

Chapter Four

The knocker was off the door, which indicated that the resident was away from home. Good. That meant Rex did not have to face Lady Royce. Not that he never saw her, simply that he saw her as rarely as possible, more often by accident than design. When he was at university, a scholar on a spree, or later, a young man about Town, avoiding encounters was easy. Countesses seldom frequented gaming hells or whorehouses or sporting events. Young bucks and beaux did not attend debutante balls and afternoon teas and musicales unless dragged by their female relations. Lady Royce knew better than to try to drag Rex anywhere. She did send him letters, which he answered politely on his father's orders, and packages while he was in school or with the army. Often there would be warm socks, tins of tea, a coin or a pound note tucked in, so the other lads thought Lady Royce was the best mother in the world.

She was no mother at all. Right now Rex was pleased he did not have to make stilted conversation with the stranger who gave him birth. It was enough that he was here at her bidding, cradling an unconscious convict.

On the other hand—the one holding his coat closed

over the young woman's torn gown so he had to kick at
the door instead of knocking—with the countess away,
who was going to take charge of Miss Carville? He almost
dropped her, panicked at the thought that no one was left
at the London town house to answer his call. No, the
housekeeper would be somewhere, Rex decided, or the
cook. There were competent women in most households,
experienced with invalids and infants. He kicked at the
door again.

Both were away, the butler announced when the man finally opened the door, aghast at the foul sight in the im-
maculate doorway of his domain: a dusty soldier in
shirtsleeves, a filthy urchin in his arms. He sneered.

Rex frowned at the butler's bare feet.

The major domo wrinkled his nose at the stench of
horse and worse. Rex raised his eyebrow at the scent of
patchouli that wafted from the bewigged butler, but he
again demanded a woman to look after Miss Carville.

According to the butler, Dodd, Cook was with the mistress in Bath, as were Lady Royce's dresser, her companion, and the upstairs maid. The housekeeper was visiting
her sister in Richmond and the parlor maids were on holiday. So the young female could not be brought into
Royce House, no matter who she claimed to be.

"She claims nothing. She is too ill."

"Then she belongs in a hospital, sir." The butler started
to shut the door in Rex's face.

Still holding the woman close to his chest despite the
cramp in his right shoulder and the trembling in his left
forearm, Rex kicked the door fully open with his good leg.
He would have kicked the blasted butler if he could have
reached. As it was, the man had to leap backward to avoid
the heavy door connecting with his bare toes. "I'll call the

Watch," Dodd threatened. "We don't allow vagrants and vermin around here. This is a house of nobility. Lady Royce knows only the finest people, not criminals and cutthroats."

"Do you know who I am, you sanctimonious prig?"

The butler curled his lip again. "No one who should be calling on a countess, that is for certain."

"And I wouldn't, had I any choice. Your countess is my mother, confound it!"

The butler's face went pale. His toes curled under his feet as he finally recognized the air of authority under the grime—worse, the likeness to a boy's portraits in the sitting room and the parlor. "I . . . I do not believe you," he said.

Rex was seeing red. Not just at the lie, but out of anger. Miss Carville could be dying for all he knew, or dead already, while this supercilious servant worried about her presence and his pedigree. And whoever heard of a butler going barefoot? He pushed past the man and headed for the stairs that had to lead up toward the bedchambers. "Find me a female to attend Miss Carville. Now!"

"But . . . but no one is on duty but a footman, the pot-boy, and a kitchen drab."

"Get her. And have the boy bring hot water. There is a groom outside holding my horse. Send him for a physician—whichever one Lady Royce uses. The footman can get a message to my man at the Black Dog Inn."

Instead of carrying out Rex's orders, Dodd hurried after the viscount and his burden. Rex stopped at the first door, his leg protesting the climb.

"No, no! That is the countess's own bedroom."

The next one was the earl's, it seemed.

"Has my father ever been here, then?"

"Not that I know of, but I have only been in my lady's employ for six months. Her previous butler retired."

And this one would not last long if Rex had anything to say. According to Dodd, the next door led to her ladyship's companion's room, and the following chamber was being redecorated.

Rex was too tired to care about that lie, and too concerned about getting Miss Carville onto a bed before his arms gave out. Dodd finally rushed ahead to open a smaller room done up with rose-painted wallpaper and roses on the fabric hangings. It was as feminine and frilly as the rooms that stayed closed and clean next to the earl's bedchamber at the Hall.

Rex placed his burden on the bed and removed his coat from around her, then stood back, shrugging into it, waiting for the scullery maid.

The girl took three steps into the room, pointed at the figure lying so still on the bed, and screamed "Murderess!"

"She is an accused murderess," Rex countered, buttoning his uniform coat so he would feel more in command of a situation that was far beyond his ken. "First she is Lady Royce's goddaughter and she is ill."

"Gaol fever!" the maid yelled. She threw her hands in the air and fled, almost knocking the bucket of water out of a wide-eyed boy's hands. Rex grabbed for the bucket as the boy stared at Miss Carville's half-naked body. Rex hastily pulled down the remnants of her skirt to cover her legs.

"You, out!" he bellowed at the boy. "Fetch more water, and some soup if you can find it, or biscuits and tea." Then he once more ordered the butler to send the footman for

Murchison, a woman—any woman—and his cousin Daniel, in that order.

"I . . . I know of a woman nearby. My, ah, sister."

"Get her, man!"

In mere seconds—and mere doors away, obviously the one Dodd claimed was being redecorated—a female staggered into the room. She did not look like Dodd, but the patchouli she must have bathed in did smell like him. Dodd suddenly had his shoes on, Rex noted, but the female did not have her gown fastened. Her face paint was smeared and her lips were swollen. She had a bottle of wine—from the Royce wine cellars, Rex guessed—in her hand while the other hand held the gaping front of her gown over fleshy, flabby breasts.

"You've brought your whore into my mother's house?" Rex shouted at the butler, who was edging toward the doorway. Even Rex, as far from polite society's ways as he could get, knew that was an outrage. "And here, to tend to a lady?"

"Lady, my arse," the female said. "She's nobbut a light skirt from what they say, and a cold-blooded murderer to boot. Who's to say she's better'n old Nell?"

"I say it, damn it! Get out, before I throw you out. And you"—he turned toward Dodd—"if you want to keep your post past tomorrow, you'll make certain your doxy is gone without lifting any of the countess's silver, and then you will find a respectable woman to come help. Try next door if you need to. And when the footman gets back from finding my cousin and my valet, post a message to Lady Royce, saying that her goddaughter has arrived."

He did not speak his thoughts, that the countess should have been in London while her godchild was in peril, not leaving him to comfort a delicate female, not abandoning yet another innocent to his or her fate.

If Miss Carville was innocent. He still did not know.

"Tell Lady Royce to come home now."

"I cannot give orders to my mistress!"

"She sent for me. Now send for her. Miss Carville is her responsibility."

Dodd bowed, shoved Nell ahead of him, and ran to do Rex's bidding. "Yes sir, my lord. Right away, Captain, ah, your lordship." Good positions were hard to find. Besides, Viscount Rexford looked like he'd have Dodd's head if his demands were not met, no matter how unreasonable. The butler had heard the war reports as well as the rumors. Everyone had. No one, it seemed, disobeyed his lordship, not ever. Or else. Murder and mayhem flashed from those ice-blue eyes, for certain. Dodd vowed to get the housekeeper back if he had to drag her himself. Yes, and Lady Royce, too.

Once the room was empty of servants, Rex stared at the unmoving form on the bed. "You are Lady Royce's mess," he declared, more for his own sake than the febrile woman's. "Not mine."

But the countess could not come fast enough, and Rex could not walk away or lie to himself, which made it his mess after all.

He repeated Murchison's French blasphemies, then a few of the cavalry's finest curses. The woman was still lying atop the covers, in rags and in need. Damn. He could not leave her like that. He could not wait for a maidservant, either. Murchison was an hour away, at least. Who knew how long before the doctor would arrive? The female was shivering, despite beads of sweat on her forehead. He lit the coals in the room's fireplace.

Oh, lord. He gave up the curses and prayed harder than when he'd found himself facing that party of advance French scouts.

Hell, they were the enemy; Miss Carville was a lady, which was far worse. Rex had never undressed a lady in his life, much less washed one. He looked at the bucket of water, which was cooling, and the towel on the washstand. "Miss Carville? Please, miss, please wake up."

She did not open her eyes. So much for swearing, praying, and begging.

Rex took his coat off again, feeling perspiration dripping down his own back, but not from the heat of the room. He took a deep breath and straightened his spine. "Very well, please do not wake up then. That will be easier on both of us."

Like a general studying his maps and maneuvers, Rex planned his campaign. First he fetched a nightgown from the countess's room and a bottle of brandy from the earl's. Then he turned down the covers on the other side of Miss Carville's bed so he'd have some place to roll the female onto when she was clean. He had a sip of brandy.

He brought the water and towel closer, and had another swallow. He'd wipe her face and hands first. How bad could that be? The brandy was good.

As gently as he could, Rex wiped at the dirt and scrapes, avoiding the swollen, discolored skin around the woman's left eye and the bruise on her chin, her cut lips. The doctor would have to prescribe salve and ointments for those. Rex carefully cleaned her hands—how small they were in his—and marked the raw place where someone had pulled a ring off her finger, and the sores on her arms from what he assumed were manacles. Her wrists were so narrow he could reach around them with his fingers and still have room. Shackles on this wisp of a girl? The notion turned his stomach, or perhaps that was the brandy. No, he was queasy at his next job.

Where the devil was Dodd and a decent woman?

Rex took a long swallow and set the bottle aside. A man needed a clear head to face the enemy, and his demons.

He raised Miss Carville and slipped the nightgown over her head, stuffing her arms into the sleeves, which were much too long. The countess was far larger, and far away, blast her.

Rex's strategy was to cut away the rags of Miss Carville's gown, lowering the night rail as he went to pre-serve her modesty as much as possible. He'd leave the washing of her body to whatever woman Dodd found. He thought he could hear voices in the front hall, a door shut-ting, footsteps on the stairs. Reprieve! He reached for the brandy again.

Of course that was when Miss Carville opened her eyes. And saw a rough-looking, long-haired man bending over her, a bottle in one hand, a knife in the other.

She shrieked. What else could Amanda do, when she was too weak to raise her arms, and they seemed to be swathed with cloth bindings anyway, with more wrapped around her throat? There she'd been, safely cradled in her father's arms, tenderly comforted by her mother's cooling, soothing touch. Someone cared for her; someone loved her. How sweet her dreams. Then she awoke to yet an-other nightmare of stabbing, strangulation, torture. The loathsome demon's eyes were wide with evil intent. An angry scar ran down his cheek and he stank of spirits. A guard? A prisoner? Amanda had no doubt he meant to rape her, then kill her. She shrieked again. No one was going to hear and help her, but what did she have to lose?

Rex slapped his hand over her mouth. Then he apologized when she winced and tried to pull back. "Sorry. But think of your reputation." No, that was so far blackened, she might as well be dipped in tar. "Think of mine." Which was worse. Lud, her eyes were wide and terror-filled, except for the one that was half swollen shut. That was brown, but bloodshot. "Please do not be afraid. I am trying to help you."

She stayed rigid, gathering her breath for another scream, he thought. "Please. My . . . mother sent me to help." The words were almost as painful as this little kitten's fear of him. "I would not hurt you."

"J-Jordan?"

He sighed in relief, that she was not out of her mind in a blind panic. A rational creature could be reasoned with. "That is right. Jordan, Lord Rexford, Lady Royce's son." He tried for a smile to reassure her while he put the bottle on the floor. He bowed and said, "At your service."

Amanda blinked and tried to focus on the man's features, not the knife in his hand. He was dark while the countess was fair, and his eyes were a bright sapphire, unlike Lady Royce's baby blue. But there was something about his mouth, and the smile, that seemed familiar. Perhaps she was thinking of the portraits on Lady Royce's walls. She almost smiled back, except for the pain in her split lip. "She must be so happy to see you."

"Not if I let you sicken worse," he muttered, not wishing to discuss the countess or their eventual meeting. To avoid any talk of Lady Royce, Rex busied himself putting the knife away and searching for a cup near the washstand, then pouring a tiny bit of the brandy into it. "Here, have a sip. Lord knows you deserve it."

She swallowed and sputtered, then looked around. "I am not in prison?"

"No."

"Then it was all a bad dream?"

"I am sorry, but I cannot lie to you. You are not acquitted."

A tear ran down her cheek, so Rex hurried to add, "But I will work on it. I swear, on my honor."

Amanda brushed at her eyes with the sleeve of the voluminous gown she seemed to be bundled into, clean and smelling of lavender. "Your mother always said you were an honorable man, one who could be trusted to tell the truth. She thinks you can accomplish anything you want."

"Not quite." Or else he'd be in China right now instead of Grosvenor Square. "But before I can hire barristers and such, we need to get you well. And clean. Your clothes have to be burned to protect against the spread of disease." He did not mention the possibilities of lice and fleas.

"Lady Royce?" she asked, looking around the room for her godmother.

"She is on her way." Like lice and fleas, the details were not important right now. "As are a physician and hot tea."

Ah, the maid must be bringing the tea. "Thank you."

"Unless the potboy does not know how to fix a tray."

"No maid?"

"I am afraid not. Not yet, that is. Soon, I pray. I was, ah, attempting to cut off your clothes in the meantime," he tried to explain, holding up his knife again.

Could a ghost get any whiter? Miss Carville matched the color of the sheets. To distract her, Rex decided to ask his questions. To hell with her modesty and her virginal fears. He had to know if she killed Sir Frederick. "Miss

Carville, you need to tell me about your stepfather's death. I do not care much what you say, as long as it is the truth. I will help you either way, but I must hear it from your own lips. And believe this if nothing else: I will know if you lie."

Her mouth opened as if she were going to speak, but then her eyelashes fluttered closed and her hands fell back to her side. Miss Carville had fallen back into her fevered stupor—or else she was evading his question.

Chapter Five

Rex cursed. He cursed the sick—or sneaky—female. He cursed the countess for calling for help—and his father for giving it. Mostly he cursed his own traitorous body for assessing Miss Carville's body while he quickly cut the clothing away, hastily swabbed at dirt and dried blood, hurried to pull the nightgown down. Damn, for all he'd done, for all his freakish quirk, Rex still considered himself a gentleman. Not a voyeur, not a rake, not a lust-driven despoiler of virgins. Of course Miss Carville might not be any pure maiden, not if the rumor mill ground true. Virgin or not, murderess or not, she deserved better than being ogled while she lay ill. That was a reprehensible breach of honor. Yet Rex could not help noticing her high, firm breasts and her narrow waist, flat belly, and long, shapely legs. The female might be small, but she was perfectly formed. And blond.

He pulled the countess's overlarge nightgown down so fast and so hard the shoulder might have ripped. Miss Carville was clean enough in his view, and far too long in his view, also. He did not think any of her ribs were broken, nor were any of her cuts deep enough to need stitches. He moved her over, between the sheets, and covered her to the chin with the blankets. Then he could breathe again.

When he gathered her ruined garments to toss out into the corridor for burning, Rex heard steps on the staircase again. This time Dodd brought the doctor up. The butler did not meet Rex's eyes when he mumbled that none of the neighbor ladies agreed to come, and none of the nearby maidservants, either.

"Perhaps the doctor knows of a willing woman," Rex said, looking toward the older man in hope. "An experienced nurse, fit for a gentlewoman's care."

The physician was already examining Miss Carville, making snorting noises, while Rex kept his back turned. "I'll try to find one who isn't a drunkard. The countess wouldn't want one of those in her house. Not that she'd want this, either, poor lady."

"Are her injuries that dire, then? Or is it the fever?"

"Hmph. I meant Lady Royce, not the murderess. This one will do, with some willow bark tea for the ague, laudanum for her nerves, basilicum ointment for everything else." Rex could see the man's certainty in bright color as he laid out the powders and potions, and was relieved until the doctor said, "But I still say it seems a shame, the same as I told Dodd here when I arrived."

"That a gently bred woman could be treated so savagely?"

"No, that Lady Royce will be bothered with such a mare's nest, and that I have to waste my time over a killer."

Rex turned and glared at the physician. "Thank you for coming. You need not send over a nurse. We'll manage. You may send Lady Royce your bill. Good day."

"Hmph."

"How?" Dodd wanted to know, despite the imperti-
nence. "How are you going to take care of the female?
There is already enough scandal to see Lady Royce's good
name destroyed." What use was a good position if he was
laughed at when he visited the pub his fellow butlers frequented? How was Dodd to collect vails from callers if no
one visited her ladyship?

Rex wanted to say "Hmph" himself. Reputations be
damned, he would not see Miss Carville ill-treated or
insulted. He could not say precisely why he felt protective of the girl, but it was certainly not because he'd
touched her soft, silky skin, or that her appearance, battered and bruised with her hair lopped off, appealed to
him. Even clean she still looked like something the cat
dragged in, and then dragged outside again as unappetizing. No, he'd felt the surprising tug of tenderness the
moment he'd glimpsed her in prison. Why, he could
have bribed the warder to have her moved to a more
comfortable cell. He could have paid a matron to tend to
her, and see that she was fed and bathed and doctored.
Maybe he should have done just that, leaving her there.
No one, not even his father, could have expected him to
do more. He was in London to determine guilt or innocence, to investigate a murder, to hire a competent barrister. Lud, he was not here to play nursemaid to a
wench weeks away from the hangman's noose. Rex
looked at Miss Carville, pale against the pillow, though,
and knew he'd had no choice. It was as simple as that,
not a matter of duty or chivalry or justice. He, and no
one else, had to make her safe.

He smoothed the blankets around her and told the butler, "Caring for Miss Carville is not your concern. Just
find someone to cook a meal—porridge or something that

a sick person can eat. Find a coffeehouse or a bakery if you need to. And find me another bottle of brandy."

Dodd shook his head on his way out. "There'll be the devil to pay, for sure," he muttered, whether Lady Royce found out about Nell or not.

Rex did not have to see any colors to know the truth of that.

He waited until Dodd's footsteps echoed down the hall, then grimaced at the stuff the physician had left. The tea he could brew, the laudanum he could dose, but damn if he did not have to half undress Miss Carville all over again to spread the healing salve on her wounds. He'd done the same many times for soldiers, he told himself. And for his horses. This was another act of charity, nothing else.

Then why was his sight swimming in a sea of red lies? Because no matter what he told himself, he wanted another glimpse of Miss Carville's delectable body, hoping the sight was not half as lovely as he recalled.

It was.

Murchison finally arrived. The valet clucked his tongue when Dodd brought him to Miss Carville's bedchamber, but blessedly did not say anything about the highly irregular situation. Verity the mastiff skittered around the room in joy at being reunited with Rex, then took an interest in Miss Carville—or the salve on her face. She was fast asleep. Rex had spooned some food into her, a thin soup that was all the weepy scullery maid could manage, along with the physician's powders. Her skin was cooler to the touch, her breathing more even, the pucker between her eyebrows smooth, her cheeks showing some color besides the purplish bruises.

"She'll live to the trial, at any rate. Call me if she wakens."

Murchison's jaw dropped open, but with Dodd in the room he could not curse or complain in any language.

Rex took the opportunity while Miss Carville slept to claim a suite of rooms across the hall for himself, one with a dressing room with a cot for Murchison. He desperately needed to wash and eat and rest his leg, too. And figure out how he was going to find a respectable woman to come take over the sickroom until the countess returned. He refused to think about the situation if Lady Royce, as was her wont, turned her back on her responsibilities. Heaven help them, but Murchison would have to do for now.

But the mademoiselle slept on, and Murchison's duty was to his master, whose instructions were to keep the viscount looking and acting as civilized as possible, like a proper heir to an earldom. So the valet left Miss Carville's door open and went across the hall to unpack a change of clothes for Lord Rexford, while his lordship bathed. The captain's uniform, to Murchison's disgust, was covered in dirt and soup and dog hair, with a trace of Miss Carville's blood. At least Murchison hoped it was Miss Carville's, lest Lord Royce's son be charged with murder, too. He took the coat below stairs to sponge it off and press it.

Amanda was having another dream. She was drifting on a cloud; no, she was being carried aloft by a great bird, held gently between its feet. The giant eagle would never let her fall, never let her grow cold or weary or hungry. When the bird bent its neck to look down at her, she smiled. Then she noticed that her winged companion had flashing blue eyes, not the fixed, staring golden ones she expected. The bird's eyes were brighter than the skies they flew through, circled with a black rim, and shielded by thick black lashes. She laughed out loud. Eagles did not have blue eyes or eyelashes, but this was her dream, and the bird could have a mustache if she wanted, or a scar down its cheek. Either way, she could sleep in safety and wake in peace, watching soft white clouds pass by.

She never wanted the dream to end, but her mother was washing her face. "Do not scrub so hard, Mama. I am too tired to get up now. My head feels heavy. Maybe I do not need to go to church this morning."

Her mother did not listen. She never did. Amanda opened her eyes to argue some more—then screamed. No gaunt, scarred pirate with a knife hovered over her this time. No calm, confident soldier, either. No blue eyes looked at her with concern. Instead, beady, bloodshot eyes watched her from mere inches away from her face.

Great gods, a hound of hell was about to claim her soul for the Devil! Huge, slavering jaws opened, showing long white fangs in the wrinkled, Stygian dark face. She screamed again.

The beast let out a howl, then scrambled under the bed, thumping and bumping until Amanda feared the whole structure would collapse, tossing her to those gnashing teeth. Should she try to escape out the door, or look for a weapon? What weapon was effective against a demon sent by Satan? How could she hope to outrun her fate? The demon was keening loudly enough to wake the dead anyway.

Then the door burst open. "What the deuce?"

The beast bounded up from under the bed and threw itself at a man wearing nothing but a towel and a few drops of water. He was Lord Rexford, Amanda recalled, Lady

Royce's son, her own rescuer. Now she had to rescue him. She grabbed up her pillow, to go to the viscount's aid. Maybe together they could smother the creature. No, there was water in the pitcher by her bedside. Perhaps she could blind the creature, or bash it over the head.

But Lord Rexford was petting the beast, telling the huge animal that she was safe. "Good girl."

"Good . . . girl?"

He nodded, one hand on the dog's collar, the other at the towel at his waist. "Her name is Verity. I am sorry if she frightened you, but she means no harm. And I can see you are feeling more the thing. Your lungs are working well, at any rate."

Now Amanda felt a blush rising from her shoulders to her cheeks. She was standing atop a mattress in a too-large borrowed night rail, brandishing a pillow and a pitcher of water. And a half-naked man was watching her chest heave with each gasping breath. She could not help but notice that his own chest—with its downy black line of hair and sharply defined planes and hollows—was also heaving, likely from a mad dash from his bath. The idea of Lord Rexford at his bath was enough to make her already reddened cheeks turn scarlet. Not that she took her eyes away from the rippling muscles and broad shoulders. Oh, no. Who knew when she would get another chance to see a gentleman's bare chest again, if ever? Whatever precepts of polite behavior she'd had drilled into her head since she could walk and talk flew right out the window, with the eagle of her dreams. Lord Rexford was flesh and blood, and she was no longer constrained by the tenets of the *ton*. No one expected an accused murderess to simper. So she stared.

Now it was Rex's turn to blush—for perhaps the first

time in ten years. Lud, the female was looking at him as if he were a fancy bonnet in a shop window, no, a bonbon on a platter that she was thinking of tasting, of biting and licking and—and if she wet her lips one more time with her pink tongue, the towel was not going to be enough to save both of them from more embarrassment. "I apologize for my undress, and for Verity's disturbing your rest. Please get back under the covers." Where the fire's light could not outline her slender figure through the white lawn nightdress. She bent to put the pitcher back on the bedside table and he drew in a breath at the sight of her rounded bottom. Good grief, he had been without a woman too long if he was drooling over a sickly female with a noose hanging over her head, almost literally. "Please get down, you have been too sick to be so active." He'd help her, but that would take two hands, and he needed one at the hastily tied knot of the towel.

She was feeling dizzy, actually, but she did not want to go back to sleep, or to have him leave. "That is your dog?"

"Hm?" He'd been watching her smooth out her nightgown, then gracefully slide under the blankets. She was sitting up, though, with her breasts uncovered except for the gown's thin fabric. He could make out the dark shadow of her nipples, and wondered if she really was a virgin, or a hardened seductress. Rumors had her meeting a lover, according to his information. If she were already bachelor fare . . .

"I suppose the beast must be yours, the way it is drooling on your foot."

Rex tore his gaze away from the woman's breasts and his thoughts away from the gutter. Who was the beast? Him? "Oh, Verity. More like I am her person. She found me one day and has hardly left my side since. I apologize for not warning you. You were sleeping soundly, so I saw no reason to disturb you from the rest you need."

Amanda looked at the dog with distrust, then scrubbed a hand over her cheek. "I am sorry if I bothered you, after all your kindness. I think she must have been licking my cheek. The unexpected wetness startled me, that is all. I do like dogs."

The muddiness in Rex's mind cleared when she added, "Small, friendly ones. I should not have screamed."

He shrugged. What was one more earsplitting shriek? "Half of London already believes I am torturing the truth out of you."

"I do not understand."

"That is a godsend. But speaking of the truth, will you tell me now how your stepfather died?" Rex knew he should wait until they were both properly attired, but she seemed alert and eager to talk. And he did not want to leave yet. "Did you kill him?"

"I—"

"Well, I have never seen the like, in all my born days! You know better than that, Master Jordan, prancing around in your altogether—and in a lady's bedchamber besides. Why, I'd think you were raised by wolves if I hadn't done the job myself!"

"Nanny?" Rex hardly recognized the gray-haired woman who had been the nearest thing to a mother he had after the countess left. She was a great deal smaller than he recalled, and stooped over. For all her bent back, she tossed her own plaid woolen shawl over his shoulders to cover his bare skin.

"Who else do you think would come when that fool Dodd sent a man blathering about murder and disaster and the downfall of the countess? He was right, too, from the looks of things. Why, I would be mortified if the countess found out I let you compromise her goddaughter."

Rex ignored the bit about compromising. "But how? I mean, how did Dodd know to send for you?"

"Tsk. My sister is your mother's housekeeper, don't you know. Sadie stays with me in Richmond while the countess is away."

"I did not know you lived so near to London. I would have visited."

"Like you visited your mum, then?"

"I do not wish to speak of that." Rex noticed that Miss Carville was following the whole conversation, her brown eyes shifting from him—and his bare legs, damn it—to Nanny Brown.

"Don't you go getting all niffy-naffy on me, Master Jordan, me who wiped your bum when you were born."

"Nanny!" Rex saw Miss Carville hide a smile behind her hand. Lud, he wished he had his breeches, or a bigger towel.

There was no stopping Nanny Brown. "But the trouble between you and the countess is for another day. Today is for the kettle of slops you've landed in now."

That took the smile off Miss Carville's face.

"Well, you always were one for trouble, weren't you? At least this time you knew enough to come to your mum's house. My sister is already taking over the kitchen until Cook comes back, although Sadie never could cook worth a ha'penny and she gets bilious, don't you know. I'll take over with the young lady."

That was a dismissal, so Rex headed toward the door. Nanny followed, until they were out of Miss Carville's hearing. Then she wanted to know what the doctor said.

"He said that she'd live long enough to hang."

"You won't let that happen."

Her words showed as a bright yellow to Rex. Nanny really believed he could alter the course of British justice. "I'll try."

"Well, get on with you then. You won't find the guilty one sitting here. And you don't belong in a young lady's bedchamber in the first place. You should know better."

"Yes, Nanny. But—"

"And without your clothes? Heaven help us if that's what they teach young gentlemen in university. Or did the army give you bad manners along with a limp? You need fattening up, besides." She poked a bony finger in his ribs.

There was nothing like being treated like a little boy, right after acting like a rutting stag. Since he had not received the answers he needed from Miss Carville, though, Rex asked for Nanny's opinion. "You don't believe she is guilty?"

"Why, look at the little lamb. And I don't mean the way you were gawking when I came in, either. No, if she did shoot the cur, she'd have good reason. Your mother adored her, Sadie says, so there cannot be a mean streak to her. Now get on with you. Sadie is heating some stew for all of us. I made it, so you'll like it. Until we get more help, you'll have to take potluck—once you are decent."

At least Miss Carville was in good hands. Now Rex could start unraveling the knots in her tangled circumstances. Nanny seemed confident he could. The stew was indeed good and filling, and Murchison had packed some of his old, comfortable clothes. His leg felt better for the hot bath and the rest.

He had no more excuses for staying in, or for not finding his cousin Daniel.

Chapter Six

The footman who was sent to find Daniel came back with his current address, but not his present whereabouts.

"One of the other boarders says as how Mr. Stamfield oftentimes drinks and dices at Dirty Sal's, a low den in Seven Dials where no gentleman less'n his size and reputation would dare walk," the footman reported. "I wouldn't put one foot there."

Rex had no choice but to leave Miss Carville alone with the servants although he worried about her welfare with such watchdogs: a philandering butler and a cowardly footman, a sniveling kitchen maid and a pimply potboy, a masquerading French valet, a housekeeper who could not cook, and a bent old nanny. Meanwhile the real watchdog, Verity, hid under the bed at the first sign of trouble.

They'd have to do, Rex decided as he tucked a pistol into his waistband and secured a dagger in his boot. His jackass of a cousin had to be stopped from committing suicide in a slum. That, too, was now Rex's responsibility. Last week he'd been riding and sailing, with nothing but his thoughts and his dog for company. Granted his thoughts were dismal, but now he was in the metropolis, with people depending on him again, fools that they were. He'd sworn to take orders from no one, be beholden to no one, and have no one's welfare depending on him and his one freakish talent.

Once again, his wants and wishes were blown about like leaves in autumn.

"Shall I call for your carriage, my lord?" Dodd asked, all respectful in hopes of keeping his position.

"No, the crested coach would be set upon instantly, if it could fit through the narrow streets, and a horse would be stolen as soon as I dismounted. I'll take a hackney as far as the driver will carry me and walk the rest of the way." He practiced sliding the case off the cane he carried, revealing the sword hidden within. His clothes were plain country wear, with no gleaming rings or fancy buckles to tempt the denizens of London's underworld, but if anyone should challenge him, he'd be ready. He half wished some thug would try to pick his pocket or steal his purse. Heaven help the poor bastard.

Maybe the scum who hid in alleys had unspoken talents of their own, like reading danger in the set of a man's jaw, or seeing murderous intents like sparks in his eyes. No one bothered Rex. For a coin, a street urchin led him straight to Dirty Sal's, after asking twice to be sure the toff really wanted to go inside that sinkhole. For another coin, the boy offered to take a message to the gent's family, for when he didn't come out.

Rex tossed him a coin without answering, and stepped through a cloud of smoke and sour ale and sweat. He waited for his eyes to grow accustomed to the gloom and his nose to the stench, while he kept his back to the wall near the doorway. The gaming tables were full. So were the spaces at the long plank bar against the opposite wall. Rex could not make out every face, or see into every corner, but Daniel's size usually made him more easily spotted than most. Rex noticed a man with an eye patch leading a woman in a loose blouse up rickety stairs to the floor above. Perhaps Daniel was taking his pleasure—and the pox—there instead of at the dice tables. The viscount ordered a mug of ale while he waited. The barmaid leaned forward so he could see where she tucked his coin, and offered him more than a drink. He smiled and shook his head.

From his position, Rex could overhear some of the conversation at a nearby card table. Without even trying to pick colors from their words, Rex knew at a glance which of the players were cheating. They were all cheating. Marked decks, hidden cards, signals passed across the table—just a friendly game among pals. An argument ensued over how many aces were in the pack. Heated words turned to a shove, which turned to a punch, which pushed a chap at the next table into dropping his dice, which came up sixes for the fifth time, which led to more shouts, more punches, and more of a melee, with his cousin Daniel in the middle. Of course.

Chairs were flying, tables were overturned, the barkeep was swinging a club, and Dirty Sal herself—or so Rex thought she must be—was waving a musket around.

Now this was the very entertainment Rex had been missing. Slashing out with his cane, he cleared a path to his cousin and got between him and the owner of the establishment, who appeared ready to shoot the next rotter who broke a chair. If there was one glass left unbroken at the end of the night, that would be a miracle.

"I've got your back," Rex shouted over the din of the fight.

Daniel turned and grinned, using his thick upraised arm to fend off a tossed stool. "Just like old times, you little nit. You need me to save your skin."

"Hah!" Rex punched a ferret-faced man in the midsection.

Daniel threw another combatant aside as easily as he'd thrown the stool. Rex used his cane to trip a charging drunk. Daniel banged together the heads of a pair of men who did not have seven teeth between them—and Rex lobbed a pitcher of ale at Dirty Sal and her musket, dampening the powder enough to render the fight less deadly.

Daniel laughed his loud, deep laugh, and Rex had to laugh, too. The Inquisitors were together again, in the middle of a fine rowdydow.

When it looked as though the establishment's regulars were going to join forces against the newcomers, Rex shouted, "Had enough?"

"Unless you want to go one on one, little coz."

"Not this minute, bullyboy. We need to talk."

"Not here."

A French cannon wouldn't be heard in the place. The cousins waded toward the door, dodging fists and punching back when they couldn't, sticking close together. "Just like old times, eh?"

Rex shook his hair out of his eyes. "Better. No one is shooting at us anymore."

Daniel suddenly stopped just as they reached the street. Unmindful of the fighting spilling out of the doorway behind them, he took Rex's chin in his broad hand and turned it to the lantern hanging by the entry, so he could see the scar. Then he looked at Rex's leg and the cane now bearing his weight, while Rex stayed quiet, breathing hard. "I should have been there with you. This wouldn't have happened."

Rex pulled away and started to walk across the street from the gambling hell. He hid his limp as much as possible. "No, we both would have been shot. No one saw the Frenchies creeping around camp until too late."

"I should have been there," Daniel insisted in his mulish way. "Your father told me to look after you."

"Dash it, I was not a child needing a nursemaid. And your mother and sister needed you at home."

Rex was watching his cousin, not the fight at their backs, so he never saw the thug come at him with a raised bottle. Daniel did and bellowed. Rex turned in time to feel the brunt of the bottle on his nose. Daniel roared a curse, dove at the man, and started pounding at him on the ground.

"Let him go. I don't think my nose is broken," Rex said, trying to stop the bleeding with a thin monogrammed square.

Daniel lumbered to his feet and handed over a sturdy spotted handkerchief. "You shouldn't have called me a useless dumb lummox."

"I didn't mean it."

"I knew that. Didn't like hearing it anyway."

"You were too damn stubborn to go home any other way."

"I am not stubborn, damn you!" Daniel drew his hamhock fist back and made sure Rex's nose was broken this time.

"Oh, hell," Rex muttered through the kerchief, which was joined by Daniel's neckcloth, then his own. "I thought my father told you to look after me."

"I am," Daniel said, hauling Rex to his feet and pulling him along before the Watch came. "You are too damned handsome for your own good."

Rex stumbled at first at his cousin's longer stride, but kept up. "What, with the scar? Women tremble at the sight."

"They'll tremble, all right, but with eagerness to sink their claws into you now that you are in London. What's a little scar compared to your title and fortune?"

"That's not why I came. I have another mission in town. My father sent me to rescue a damsel, and I need your help to fight off the dragon."

"Damsels and dragons, eh? I suppose you get to play the white knight and you expect me to be your loyal squire as usual? I won't do it. Ain't in the petticoat line, and ain't wearing armor. I like my freedom and my comfort too well."

"This is different."

"Not army work, then? I sold out ages ago, you know. Soon as I came home, and glad of it." Daniel kept walking, leading Rex toward a better section of town, thank goodness. Too many eyes stared out of too many alleys for Rex's comfort. No one had challenged them yet, but a limping, bloody nob was an easy target for a gang. Daniel was a large target for a thrown knife or a pistol.

"I am going to resign my commission as soon as this is over. I've had my fill of being treated like a barbarian." Not that this evening was any indication of a more civilized existence, but it felt better, except for his nose.

"We saved a lot of English lives with the information we got for the generals," Daniel said, "no matter how we got it."

"But we lost the respect of those very lives we saved, and well you know it. This is a more personal battle."

"Very well, who is the dragon, then?"

"Lady Royce."

"Your mother? You've reconciled with Aunt Margaret? That's grand."

"No, I have not reconciled with that woman. She is not even in Town yet. She's flitting around Bath while there's a cyclone brewing here. It's her goddaughter, Miss Amanda Carville."

Daniel stopped walking. "The female who shot that dirty dish Hawley, her own stepfather?"

"The one who was charged with the crime," Rex amended. "And charged in a hurry, I might add, by Sir Nigel Turlowe."

Daniel whistled, then regretted it, discovering a split lip. "So that is why your father sent you. Did she do it?" Daniel knew that Rex would have the truth, if anyone did.

"She was too ill to tell me. Then she was frightened by the dog, then Nanny Brown threw me out of the room." Rex swung his cane at a street lamp in frustration. "We have to find out."

Daniel leaned against the lamppost. "We?"

"I do not know my way around Town the way you do. And if Miss Carville did not commit the murder, then someone will not want us looking into it. Nor will Sir Nigel."

"You need me."

"That's what I said, you big oaf."

"Are you sure your nose is broken this time? I could . . ."

They went to the boardinghouse where Daniel rented a

set of rooms, to pick up his things. At first Daniel was not happy at the idea of staying at Royce House.

"I'm not, either," Rex said in an understatement. He'd rather have slept on the sagging sofa in Daniel's sitting room, but neither one of them had a choice, not if they were going to settle the court case as soon as possible. "But I vouched for Miss Carville, so I have to stay close at least until the countess returns."

"She'll be mad."

"Miss Carville? How can she complain of another champion? Besides, she is too ill to notice your presence."

"No, Aunt Margaret."

"What, that you've turned into a sot and a brawler?"

"No, that I broke your damned beak. I promised to look after you."

"That was on the Peninsula, not in London."

"I promised your father about the army. Your mother about everything else."

"Well, I promised your mother and father, too. And I never broke your nose, so you deserve the guilt and the anger."

"You couldn't break my nose if you wanted to."

Rex did not bother refuting the boyish taunt as he sipped at the wine Daniel brought. "I did not know you corresponded with the countess."

"She's my aunt, don't you know. She always wanted to hear about you."

"She could have asked me."

"Would you have answered?"

"No."

Rex sank into a chair and gratefully accepted the wet towel Daniel handed him to put over his aching nose, and another glass of wine.

While Daniel packed—if throwing clothing and papers and books into a trunk could be called packing—he wanted to know their plan. Rex always did have a plan, hey-go-mad or hell-born, and Daniel always went along with it.

"Well, until we know if the lady is innocent or not, we cannot mount a defense. We'll need to talk to the servants at Hawley's house, and pick up Miss Carville's belongings while we are there. And I want to know why the stepsister and -brother never visited the jail, and what man Miss Carville was supposed to be meeting on the sly."

"I never heard a name in the clubs and coffeehouses when everyone was talking about the killing. Mostly they were all glad Sir Frederick was gone."

"That's what I heard too, so far. But someone has to know more. Then there is the little problem I might have with the Lord High Magistrate or the sheriff's office, for nearly kidnaping Miss Carville out of Newgate."

"You didn't go bail for her?"

"There is no bond set for a killer—an accused killer. I suppose they figure the accused would all scarper off to the colonies or something."

"Right. I would be running too, if I had the gun in my hand at the scene of the crime." Daniel grinned, then found another towel to hold against his split lip. "So you stole the woman like a ravaging Hun?"

"Not exactly. I paid the guard and claimed I was taking her for medical treatment. So I might have to call at the War Office."

Daniel took a long swallow of his wine, deciding that would work better than a towel. "The Aide?"

Rex nodded. No one voluntarily called on the secretive figure behind the covert operations of the army's

Intelligence division. "I am on sick leave still, so he cannot order me back to the Peninsula. On the other hand, he will not want me arrested for obstructing justice."

Daniel put on a clean jacket—cleaner, at any rate—and said, "With friends like that, who needs maggots?"

"Right."

"Tell me about the woman."

So Rex told what little he knew. Of course he did not describe the woman's figure or soft skin, only her condition, the rescue, and the few words they'd exchanged.

"Have you a guess?"

Rex knew Daniel meant about the murder, not whether Miss Carville was a virgin or not, which kept rattling around Rex's brain like a loose shutter on a windy night. "My gut says she's no cold-blooded killer, and Nanny Brown swears the countess would not have sent for us if she were. Other than that, the lady might have had good reason."

"Good enough for Sir Nigel and the courts?"

Rex did not know, which worried him. "Are you ready? I do not like leaving her alone in that household. Most of the servants are on holiday." He stood, with effort. Damn, but his bad leg was not up to this much activity. He took a last swallow of his wine for the trip back to Mayfair.

Daniel watched, without offering a hand. "Well, if she is convicted, at least your mother won't make you marry the chit."

The wineglass slid out of Rex's fingers. "What do you mean?"

"Stands to reason Aunt Margaret won't want a killer in the family, even if the gal is her goddaughter. Might shoot her husband next. That'd be you," he added, in case Rex missed the barb.

Rex was still on the dire word. "Marry?"

"Well, the wife of a peer gets special privileges in the courts, doesn't she? And there's no doubt that you compromised the female. Took her off on your horse, brought her to your mother's house with no respectable female present. Undressed her, too. If that's not compromising a lady, I don't know what is, unless you raise her skirts on a park bench in Hyde Park."

While Rex sputtered and tried to explain the situation, Daniel tied another spotted kerchief around his neck in lieu of a cravat and then hauled his trunk onto his shoulder. He looked more like a dockworker than a gentleman, but Rex was not in any position to cast aspersions, not with his shirt and coat stained with blood, his red-soaked neckcloth tossed in the trash altogether. Besides, who cared about neatness when Daniel spoke of nuptials?

"Deuce take it, I saved her from being beaten and raped! I took her to where she could be tended and healed."

Daniel headed down the stairs with his burden, as if he carried a bandbox instead of a trunk. "You ought to know the *ton* don't care a whit about the right or the reason. They only care about the looks of the thing. An earl's son, a spinster lady alone in a house. Sounds like wedding bells to me. You better hope she's guilty."

"No, I shall not hope for that. And no one can force me to the altar."

"I don't know about that," Daniel called back over his shoulder. "Your mother is a powerful woman. Made me take tea with her cronies and their daughters a few times. You know how I hate that kind of thing. Makes me break out in a rash."

"That's not pushing you to wed one of them."

"I don't know. Your mother had that look in her eye. I was glad she left for Bath when she did, except she did set a fine table. Oh, pull the door shut behind you, there's a good fellow."

There's a wed man walking.

Chapter Seven

Nanny Brown clutched her heart when she opened Miss Carville's door to see Rex looking as if he'd been run over by an oxcart.

Rex almost had palpitations too, when he saw the gun wavering in the old woman's gnarled fingers.

"My stars!"

"My pistol." Rex still had the mate tucked into his waistband. He gingerly reached out to take the weapon.

Nanny almost dropped it before he had his hands on the barrel. Daniel ducked, behind him.

"Oh, it is not loaded, but I thought it best to keep the thing nearby. My knitting needles are in my pocket and the warming pan is next to my chair."

"You needed a weapon to defend yourself from Miss Carville?" Good grief, had he carelessly left his former nursemaid alone with a homicidal maniac? He'd supposed that the younger woman had a good excuse for shooting Hawley, if she actually did commit the murder. Not that she was liable to murder a frail old woman in her sleep along with the rest of Lady Royce's household.

Rex shuddered to recall his last day in the army, when the same overconfidence in his intuition almost let a troop

of French scouts fire on headquarters. He was the only ca-
sualty, thank goodness, or he never would have been able
to forgive himself. Lud, if something happened to Nanny,
he'd be in worse straits. She was not even a soldier.

He should have waited for morning to find his cousin,
or left a message at Daniel's rooms. He should have
posted guards, or stood sentinel himself. He should
have—

Nanny sniffed, then scowled at the odors of cheap ale
and fine wine and clucked her tongue. "How much have
you been drinking to come up with such a foolish notion?
Of course I did not need to fend off Miss Carville. She is
a lady, not a criminal. But someone loose in London killed
that unfortunate man." She stepped closer and peered up
at Rex. "Did he attack you?"

"No, we encountered a spot of trouble at a gaming
club, that's all." Rex touched his swollen nose. "A, um,
discussion about the dice used."

"It looks broken, which is no more than you deserve,
gambling and drinking and brawling, on your first night in
London. What will her ladyship think?"

Rex was about to say he did not give a rap for what the
countess thought when Nanny caught sight of the large
man standing back in the shadows of the hall. She clucked
again. "I should have known. Daniel Stamfield, you always were up to no good. From what my sister tells me,
you are no better now than the nasty little boy you always
were, getting my lamb into trouble."

Instead of taking offense, Daniel laughed and rubbed at
his chin. "You always were blind when it came to your favorite. Everyone in Royston knew Rex was the ringleader.
You must be the only one who thought he was an angel."

"I'll have you know I still do. Except for the gambling and drinking and brawling, of course."

"And Daniel was never little, Nanny," Rex put in, before he received another scolding.

"No, and he has never been other than a heathen, either. Is it true what my sister says about the night last month when you escorted Lady Royce to Almack's?"

Rex looked back at his cousin in amazement. "You actually went to that pillar of propriety? The place they call the Marriage Mart?"

"I told you, your mother is a strong woman."

Nanny poked at Daniel's chest, but she was too short and stuck her finger in his stomach, grown soft in London's clubs and pubs. "She said you scratched your arse right in front of your aunt's friends and Princess Lieven."

"I warned her that all that gossip and sham politeness made me itchy. It always did, but she insisted. Said I had to have outgrown throwing spots like a high-strung debutante. At least she never bludgeoned me into going again."

Rex was laughing out loud. The wine at Daniel's house might have had something to do with his hilarity, but the thought of his bumbling giant of a cousin among the dainty manners at Almack's cheered him up considerably.

Daniel muttered, too low for Nanny's hearing, "Keep laughing if you want your arm broken, too." To Nanny he said, "I apologized to Aunt Margaret."

"A great deal of good that did. Why, my sister said the poor lady decided to leave for Bath the next day, so she did not have to face any of her acquaintances. Which is why she wasn't in Town to help Miss Carville last week. As for you, Master Jordan, you ought to be ashamed of yourself, getting into a nasty brawl at your age. Why, you are supposed to be an officer and a gentleman, not sowing wild oats. For that matter, you are supposed to be proving Miss Carville's innocence."

Which reminded Rex of why they were all standing in the hall outside the woman's door. "We have come to see about that very thing, Nanny. Is Miss Carville able to answer a few questions?"

"At this time of night? I should say not. She is fast asleep."

Rex could tell by the red flashes that sweet old Nanny was lying through her false teeth.

"We'll just disturb her rest for a moment."

Nanny crossed her arms in front of her age-flattened chest and barred the door. "You will not come into a gentlewoman's bedroom looking like a prizefighter, the one who lost the bout. You will not come into a proper young lady's chamber at night at all, ever. Now you go on and get that man of yours to do something about your face before you give the poor girl more nightmares in the morning."

With Daniel's words about compromise and marriage echoing in his mind, Rex nodded. "We shall speak with Miss Carville early then. We have a lot to accomplish tomorrow."

The ancient martinet shook her head. "I promised the lass a bath and a hair wash if she has no fever in the morning. That will make her feel better about things. So you'll just have to wait."

"Devil take it, I have to insist."

"Insist all you want, my lord. I do not take orders from you, no matter how much you glare at me. I'm here because you need me, young man, not because I need a salary. Your father made me a generous pension, so mind your tongue."

"Yes, ma'am," Rex answered, stepping back on

Daniel's foot to stop his cousin's snicker. "You will tell us when it is convenient to begin trying to prove Miss Carville's innocence. I am certain her clean hair will impress the judges."

Nanny used her pointing finger like a poker to Rex's chest. "And I won't have you dressed like a stable hand in my lady's chamber, either. You tell that valet of yours that, too, unless he's deaf as well as dumb. He refused to listen when I asked for your pistol, so I had to fetch it myself when he was out."

"Out as in out of the house? Or perhaps in the kitchen or the laundry room?"

"How should I know? The fellow does not talk, does he?"

He did when he got his first look at Rex and what he'd done to yet another suit of clothes, to say nothing of his face. *"Sacre bleu!"* Murchison yelled before he could recall himself, which Rex felt was worth the sore, swollen nose.

"He can speak?" Daniel whispered.

"In French," Rex whispered back, knowing full well that Murchison could hear every word. "But don't tell anyone. We'll have to puzzle that business out, too." Which, Rex reasoned, was fair notice to Murchison that he meant to investigate the gentleman's gentleman. Rex disliked secrets almost as much as he disliked lies.

"He ain't a spy for the Frogs, is he? I told you, I'm out of the espionage business for good."

"I doubt my father would keep on a traitor, but then again, I never considered that Lady Royce would befriend a convict."

"Well, I never thought I'd see you at your mother's

house, either, so I guess you can't trust your gut. Except when it's telling you it's hungry."

With his size, Daniel needed far more sustenance than Rex. Hell, he ate enough for two men, and never seemed satisfied.

"Maybe there is some of Nanny's stew left."

There wasn't, but they did find a cured ham in the larder, a tin of biscuits, some fruit preserves, a wheel of cheese, and a bushel of apples.

"I told you your mother sets a fine table," Daniel said between mouthfuls, washed down with a bottle of excellent wine. "Even if it is the kitchen table."

"I saw no reason to stir up the butler and the footman to serve us in the dining room. Do you mind?"

Daniel laughed. "After sharing half a scrawny chicken with you in a sweltering tent, this is heaven. As long as the monster you call a dog does not steal from my plate."

Verity did not need to steal, not with Daniel sliding slices of ham across the boards to where her chin rested on the wooden table.

Rex relaxed and cut off another slice of cheese, pleased his two friends were getting along. He should have known they would, since both were more interested in food than conversation or physical activity.

He was pleased, too, with the meal. Daniel was right: The food did taste better than any Rex had eaten in ages. He ate more than usual, his appetite encouraged by Daniel's enthusiasm. Or else the fight had reinvigorated him. Yes, Rex thought, being hit in the head must have knocked some of the cobwebs out of his skull. Instead of that aimless wandering, that dreary melancholy he'd fallen into, he felt more like himself than he had since being shot. Perhaps better, since he was not interrogating captured soldiers; having the generals press him for faster, more detailed, results; or pretending not to notice the disdain of the other officers.

He could laugh, even, as Daniel and Verity both gazed longingly at the last biscuit, which happened to be on Rex's plate. He ate it.

Lud, a man could not stay in the doldrums with Daniel and a dog around. Besides, now he had a mission, and a partner.

All in all, Rex decided, he'd had a good day, his most productive in months. He found it hard to believe so much had happened—had he truly just arrived in London this morning?—in so short a time. A jailbreak, a scandal, and a bar fight, plus finding out that his cousin had been banned from Almack's. The day was almost perfect, especially if one did not consider the sins of ogling an unconscious female or lusting after a helpless woman in his care.

Maybe he should get into brawls more often.

Her hero was a drunken brawler? His cousin was a social pariah, a troublemaker since birth, and a gambler? Amanda had heard every word between Nanny Brown and the gentlemen through the open door. Now she could not hold back her tears.

When she'd woken from her stupor to find herself at Royce House, she began to think she had a chance of living until her next birthday. She would not have made next week in prison. Why should she struggle to survive there, anyway? They were only going to hang her. The formal conviction appeared irrelevant.

At her godmother's home she'd felt a spark of hope, a tiny glimmer of optimism. Lord Rexford had seemed so

competent, so confident, she had to believe he would rescue her. That flicker of faith was doused by the cold wind
of reality. No one was going to be able to save her, especially not a ruffian and his unmannered kin.

She had no money, no friends or relations to call on.
Only an old woman with an unloaded pistol stood as her
defender. Why, she had to sleep in a borrowed nightgown.
Amanda wiped her eyes with the corner of the sheet. She
did not even have a handkerchief. Perhaps she'd go to the
gibbet tripping over one of the countess's old frocks.

What was the point of waiting for them to hang her?
She eyed the window of her room, but knew that shrub-
beries surrounded the entire house, thick enough to break
a fall. The bottle of laudanum? She had no idea how much
was needed. If Nanny Brown brought the pistol back . . .

The coward's way out? Yes.

A sin? Yes.

But it would be proof of her guilt, too. That's what
everyone would believe, anyway. Lord Rexford would
look like a fool for coming to her aid. He had come,
though, so she supposed she owed him better than that.

He should have left her in that wretched cell. She'd
been so close to escaping it all there, so distant from her
misery, almost in her parents' arms. Now she was suffering worse, because he'd thrown her a life preserver. Her
ship was sinking and sharks were circling, but she'd
grabbed hold with both hands. Now the rope was fraying,
and the viscount was not going to bring her to shore. She'd
have done better letting the waves wash over her. Hope
was gone. Hope was a demon, a devil, a cheat.

When Nanny came back into the room she found Miss
Carville curled into a ball, sobbing.

"There, lambie. He'll fix it, I know he will."

Amanda looked up, checking for the pistol. "He's drunk."

"Pooh. He's a gentlemen fresh come to Town, seeing his best friend after months. I doubt they have been apart so long since their crib days. And he has burdens of his own to carry. But the boy I knew is good at heart. And nearly as wise as his father. Tonight's nonsense is nothing to fret over. You'll see."

"No," Amanda said with a sniff and another sob. "There is nothing he can do. And why should he put himself to the trouble? I am nothing to him."

Nanny handed her a handkerchief. "He will help because he is an honorable gentleman. And because his mother asked, that's why."

Amanda blew her nose and asked, "He does not like her much, does he?"

"He has his reasons, and none of them for us to discuss. It was sad times for all of the family. I doubt any of them will ever recover, but that doesn't mean his lordship won't do his duty. He served the country proud, no matter what anyone says. And that oversized oaf Daniel wouldn't hurt a fly, unless someone threatens his friends. Close as brothers they always were. Where one was in trouble, the other'd be there, too." Nanny sat by Amanda's bedside and took up her knitting. "Why, the stories I could tell about those two rapscallions."

Amanda envied the cousins that closeness. She was too much older than her stepsister to be friends, and was more of an unpaid companion to Elaine these last five years. Thanks to Sir Frederick's penny-pinching ways, Amanda had never gone to school or had a proper come-out, where she might have met girls her own age. Elaine had not even sent her a note in jail, much less a change of clothes or a coin to purchase better treatment. Amanda started weeping again.

Nanny was going on about her favorite topic, it seemed, while her knitting needles clacked. "Master Jordan was a good boy, as smart as could be. And the best rider in the shire. The best swordsman, later, too. I know he must be bothered, limping that way. But he'll be as steady as a rock. And that clodpoll cousin will prop him up if he falters, never you fear. They are good men, both of them."

If they were all she had, Amanda thought, heaven help her.

Nanny poured more laudanum and Amanda swallowed it gladly.

Chapter Eight

The primping took most of the morning. Even then, Rex was barely fit for polite company.

His hair was trimmed and his uniform was neatly pressed, but his head ached from all the liquor, his nose looked like part of a clown's costume, his bad leg had stiffened in London's perpetual damp, and his dog preferred Daniel. He felt wretched.

"I always have a roll in my pocket, or a meat pasty, that's all."

"Do not shout." Rex held his head in his hands, cringing as Daniel took his third helping of eggs and what was left of the ham from the night before. "And I am glad the mongrel is drooling over someone else's clothes for a change."

"You used to be able to hold your liquor better."

"I used to be able to do a lot of things better." Rex took a sip of his coffee. It tasted as if the housekeeper had used fairgrounds instead of coffee grounds. He shoved it aside and poured a cup of tea.

"Tea? You are acting and sounding like an old man, coz. Hell, you're not yet thirty years old."

"I will be soon."

"Three months later than I will, and look at me."

Rex tried not to. His cousin's face was not as lurid as his own, but Daniel's apparel hurt the viscount's eyes. Wide yellow Cossack trousers, a turquoise and puce striped waistcoat, a peacock blue coat, with a spotted kerchief instead of a neckcloth, might have looked dashing on a trick rider at Astley's Amphitheatre. On Daniel? "You look like a hot-air balloon."

"That shows what you know. My outfit is all the rage, the height of fashion. And a deuced sight more comfortable than the fancy rig you're sporting."

There was no getting around the strangling high knot Murchison had tied at Rex's neck, or the close fit of the heavy woolen uniform coat, with its brass and gold trim. His glossy high boots aggravated his sore leg, and the knit pantaloons emphasized his limp.

"I thought I better look the proper officer if I'm to call at the War Office immediately after we speak with Miss Carville."

"Oh, I thought you were dressing for your visit to the sickroom."

"Don't be more of a gudgeon than you have to be. I am still part of the army."

"And here I thought you were still Nanny's lambikin. Since when do you march to petticoat orders? You haven't listened to Nanny Brown's nattering since you were in leading strings."

"She's old."

"And Miss Carville is young."

"I did *not* dress for Miss Carville or Nanny Brown." He quickly shoved the plate of sweet rolls in Daniel's direction when he saw his cousin start to scratch at the top of his hand. "I am merely trying to do my best for the lady, guilty or innocent. I think that we might need all the forces we can muster, and all the resources of the Special Section, too."

Daniel swallowed a bite of roll, then handed the rest to the mastiff. "I've been thinking, too"—he ignored Rex's snort of derision—"about what's best for the lady."

"The last time I let you think I got coshed with a bottle."

"But you got shot on your own."

That was true. "Very well, so what are the results of your mighty musings?"

"I think you should get betrothed to her."

Rex set his teacup down with a thump and a splash onto the tablecloth. "Now that is more idiotic than your usual ideas. I might have expected such rubbish from Lady Royce, seeking to shift her responsibilities onto my shoulders, or even from Nanny, but you?"

"Think on it. People will believe she's innocent if you propose. No viscount would court a killer, would he? And he wouldn't affiance himself to someone about to dance with Jack Ketch. At least it would get people wondering, instead of hanging her in the press. Public sentiment can sway a judge. Mightn't be the right way to decide a case, but it's better than trying to discredit the witnesses."

Rex blotted at the stain on the linen tablecloth without answering.

"And you know how peers get preferential treatment. You nobs get to be tried by the Lords instead of the courts. No one is going to convict a countess's daughter-in-law. Granddaughter to an earl, isn't she?"

"Something like that. But I doubt those rules apply to a viscount's fiancée, even if I were willing to go along. Which I am not."

"You wouldn't have to call the banns or anything. As soon as she's cleared of the charges, you go your own ways."

"You know better than anyone that I could not take part in a sham engagement. Lie to the courts, to the *ton*, to Lady Royce? My head would burst with the fireworks of color."

"Then marry her. Then she'd be a titled lady, and you wouldn't be living a lie. Yes, that is the better idea. You know you'll have to marry sooner or later anyway. Sooner, if your mother learns you undressed the female."

"I will never marry."

Daniel set down his fork. "What, never? What about the succession?"

"The Crown can have the earldom when I am done with it. The prince can reward some jumped-up industrialist with a title and an estate, in exchange for having his own outrageous bills paid."

"But your father will—"

"He will be long gone before that time."

"But why, Rex? You've always known you had to marry. It's part of the requirements for being the heir and all. Like wearing your sword into battle. Lordlings have to produce the next generation."

"This lord shall not. The world does not need another freak in its carnival show. The haut monde does not need another target for its vicious gossip. What did the earldom gain my father? Nothing but ignominy and insult for his so-called gift. My own reputation is lower than a lizard's, and yours not much better by the mere association. And if the truth were told? Royce Hall and all of its inhabitants would be burned to the ground, aye, and this house with it. The countess would be tarred with the same brush of witchcraft and devil's work. Perhaps that was why she left my father. He never said. But I will not bring another Royce male into this world, to suffer the way we have."

Daniel pushed his plate away. "Well, I still say it was a good idea."

"Then why don't you wed her?"

"Me? A onetime junior officer, a country nobody? What good would that do the female? I've got a tidy manor house and the farm, but that's all. No title, no fortune, no influence anywhere. No fit lodgings here in town, no invites to fancy parties. I doubt I'll be permitted back into Dirty Sal's. I don't have your pretty face, what once was, anyway. I'll wed when I'm ready—promised my mother, don't you know—to a plainspoken lass from the country who won't think I'm a great hulking looby like the London twits do. Your Miss Carville needs someone who can help her cause, not stumble over it."

"She's not my Miss Carville."

Then why, Rex wondered, was he so relieved when Daniel refused to marry her?

Nanny Brown had magic in her long bony fingers along with the arthritis.

Amanda felt almost alive the next morning after the old woman was finished with her. She was still slightly feverish and weak and weepy when she awoke, but Nanny would not permit her to feel sorry for herself.

"And what else should you be but blue-deviled, what with the sights and suffering you've seen?" Nanny asked. "But a bit of prettying up will make you feel more the thing, I swear."

The bath was heavenly, the shampoo sublime, and the sweet scented oils Nanny rubbed into Amanda's skin divine. What most made Amanda feel better, though, was the pampering. No one had paid her this much attention since her mother's death. She and Elaine shared a maid, but the servant knew who was favored in the house, and did as little for the poor relation as possible.

"A woman always feels better with clean hair and fresh underthings, I always say," Nanny told her, laying out Amanda's own silk petticoat and lace-edged chemise.

Someone, most likely Lord Rexford, Amanda thought, had sent for her clothes at Sir Frederick's. The single trunk could not have contained her entire wardrobe, and the surly maid might have run off with the rest, but Amanda was grateful to see some of her own things, especially her mother's pearls. Just knowing she would not have to face her future in rags or borrowed apparel raised her spirits another notch.

She chose her favorite gown for the interview with Lord Rexford, a rose-colored muslin with tiny flowers embroidered at the hem and the neck. As it happened, her wardrobe was now far more fashionable than in previous years, for she had been escorting her seventeen-year-old stepsister on Elaine's come-out Season. Sir Frederick had been determined to snare a well-born beau for his daughter, and needed Amanda's connection to Lady Royce to procure vouchers and invitations. He could not let the beau monde see Amanda in faded frocks or mended gloves or styles of five years ago, lest they label him a pinchpenny, which would ruin his daughter's chance of marrying a title. So for once he gave Amanda a generous clothing allowance, likely from her own funds.

Amanda had had plans to catch a husband of her own this Season now that Elaine was old enough to wed. With freedom from Sir Frederick in her mind, she'd selected her new gowns with an eye to style and color instead of the serviceable fabrics and modest gowns she'd chosen in the past, knowing they had to last. Her new clothes were in the latest mode, with a graceful, airy look that became her slight figure and made the most of her rounded bosom, which, the modiste assured her, was more liable to attract a gentleman's eye than all of Elaine's frills and furbelows. Elaine's gowns were white and the palest pastels; Amanda's were in brighter, more vibrant tones.

Nanny shook out the deep pink gown to check for creases. "This will put roses in your cheeks for sure."

And the face powder Nanny borrowed from the countess's vanity would hide the bruises on her skin and the shadows under her eyes.

Nanny trimmed her hair, too, tsking over the uneven lengths. "Looks like goats have been nipping at it." She and her sister mixed eggs and ale and lemons into a frothy shampoo, then twisted the short locks around their fingers into tiny ringlets. They fed her and dressed her and put her mother's pearls around her neck, before seating her on the chaise longue in the countess's sitting room near the fireplace, with a blanket across her knees.

Despite the blanket, Amanda started shivering.

Nanny added more coal to the fire. "Maybe we did too much. I worried that we should have waited another day."

"No, Nanny, you did wonders. And you were right, I do feel human again, simply being clean and neat."

"Neat and clean? Why, I swear you look like a princess, only prettier. No one could suspect you of an evil thought, not with that sweet smile, much less murdering anyone."

"Thank you, for what you have done and for what you believe." She held the old woman's hand and started weeping again. "You—you have been so kind."

"Go on with you, lass," Nanny said, dabbing at her own eyes with her apron. "Now I'll just change the bed linen so it will be ready for you as soon as the gentlemen have the information they need."

Alone, Amanda thought that although she felt better and looked better, her prospects were just as dim. She did not know what Lady Royce's son could do, if anything, but no one else would try. If Lord Rexford did not believe her, her chances were nonexistent.

Amanda twisted her hands in the blanket, afraid he would not accept her word of what happened. What if his reputation for brutality was valid? She would not think of that.

He had been kind and sober. Maybe he only turned savage with the drink in him. Like last night and the barroom brawl. She could not think so badly of the man who had carried her on his horse, put ointment on her cuts. Oh heaven, she so wanted to believe he was a gentleman, but perhaps a barbarian could do more for her.

She blotted her eyes with her own handkerchief, one she had embroidered herself, and straightened her spine. She looked like a lady and smelled like a lady. She was determined to act like one, too, not fall to weeping and wailing as she waited for two of the most dreaded men in the King's army, the Inquisitors.

Rex was speechless. The reclining woman could not be Miss Amanda Carville, accused murderess. She was an angel, all tousled blond curls and big brown eyes. She was a raspberry pastry in deep pink. She was a china figurine, so still and perfect. She was spun-sugar delicate and gossamer soft and, hell, her breasts were larger than he remembered, overflowing the bodice of her gown. She was—waiting for him to introduce his cousin, who nudged him in the back.

Rex bowed and stepped farther into the room. At least he must have, because he had her hand in his, and was raising it to his lips. "I am delighted to see you looking better," he said, in what had to be one of the world's greatest understatements. She looked like—No, he could not fall into that abyss again. He was a soldier, not a poet. "May I present my cousin, Mr. Daniel Stamfield?"

Daniel shoved him aside, which reminded Rex to relinquish her hand, so small, so fine-boned that it got lost in Daniel's huge paw. "I promise he is a gentle fellow, for all his great size." His scowl said it better be so.

Daniel made a proper bow and said, "I am at your service, miss."

Mr. Stamfield's breadth and bulk were intimidating, Amanda decided, but his smile was genuinely friendly, unlike Lord Rexford, who did not smile at all, but glared at her and his cousin and the very room as if he hated being there. He was looking as cross as a bear with a sore foot, which she supposed was understandable, with his nose all red and swollen. He might have the headache, too. Sir Frederick often had, after a night of overindulgence.

Despite his frown and his spotless uniform, Captain Lord Rexford still appeared the buffoon. His cousin wore the clothes of a clown. And these were the army's invincible interrogators? For that matter, these were her only hope of rescue?

She turned her attention back to Mr. Stamfield, who politely raised her hand, and said, "Anything you need, I shall see that Rex provides."

She did not laugh at the teasing. "You are too kind."

"Any friend of my aunt's is my friend," he insisted,

lowering his body carefully into a chintz-covered chair. Lord Rexford chose to stand near the hearth.

"Then you believe me innocent?" Amanda asked.

"I did not say that. Some of my best friends are scoundrels, and my own aunt is not above blackmailing a chap to get her own way. Not that I am saying you aren't innocent. That's what we're here to find out. Then we can decide the proper course to take."

Now Lord Rexford stepped closer. Amanda could see the strain in his blue eyes, and the scar showing white against his tanned skin. "I suppose you have heard of our reputation?"

She would not flinch. "That you get the truth any way that you can?"

He was the one who winced at the bald statement. "You need not be afraid. Just answer our questions honestly, that is all I ask. As I promised, I will still help you no matter what you tell me, even if you say you have been planning to murder your stepfather for months and do not regret it now."

"I have told the truth to everyone," Amanda said, hating the catch in her voice and the dampness in her eyes. "I never attempted to lie about anything. No one listened to me. Now you tell me to speak honestly. Why should I think that you will believe what I say?"

Rex brushed his thumb across her cheek, catching the tear that fell. "Because I know it will be the truth."

Chapter Nine

I do not understand."

"No, I cannot suppose you do."

Amanda waited for an explanation that never came. Instead Lord Rexford seemed to grow angry again. "It is irrelevant, and we are wasting time. Sir Nigel Turlowe wants a conviction, damn his black heart to hell. Begging your pardon."

Amanda nodded, wishing she could curse, too.

Lord Rexford had turned from gentle shepherd to the wolf that ate the sheep. He started pacing, while his dog watched from beside Daniel's chair. "The trial is set for almost a month away, but every day that passes makes the task of an acquittal more difficult."

"I . . . I see." Amanda saw the hangman's noose, the crowds coming to watch, the thick rope dangling, waiting. She clutched the blanket again.

"Stop, Rex, can't you see you are frightening the poor woman?"

He was frightening himself, too, to have her very life depending on him. "I apologize once more, Miss Carville."

"There is no need. I am aware of my dire straits and your uncomfortable position in assisting me."

"But you might not be aware that Sir Nigel despises my father and wishes to discredit him further for some reason. Embarrassing Lady Royce would suffice, I suppose, or dragging me into his vendetta."

"Then I am a mere pawn in his grudge? I would not be in this fix if two men were not feuding?"

"Sir Nigel did not put the gun in your hand, did he?"

"No, I did that."

"Very well. Let us begin there. The weapon was in your hand. Sir Frederick was shot. Did you shoot him? This is a simple question, answerable with no roundaboutation, if you please."

"No. I wished him dead many times, but I did not kill him. I did not!"

Rex looked toward his cousin who held his hands up, palms out. "No rash."

Rex nodded. "True-blue," was all he said. Everyone was silent for a minute, thinking.

Amanda was thinking that her saviors were crazy.

Finally the viscount said, "In a way it would have been easier if you had shot the lowlife."

"How could that be better for me?"

"Because then we could have pled self-defense, a threat to your life, extenuating circumstances. You might have thought he was a burglar. Anything. We might manage to have you sentenced to parole, perhaps in Lady Royce's care, or sent out of the country for your lifetime."

"Botany Bay?" she asked with a gasp. "Few men live through the voyage there, fewer women."

"No, I meant India or the colonies. Or even one of my father's outflung properties."

"But I could not live as your family's pensioner. Or subject your mother to social death here in London." She turned toward Daniel. "You saw what happened over your little faux pas. Lady Royce would be ostracized if she harbored a confessed killer." She raised her chin. "I am not guilty. I shall not confess."

"Very well. If you are not guilty, who is? Do you know?"

"No. I have been racking my brains, and I cannot think of a single person. I did not know my stepfather's associates. He seldom entertained at home, and whatever business he conducted would have been at his clubs. "

"What about the butler?" Daniel wanted to know. "It's always the butler, isn't it, except when it is a jealous spouse."

"Hareston is a fussy, sneaky sort, who would never have left the gun on the floor."

"Perhaps you surprised him and he panicked."

"But why would he shoot his employer, putting himself out of work?"

"Why indeed?" Rex asked, searching in the countess's escritoire for a pencil and paper. He ignored the small packet of letters tied with a blue ribbon in one of the upper drawers. They looked suspiciously like the twice yearly letters of obligation he had sent in reply to birthday and Christmas gifts. He slammed that drawer shut and found what he wanted in a lower one. "And we can leave your stepsister and her aunt off the list because I understand they stayed on at Almack's until someone sent for them, after the Watch arrived. Odd."

"No, I doubt they noticed I was gone."

"That caring of you, eh?" Daniel wanted to know,

looking like thunderclouds. He would not have let his sister out of his sight in London.

"My stepsister was too excited about her first evening at Almack's, and her aunt, Miss Hermione Hawley, Sir Frederick's sister, was sitting with the chaperones, scrutinizing the eligible bachelors. Elaine cares for me."

"Yet she did not help you when you were arrested." That was a statement from Lord Rexford, not another question.

Amanda glared at him. "She is seventeen. What should she have done? And her father was dead, horribly. I think someone told me that she and Miss Hawley left London the next day, conveying the baronet's body to his family's cemetery in Hampshire."

"Very well, they are not suspects or witnesses. Why do you not start in the beginning."

"But I have told my story over and over again. Surely you have heard all the details from the newspaper and the servants and town gossip."

Daniel was nodding, but Rexford did not pay attention, making notations on his pad. "I need to hear it from your own mouth because proving innocence in this case is going to be far harder than proving guilt."

"But I did not commit the crime!"

"I know." He touched her hand, then jerked his away, as if he had not meant to touch her. "But think on this. What, say, if your pearls were in question? You can prove you have a set by the necklace itself, or a bill of sale."

"They were my mother's."

"A will, then, or a houseful of servants recalling them. Easy proof. But what if someone said you had a diamond necklace?"

"I do not. Sir Frederick sold it and my mother's other jewelry, to pay for her doctors, he claimed."

"Ah, but you could have sold the necklace, or tossed it in the dustbin. Then it would be your word against the prosecutor's case."

Amanda fingered the pearls at her throat. "I see."

He nodded. "The negative is far harder to prove, but it is not impossible. Now start at the beginning of the unfortunate events. No, start with your life with Sir Frederick and his household."

So Amanda told him about her mother's marriage, her fading away, and Sir Frederick's anger. She told about his misappropriating of her inheritance and stealing her dowry, and how she was relegated to a poor companion in the house.

Daniel asked, "Why did you not leave? My aunt would have taken you in."

"And left little Elaine to face her father's rages, his skimping on her clothes and education and even simple entertainments? I could not abandon her when she was so young."

"Admirable, I am sure," Lord Rexford said, "but then she grew up enough to enter the Marriage Mart."

"Yes, her father wanted her to marry a title. She liked the idea of becoming a marchioness or a duchess."

"Not likely, a filly coming from that stable."

Rex frowned at his cousin's interruption. "Go on."

"With Elaine grown and her father attending to her future, I hoped to marry myself. Sir Frederick swore none of my suitors was good enough. In fact, that very afternoon he admitted that he would never part with my dowry. I was not of age yet, and he would see it diminished to nothing by my twenty-fifth birthday. My inheritance was already gone, he said, for my upkeep." She ignored Daniel Stamfield's angry mutterings and watched Lord Rexford add another note to his list. When he looked up, she continued. "I thought a particular gentleman of my acquaintance would not care about the money. He was well-off, and had expressed his interest."

"Did you speak with him that night at Almack's? Was that why you left so precipitously?"

"Yes, and yes." Amanda bit her lip while the two gentlemen waited. She told them about Mr. Charles Ashway and her expectations. Her voice trembled when she spoke of receiving the cut direct from him.

Amanda swore the floorboards shivered when Mr. Stamfield jumped to his feet. "That cad. I shall call him out for you, Miss Carville. No gentleman leads a lady to await an offer, and then treats her so abysmally."

"He had his reasons. I demanded an explanation, you see." She blushed and stared at her hands, but she managed to whisper the slander Sir Frederick had told Charles.

"And he believed your stepfather's lies? Anyone can tell you are a lady, not any barque of frailty. I will not bother challenging the mawworm, then, I shall just pound him into the ground. Dueling is illegal anyway."

Amanda had to smile. "I thank you for the thought, Mr. Stamfield. I wished to hit him myself."

Rex wanted to wring the dastard's neck, but that was for another time. "You must have been furious."

"Oh, I was worse than angry. I wanted to shout and stamp my foot and throw that insipid orgeat they serve right at him. But there was Elaine to consider. Besides, I knew Mr. Ashway was not the culprit. He simply did not trust me, and he cared more for his family name than he did for me."

Daniel sat back down. "That whole family is a bunch of bobbing blocks. You are better off without him."

Rex thought so, too. "Go on."

In firmer tones, Amanda told them, "My stepfather was entirely to blame. So I went home, alone, to confront him once and for all. I was going to go to the solicitor's in the morning, and the bank. And I intended to write to Lady Royce in Bath, asking her advice and assistance. I hated Sir Frederick more than I thought possible at that moment, and I did wish him dead."

"Perhaps you ought to keep that thought to yourself from now on," Rex warned. "Not that wishes equate to deeds, but it looks bad." He asked the name of her bank and which solicitor handled the family's affairs, then brought her attention back to Sir Frederick. "He must have been upset when you said you were going to expose his thievery. That would not have helped his daughter make an advantageous match."

"I did not get the chance to threaten him. He was already dead."

"So there was no struggle, no physical violence on his part?"

"No." In a voice as thin as a thread, she repeated, "He was already dead."

"Then how did you happen to have the gun in your hand?"

"I thought he was in his cups and had dropped it. I wanted to protect the rest of the household." She paused. "Then I saw him."

Rex saw her shudder and exchanged a glance with his cousin. "There is no need to tell us more. We can speak to the coroner for the rest. You had cause to shoot the dastard but you did not."

Now Amanda started crying again. "You truly believe me?"

"Of course. True-blue, like I said."

"No one else did."

"Well, we shall have to change their minds. Let us start with the gun. Was it Sir Frederick's?"

"I have no idea. I know he owned a brace of pistols because he mentioned shooting at Manton's Gallery a few times, but I never saw them."

"Can you describe the murder weapon at all?"

"It was cold and gray and heavy."

"No pearl handles or carvings? Some pistols have fancy work on them."

"I did not notice. I was too angry, and then . . ."

"Yes." Rex made a note on his paper to examine the gun, and to check at Manton's. "Sometimes they can be identified by their markings. A gunsmith will recognize his own work and recall who bought it. A weapons dealer might have records of the purchase. We'll start there. Now, who else would have been at the house that evening?"

He wrote down the servants she mentioned, noting that they had been given an evening off, with the ladies at the assembly rooms. "Sir Frederick did not sound like the type to be generous to his staff."

"I was surprised, but glad for them."

"It might be that Hawley was expecting company he wished to keep private."

"A whore?" Daniel asked, then blushed and begged Amanda's pardon.

"Or a partner in more shady dealings. We can easily find the men he drank with and gamed with at his clubs.

We'll need the names of his friends, his investment advisors, his tailor." Rex turned the page and added more avenues to pursue.

"What the deuce do you want to know his tailor for? I can give you the name of mine if you want to cut a dash."

Rex raised his eyebrow at his cousin's ensemble. "I want to know if the baronet paid his debts. A man's tailor can tell a lot, if he wishes. So can his valet. Where was his man that evening?"

"I do not know. I think I saw him in all the confusion, after." She gave him Brusseau's name.

"Another French valet? Hmm."

"Do not make too much of it, coz. French servants are all the thing; the Quality think it gives them style."

"Did Sir Frederick dress in the latest fashions?"

Amanda and Daniel both shook their heads.

"What of Sir Frederick's son?"

"I do not know Edwin Hawley's mode of dress or if he has a valet. Edwin and his father were estranged. He moved out several years ago and I have not seen him since. I believe him to be residing at Hawk Hill, the Hawley seat in Hampshire. Sir Frederick hated the country and bled the estate to finance his investments. He could not sell the entailed property, or cast Edwin out of the succession to the baronetcy, of course, although the servants hinted that Sir Frederick borrowed heavily against the income. I thought they must have argued over the rents and mortgages but I never knew."

"He had motive to get rid of the drain on the estate, then, and claim it for his own?"

"Oh, not Edwin. He is such a nice young man."

They all knew nice men did awful things when forced

to it. Watching one's fields go fallow and one's tenants go hungry could make a fellow desperate.

"I would have known if he was in Town. Elaine would have told me."

Rex would send a man to Hampshire to check. "Very well, one last question. Who was the gentleman you were seeing?"

"I told you, Mr. Charles Ashway, of the Derby Ashways. The family holds a distinguished barony."

"No, not that man, the other one."

"I had no other suitors. Sir Frederick discouraged them all."

Rex studied his notes. "They said you went out at night on occasion."

Now Amanda looked at the fire burning in the hearth. "That has nothing to do with the murder."

"Of course it does. The talk leaves you looking no better than you ought to be. Did you meet a man outside your house?"

"I shall not speak of it."

"But you will not deny it, in words?"

She did not say anything.

He cursed under his breath. "Do you own a blue cape?"

"You must know I do."

"Is it with your belongings sent over from your former home?"

"I do not know. I did not unpack. Nanny did."

Rex made a note to look into that, too. "The blue cape was how you were identified in the park across the street from Sir Frederick's house on several nights."

Again she said nothing, just rubbed at her forehead and the headache forming there.

The interview was over.

Chapter Ten

Everything she'd said was true. Everything she had not said was damning. It appeared Miss Carville was guilty of something, after all.

More secrets, damn it.

"What do you think?" Rex asked his cousin after Nanny helped the woman back to her own bedchamber, wrapped in the blanket. He was ready to carry her, but Nanny glowered at him, as if the shady female's exhausted, teary condition and pained expression were his fault. He stepped aside, holding the door.

"I think she is a diamond of the first water. Those golden curls look soft as silk, and that little nose has an enchanting tilt. She has the sweetest brown eyes, when they aren't filled with tears, and as for her shape . . ." Daniel held his hands in front of his chest instead of discussing a lady's bosom in his lady aunt's sitting room. "Of course I prefer my women on a larger scale. Why, I'd be afraid of breaking that little china doll."

Rex knew Miss Carville was soft, not at all brittle like a porcelain figurine. "I meant what do you think about her avoiding questions about the man she was meeting?" Rex was prowling the sitting room, picking up this book, that ormolu clock on the mantel. He was thinking more about the woman who had just left than the woman who resided here, though. He had stopped wondering about Lady Royce years ago, or so he told himself.

"She refused to discuss why she was going out alone at night, breaking every rule for an unmarried miss. At the same time she was chasing after Ashway for his ring." He could not decide which was worst—Miss Carville's lack of candor, her lack of morals, or her lack of honor.

"Perhaps the chap is unsuitable, a servant, say, and she knew her stepfather would never give his permission. Or he could be a married man. She could be keeping his identity hidden so his wife doesn't find out."

"Or she is protecting her lover from the law." He checked his notes. "Yet she said she did not know who killed Hawley. It was a clear blue, with no muddied maybes."

"Well, then, she does not know and does not suspect the fellow in the park. And you are damning her for a light skirt without knowing the facts of the matter. She might have a fine reason for going out, not to meet a lover at all."

"Name one."

Daniel lowered his brows in concentration, without coming up with a single possibility. "Why don't you ask her?'

"I did and she refused to answer."

"No, ask her if she has a lover, not who he is. That's what has your ballocks in a bind."

"It is not!"

Daniel smiled and scratched his armpit. Verity the dog, whose only truth was a bone with meat on it, sighed and slumped at Daniel's feet.

Rex glared at both traitors. "Furthermore, Nanny

Brown managed to drum the basics of polite behavior into my head. One does not ask such questions of a lady. Can you imagine? How do you do, Miss Furbelow. May I have this dance? Oh, and by the way, are you a virgin?"

Daniel laughed. "Such honest dealing might make for happier marriages, without some poor nodcock finding out on his wedding night that his blushing bride has been gathering her rosebuds with the gardener."

Rex was not laughing. He had more riddles than a Sphinx and did not need another puzzle. He already had to consider why the countess kept his few, coldly courteous letters in her desk, or why his boyhood portrait hung in her sitting room. Or why Miss Carville would not name the man in the park, even to save her own neck. Did she love him that much—and why did that notion bother Rex so much? Then there was the question of why French valets seemed to be cropping up like mushrooms.

The most important mystery, of course, was who in Hades had killed Sir Frederick Hawley. Rex had less than a month before the trial, but he hoped to solve the riddle by week's end. Once he did that, he could wash his hands of all of them.

Nothing could be done until after nuncheon, not with Daniel's stomach growling. While they ate Rex consulted his lists and divided the tasks. Daniel could search Hawley House and find the names of Sir Frederick's associates at the gentlemen's clubs, including any he might have owed gambling debts. Murchison could listen for word of that valet, Brusseau, who was in need of a new position. Rex would go to the bank and the solicitor's—after he did his damnedest to keep out of prison for obstructing justice.

With their battle plan in place, Rex knocked on Miss

Carville's door. Nanny Brown opened the door, then stood in the entry, refusing to leave.

From the hall, Rex asked if Miss Carville wished anything else brought from her former home. "That will give Daniel an excuse to look around for the baronet's guns, signs of struggle, that kind of thing. He might get lucky and find the estate books to, ah, borrow. I would like to see how Sir Frederick managed his finances."

"The servants would never let Mr. Stamfield pry into family matters."

"They will if they know my cousin's reputation. Few people argue about the niceties when Daniel is around. His size alone usually makes folks extremely cooperative."

She gnawed on her lip. "What if they do not let him in? Will he resort to fisticuffs again? I would not want more mayhem attributed to me."

"I doubt it will come to that. Daniel can be very persuasive, and I gave him a purse full of coins to buy the information he needs. If worse comes to worst, we will break in when everyone is asleep."

Amanda gasped. "You could be arrested! Dear Lady Royce would be horrified. No, it would be far better if I went. I should not like your cousin accused of wrongdoing, and I know where to look."

He could tell that she could barely lift her head. The pucker was back between her eyebrows, and she was back in bed, in a nightgown. This one was a bit of lace, not plain and concealing like the borrowed one he'd bundled her into. Nanny caught him looking and hurriedly pulled the covers up high, but not before he wondered if that other man had seen her like this.

"I was merely teasing. Daniel will find what we want or the barrister we hire will ask for a warrant. He may have to get an order from the courts to inspect the bank-books, but I am hoping for cooperation there, too, before we have to resort to official means. Lawyers have their own ways of doing things, usually slowly. And I'm hoping to avoid the sensation of a public trial by finding enough evidence to see the charges dropped altogether."

"I wish to help," she insisted. "The last barrister I had never let me speak."

"You can help by writing a note to the butler there, giving us permission to fetch your things. Daniel knows what to do after."

"Miniatures of my mother and father are in my bedroom. Those are what I miss most. But this is my life, and I should go."

"You are not well enough yet, and there is your reputation to consider, what is left of it anyway. Out and about with two single gentlemen within days of your stepfather's murder? There is no reason to bring to the *ton*'s attention that you are without chaperonage here."

"Nanny could come."

"Lord love you, lambie," Nanny spoke up. "You know I don't count. The toffs think only one of their own can guard a lady's virtue."

Amanda sighed, conceding that she was not up to much more than holding a pen. She wrote the note despite the headache that pounded at her temples.

Nanny was already mixing her powders and drops. "You leave everything to his lordship, pet. He'll see you through."

Rex wished he could see through the covers.

Amanda scrawled the note with shaking fingers. It was barely legible, but Hareston, the butler at her stepfather's house, could barely read. If he was still there. He might have decamped with the good china in lieu of his quarter pay, knowing Edwin would not keep him on even if the new baronet did not shut up the London town house to save funds.

Amanda fleetingly worried about Elaine, immured in the country. She had always feared her father, who'd ignored her as much as possible. The two had been rubbing along better this year, with Elaine delighted with her new gowns and finally having a social Season, and Sir Frederick viewing the girl as a way to better himself. Perhaps Elaine was grief-stricken at her loss, both of her father and the entertainments of the city. She would have to go into mourning either way. At least she would have her own brother to look after her. Amanda hoped Edwin would not push the seventeen-year-old into an unwanted marriage, the way his father had planned. Then she worried that she was putting too much confidence in the young stepbrother she had not seen in two years, and rarely before, while he was at university. She was counting on his honor to restore her own fortune; she was assuming his family feelings would protect his sister. She could be wrong.

Why borrow trouble? The Hawleys were no longer her business. Staying out of jail, proving herself innocent, those were her concerns. Granted, she was too weak to make inquiries, and the gentlemen's clubs' doors were locked to women, but she could examine the accounts books when Lord Rexford brought them, if she could keep her head clear.

"No more laudanum, Nanny. I need to be able to think."

"Oh, you can let Lord Rexford do that, too, I swear."

Amanda had to smile at the old woman's confidence in her former nurseling. He was a large man, not as big as his cousin, of course, but still tall and commanding. He was not, however, a god. "He is being immeasurably helpful. He believes me, which is more than anyone else does. But if he manages to free me from the charges, I still have to plan my future. I cannot be a weight around Lady Royce's neck, and my soiled reputation will prevent Elaine's finding a husband, if I were welcome to stay with her at all."

Nanny smiled. "I am thinking you can leave that to his lordship, too. He'll do the right thing."

"The right thing . . . ?"

"Of course. He helped ruin your good name, didn't he?"

The old woman could not be thinking what Amanda thought she was implying. "But I am an accused murderess."

"Not for long, if I know the lad."

But what Nanny did not know was that the viscount believed her another man's mistress, no fit bride for a gentleman, no fit mother to his heir. He might not believe Sir Frederick's slanders like Mr. Ashway, but neither did he believe her untouched. She'd seen the shadows fall over his face when he spoke of the man in the park. She feared for a moment he'd grow violent when she could not, would not, answer his questions. Besides, he did not seem to like her. She was a chore to him, like mucking out the stables. Why, he had not so much as blinked an eye at the change in her looks, after an entire morning of Nanny's fussing. He could have smiled or paid her more than the cursory compliment that she looked better. A small smile of approval would have been enough. His cousin was gallant, but that did not count.

No, Captain Lord Rexford was not the least interested in Amanda as anything but an investigation to pursue;

afterward, he could close his notebook and go back to whatever he did in whatever rural fastness. Perhaps he would rejoin the army and torture prisoners.

She shook her head, then regretted the pain that caused. Still, she refused to believe that last, not when the viscount was here at his mother's house, which obviously bothered him, on a stranger's behalf. There was only so much, though, that anyone expected from a good Samaritan. No one would possibly demand that he wed a fallen woman, least of all Amanda.

If some misguided smidgeon of chivalry forced a proposal out of the man, Amanda would refuse. She did not want to be married to a fiercesome gentleman subject to black moods and bouts of drinking. Her mother had made that mistake, and Amanda had seen the results. Worse, Lord Rexford was reclusive and bitter and wont to batter opponents with his fists and his nose. And he had secrets of his own. She doubted he would ever reveal himself to anyone other than his cousin, not even his future wife.

She knew that any number of females would leap at the chance to be a wealthy countess eventually, no matter the costs. Amanda pitied that poor woman, whomever she turned out to be. Marriages of convenience seldom turned out to be convenient at all, especially for the wife.

No, if she could stay out of prison, and out of the hangman's clutches, she could stay out of a lifetime of misery.

"His lordship did not destroy my reputation," she told his doting old nurse, who only wished to spoil another generation of Royce infants. "He saved my life. I can never ask for more. I will be forever in his debt for that alone, and longer if he helps clear my name of the murder. What reward would that be, to demand his bachelor life, his name? Even if he does not wish me near his family,

Edwin will assist me, especially if I can show that his father misappropriated my fortune. Any honorable man would make amends, wouldn't he?" she asked, more to convince herself than Nanny. "Perhaps I can recover enough of my father's fortune or my dowry to live quietly somewhere."

Nanny tsked and took up her knitting. Amanda slept, without the drugs, and dreamed of blue capes and blue-eyed babies.

Chapter Eleven

He should have gone through proper channels. He should have made an appointment. He should have reported to the officer in charge. He did nothing of the kind. Damned pettifogging politicians, all of them. The real soldiers were at the front, fighting the bloody war.

Hell, he should have resigned his commission first, in case they wanted to court-martial him.

Instead he asked the subaltern at the door for Major Harrison. There was no Major Harrison, of course; he'd checked the roster of officers. The name was a code to open doors, a great many successive doors, at which he had to identify himself with the proper answer to the query: "What is the nature of your business with Major Harrison?"

The proper response was: "I come in aid of my country and the war effort." Rex supposed that was how the man he wished to see became known as the Aide, although he served no general in London and wore no uniform. Rex had been through the intricate rigmarole once before, when he was given his orders to report to General Wellesley himself. His father had given him the passwords. To this day he wondered how the Earl of Royce had come to know the key to the most secret of England's hidden defenses. He also wondered if the codes had changed, or if his own name would be enough to deliver him to the innermost sanctum.

He was passed from one junior officer to another, each waiting for instructions to proceed. Then he was handed over to a higher-ranking flunky who led him up stairs and down corridors in the vast building, with no concern for Rex's leg or his limp. If he was not fit for duty, the attitude seemed to be, he should not be wasting the Aide's time.

Rex made no complaint, nor did he when left to wait in a small office empty of everything but two hard wooden chairs. He sat on one and put his aching leg on the other. To the devil with protocol and politeness. Of course he had to jump to his feet, doing his leg more insult, when a lieutenant colonel he did not know entered the room.

He saluted, gave his name and rank and unit, to the officer's grim disapproval and rigid posture. Then he repeated that he had come in aid of the country and the war effort but added: "And please inform Major Harrison that I have come about the truth." That way Major Harrison, who did not exist, would be sure of his caller. The officer left without saying a word.

A man in rumpled civilian clothes hurried into the room next, nodded to Rex and said, "Follow me," without giving his name. Ah, Rex thought as he went up corridors and down stairs, he had finally reached the inner level of the spymasters, where the real work was accomplished.

As they neared the very hallway where Rex had begun his journey, he began to wonder if he was being shown the door. He'd never find the office he wanted on his own, and doubted if shouts or orders, threats or bribes, would bring him any closer to a man who existed only as a myth to most of the army.

Instead of leading him to an exit, however, his guide took Rex through a dining hall, through a kitchen, and then down what appeared to be service stairs. They went past a wine cellar, munitions rooms, and a series of barred cells. Then the man used a key to open a door that led to more downward stairs, with twists and turns and dark corridors, which was not at all the way Rex had come the first time. He thought they must be in the catacombs beneath London's streets by now, judging from the dank and damp air. They trudged so far he felt they might be in another country soon.

Just when he thought his leg would stiffen entirely from the cold or collapse beneath him from exhaustion, his guide used another key at another door. This one led up several sets of stairs that finally, thankfully, ended at a door opening into a dimly lit but ordinary-appearing book room. Draperies were drawn across the windows, and only one shaded oil lamp burned on a wide wooden desktop covered with papers. The lamp did not give off enough light to read any of the titles on the floor-to-ceiling bookcases, or to see into the darker corners—all on purpose, of course, to obscure the room's sole occupant.

The gentleman behind the desk rose and held out his hand before Rex could salute. "Ah, Rexford, I have been expecting you."

Major Harrison, which was surely not the man's name, but was the only one Rex knew other than the Aide, had a firm grip for a man who appeared to be in his dotage, with an old-fashioned gray wig and thick, tinted glasses and a silver-streaked beard and mustache. Of course, they could all be fake.

Rex shook the hand, bowed, and took the seat he was offered in a comfortable leather armchair, too far away across the desk to make out his host's features or expression by the meager light. "I do not see how you could be expecting me, sir, when I did not know I was coming."

Harrison tapped one opened letter in front of him. "From your father, who asked me to lend what assistance I might." He tapped another. "From a justice of the court, demanding satisfaction." Another: "From the Lord Mayor's office, in reference to a public disturbance. And this one?" He stroked it gently, as one might a lover's cheek. "Well, let me simply say that I have indeed been expecting you." He poured wine into two glasses waiting on the side of the desk. "How is the leg?" He politely ignored the nose and the scar, unless he truly had such weak eyesight he could not see them. That might explain the darkness, Rex considered, if light exacerbated the problem. On the other hand, not a single drop of wine went awry.

"It is healing, sir, thank you." It would never be the same, and they both knew it. "But I have not come for new orders."

"No, I had not supposed you had. I do not know that I could have given them at any rate. No one was happy to hear that the heir to an earldom—the only heir, I must add—was shot. You were supposed to be safely behind the lines. So no, I dare not send you back where you can do the most good. His Majesty causes enough trouble for my department as is."

"I have been thinking of retiring from the army."

"Good, good. Then I do not have to make any unpopular decisions. What shall you do?"

Not make small talk with the devil in disguise, Rex

swore to himself. The Aide's accents were educated, but not quite those of a gentleman. His clothing, not a uniform, was neat and well tailored. And he held England's safety in his manicured hands, as well as Rex's secrets.

"I am not certain." He nodded toward the topmost letter, the one from Lord Royce. "I cannot think of my own future until I resolve the situation I assume my father must have discussed with you."

"Ah, yes, Miss Amanda Carville. I trust the lady is well?"

"As well as can be expected after her ill treatment." Rex did not bother to keep the anger from his voice.

"There are those of us working for reforms of the prison system, but Parliament acts slowly. When it is your time to take your place there, I hope you will be more diligent about attending than your father."

Rex would not hear disrespect of his sire. "My father is ailing."

"More so than in recent years?" the Aide quickly asked. "I had not heard."

"No, he is not much worse, except for a troublesome cough that has lingered far too long."

"Let us hope the warmer weather will help. Meanwhile, I have a notion of a course that might appeal to you until that sad time in the far distant, I hope and pray, when you become earl."

"I am not seeking a career. I thought I might devote myself to the estate, study the latest agriculture advances and implement scientific discoveries."

"That would be an unforgivable waste."

And that was none of this man's affair. Lord Rexford brushed at a speck of dust on his boots.

The Aide changed course: "In the matter of Miss

Carville, I have already smoothed feathers at the Magistrate's office. What further assistance may I be?"

"I need access to the evidence and to Sir Frederick's accounts."

"If you are planning a defense, you must think the woman is innocent."

"I know she is innocent."

The Aide did not question Rex's knowledge or assurance. He steepled his fingers on the desk and said, "Ah, that does make the case more interesting."

"Not for Miss Carville. She could hang."

"Quite. But for the department. I have wondered about Sir Frederick Hawley's loyalty for some time now. A few overheard conversations among smugglers aroused my suspicions."

"I thought your field of operations was the war."

"They are all interconnected."

Indeed they were. Rex was familiar with the practice of free-trading, having lived most of his life along the coast. He did not approve of paying for French goods in good English gold to be used to buy guns, to kill good English soldiers. He knew whole villages would not survive without the illegal income, however.

The Aide was going on: "We have listeners tucked among the various gangs. Some of our men work for the money while others are true, loyal Englishmen, despite their chosen careers. A bit of contraband may be overlooked by my department, and any information the smugglers bring back is always welcome. But transporting spies into England? Sending weapons and stolen military documents back to France? No, we cannot have that. I had an excellent man placed quite near your home, in fact, but he is involved in other duties now, to my regret."

Rex doubted any arm of the government could stop the flow of traffic between the two countries, not while there was money to be made. Nor did he care about staffing woes in the ranks of spies. "I cannot see why you would believe anything an informant says. They are traitors to their partners, if not their country. Why do you think they give correct information?"

"We are not all as fortunate as you in determining truthfulness, but who says we believe everything that we hear? We investigate as much as seems plausible when we can, in case it is accurate. The course of the war might depend on hearing a bit of gossip about a heavier-than-normal shipment, a passenger wearing clothes fit for court, men killed for knowing too much, that kind of thing."

Rex supposed the man had a point. Not every Englishman supported the war or the mad king or his profligate son. Still, of all the crimes Sir Frederick might have committed, Rex had not suspected smuggling or treason. "He did have a French valet."

"I have a French valet, also. Many loyalists fled France to save their lives. That does not make them smugglers or spies. Many, in fact, are vastly eager to aid in overthrowing Bonaparte so they can return to their homes and claim their own properties."

"Sir Frederick and his man never left London, from what I hear. His estate is in Hampshire, not far from the coast, but he never goes there."

"But London is where smuggled goods eventually come to be sold for the highest profit. A man in the city is necessary to expedite deliveries, arrange for storage, pay the carriers. I have no proof that Sir Frederick Hawley was connected in any way to what we suspect is a well-organized band, but if his murder was not a domestic matter, all in the family, I should like to know who actually shot him, and why."

"So would I. I also am curious as to why Sir Nigel Turlowe bestirred himself in the case. He seldom notices the workings of his own offices."

The Aide shuffled some papers. "Unlike myself." He straightened the documents into a neat pile, then pulled one out to study, scattering the others back across his desk. "Well, it is an excellent thing that you are looking into the matter. Both for Miss Carville and for the country. And if you hear of anything untoward, you will let me know?" He peered at the page, indicating he'd rather get back to his own work than entertain Rex any longer.

"Of course. How may I contact you?"

"You can leave a message for Major Harrison at Whitehall. Or simply Mr. Harris here, at McCann's Club. I'll be sure to get it."

They were at McCann's? That was a few streets away from Whitehall. Rex could have reached it in ten minutes, not the half of an afternoon he had wasted playing at espionage. "I can call on you here?"

"Without an appointment? You'd be lucky to be turned away without a knife in your back. My guards are very careful, you see. In addition, I seldom spend time in any one place. There are too many people who want to see me dead."

Rex was almost counting himself in that number. "Is your name Harrison at all?"

Without saying yes or no, which Rex could have judged, the Aide said, "It is as good a name as any."

Rex nodded. Let the man have all the secrets he wished behind his green-glass spectacles, and cast his webs as far as he could throw them. Rex merely needed his influence.

He stood, obviously dismissed as Harrison read the message in front of him. "May I count on you to clear my path with the courts?"

The older man looked up. "Well, that is not as easy as you make it sound. You might need to lend a bit of assistance in return."

Rex raised his eyebrow, but the man either did not see or pretended not to. "Oh?" Rex asked in frigid tones.

"It is that job of work I mentioned."

"And I mentioned I was no longer interested in the army. I am on sick leave, and shall resign as soon as I am done with this ugliness."

"You are in uniform. And capable of fighting." Harrison tapped one of the letters again. "I could ask the general to put you under my command, of course."

Rex sat back down, glaring.

This time Harrison must have noticed. "I am not speaking of the army, Captain, but Bow Street, which is where you need to go anyway. I believe they are holding the murder weapon, and they have the depositions from the witnesses."

"Why am I not surprised that you have something to do with the new police force also?"

"I have something to do with a great many fields of the kingdom's well being. But I have a friend, an old friend—"

Now Rex pounded on the desk, not caring that this was, more or less, his superior officer, and the most powerful man who did not exist in all of Britain. "You told him about me? How dare you! My father said you could be trusted with the truth that could see the house of Royce destroyed."

"No."

Through his anger Rex could see the blue of the truth. "No?"

"No, I did not tell my friend about your gift, only that you had extraordinary instincts and had conducted scientific experiments while with the army, experiments concerning the timbre of a suspect's voice, the tempo of his speech, the amount of times he blinks his eye. I made up as many possibilities as I could, so no one would suspect the truth. I doubt anyone would believe it without proof anyway, so your secret is safe."

"Then what do you want with me?"

"Think, Lord Rexford, instead of going off half cocked. Imagine if an investigator could ask a few questions to know if he had arrested the right suspect? Or if a witness is lying? How many more could be put behind bars? How many innocent men freed? How much time gained by the few detectives we employ? Your skill could revolutionize thief taking and make London a far safer place."

"I am one man. What could I do?"

"You could get on about your business of begetting sons, that's one thing, so there are more of you. And you can give Inspector Josiah Dimm a few hours of your time. You are asking me to bend the law in your favor, and asking him to share evidence in a capital crime. You can repay the favor, while still doing service to your country."

"I have served!"

"Yes, but now you are quitting. I cannot permit that. You, sir, are a national treasure." He held up a hand, which had none of Nanny's swollen knuckles. "No, not like a masterpiece to be displayed at the Royal Gallery, or the Crown Jewels, on view at the Tower of London. You are rarer, actually. I shall not, will not, see you squander the gifts you have been given by wallowing in self-pity."

"Recovering from my wounds and tending my father's holdings is not wallowing."

"Rat rot! Next you will be milking the cows! Anyone can be trained to manage your estates. No amount of training will yield England another truth-seer. Your country needs you."

Rex had no choice, as far as he could see. He needed the weapon and the search warrants.

Harrison—or whoever—held the sheet of paper closer to his face, as if anyone could read it by the one small lamp, especially a man in tinted spectacles.

"Very well."

"Excellent. Give Inspector Dimm this letter."

The letter was already prepared and addressed. "You knew I would agree?"

Harrison smiled. There was something familiar about the smile behind the mustache, but Rex could not place it. Perhaps what he recognized was the sense of being managed, the way his father had manipulated him into coming to London and helping Miss Carville. Which reminded him: "If I chose not to accept this assignment, would you let Miss Carville hang, knowing she is innocent of the crime?"

Again the spymaster did not say aye or nay.

"Damn you for a blackmailer and a blackguard."

Harrison stood and sketched a slight bow. "We all do what we must, in service to King and country. Remember that."

Chapter Twelve

Rex had done enough, he thought, as he made his way to Bow Street. He was doing enough for his father, too, limping his way through London. When was he to be left in peace, to find his own path?

Granted he hadn't found any direction yet, but that was not to say he mightn't enjoy counting sheep and deciding whether to plant mangel-wurzels or maize. He was tired of others deciding for him. Yes, he had joined the army willingly, anxious to prove his worth and his courage like every other red-blooded—and blue-blooded—Englishman. What, should he have become another park-saunterer wasting his patrimony in idle pleasure while others died to keep the Corsican from British soil?

They had not let him fight.

Now they wanted him to become a Robin Redbreast. The populace hated and distrusted the new police department as much as they despised spies. The beau monde looked upon the Bow Street Runners as little better than ferrets set out to kill mice, one kind of vermin set out to kill another kind.

Rex slashed with his cane at a scrap of paper swirling through the filthy London streets and almost stumbled while two clerks watched and snickered, thinking him drunk. He wished them to perdition.

What he really wished to do was return to the Hall and sail his boat away from everyone, those who pitied him, those who worried about him, those who thought he was wasting his life. No, that was a lie he could not tell, even to himself. What he truly wanted was to return to Royce House and make sure Miss Carville was not set back from the morning's interview. She was ill; he had been harsh. He ought to apologize and make certain she was comfortable. He could find another, less finicky physician if she still had the fever. He could hire more maids if Nanny was too old. Zeus, he ought to help Daniel bring back her parents' portraits that she valued so highly, if they would bring her solace. Perhaps he should stop at a bookseller and find her the latest novel to read during her convalescence. Or did she like to have flowers about her?

He stumbled again when he realized where his mind was wandering. What he had to do was find the killer— soon—not find out if Miss Carville liked roses instead of lilies. If the price of information was a few hours playing at policeman, so be it. Far better to serve his country that way than by siring more misfits, no matter what the Aide thought. Or his father. Or Nanny. Or Daniel.

He wondered what Miss Carville thought.

Where were they? Amanda had napped; then she'd forced herself to eat some biscuits along with her tea. She had to get better, stronger, so she could act on her own behalf. Her headache was gone, but her worries were not.

Why had they not sent word? Surely Lord Rexford and his cousin knew how desperate she was for good news. She did not wish to be ungrateful, but she could not help fretting that the two men were what Aunt Hermione Hawley called choice spirits, hey-go-mad gentlemen out on a lark. A lark? To her it was life or death.

She dismissed her lack of trust. Lord Rexford took her situation seriously, enough to break the law, jeopardizing his military career. Mr. Stamfield was willing to break a few more laws, plus windows. Good grief, what if they were arrested? How could Amanda ever explain to Lady Royce that her son was in prison? Who could she ask to bail him out? How could she console the viscount's dog, who was resting on her feet, watching the door mournfully and whining occasionally. Who, by all that was holy, would help Amanda if Lord Rexford could not?

Amanda pulled at a thread on her handkerchief, half unraveling the hem. "Why haven't they come back? It has been so long."

She must have spoken aloud because Nanny looked up from her knitting. "Long? It has only been an hour, dearie."

The Bow Street building was crowded, noisy, dirty, and the people there were more discourteous than Rex was used to as a dignified gentleman or as a military officer. No one dropped what he was doing to rush to Rex's assistance. No one stood or saluted. Everyone seemed too busy solving crimes or planning new ways to commit them. Rex appreciated the industriousness of the office, if not the wait until someone directed him toward the back of the long room.

He tried to close his mind to the clashing colors of outright lies and half-truths as he walked past rows of pickpockets and prostitutes to where Harrison's friend, Inspector Dimm, rated a private cubbyhole. A very young assistant working at a battered desk outside the door directed Rex to knock, then enter the tiny office that contained two chairs, a desk, and files and folders stacked floor to ceiling.

Inspector Dimm was old, with no pretense of being anything else. What hair he had was grizzled gray, his hands had age spots, and his face was creased with lines of experience. His body had lost its shape to good eating and a lot of sitting.

Dimm took his stockinged feet off the desk, the unlit pipe out of his mouth, and heaved himself out of his chair to welcome Rex. As soon as he heard Rex's name, before reading Harrison's letter, he was beaming like a boy with a new pony on Christmas morning. His eyes twinkled, and Rex thought he might have rubbed his hands together in glee if they were not filled with his pipe and the letter.

"I was hoping Himself could convince you to stop by," the Runner said, offering Rex a glass of ale and the other chair, once it was cleared of yet more papers and reward posters. "Just put them on the floor. And do forgive my bare feet, my lord. Or is it Captain? Two many years walking the streets as a Runner, don't you know."

"Rexford will do," Rex said, unwilling to meet the other man's friendliness and familiarity.

Dimm noticed the lack of warmth in his guest as he filled two glasses. "I suppose Harris had to twist your arm?"

"Do you speak of Harrison?"

"The chap has many names, many enemies, and many ways of solving problems, thank goodness."

"His ways are not always aboveboard." Or else Rex would not be here now.

"With the weight of the world on his shoulders, how can he worry over minor details?"

This told Rex much about Dimm's flexible notions of justice and law enforcement. While Dimm found a pair of spectacles under the papers and read Harrison's note, Rex's uneasiness grew at the idea of being associated with yet another authority who believed the ends justified the means.

After asking Rex's approval, Dimm relit his pipe and puffed for a moment to get it going. Then he sighed in contentment. "I am deuce glad you came, Captain. We are overwhelmed. The criminals are beginning to outnumber the law abiders, it seems."

"I am interested in one particular case that—"

Dimm set his spectacles back on the desk. "He says to trust your findings. I tell my trainees that an officer of the law has to keep an open mind, to consider every possibility, to look at the facts from every direction, and then trust his own instincts. No explanation for a man's instincts, eh? And no way to prove they work, either. But now you are adding a scientific bent from your research with the army. Facts and figures don't lie, eh? All in black and white."

Not quite, but close.

"Excellent. The world is a better place for the new sciences."

Science? There was no science to the magic of truth-seeing. It was simply there. But Rex was saved having to lie.

"The letter also says not to discuss your work with any-one."

Thank goodness. "Major Harrison, or Mr. Harris,

considers that spies and assassins are everywhere. This new, ah, science could be a target."

"Hm. He might have a point, if word got out that honesty was measurable, like time. There are people whose livelihoods depend on bending the truth."

Rex thought about the spymaster. "Or hiding it."

Dimm changed the subject. "My superiors do not approve of beating confessions out of suspects, you know."

So he had heard the rumors, the damning reports of Rex's military career as an interrogator and gatherer of the enemy's secrets. Rex supposed everyone knew of the feared Inquisitors. "Nor do I."

"Good, good. As long as we are in agreement, then, let us see what you can do, eh? Then we can decide how best to use your skills."

He called out for Clarence to bring in Nate the Skate. While they waited, Inspector Dimm explained that Clarence was one of his grandnephews. "Although the devil if I can remember which nevey's son he is. I train up a lot of the family. Letting Bow Street give them a salary is easier than paying their room and board myself. Asides, I always say that if you want to see the job done right, use your own relations. The trustworthy ones, at any rate."

Rex's father would approve. Out of politeness and a little curiosity, Rex asked the inspector if he had a big family.

"More than I can keep track of. It's a mixed blessing, never a Sunday without an invite for supper. Never a moment when some whelp isn't sleeping on my couch or some gal isn't getting wed or giving birth. They always expect gifts, don't you know. What of yourself?"

"I just have my father and two cousins."

"No wife?"

A gleam came to the old man's eyes that reminded Rex of the French soldiers, before they shot at him. "Not yet. I have been off to war."

"Quite right, not leaving a poor lass behind to fret. What of your mother?"

Rex did not count the countess as kin. He shook his head, no. He doubted she cared enough to worry.

Dimm must have misunderstood because he said, "My beloved wife, may she rest in peace, had a score of brothers and sisters herself. So did I, so there is no dearth of new recruits to train every year."

Before Rex had to correct Dimm's assumption, young Clarence came back with a small man in scuffed boots and tattered frieze jacket, his hands cuffed behind his back. Dimm waved Rex to the corner of the room.

"Now Nate, I am going to ask you a few simple questions and I want you to answer honestly."

"I did it."

"Dash it, Nate, I haven't asked the question yet. Did you break into the warehouse on Donegal Street?"

"Yes, sir, I did."

Behind Nate's back, Rex shook his head, no. The man had lied.

"What about the robbery at Lord Peckenham's?"

"I did that one, too. Got a satchel full of silver. Platters, the tea set, spoons."

Rex saw nothing but red. He did not understand why the man confessed to crimes he did not commit.

"Because he'd be on the street otherwise," Dimm said after Nate was led away, "cold and hungry and in constant danger from the other alley dwellers. He comes in once a week, confesses to some crime that made a splash in the newspapers. We give him a hot meal and let him sleep in one of the empty cells. No harm done."

But a lot of kindness. Rex relaxed. "So did I pass the test?"

"That was too easy, I am thinking. Clarence, bring in Butts."

The next suspect was not half as innocent as Nate the Skate. Butts was a surly dockworker with tattoos everywhere his clothes weren't. He spit at Dimm's feet when the inspector asked if the man had killed his partner.

"No."

Rex knew instantly that the man was lying, but tried to appear as if he were studying Butts's mannerisms. There was not much to study in "No."

Dimm helped him by asking more questions. "How did that crate happen to fall off the ladder just when your partner walked by?"

"How should I know? I weren't anywhere near."

Another lie.

Then Dimm asked—an experiment of his own, Rex knew—"Did you kill Sir Frederick Hawley, too?"

"Hell no, why would I? He weren't bedding my wife too, was he? 'Sides, you can't pin that on me. Everyone knows the gentry mort did it."

Now he was telling the truth, and Rex regretted that he wouldn't get to see Butts hang for his partner's murder.

When Butts was dragged out, after his near confession, Dimm asked, "Did the mort—that is, the lady—kill him?"

"No."

"You are certain?"

"As certain as sin."

"Very well. I can get you the files and the evidence as

soon as I clear some of these other cases. Are you willing to help?"

Despite the urgency to get back to Miss Carville, Rex found that he was willing. Interested, even. Dimm accepted his judgments on the next two suspects brought in, because they tallied with the evidence and his own instincts, but the Runner was stymied. "I've seen everything in my time, don't you know. This is something beyond my ken. 'Course, I can't convict anyone on your say-so."

"I wish you would not use my name at all."

"Well, I won't admit I listened to your guesses. I might as well say I consulted a gypsy fortune-teller. I still need evidence to make a case. But now the field is a lot smaller. I don't have to look for other suspects, and don't have to accept any more beggars' confessions, instead of looking for the real thieves. Harris was right, you are a very handy man to have around. Another hour, shall we say?"

Rex stayed in the back corner, giving thumbs-up for truth, thumbs-down for a lie. He consulted his notes a time or two to try to look official, if not scientific. He could have come to the same conclusions without seeing the men's faces, but if Inspector Dimm pretended to accept the notion of a learned experiment, Rex was willing to pretend he had a technical system. In fact, he found the experience fascinating.

The French officers and messengers he'd questioned on the Peninsula had to be threatened—and then convinced to cry out as if they were being tortured—rather than let anyone think they had willingly given up their country's secrets. Most crossed themselves when Rex declared he knew they were lying, or threatened to set Daniel on them. After a bit, the cousins' reputation preceded them, and the prisoners needed less prompting.

London's criminal class had less honor. Or less intelligence. Their lies were more creative, but few had the sense to refuse to answer. Many of the suspects were guilty, and Dimm quickly came up with a solution to his dilemma of how to use Rex's pronouncements. He told the ones Rex gave a thumbs-down that there were witnesses to the crime. If they confessed, he'd see they were conscripted into the navy instead of standing trial and taking their chances, which were next to nil.

Rex wasn't so pleased about sending cutthroats to the navy.

"The admirals know how to manage reluctant sailors, and they need every able-bodied man they can get. As for the culprits, they stand a far better chance of surviving the navy than they would facing the noose or the hulks or transport to Botany Bay."

They cleared away a whole stack of open cases without costing the Crown the price of a trial, while filling His Majesty's warships. Dimm freed a handful of others and set various nephews and sons-in-laws to finding support for the few of Rex's judgments where no one confessed.

Dimm was thrilled. "We got more work done in the past three hours than possible in a week."

"It has been three hours already?"

"Aye, and time I got home to my own dinner. Of course you'll be wanting to clear your own case first."

He had Clarence find the murder weapon in the evidence room. "There was fresh powder on it, so the officer in charge declared it definitely the murder weapon. No one looked much further, I am sorry to say. The lady denied the accusation—you saw that they all do, guilty or innocent—but the prosecutor came to Bow Street himself and he was satisfied with the evidence and the witness reports and how everyone knew the victim and his accused killer had argued. He said he wished a speedy conclusion, because the man was a gentleman. He didn't want to give the public the idea that it was anything but a domestic dispute, less'n common folks think they can get away with shooting the swells, like the Frenchies."

"She did not do it."

"I believe you. I've got instincts of my own, and daughters and nieces. But it weren't my case, don't you know." He copied over some names and handed the page to Rex. "Here are addresses for the servants, although I don't know what good they'll do now."

"I can talk to them, get an impression of Sir Frederick, find out who stood to benefit."

"And who's telling the truth, eh?"

"Exactly."

"Well, if you come back tomorrow, I'll try to have warrants for you to search the premises, open the man's records and such."

"Thank you. And I can devote another couple of hours to crime fighting, in return, if you wish."

Dimm relit his pipe. "Be happy to have you. Don't suppose you intend to publish any findings of your experiments? Any way I could teach the young ones to look for your signs of lying?"

"I am afraid not." Rex wished he could explain.

Dimm sent a cloud of smoke into the air. "I watched, you know. You never even looked at their eyes. They say eyes are the windows to the soul. I can usually tell a cold-blooded killer by looking at their glims, but I'm never as fast or as confident as you seem to be."

"It's not the eyes, it's the voice." And the colors.

"You must have done a powerful lot of research,"

Dimm said, a hint of wistfulness in his own voice mixed with a heavy dose of disbelief. "Bless you."

Rex walked a little jauntier as he made his way back to Royce House. He hardly noticed his bad leg or who was watching him limp. He stopped at a nearby bookseller and asked what the ladies were reading nowadays. He bought two, so Miss Carville could have a choice. Then he bought flowers to bring to her, roses and violets because he could not decide which. Now he had gifts to bring, along with information, the support of two vastly different but powerful men, and the gun.

Chapter Thirteen

He brought her hope.

Amanda felt a warmth she had not known in ages, long before the current disaster. Lord Rexford did not have to bring flowers and books. Gracious, he did not have to do anything at all. He was helping her to satisfy his father's demands, his mother's pleas. But the flowers? They must have been because he wanted to, nothing else. Charles Ashway, her onetime suitor, had sent her a bouquet after a dance, out of politeness. Rexford was not polite by any means. Ashway had never made her feel special—or atingle—not even when he came close to an offer of marriage.

Amanda wanted to throw herself into Rexford's arms, an impulse she had never felt for Ashway, not even when she contemplated accepting the offer that never came. She might have done such a hoydenish thing—her reputation was gone, what did it matter?—except the viscount was holding a gun.

Then Mr. Stamfield came home, and she did throw herself at him when he brought her parents' portraits. He turned as red as Lord Rexford's uniform coat. His lordship turned green, it appeared, scowling and tapping his cane on the floor, which made Amanda's smile grow brighter. He did care!

She propped the small paintings on Lady Royce's sitting room mantel, since Nanny refused to allow the gentlemen into Amanda's own bedroom. "Oh, you have both made me very happy! I know these are the first steps, but I was stuck in a morass, unable to move. Now we can find the owner of the gun."

The viscount stopped tapping. "What if it proves to be your stepfather's? Then the evidence still points to you. I do not want you to get your hopes too high. There is not much distinctive about the pistol. We might not be able to trace its ownership at all."

She sniffed first at the violets, then at the roses, refusing to be defeated. "But we might, and that is more than I had yesterday. And now I have the paintings, too." She lowered her eyes. "And I have friends in you, Mr. Stamfield—"

"I wish you would call me Daniel, if we are to be friends."

"Then you must call me Amanda, because I will cherish that friendship no matter what happens. And yours, Lord Rexford."

"Rex. That is what my friends call me."

The king—how fitting. Except for his swollen nose, his lordship looked regal enough for royalty, tall and strong and in command. His bearing held more authority than the foolish prince could muster, in all his medals and ribbons. "Rex." She tasted the name on her tongue, drawing out the final sibilance. "It is my pleasure to be given the privilege of first names." She had known Charles Ashway two months before they became so familiar, and then only in private.

"The pleasure is mine." Oh, how Rex wished it were, to hear his name on her lips, on his pillow. The woman was looking healthier, although she was still pale, still too thin. Jupiter, was it only yesterday that he'd pulled a limp rag out of the trash heap of Newgate? The flowers and portraits—or the gun—had brought an animation to her face that he found irresistible. The sight of her smile had rendered him near speechless. For that matter, the sight of her in Daniel's arms had made him murderous.

Daniel was grinning, so Rex gathered what wits he had after her declaration of friendship. One wrong move, he knew, and he'd be stepping into the parson's mousetrap. "Very well, we are friends. Now let us discuss our findings. Daniel, were any of the servants still at Hawley House? I have possible addresses for some who told Bow Street they were leaving."

"A stiff-rumped butler, Hareston, opened the door. Reluctantly, I might add, until I showed him a coin and Miss Carville's—Amanda's—note. A nasty piece, that one. My money is on him for the killer. He watched me every second, so I never got a chance to look for a safe or through Hawley's desk drawers."

"The safe is behind a hunting scene in Sir Frederick's office," Amanda told them, "but I do not know where the key is, or if it has a combination."

"I should have a warrant tomorrow," Rex said, "a legal writ so no one can deny us access. As soon as we have that, we can go back, and to the bank also. Who else was there besides the butler?"

"According to Hareston and another coin, Brusseau the valet left to take up a post elsewhere," Daniel said. "Hareston said he did not know with whom."

"That was fast, for a man whose last master could not

give him a reference. His name is not on Bow Street's list. We'll see if we cannot discover who hired the valet. I'll put Murchison on that."

"Murchison, your valet who Nanny says does not speak?" Amanda asked.

Rex shrugged the question off. "Who else was at the house, Daniel?"

"A couple of footmen. A housekeeper."

"That would be Mrs. Petcock," Amanda explained to Rex. "She sleeps near the kitchen, so could not have heard anything."

"That's what she said, and added a few uncomplimentary words for her late employer. She is staying, she says, in hopes of being kept on when the place is rented out."

Amanda clutched the bouquet of violets tighter. "Has she heard from Edwin already then? He does not have plans to come to London?"

Amanda was disappointed, thinking her stepbrother would come to town to settle his father's affairs as soon as the funeral was over. Edwin might believe her, might help her, might give her a home with him.

"I do not think the housekeeper knows anything definite," Daniel said. "More what she wants to see happen. She hasn't been paid since the new year."

"But we had new gowns and new upholstery in the drawing room."

"The better to make a good impression on Miss Elaine Hawley's callers, I suppose. Everyone seemed in agreement that she was to marry well—not just a title but money also—to pull her father out of River Tick."

Amanda knew Sir Frederick was miserly, but she thought he had funds enough. "He had my mother's money, and my dowry, plus income from his own estate."

"Well, perhaps he kept a fortune tucked away in his safe or the bank, but he was not generous with his gold."

"No, he was never that."

Daniel suggested perhaps someone was blackmailing the baronet, bleeding him dry.

"And I frightened the extortionist away when I arrived home early," Amanda guessed.

Rex put a stop to their musings. "No blackmailer would kill his source of income. What else did you discover there, coz?"

"The butler gave me itchy feet."

"Ah."

Amanda offered to search the countess's dresser for talcum powder.

Daniel shifted in his chair. Wood creaked, so he stopped his embarrassed twitching. "You see? I'm not fit for polite company. Shouldn't have mentioned my feet."

"Or your itch," Rex added, with a narrow-eyed warning.

Amanda looked from one to the other. "But I am not missish, and we must not stand on ceremonies while discussing my case. We are friends, aren't we?"

Daniel smiled. "I knew you were a right 'un. I just felt he wasn't telling the truth. No, that he wasn't telling all of the truth. I'd wager he knows who hired that valet Brusseau in such a hurry. I never thought Sir Frederick was so well turned-out that his man should be in demand."

Rex made a note in his pad. "I'll try the butler tomorrow. Do you know if he's been paid?"

Daniel shook his head. "Not in a while. I believe he is skimming enough off the household budget to survive, but he will be below hatches if a tenant or the new owner does not arrive soon."

"What about the grooms and the footmen? Did you question any of them?"

"What do you take me for? A novice? Of course I did. The ones who were not attending the ladies at Almack's say they were all in the mews, throwing the dice. It's too far away from the house to hear a pistol shot or a solitary horseman. No one called at the house that they remembered; no one came near with a carriage or a horse needing stabling."

"Drat. Do you think they were lying, too?"

"Unfortunately, no. They knew nothing."

Amanda asked, "You are sure?"

The cousins looked at each other. "We are sure."

"But how?" she wanted to know. "People lie all the time."

"Not to us, they—" Daniel started, to be stopped with a glare from his cousin.

"It's a, uh, a scientific thing."

"It is?" Daniel and Amanda both asked.

"Yes, we made an extensive study in the Peninsula. People who lie give clues. Like blinking faster, or shifting their eyes, or breathing hard. Their voices change, too."

Daniel started to rub at his ear.

Amanda was fascinated. "So you did not really torture prisoners."

"Of course not!"

Indignation cured Daniel's itch. "I would challenge anyone who claimed to my face that we did. Can't stop whispers behind our backs, but that's all it is."

"I could not see how such accusations could be true, you have been so kind. But why let the stories of cruelty last?"

Because they had not thought of the Aide's brilliant

pretense of research, Rex thought. Aloud he said, "Because the rumors worked in our favor. If enemy prisoners were afraid I would slice off their, ah, ears, or Daniel would sit on them, they were more liable to tell us what we needed to know. Flashing a knife"—he pulled one from his boot in a streak of light—"or swinging Daniel's anvil-sized fists was intimidating enough. They talked. Every minute mattered when the generals were waiting to deploy our own troops or defend a position. They needed to know where the enemy was, what his plans were. If the prisoners knew, we found out."

"I did not believe anything else."

Well, she almost disbelieved the gory tales, Rex could tell from the orangish cast to her words.

"And your mother never credited a single one of the rumors."

Lady Royce knew the truth, but Rex did not wish to think about that.

Amanda was asking, "Can you show me?"

"Show you?"

"How to judge the truth."

"Hmm. The research has not been made public for national security reasons, but perhaps, since we are all friends . . . Look at Daniel carefully. I am going to ask him simple questions, and he is going to lie sometimes, say the truth sometimes."

"I am?"

"Yes, you are. What is your mother's given name?"

"Cora."

"There, did you see that?"

"What?"

"Watch again, more closely. Daniel, what is your mother's given name."

"C—" He saw Rex shake his head and changed his reply to Carolyn. He scratched his nose.

"Aha! You see, he blinked more."

"I must have missed it. Let me try. Daniel, what is your middle name?"

"I never tell anyone!"

Rex laughed. Amanda pleaded. Daniel looked over at his cousin who silently mouthed, "Lie."

"Ralston."

Amanda set the violets aside. "I cannot tell."

Daniel said "Good," and stopped rubbing at his nose.

Amanda turned to Rex. "Do you like me?"

"Great gods, what kind of question is that?" Rex was blinking. His voice had raised an octave. His eyes were shifting from her to a grinning Daniel to the Staffordshire dogs on the mantel.

"Yes," he croaked. "Do you like me?"

She did not hesitate, blink, or bleat. "Yes."

Blue, and Rex's heart swelled in his chest.

Amanda never knew she could be so forward. The proper young lady she'd spent twenty-two years refining seemed to have disappeared in jail. No female of breeding asked such personal questions of a gentleman she had known for two days, and without a proper introduction, to boot.

Amanda was no longer a lady in the eyes of polite society, whichever direction the trial took, so in a way she was more free to say what she thought, to think what she felt, to feel. Staring at the possibility of a sentence of death, or a short, brutal lifetime in prison, refocused one's sights. Politeness, conventions, missishness—heavens, she had no time for that nonsense.

Lord Rexford—Rex—liked her, which somehow made her less of a burden to him. She could almost believe that a wealthy, well-born gentleman might truly befriend a penniless woman of no distinction but a murder charge and a blackened reputation.

He'd brought her gifts. He'd said he liked her. The world was not entirely bleak; not when violets bloomed and honest blue eyes smiled at her.

Chapter Fourteen

Nanny shooed the gentlemen on their way and ushered Amanda back to her bedroom. Tomorrow, the old nursemaid declared, missy might be permitted downstairs to take luncheon with the viscount and his cousin, although there was no guaranteeing the quality of the meal with the housekeeper doing the cooking.

And tomorrow, Nanny muttered on her way out, the countess had better come home, for all their sakes.

"She's right, you know," Daniel told Rex over a glass of sherry in the formal drawing room.

"That Miss Carville, Amanda, will be vastly improved by tomorrow? She has made a great recovery, hasn't she? The lady looks as if a gust of wind could blow her away, yet she has withstood the storm. I think she is brave, for a female. Don't you?"

Daniel scowled over his wineglass. "I think you aren't thinking with your head. What I meant is Nanny is right that you need a proper chaperone here. Not good for the gal to be alone with us, you know."

"Why? We're here to help her, not destroy her health altogether."

"When did you get so dense? It's the chit's reputation that has Nanny in a swivet, not her health."

"When did you start worrying over the punctilios of polite society?" Rex countered. "And you such a pillar of respectability. Wasn't it you swilling gin in a sty of swine a day or two ago?"

"I never said I was a model of proper behavior, and that's the problem. Neither one of us is fit company for a gently bred female. A young, unmarried female," he added, in case Rex had forgotten.

Rex raised his glass to that. He could barely trust himself not to bash her door in just to see her angel's curls and sweet smile. Of course he wouldn't stop in the doorway; not in his dreams, at least. In reality, he would never step over the line, figuratively or not. He did know the dangers, without any reminder.

Daniel was going on: "Rumors are already starting, that you're setting her up here as your mistress."

"Damnation!" Rex might wish it, but how dare anyone speak so ill of Miss Carville. And of him. "They think I would ruin a lady? And bring my lover here to the countess's house? What kind of loose screw do they take me for?"

Daniel hunched his broad shoulders. "A spy and a slime, same as me. It's a bad reflection on your mother, too, or that's what the clucking tongues will say, with Aunt Margaret turning a blind eye on the situation."

"The countess is not even here!"

"Exactly. I suggest we change a few minds tonight."

Rex squeezed his still-swollen nose. "I am not ready for another bout of fisticuffs. And I do not see how drawing anyone's claret will change the *ton*'s opinion of me or

Amanda. Or Lady Royce." Although the last was the last on his list of worries.

"Fighting won't, but if you are seen out and about, at the clubs, a party, something fashionable, people will see that you aren't hiding away, slinking in shadows. You have to assure them that you and Miss Carville are mere houseguests together, strangers under one roof, only until her health is restored and her situation is resolved."

"That is what we are, strangers to each other."

Daniel rubbed at his ear. "Best if you tell people she's been near unconscious, under constant care of nurses and maids, which is almost true. You can spread that around Lady Arbuthnot's daughter's come-out ball tonight. Your mother would have been invited. Bosom bows, don't you know."

How would Rex know the countess's friends? "A ball? You and I?"

"Actually, I thought you'd toddle 'round by yourself."

"Think again. If I go, you go. Or else people might think you are back here, seducing the lady."

Daniel smiled at the idea. "They might, mightn't they?"

Rex vowed not to leave his cousin alone with Amanda ever again. "You are coming. We'll do the pretty, act unconcerned, and tell people that Amanda is sick abed with Nanny watching, without bending the facts. Now that I think on it, going out might serve other purposes. We might learn something about Sir Frederick, too."

"And we might get a better meal than the housekeeper here can provide. I hope your mother gets home soon, with her cook."

Rex was looking forward to the countess's return about as much as he looked forward to putting himself on display at Lady Arbuthnot's. Both were necessary evils.

*   *   *

Daniel was starting to pull at the neckcloth Murchison had tied in an Oriental knot. They were barely through the receiving line where Lady Arbuthnot had lied through her teeth in greeting. The only truth she spoke was that unattached gentlemen were always welcome at debutante balls. Unattached gentlemen of means, they all knew she meant.

She promised to introduce them to suitable partners as soon as the dancing began—not her daughter, of course, whose card was already full. Her regrets for that circumstance were as red in Rex's mind as the rash on Daniel's neck. They, and their titles and estates, were good enough for someone else's daughter despite their reputations, but not her own little chick.

The men murmured their gratitude for the lady's kindness, and promised each other to play least in sight when she came matchmaking for her wallflowers. Rex was all for finding the card room. "It's the men who will know about Sir Frederick's debts."

"But it's the ladies we have to impress with Miss Carville's respectability."

They looked around the crowded, flower-bedecked ballroom, the young women like so many more blossoms in their frilly pastels. They were all fluttering lashes and fans, while their mothers gossiped, relating to each other every bachelor's interests and income. A great many—too many for Rex's comfort—calculating glances were directed at the cousins.

"Oh Lord," he said, "we'd do better back at the front. The French have a whole army to aim at. We're standing targets here."

"It's your red coat and all that gold braid."

"It's your great size. No one can miss you."

Without further consultation, they retreated to the refreshments room.

"Lobster patties, my favorite." Daniel forgot about the matrimonial-minded mamas and took half the platter onto his plate, itch also forgotten. Rex was too on edge to eat, but poured himself a glass of punch, which turned out to be sweet and insipid. They stood to the side, watching the crowds, noticing everyone noticing them.

A few older women, not wearing the white and pastels of the debutantes, smiled in their direction. The females did not have to say a word to make their intentions, and invitations, as clear as day. A few gentlemen came by on their way to the food table and nodded, more out of respect for Rex's uniform, he thought, than for the cousins. They frowned at Daniel's plate on their way back, sans lobster patties. One man asked after Rex's father, after looking over his shoulder to make sure no one heard him. He scurried away as quickly as he could, without the glass of punch he'd supposedly come for.

"We'd do better at cards," Rex decided out loud. "No one will speak to us here."

Daniel was off refilling his plate and did not answer, but someone else did.

"Can you blame them for not speaking? I am astounded you had the gall to show your face at a respectable gathering."

Rex looked over, to find himself the subject of a sneering scrutiny, through Sir Nigel Turlowe's quizzing glass. Sir Nigel was the knighted barrister who had ruined his father's career, who had rushed Miss Carville into jail, who appeared to have a grudge against the entire Royce family. He was a man of middle years, with his brown hair parted

in the middle to make it look fuller. He had thin lips, too, a
sharp, pointed nose and pale eyebrows and lashes. He reminded Rex of a lizard.

Rex did not bow. He curled his lip in return and said, "I
myself am surprised at the indiscriminate quality of Lady
Arbuthnot's guests."

Sir Nigel's watery eyes narrowed. His nostrils flared.
Rex expected a forked tongue to come out of his lips.
Instead the man said, "I do not appreciate your interfer-
ence in my court case. Miss Carville's guilt is a foregone
conclusion and an easy conviction. Stay away from it."

"I do not see the case that way." Rex saw the man's own
yellow belief in his words, with a tinge of orange doubt,
likely because of Rex's involvement. So Sir Nigel believed Rex's actions could change the outcome, which
was encouraging.

Sir Nigel sneered again. "I do not care what you think,
or what outlandish notions you have. Sympathy, chivalry
toward Lady Royce's connection, or your deviltry, nothing
affects the facts. The woman is guilty and belongs in jail.
If she does not appear for trial then it is on your head and
on your honor, what there is left of it."

Rex put his hand down, to where his sword would have
been. Then he raised his other hand, the one with the cup
in it, ready to throw punch in the dastard's face along with
his challenge. No man who considered himself a gentleman could accept such an insult. "Name your sec—*Agh.*"

Daniel's elbow had landed in Rex's ribs. The punch
sloshed over onto Rex's hand. Sir Nigel snickered.

"Don't do it," cousin Daniel whispered, cutting his eyes
toward the gathering crowd. "He's wanting you to make a
fool of yourself, can't you see? Besides, it won't help
Miss Carville's cause to be defended by a hothead. And if

you kill him, you'll have to leave the country. Then what will she do?"

Rex raised his eyebrow as if to comment on Daniel's sudden wisdom, which he accepted, given the moment to think. He dabbed at his hand with a handkerchief, then turned his head toward the barrister knight. "Perhaps you might wish to discuss my honor at Jackson's Boxing Parlor. You'll appreciate the odds, I am sure, fighting a cripple. No? Then Antoine's Fencing Academy? Manton's Shooting Gallery?"

"Everyone knows you are a crack shot."

"And now everyone knows that your mouth is bigger than your manhood." Rex spotted Lady Arbuthnot hurrying over, attracted by the circle around the two men. "That is," he added for the lady's sake, "your manners. It cannot be quite *convenable*, can it, insulting a fellow guest in our charming hostess's home?" He bowed to that lady. "Especially since she was kind enough to accept myself and my cousin instead of Lady Royce, her original invitee. My dear Lady Arbuthnot, please accept my apologies." He bent over her hand, but kissed the inside of her wrist, above her glove, instead of the air above her fingers as was customary. Then he winked at her.

"Dear boy. Of course I accept your apology." She turned to Sir Nigel expectantly.

The knight pursed his thin lips. "I have done nothing for which I need apologize."

Rex pointedly refused to look at the reptile, or address him. "No, my lady, he merely throws insults rather than punches. Luckily for him dueling is illegal."

"Since when does the law matter to you?" Sir Nigel sneered again, turning to the crowd for their approval.

The gentleman who had asked after Lord Royce shook

his head and said, "But it should stop you, sir, an officer of the court."

An older man laughed out loud. "Seems more than Sir Nigel's position keeps him from answering a challenge, eh?"

Sir Nigel turned apoplectic, with high color and heavy breathing. Rex wondered if he would save them all the cost of a bullet. Regrettably, Sir Nigel recovered enough to turn on the older gent. "I am no brute, proving my worth with my fists. Or bullying my way through life as if a title and wealth gave me the right." He pointed back toward Rex and spit out, "Hear this, Rexford. That murderess's parole is on your head. I will see you behind bars if she gets away—see if I don't. And I'll have that Dimm-wit Runner's job, too. The old fool should have retired years ago."

"Instead of catching scores of felons to make London safer for all of us? Perhaps you ought to inquire at the magistrate's office how many crimes he has solved this week alone, how many true miscreants he has seen sentenced, with facts and confessions to prove his cases, not smoke and mirrors and personal vendettas."

Sir Nigel ignored the interruption. "And that shady character connected to Whitehall who pulled strings for you. I'll see him brought down, too. Why should anyone trust a fellow who always stands in darkness?"

"Strange, I would trust him with my life, and have. As has General Wellesley, along with the lives of half the army. Any foul attempt to discredit the Aide might very well sacrifice our own soldiers."

Sir Nigel waved his fist in the air. "Justice, I say! Justice will be done."

"Justice? Is it justice to abuse a gently bred young lady

of two and twenty years by tossing her to ignorant guards and common thieves without a conviction? She could have been placed under house arrest, or remanded to a family friend."

"Everyone knows she is guilty."

"Now you are judge as well as jury? I thought the lowest cutpurse or pickpocket got a fair trial."

The onlookers were shaking their heads in disapproval.

Like the experienced barrister he was, Sir Nigel sensed he had lost the goodwill of the listeners. "Bah!"

"Bah, indeed, traducing the justice system you say you hold dear. But let us ask our charming hostess."

Lady Arbuthnot was looking anxious, with her ball turning into a political debate, if not a duel.

Rex asked her how old her lovely daughter was.

"Nineteen," she answered with uncertainty as to his purpose.

"And if she found herself in the wrong place, at the wrong time, in a situation far beyond her understanding or experience, would you not expect her peers to deal with her as a lady?"

"Of course." She glared at Sir Nigel. "I have known Amanda Carville her entire life. She is a sensible, kind-hearted miss who always acts just as she ought. If she claims she is not guilty, and Lady Royce shows she believes the girl is not guilty by taking her into her home, and a brave officer from the general's staff puts his own honor at stake for her, I, for one, am willing to believe her."

"She is innocent." Rex stated without hesitation. Daniel nodded his head in agreement.

"Two officers."

"Bah!" Sir Nigel repeated. "Of course the young bucks

will back her story. Amanda Carville is nothing but a light skirt."

Rex held onto his temper with effort—and with another jab in the ribs from his cousin. He might be black and blue in the morning, but he would not be counting twenty paces, leaving Amanda without protection. "No," he told Lady Arbuthnot and the circle of eager guests who surrounded them. "The only one who claimed Miss Carville's disgrace is the man who wanted to keep her dowry for himself, after he stole her inheritance."

"He did?" Lady Arbuthnot gasped. A few of her friends fanned themselves with their hands. "I never knew. But I never did like that Hawley monster. That poor child." She glared at Sir Nigel, who made her a cursory bow, turned on his heel, and left without another word, shoving one portly matron aside.

Lady Arbuthnot asked Rex, almost as if he had prompted her, "My dear Lord Rexford, when did you say your mother was due to return to London?"

"Momentarily, depending on her own health and the weather," he said, trying for any plausible excuse for the delay. "Meanwhile she has ordered her beloved godchild placed under the care of thoroughly trustworthy women, who watch over Miss Carville's sickroom night and day."

Lady Arbuthnot beamed at Rex and Daniel, then at her friends. "Excellent. Do you know, I believe my daughter has a dance open after all?"

"So does mine!"

"And mine."

Oh, Lord.

Chapter Fifteen

They went to the Cocoa Tree next. The gamblers and gossipers there were not as fusty as the members at White's Club or Boodles. The cousins' reception was not warm, but their money was welcomed at the tables, especially when word arrived, as it always did, of the confrontation with Sir Nigel Turlowe.

"What did that Shakespeare chap say?" a castaway gentleman watching their game asked. "Something about, first, kill all the lawyers." He raised his glass. "Here's to the downfall of that social-climbing jackass."

The son of a marquis, the drunk had never worked a day in his life. The son of an earl, Rex understood about wanting to make something of oneself, but not on the backs of others. He raised his own glass, although he took a mere sip. "May he at least be proved wrong about Sir Frederick Hawley's murder."

"You say the gal did not blow his brains to smithereens?"

One of the card players gagged.

Rex frowned and said, "No, Miss Carville had cause to dislike the man, but she is a lady." That stopped any possible comment about Amanda's supposed fall from grace.

Rex reinforced his point with adding, "She is Lady Royce's godchild, don't you know." He figured that the countess's social standing ought to be good for something.

"Stands to reason, with you taking up the cause."

If the man was hinting for more gossip, he was wasting his time. "Family," Rex said, almost choking on the foreign word. "I never met the female before."

The cousins earned their acceptance at the table by losing, and by paying in coins, not in vouchers to be collected some time in the vague future. "Not like Sir Frederick's usual habit, eh?"

But no one claimed to hold the dead man's vowels. One down-at-heels young baronet owed Hawley a small sum, in fact, and wondered if he had to pay the heir.

A debt of honor was a debt of honor—that was the consensus among the inveterate gamblers, no matter the legality of the thing. And Sir Frederick's family needed the blunt. The son was trying to restore an ailing estate, wasn't he? And who would marry either of the girls now, guilty or not, without a generous dowry?

Rex made sure he lost to the baronet.

They moved on to a new gaming club Daniel patronized where the company was less lofty, less bound by scruples than greed. The wine was watered; the dice were likewise suspect. Again, Rex and Daniel swore Miss Carville was innocent. And an innocent. She was home ill, wasn't she? And again, they found nothing damning about Sir Frederick. No one liked the man, but no one seemed to hate him enough to kill him. As at the previous establishment, no one knew his friends, if he had any.

Their next stop was at McCann's Club, a favorite among military men. Rex wanted to look around, to spot a familiar figure, listen for a familiar voice. The Aide,

Major Harrison, or Mr. Harris, was either disguised so that Rex would not recognize him, or he was not wearing a disguise at all, in which case Rex would still not recognize him. Either that or he was not there. The manager swore he never heard of the man, by either of his names, but if an elderly gentleman fitting the description did happen to come by, the manager would give him a message from Rex. Rex held his coin away from the outstretched hand. No, he had no message. And no, he discovered, the upper rooms were not open to guests. They were reserved for the club's proprietors, with two guards watching the stairwell.

The cousins moved on to one of Daniel's more frequent haunts, a gaming hell just like the one where they'd been in the brawl, where they would not be welcome or safe anytime soon. The dive was noisier than any of the more genteel clubs, dirtier, with rougher company, higher stakes, and cheaper liquor.

Daniel was too familiar with the low clientele for Rex's comfort, knowing every serving girl by name, every sot passed out in the corners, all the toothless old gamblers, and the hard-eyed younger ones, who cleaned their filthy fingernails with stilettoes.

This was no place for his kin, no matter how big and strong Daniel was, or how friendly the whores. Rex decided it was a good thing he'd come to London when he had. Someone had to rescue dunderheaded Daniel before he caught the pox or a knife in the back.

Rex thought for a moment about going upstairs with one of the cleaner-looking bar maids, to slake the entirely inappropriate and totally unquenchable thirst for Miss Amanda Carville. He'd gone too long without a woman, he told himself. That was all it was: A man had certain needs. The only reason he thought of those needs and

Amanda in the same breath was that he'd rescued the girl. He'd carried her and washed her, and tucked her up in bed. Now he felt protective of her, possessive, even.

He felt more than brotherly, though. Amanda was vulnerable, appearing so fragile and soft, but she was deuced appealing, too. No painted doxy stood tall and straight, with a lady's careful carriage. No wench in a gaming den had that glow of intelligence about her or the educated speech. No whore wore her innocence like a crown. And no, he knew a tumble on dirty sheets would not satisfy his need.

Neither would a visit to a higher class of courtesan at one of the luxurious bordellos. For that matter, he could have answered any of the come-hither glances from the widows and wanton wives at Lady Arbuthnot's, but the lobster patties had seemed more appetizing. Damn, the only woman he wanted was the one he should not, could not have. The sooner he left London, the better.

For tonight, Rex was tired of the cards and the smoke-filled rooms. Never a gambler, he was bored with losing his brass to loosen tongues. They never found that Sir Frederick won or lost vast amounts, only that he seldom bought a round or left a coin for the dealer or paid his debts early. The man was a niggard, everyone agreed, a mean drunk, and not mourned overmuch, but he had no obvious enemies.

Rex had no idea if their appearance had changed anyone's mind in Amanda's favor. If the patrons of every walk of life, from the glittering *ton* to the gutter, felt that of course Miss Carville had committed the crime, they were wise enough to keep their lips sealed when the cousins were nearby.

So Rex felt he was getting nowhere but poorer, and

Daniel was getting drunker. "I think we have learned all we are going to," Rex told his cousin, hauling the larger man to his feet with effort. "We have done what we can for Miss Carville's reputation by staying out this late to prove we are not sitting in her pocket, or her bedchamber. So come, tomorrow will be a busy day, and I do not like leaving her alone all night."

Daniel stumbled after him, but once out in the air seemed to regain his footing and his common sense. He leaned toward Rex and shook his finger. "You are too involved, my boy. Dangerous, don't you know."

"I was speaking of my dog, Verity. She is not used to London ways or being without me. I do not know if anyone fed her, or let her out afterward."

Daniel leaned against a lamppost and took off his shoe to scratch his toes.

At home—Lady Royce's home, Rex reminded himself lest he get to thinking he belonged here, which he definitely did not—he poured two last glasses of excellent brandy while Daniel and Verity made one more foray to the pantry to see what there was to eat. Neither of them was ever full, but Rex had not eaten much that evening, so they all shared a potluck meal of cold meats and cheese and bread. Not even Nanny's sister could ruin those.

Rex consulted his notes, planning their next day's campaign. Bow Street came first, and he tried to encourage Daniel to attend with him. "It's interesting and a worthwhile enterprise."

Daniel set down his makeshift sandwich. "I get hives just thinking about all the lies they'll tell."

"But we can winnow out the guilty ones quicker than

the detectives can. You know, making the world a better place."

Daniel snorted. "Yes, and have people looking sideways at us wondering how, just like the army, where we were making the world safe from the Corsican. Research and science, my arse. And if you are thinking anyone will appreciate the effort, remember that Spanish officer at Cifuentes who kept crossing himself and praying every time we walked by."

"Well, we need the warrants from Inspector Dimm, so we owe him an hour or two. Then we can go to Hawley's solicitor, his bank, and his house to search."

"For what? You've got the gun."

"For the reason someone wanted him dead."

Daniel took a big bite of his sandwich, then broke off a piece for the dog. "What if it was an ordinary burglar who was surprised by Sir Frederick? I know the report said the windows were all shut when the Watch arrived, but the thief could have walked in and out the front door."

"Past Miss Carville? No, but a robber could have used the servant's entrance, with the staff all elsewhere, when he heard her return home. No one said anything was missing, though."

"Maybe the thief didn't have time, with Amanda storming in. Besides, if the killer was after Sir Frederick's purse, we'll never be able to prove it."

"Unless he happens to be one of the raff and scaff Dimm drags in off the streets for us to question."

"I suppose." Daniel took the rest of his meal—his fourth or fifth of the evening—and went up to bed, Verity following the scent. Rex stayed behind with his notes. They still had to find that valet. Perhaps Murchison had discovered something.

The valet had been waiting up, despite the late hour. He shook his head no. Nothing was known about Brusseau's new place of employment? Another head shake, but one word: *"Frère,"* in French.

"Brusseau has a brother? A fine lot of good that does us, if we cannot find either. Keep trying."

Murchison wrinkled his nose at the stench of cigars and cheap perfume clinging to Rex's uniform, but said nothing. There were advantages, after all, in having a valet who did not speak much.

Then Rex was alone. He ought to climb into bed and rest his weary leg. Instead he pulled the sash of his robe tighter and took his candle down the hall. He'd just check on Miss Carville, make certain she was not still feverish. After all, Nanny was getting old, and could not watch over her every minute.

He paused outside the woman's door. No light came from under the crack, but a loud sawing sound reached the hallway. Good grief, someone was trying to cut through the window. His hand on the doorknob, Rex listened again. Not sawing, he realized, but snoring. No wonder the woman was unwed, if word of that got out. She was louder than a woodsman, with a whistle here and there.

Rex smiled. So Miss Amanda Carville was not quite the delicate flower he'd painted in his mind's eye. Now maybe he could sleep without thinking of her. Who the devil wanted to share his pillow with a wheezing, gasping, whistling chorus? He might as well sleep in the barnyard.

The noise stopped suddenly. Good gods, had she choked? Knowing he was doing wrong, knowing he had no choice, Rex pushed the door in. If anyone saw him he could say he heard noises—heaven knew that was true— and came to check on Miss Carville's welfare.

He would have stumbled over the trundle bed set up right at the entry to the room, except the snoring began again, louder now that he was closer. Nanny was fast asleep, on her back, her mouth wide open, sounding like a honking goose. If the noise did not frighten intruders away, his old nursemaid had the fireplace poker on the mattress beside her, her knitting needles on the other side. Nanny was doing her best to guard her charge against fevers and marauders and rakish gentlemen.

He shielded his candle and stepped around the cot to the four-poster bed. Amanda was sleeping, lord knew how, over the racket. Then he saw the bottles on the nearby table and supposed she'd taken the laudanum again, the poor puss. She'd likely feel muzzy in the morning, but at least she would get the rest she needed.

He couldn't help noticing the gold curls flattened under a bit of a lace nightcap, or how the covers were pulled up to her chin, leaving no trace of a neckline or breast. He also saw the kitchen knife on the bed near her hand. "That's good. Sleep well, my dear, and trust no one." He turned to leave. "Not even me."

Amanda stayed awake as long as possible. She wrote letters to her stepsister and -brother, telling them of her situation, as best she could. She did not ask for their help or support. If Edwin and Elaine believed her guilty, none would be forthcoming. If they believed her innocent, she should not need to ask. And what could they do, anyway? Neither had funds or influence or understanding of the courts.

Lord Rexford had all of them.

She looked over the clothes that had been brought from Hawley House, knowing she would never get to wear ball gowns again unless Rex succeeded. She glanced at the books he had brought her, but she'd read both of the popular novels. She rearranged the roses, and moved the violets closer to her bed. She had dinner, and then tea and biscuits, and a glass of wine Nanny recommended as a restorative. It did not restore Amanda's patience.

The men did not come home.

Amanda could not complain. Of course not. They were young gentlemen, so the London night was their playing field. They had already done so much for her, and were trying their best. They were entitled to a night of pleasure. Blast them.

She decided to go to bed. A good night's rest would complete her recovery so she'd be more help tomorrow. With Nanny asleep near the door and the kitchen knife at her side, Amanda was safe, well fed, clean, and comfortable. Surely she had a lot to be thankful for in her prayers, especially Lady Royce and her son. She prayed for them, too, and blew out the candle.

She lay there, waiting for sleep to come. It couldn't tiptoe through the noise. "Nanny?"

"Mm, yes, miss?"

"You are snoring."

"Oh no, I would never do that. Good night, lambie."

The trundle bed was rocking with every inhale; the draperies were fluttering with every exhale. Dreadful thoughts came to Amanda in the dark instead of the solace of sleep. In another few moments she'd be in a panic again, worrying that Rex and Daniel would not come home, would not find evidence to help her case, would not save her. The trial was another day closer. Before she could talk herself into a waking nightmare, seeing Sir Frederick on the floor, hearing the prison guards bargain for her body, feel the filthy hands grabbing at her, she took the laudanum left at her bedside.

She pulled the twisted covers straight, tightened the bow of her nightcap, and said her prayers again, just in case no one had heard them the first time, over the snoring. Slowly she sank into slumber.

What a lovely dream! His lordship came into the room to watch over her, to whisper something. Amanda could not make out the words, but she knew they were tender, caring, encouraging. Then he left, and Amanda smiled in her sleep until the dream turned sour.

Of course he would not really come into her bedroom now that she was no longer so sick. Rex was a gentleman with a rigid code of honor, and had not a little fear of Nanny's knitting needles. But what did it matter?

Amanda had no reputation left to lose. They all knew it, whether Nanny guarded her like a hen with one chick or not, whether Rex and Daniel treated her like a lady or not. She was not a lady in the eyes of the polite world. She would never marry now that she was declared damaged goods. She'd never have a home or family of her own, no babies to nurture at her breast. So why should she not enjoy the friendship of the most interesting gentleman she had ever met, the only one who truly liked her? After all, who was she saving herself for, the hangman?

Rex had pleasant dreams. He awoke still warm with the memory of a soft body next to his, gentle breath on his cheek, a mew of satisfied contentment near his pillow.

"Damn it, Verity! You know you are not supposed to sleep on the bed!"

Chapter Sixteen

Rex found himself looking forward to the morning's work with Bow Street. Daniel was not. He grumbled about the dangerous characters they were likely to meet, and Rex nobly refrained from likening Dimm's cutpurses to Daniel's crooked dealers at his favored gambling dens. With the promise of a second beefsteak breakfast afterward, Daniel went along. Someone had to look after Rex, hadn't he? Who knew what crazy notion he'd get next. Helping the war effort was one thing; interrogating pimps and pickpockets was another; acting the mooncalf over an accused murderess was the worst of all. If playing at thieftaker would keep Rex away from leg shackles, Daniel was willing to help.

Inspector Dimm was having his doubts about his new consultant, too. Not about the results of Lord Rexford's so-called experiments; they were a success. Dimm's men had found evidence to convict most of those the viscount had declared guilty, the suspects who hadn't already confessed. Dimm puffed on his pipe in his little office while the cousins stood along the wall. "It's that there's been a pother with my superiors. One of the gentlemen"—he blew out a black cloud of smoke—"accused my department of beating those confessions out of the prisoners."

"Sir Nigel," both of the Inquisitors said at the same time.

"Aye, I expect so. No matter that I swore you never touched a single one of the lawbreakers, afore or after they confessed. I just couldn't explain how you got so good at guessing, is all. Odds were even, guilty or innocent, you'd get half right. But you got 'em all." He tapped the diminished pile of folders and papers on his desk. "And we proved most of them, without a doubt. I couldn't exactly explain the science behind your findings."

"Does it matter?" Rex stared at Dimm, waiting.

Dimm stared back through a smoke ring, as if he'd find an answer in Rex's black-rimmed blue eyes. Then the old Runner shrugged. "There's lots of things I'll never understand, like why it always rains on my afternoon off, or how a woman's mind works. The way I see it, getting the filth off the streets is my job, what I was hired for, any which way I can get it done."

For the inspector's sake, Rex and Daniel decided to sit outside his office, at Dimm's assistant's desk, playing at dice as if waiting for Dimm to be free for luncheon, say, or a visit to the coffeehouse across the street. With his office door open during his interviews, they could still conduct their "experiments."

"What, you don't even have to see the blokes face-to-face? Is it the sweat as they walk past? Do the guilty smell more than the innocent?"

"No, that was great-grandfather's gift—Why'd you kick me?"

Rex ignored his cousin's complaint. "There are many factors, as I said yesterday. Many people, honest or otherwise, will perspire under trying circumstances. So today we will listen to the voices and see what we detect. One rap on the table is for the truth, two mean the suspect is feeding you hog-slop."

There was a bit of confusion at first, what with the dice falling on the wooden desktop, but the system worked wondrously, to everyone's satisfaction except the prisoners and Daniel, who had a rash on both of his ankles.

"Sorry, there must be fleas in here," Dimm's assistant apologized. "Our visitors ain't much for bathing."

Or for speaking the truth.

Every captive and witness was also asked if he or she had killed Sir Frederick Hawley. None had. Did they know who committed the murder, if not Miss Carville? None did.

In a short time the holding cells were empty of the night's arrests. The innocent were set free, the guilty were sent to the courts for indictments.

Inspector Dimm was delighted. "I might get to spend some time at home, my feet up on a stool, a cat on my lap, with a good book to read." He was happy to hand over search warrants and writs making Rex's actions, past and future, legal. He also loaned him the use of a shriveled old man known as Duncan Fingers.

Rex took Dimm aside. "What am I supposed to do with Duncan, beside feed him and find him a place in the sun?"

Dimm laughed. "Duncan used to be the best safecracker in all of London. If you want to get into Sir Frederick's secret drawers or vaults, he's your man."

Rex already had a huge dog and his huger, itchy cousin, an ancient nanny, a silent valet, and an alleged murderess. What was a former convict, more or less?

*   *   *

If Sir Frederick's solicitor was disconcerted to have a known thief in his office, stretching his knuckles—"to keep m'fingers nimble, don't you know"—he hid it well. Either that or he was so terrified of Rex and Daniel's reputation that a cracksman was a lesser evil.

He was, truthfully, pleased to see someone looking after Miss Carville's interests. He was even more pleased to see the legal documents, so he was not forced to break his client's confidence.

"Left everything to his son, did he?" Daniel asked.

"Nothing that was not entailed. They had a falling out."

"We heard that. So whom did he name as heir?"

"He refused to name anyone or make a will. He told me that he fully intended to take his money with him. The son will get what is left, eventually."

"But what of the fortune Sir Frederick's second wife brought, which was to have been Miss Carville's inheritance? Surely that does not become part of the man's estate?"

"Bad business, that," the solicitor said. "But all legal. A husband has control of his wife's monies, of course, and no other trustee was named for Miss Carville's mother's own fortune by the late Lord Carville. Another oversight, in my opinion. Sir Frederick had himself declared Miss Amanda Carville's legal guardian, with my office's assistance, to my regret. Her funds were his to dispense as he saw fit, including her dowry. He withdrew all the money and closed the accounts, over my objections that time, I will have you know. He left no wherewithal for me to finance Miss Carville's defense beyond hiring a barrister to represent her."

A barrister who never asked if she was guilty. The solicitor could have used his own brass, Rex thought, to hire a more competent, caring lawyer, but he did not say it. "What did the blackguard do with all that money?"

"He said he was making investments, but not through my firm. It was not my place to ask more questions."

Not his place, when a woman and child were being stripped of their fortune? Rex did not hold the solicitor in high regard. Sir Frederick did not either, it appeared, since he did not confide his plans. "Perhaps his bank will know."

The solicitor looked doubtful. "Very closemouthed he was. I suspected—"

"Blackmail?" Daniel suggested, his favorite theory, after the butler and the burglar.

"Of course not. Sir Frederick was a gentleman."

Rex did not comment on how many gentlemen of title and means were mean as snakes. "What did you think he was doing with the money, then?"

The solicitor cleared his throat, then coughed. "I, ah, considered that he had another family to support. One not sanctioned by the church."

Daniel liked that theory. "And then, when he would not wed his lover, she shot him in anger. Or maybe he was growing tired of her and her demands and she refused to be dismissed."

Oh, lord. Rex changed the subject. "Did you know Miss Carville?"

"I knew her mother, and her father before. Good solid gentleman, he was, despite not making proper provisions. Of course he did not count on dying so young, but no one ever does, do they? He'd be appalled now."

"Everyone is."

The solicitor excused himself, then came back with a locked box. "I have been wondering what to do with this."

Duncan had it open before the solicitor could find the correct key in his drawer. Meanwhile the man of affairs explained that he'd kept the contents safe from Sir Frederick by writing stringent terms into Lady Carville's will, which she had dictated on her deathbed unbeknownst to Sir Frederick. She knew it was too late to save her fortune for her daughter, and her annuity had stopped on her remarriage, but she did have these, in her own name. Gifts from her own mother and her first husband, the box's contents were not entailed to any estate, so were hers to bequeath.

Duncan whistled.

Daniel's eyes opened wider. Even Rex was impressed. The box contained a dragon's horde of jewelry: necklaces, bracelets, brooches, and earbobs, set with diamonds, rubies, emeralds, and sapphires. To Rex's admittedly untrained eye, they appeared elegant and expensive, all in the finest taste and quality. Duncan swore they were genuine.

"They were not to go to Miss Amanda until her twenty-fifth birthday or her marriage," the solicitor explained, "and only I had the key to the box. I wondered if I should let Miss Carville have the occasional loan of them, for parties and such, now that she was attending more social engagements. I feared that Sir Frederick would get his hands on them, however, exchange them for paste copies or claim them to pay for the young lady's Season. He was not a nice man."

Which Rex did not need a wash of color to know for the truth.

The solicitor pushed the box toward Rex. "I am certain her mother would have wanted Miss Carville to have them now. Perhaps they will help."

"I do not see how, but she will be pleased to know that her mother left them safe for her."

"I, well, I thought she might sell them and find a place for herself elsewhere. The colonies maybe."

"She should run away?"

"I would never suggest fleeing the courts of law!"

That was a bright red lie. Financing the flight of a guilty woman was exactly what the man was proposing.

Rex stood. "I shall give them to Miss Carville, that she might be comforted. She can wear them as soon as she is cleared of all suspicion."

"Of course, of course. If you would not mind signing for them?"

"You do not trust me?"

The solicitor looked toward Duncan, who was holding the sapphires up to the light.

Rex signed.

Fine, now he had another worry. Not that Duncan would scarper off with the jewels, but that Amanda might.

"Are you going to give them to her?" Daniel wanted to know as they left the office.

"They are hers," was all Rex replied.

"There will be the devil to pay if she takes French leave."

But more if she hangs.

Sir Frederick's banker nervously licked his lips while he read the official documents. He did not like having his bank invaded by gentlemen of ill repute, or former bank robbers. Nor did he have answers to Rex's questions. He had no record of what Sir Frederick had done with his money, no transfer to another financial institution, only copies of recent withdrawals and fewer deposits, likely from the estate.

"You noticed no hint of irregularity?" Rex asked.

"Not in my bank!"

Which set Daniel to scratching his scalp and gave Rex a red-haze headache. "I wonder what would happen if we got writs to inspect the bank's books."

Mr. Breverton quickly recalled that he had once written a bank draft to a land brokerage office.

Rex was certain that Breverton could find the name of that realtor, and where they were located.

"Yes, of course. But it might take some time. That was over three years ago, I suspect. Gathering the correct books and ledgers out of storage will take a great deal of effort."

"Really?" Rex tapped the official papers he already had, indicating a few more search warrants would not be hard to obtain.

Breverton mopped at his forehead. "I'll have the information as soon as possible."

With the bank behind them, Rex and Daniel considered what they had learned. "Why would Sir Frederick be buying property when he did not care for his own estate?"

"To put his second family?"

"He could purchase a palace for the sums gone missing. I doubt he was setting up orphanages or hospitals, either."

Duncan Fingers made a rude sound. Everyone knew the not-so-dearly-departed baronet was a penny-pincher.

"So what the deuce was the man doing? I pray there are deeds and documents in his office."

There were not. All they found in the fake bottoms, hidden shelves, and locked compartments of Sir

Frederick's desk were a small purse of coins, bills, and correspondence that Rex gathered up to read later. In the wall safe Amanda had mentioned—and which Duncan had opened in a flash—were a pair of dueling pistols, not at all similar to the weapon that had shot Sir Frederick; a copy of Miss Carville's mother's will; and a small journal. The little book had sums recorded, with dates and initials beside them, but no indication of income or outlay. Rex tucked the small volume inside his coat, along with the jewelry and the letters, to take with him. Perhaps Inspector Dimm or Harrison could connect the initialed entries to known swindlers or smugglers. Rex knew too few men in town.

"There has to be another secret hiding place some-where," Daniel swore, tapping walls, moving paintings, lifting the carpet to look for loose floorboards. He avoided the section of the rug that still had bloodstains. Someone had placed a chair over the blotches.

Hareston, the butler, was not being helpful. He'd re-signed, in fact, the moment he saw that Daniel Stamfield had returned, with his scarier, scarred relation and court writs. He ignored the introduction to the wizened Mr. Fingers altogether, as being beneath his dignity, but an-nounced he would pack his belongings immediately.

Rex did not think Hareston's leaving, with his dignity or the family silver, was a good idea. He waved the legal papers in front of the fellow. "Do you know what these say?"

Hareston raised his red-veined nose. "I do not have my spectacles at hand."

Which Rex took to mean the butler could not make out the legal terms. "They give the right of search and removal of any evidence, and demand the cooperation of every citizen. That means your cooperation, or you could be held in contempt of the courts."

"I have not been paid. I am therefore no longer employed by the household. You have no right to threaten me."

Daniel's size and Rex's determination gave them the right, and they all knew it. Rex removed a gold coin from his pocket. "If you tell us where your master was hiding his cache, you will be paid, and given this as a bonus."

Hareston did not know, even for the reward. Rex sent Daniel and Duncan up to the baronet's bedchamber to search the clothespress, under the mattress, atop the canopy.

Rex kept looking in Sir Frederick's book room, and kept asking Hareston questions. He had the butler recite the details of the murder scene as he recalled them, and judged the man's statements to be true. Then he asked where the valet had been at the time. Hareston swore he did not know, which was also true. He'd been abed, himself, with a bottle, thinking he had hours still before the ladies' return.

"And Brusseau's current address?"

"I do not have it."

"But I am guessing that you might know where I can find him. Think hard before you attempt to throw dust in my eyes. It will not work, and I shall only get mad. You do not want to see me angry, so do not lie."

The danger in the viscount's voice had the butler backing toward the door. "All I know is that someone sent him to a wealthy shipowner. That's all the Frenchman said when he collected his things. That and the merchant had aspirations of being a gentleman."

"His name?"

"Johnston, or something like."

There was a J.J. noted in the little ledger book. "James? Jonathan? Joseph?"

"I do not know, and that is the truth as God is my witness."

And as Rex saw blue.

Daniel and Duncan returned then, empty-handed except for the dead man's signet ring, his purse, a pearl stickpin, which Daniel retrieved from Duncan's pocket, and a woman's pink silk stocking.

"Did Sir Frederick bring his ladybirds home to roost?"

Hareston pulled himself up. "Never. This was a decent Christian household, until recently."

Daniel and Duncan had not found any hiding spots, and no other safe. "He's got to have one, with all the money he withdrew. Stands to reason a clutch-fisted chap like Hawley would keep some home, even if he was investing most of it. Maybe it's behind the books here," Daniel said, starting to pull volumes off the shelves.

Rex agreed that the solution had to be in the office, where the baronet spent most of his time, alone. He did not entertain, according to the butler, and the servants were not permitted to clean the room, as evidenced by the dust clouds stirred up as the bookshelves were disturbed.

Rex stared around, considering other possibilities, idly trying to spin a large globe of the world on its stand in the corner. Like everything else in the room, the thigh-high globe was dusty and obviously too long without oil, so it barely turned on its axis. "Try the hearth, Daniel. Maybe you'll see loose bricks or a false back."

Daniel came out of the fireplace with his head covered in soot. "It's a wonder the place hasn't burned down, with the chimneys going uncleaned that way."

"He did not wish the bother, or the strangers, or the dirt," Hareston said with a sneer as Daniel shook soot and ashes across the room.

Rex was almost ready to concede defeat. Before they left, however, he asked the butler who he thought killed Sir Frederick, if not Miss Carville. Did he have enemies? Debtors? The butler had no guesses.

"I was not in Sir Frederick's confidence. Brusseau was. Thick as inkle weavers, the pair of them. But that woman has to be guilty, she or her lover."

Rex stopped spinning the ornate globe. "You saw her with a man?"

"I saw her sneaking out of the house after everyone was abed, all right. I knew her by her blue cape. Lined with fur, it is, and sent Sir Frederick into paroxysms when he got the bill. I saw the man in the street lamp's light, too. Fair-haired, he was."

Rex smashed his fist into the globe, which split into two halves: one filled with gold, the other with banknotes.

Chapter Seventeen

They retraced their steps, with the addition of a satchel Hareston found to put the money in.

"You are going to put the cash into that shifty-eyed banker's vault?" Daniel hefted the weighty bag onto his lap in the hackney, while Rex moved his cane to make room for Duncan on the opposite seat. "Is that wise?"

"We'll deposit it to a new account, with my name as trustee for Hawley's estate, after we watch Breverton count it and hand over the receipts. The rightful heir will be able to withdraw it, but not without my signature."

"Can you do that?"

"Legally? I have no idea. But I am doing it anyway, both to protect the money and hold it as evidence of heaven knows what. We could not very well put it back in the broken globe and leave it in a half-empty house." He eyed Duncan with suspicion as the small man looked out the window, innocently watching the scenery—or planning the best routes to and from Hawley House. "Nor would I trust the butler. As far as that goes, I do not want anyone wondering about my motives in taking the money away."

"Or wondering where you are stashing it, eh? Royce

House would be the target of every cat burglar in London."

"Exactly. The bank is the best place for it, especially until we discover where it came from and why Sir Frederick had it at home. I am hoping Sir Frederick's son will do the right thing and restore Amanda's mother's money to her, plus her dowry. I also want to read Breverton's name on the bank's door. There was an L.B. in the journal."

Daniel frowned. "I thought he spoke true when he told us he did not know what Sir Frederick was doing with the money."

"No, he said he had no record of what the baronet was doing. There is a difference. The truth can be as narrow as it can be broad. Maybe he did not even know where the dead man was stashing it, and that was the question to which he replied. Who would have thought the fool had a fortune in a globe of the world?"

"Not the butler, that was for sure. I thought the fellow would cry when the gold fell out. He must have been searching for days."

Duncan spit on the hackney floor. "He never found the journal, neither. Amateur. It took a real expert to open that safe without the combination."

"But it took a clumsy oaf to find the money." Daniel sounded glad his cousin was the bumbler, for once. "I wonder why Hawley hid it instead of leaving it in the bank?"

"Maybe he did not trust Breverton?" Rex considered. "But he could have moved his accounts to another institution more easily. Who knows if this is all of his money, anyway. He could have been investing it, and merely squirreling away the profits until the next shipload of smuggled goods or whatever." Rex was still holding to the theory that Sir Frederick was connected to the Free Traders somehow, since his name had been mentioned by Harrison. The property he was buying could have been warehouses near the docks, or isolated farmsteads on the outskirts of town, depots for unloading illegal goods for distribution in the city's higher-paying markets.

"Maybe he was just dicked in the nob. A chap would have to be batty, hoarding his gold at home like that. Someone might have found it. Or no one might ever have found it if you hadn't smashed the globe."

"No, the solicitor distinctly said Sir Frederick planned on taking the money with him. I doubt even Sir Frederick thought he could carry all of this"—he tapped the bag with his cane—"through the pearly gates. And he was buying property, remember. He had plans, perhaps ones requiring sudden moves. I wish we knew what they were."

Breverton refused to answer, if he knew. He counted the money in front of the cousins—twice, to be certain—and filled out the correct documents of proof of deposit and Lord Rexford's trusteeship, but he told them his dealings with Sir Frederick outside the bank were private, not subject to whatever writ or warrant the viscount produced. As for smuggling, how dare they ask if Sir Frederick had anything to do with that foul business, besmirching a dead man's honorable name?

Was Breverton himself connected to the illicit trade with France?

The banker angrily shoved the receipts at Rex and showed them the door, instead of replying.

"Perhaps you'd be helpful enough to give us your first

name?" Rex asked, in case the name on the door belonged to Breverton's father or brother. "I am sure that is not an insult, just idle curiosity."

"Lloyd," the banker snarled, pointing to the gilt lettering right beside Rex's still swollen nose. "As any blind man can see. Lloyd, with two Ls."

One was enough, as in L.B.

They took a different hackney to the solicitor's office next, to inform the lawyer of the transfer of monies, so he could notify Edwin Hawley, the new baronet. Rex also asked him to try to estimate how much of the money belonged to Miss Carville. The solicitor was happy to oblige, and his initials were not on the list.

Then they went to Bow Street, to deliver Duncan Fingers with a handsome gratuity for his day's work, after asking if the old man had anything in his many pockets that did not belong to him.

"A'course not. I went straight, don't you know. I works for Bow Street."

Daniel rubbed his nose. Rex picked the little red man up by his ankles and shook him. Coins, a stickpin and a watch fell out his pockets, along with files and picks and skeleton keys. Rex took the stickpin and the pocket watch to give to Amanda for her stepbrother. He let Duncan keep the coins, for a promise not to speak of what he'd seen or heard that day.

"No one'd believe me anyways," the old man said, scuttling away.

Inspector Dimm was glad to hear they'd found something. But they still needed a motive for the murder.

"Being attics to let is not call to get shot. Half the members of the royal family could be in danger if that were so. Robbery? Who would have known the blunt was there?"

He studied a smoke ring above his head, an odd halo for Bow Street's senior detective. "Maybe your young lady did, member of the family and all. She could have come to demand what was hers by right after they argued about her dowry and the to-do with her suitor at the assembly rooms. She admitted they had words. Couldn't rightly deny it, when six people heard the shouting in the afternoon."

"Words do not pull triggers, and neither did Miss Carville. Hawley was involved in something illegal, with cohorts." He showed Dimm the journal with its initialed entries.

"I still say they could be names of his mistresses," Daniel said, "and the illegitimate children he's supporting."

Dimm considered the possibility. He supported any number of nieces and nephews—all born on the right side of the blanket, thank goodness—on a great deal less money. "Hmm. Could be."

Rex disagreed. "The snake cheated his own son and heir. He wasn't liable to pay for his by-blows. No, I think these initials represent partners in some kind of crime. Any one of them could have had a falling out over shares of the profits or something."

Dimm puffed on his pipe. "Maybe they were just gambling debts. Toffs keep records, don't they?"

"Then why keep it so quiet and hidden away? Why does no one at the clubs recall him as a heavy gambler? Sir Frederick was dealing with the Devil."

"Know that for a fact, do you?"

"No, damn it, just by instinct or intuition."

"Or by wanting it to be so? That won't free your lady." Rex knew that all too well. "I'll keep looking."

Their last stop was at McCann's Club, where he left a note for a man the manager swore never came there. The manager lied. He also took the coin and the note, which consisted of the list of eight sets of initials. One was possibly the banker, Lloyd Breverton. Another, J.J., might be a merchant named Johnston, Johnson, or Johnstone, who might have hired Brusseau, the valet who might know more than he'd said. A third was N.T. The only man Rex knew with those initials was his father's nemesis, Amanda's prosecutor, Sir Nigel Turlowe. The coincidence was damning.

Daniel wanted to stay at McCann's for a snack, while Rex wanted to see if the note was delivered and where, or if an answer might come. The meal came, but no reply. Afterward, Rex wanted Daniel to take the sketch of the murder weapon to Manton's Shooting Gallery to see if anyone could identify its maker or owner, but Daniel was having none of that. "Leave you with a bad leg and a pocket full of gems for any London cutpurse to steal? After leaving that Fingers fellow to spread the word among his cronies? I ain't the one with a breeze in the belfry."

So the pistol would have to wait for another day. Still, they were closer to unraveling the knots; Rex felt it. He could go back to Amanda with good news, and bad questions.

Amanda was waiting with his dog in the front parlor. The drugged sleep had not refreshed her, so she had gone back to bed in the morning. The gentlemen had already breakfasted and left without telling her their plans, according to the butler, saying only that they expected to be back before dinner.

After her nap, Amanda helped Nanny move her things to another chamber, insisting the older woman would sleep better on a full bed and a softer mattress, and truly, Amanda was well enough not to need constant nursing. She did not say that the noise of Nanny's snoring would set her recovery back a week, at least.

She ate and rested, and dressed in a muslin gown sprigged with blue flowers that reminded her of the color of Rex's eyes. She found a workbasket and some sheets that needed darning, so she sat with that, as a tiny way of repaying Lady Royce for her hospitality.

Verity waited by her side, occasionally pacing to the window or the door, whining. The big brown dog wanted her master to come home. Amanda could sympathize with the mastiff's sentiments. Then she thought how lucky Rex was to receive such unconditional love, from anyone.

A dog did not care if its owner was guilty or innocent, of high birth or low, wealthy or impoverished, brilliant or as dumb as a brick. People were far more fussy and far less faithful. Amanda contemplated having a love that lasted, dreaming of a gentleman who did not care that her reputation was gone, along with her dowry. He would not mind that her hair was cut as short as a sheep's, or that her fingernails were broken, her education incomplete. He would love her anyway, with his mind and his body. He would love her for who she was, not what she looked like or what she could bring him, and love her when she grew wrinkled and gray, or big with child, or seeped in scandal.

Her chances of finding such a constant companion were poor to nonexistent. Unless she got herself a dog.

Then the dog drooled on the sheet she was mending,

shed brown hairs on her pale skirts, and left a dirty paw print on her slipper. Perhaps she needed a cat.

Verity cocked her head and perked her ears, as if she could somehow recognize which carriage passing by carried her master. "Silly dog."

Then the carriage stopped, Verity barked, and the front door opened. The dog was not so silly after all. Rex was home.

Verity bounded to his side, then Daniel's, barking in excitement, leaning against Rex for a welcome pat and almost knocking him over in her exuberance. One would think he'd been gone a month, instead of a day.

The hours had seemed that long to Amanda, too, and she hoped she did not seem as obvious in her welcome. She might want to throw herself at Rex, rub her face against the wool of his uniform, drinking in his scent, wriggling for his touch, craving his attention and his approval.

"Good girl, Verity."

Amanda was a lady, not a dog. She rang for tea instead. According to Nanny, tea was best for removing those tired lines from his face, the worried look from his eyes. The starchy butler had not been eager to serve her, so Amanda had fetched her own meals from the kitchen, but Rex was Lady Royce's son, and a viscount, and Dodd's employer for now. Besides, she did not want to leave his presence, not when he looked over from the dog's ecstatic greeting and smiled at her.

Good girl, Amanda. She thought—half hoped—he might come pat her curls, or scratch her neck. Then she blushed at her wayward thoughts. Where was that tea tray anyway?

*   *   *

Rex thought Amanda looked exquisite, her hair shining, her skin glowing with health. Her eyes had lost the purple shadows beneath them, her face had almost lost the gaunt sharpness. In just the last few days she had gained a bit of rounded softness to the bones at her neck above her gown's collar and at her narrow wrists. Lud knew Verity must have added a few pounds now that she did not have an entire estate to patrol. The unmannered beast had almost shoved him over, which would have made him look like a clumsy cripple to Amanda.

"Down, Verity."

The dog obediently sat near Daniel, as if it knew food was coming soon. Rex made his careful way to a seat in the parlor, concealing his limp as much as possible, knowing Amanda was watching. Then he chided himself for foolish vanity and put his leg up on the footstool she thoughtfully slid over. He thanked her and waited for the tea to come, then watched her pour it out with the elegance he had come to expect in her graceful movements. A man could get used to such domesticity.

As usual, Daniel complained about the dearth of raspberry tarts, macaroons, or poppy seed cakes. He made do with toast fingers and jam.

Dodd fussed with the silverware and the serviettes, obviously hoping to hear what news the cousins brought, but Rex dismissed him, sending the man for heartier fare for his cousin. After all, Daniel had not eaten for at least an hour.

When the butler had gone, and Daniel had shut the door firmly behind him, they could finally discuss the day's discoveries. Rex mentioned the notebook and the money in the globe, now in the bank waiting for Edwin Hawley. He explained his theory of an organized

crime cartel, although Daniel still clung to the idea of
other sons and daughters. Rex explained about needing a
motive that might lead to a suspect, and recited the initials to her from memory. Other than Breverton, Amanda
had no guesses as to identities. Sir Frederick never spoke
to her about his affairs or interests or acquaintances.

Daniel wiped a dab of jam from his chin. "The fellow
had deuced few confidantes, it seems."

"So we are no further along to finding his murderer?"

"A bit further," Rex told her. "But not close." Then he
set his cup aside. He hated to be hard with Amanda, but
he had to know. "Do you understand what would happen
if you fled the country?"

"You mean if I ran away? I expect everyone would believe me guilty, if they do not already."

"They would be certain of it. But they would also put
up reward posters with your picture and send bounty
hunters to track you down, for the rest of your life. You
would never be free, not really, no matter how far you
ran. There are other aspects you might not have considered, since they affect you less. If you took flight, you
see, I would be found guilty of reneging on my vows to
produce you for trial. Sir Nigel has sworn he will prose-
cute me if he is denied his day in court, although I doubt
it would come to that. I do not care about that worm. I do
care about my honor."

Amanda bit her lip. How could she swear not to flee,
if the alternative was hanging or deportation or life on
the prison hulks? What sane person would not run away
if the alternative was inevitable death? "I understand that
a gentleman's word is his bond."

"For my family, especially."

Daniel nodded around a mouthful of toast. He fed a

slice to the dog, then said, "Very honorable, the Royce name, for centuries back."

"We have always defended the innocent," Rex added, "no matter the consequences. We are already mistrusted and feared for our, ah, beliefs. My father lives as a recluse because of his love of the truth. Since the murder of a baronet has become so sensational, so would your escape from justice. The Crown would demand satisfaction, urged on by Sir Nigel, I do not doubt. The earldom could be attainted, which would kill my father. Lady Royce, your godmother, would suffer also, for harboring a killer."

"I . . . I do not understand why you are saying all of this. I thought you trusted me. Have I not said how grateful I am? Do you not realize that you, and you, Mr. Stamfield, are the only ones who have stepped forward to help, the only ones who believe me."

Amanda was upset and hurt. Last night he'd said he liked her. Now he was treating her like an actual criminal. She looked from Rex to Daniel, to find both of them staring intently at her. "Have you found something that leads you to disbelieve in my innocence, in my word to you, in my own honor?"

Lord Rexford was the one to ask the question: "Will you tell me about the man you met at night?"

She could not meet their similar eyes, Rex's so vivid a blue, Daniel's a bit paler, but both with dark rings surrounding the irises. "No."

Rex tossed his toast to the dog. "Then how can I trust you?"

She laughed, without humor. "You can trust me because I am at the mercy of the courts, and you. You know I am reliant on you for everything, your rescue, your investigation." She picked up a sliver of toast. "For my very food. My stepfamily—what there is of it—has not replied to my pleas. Flee? I have nowhere to go, and no wherewithal to get there."

Rex stood with effort, his leg gone stiff, and poured the jewels into her lap. "Now you do."

Chapter Eighteen

Amanda held up the ruby pendant and its matching earrings, then the diamonds. "But these are my mother's. She is wearing this necklace in the portrait I have. I do not understand."

"Your man of business was holding them for you."

"But Sir Frederick claimed they had been sold. To pay for my mother's nursing, he said."

"He lied, most likely so you would not have them, either, or make awkward inquiries of the solicitor."

"But how?" She spread out the sapphire set, and thought the deep blue looked very much like the color of Rex's eyes, but without his tiny flecks of silver.

He was looking over the treasure in her lap, as if assessing its value. "Your mother realized she had made a bad bargain, according to the solicitor. Her widow's portion and settlements from your father were long gone, but she still had her jewelry. The ones here were hers by right, belonging to no estate or entailment. They were hers to leave to her daughter in her will, which is what she decided to do, instead of giving them to you outright. She made the lawyer take the jewels away for safekeeping before she died, before Sir Frederick could get his greedy hands on them. The solicitor swears her will was ironclad, witnessed and filed with the authorities, which was how he kept the gems from your stepfather."

"And from me."

"You were, what, seventeen when your mother died? Sir Frederick would have had them out of your hands and to the pawn shop before you could count them. Your mother knew that. She meant her bequest to come to you when you turned twenty-five, or when you wed."

"When Sir Frederick could not keep me from leaving his household and his guardianship. But you say the man gave them to you now, for me. Does he not think I will live the three years until my twenty-fifth birthday?"

Rex sat back down again, looking at his cousin, debating what to say. "He, ah, thought you could use the jewelry to finance an escape."

"Oh. In case you cannot find proof of my innocence. Now I see why you were so concerned." She did not deny the possibility of bolting, but went back to sorting through the necklaces and bracelets, putting matching sets together on the table beside her chair, next to her forgotten teacup. She started to sniffle as she raised each glittering piece to the light, recalling her mother going off to this ball or that dinner party wearing the beautiful baubles. She remembered being allowed to play with her mother's jewel box as a small girl, thinking she had never seen such glitter, such glory. They were tokens of her father's affection, her mother had always said, although her favorite gift from Lord Carville was Amanda herself. Amanda would have better someday, her mother had promised.

"I never thought to see any of these again, not even the emeralds, which had been my grandmother's, handed down to the first daughters of my mother's family. I was

left with nothing from either of my parents but my pearls."
She fingered the strand around her neck. "I suppose they
were not valuable enough for Sir Frederick to bother
about. Or else he thought he'd have to purchase me some
piece of trumpery if he took these, to make me look fashionable and prosperous enough in front of my mother's
friends." She sniffled again, louder.

"Great gads," Daniel swore. "You ain't going to cry, are
you?"

"Of course not," Amanda said, tears running down her
cheeks. "It is simply so . . . so heartening to discover how
much my mother cared, how much effort she took to look
after me, even years later, when I need it the most. She did
not want me dependent on Sir Frederick or anyone else,
and now I need not be. I can pay my own way, hire my
own barristers. This is like a gift from heaven. I am happy,
truly."

"Damn, you don't look happy." Daniel spoke with a
brother's bluntness. "All splotchy and red-faced, in fact. I
cannot stand to see a female cry. Makes me blubber myself, don't you know. And makes me hungry, too. I always
eat when I am sad—disheartened, that is. Ask Rex."

"He's hungry when he's happy too, so ignore the gudgeon. And there was never a question of affording the
finest barrister in the land. Lady Royce can afford it, for
her godchild."

Amanda nodded, but kept dampening the heirlooms
with her tears.

Daniel jumped up, scattering crumbs, and headed for
the door. "I know just the thing. An ice from Gunter's always cheers me up, it does." He whistled for the dog.
"Come on, Verity, let's go find some better fare than but-

tered toast. We'll come back with a pail full, if it doesn't melt."

"Coward," Rex whispered as his cousin rushed past him.

"Every time," Daniel admitted, handing over a spare handkerchief. "You're going to need this if she's anything like my sister."

Amanda was sobbing openly now, her shoulders shaking, without pretending otherwise.

"Shall I ring for Nanny? Would you take some laudanum?" Rex asked, helpless. "What can I fetch for you? What do you need?"

"I . . . I need a dog."

A dog? The woman had a death sentence hanging over her head, a fortune in jewels at her side, and she wanted a dog? He decided the events were finally too much for her fragile senses. At least they could plead guilty by insanity if all else failed. "I think you need the laudanum. Perhaps a brandy?"

"No, I need someone to love me, the way my mother did. The way your dog loves you."

"You might not have noticed, but the traitor scampered right after my cousin at the first mention of food."

"But Verity will be back. All I have are these cold stones from my mother."

They were worth a king's ransom, but Rex could comprehend her meaning, at least he thought he could. "She loved you very much."

"I have never missed her more, but you will not understand that."

She was wrong. He did understand, all too well. "My mother left when I was a boy."

Amanda did not know the whole story; no one did. All she could say was "I am sorry."

"Do not be. We managed. I had my father and Nanny; and my aunt, Daniel's mother, lived nearby."

She cried harder, for him, for her. Hell, he thought, she might be crying for every motherless urchin in the streets, there were so many tears.

Any gentleman would gather her into his arms so she could cry against his shoulder. But only a swine like Rex, he decided, would be glad of the excuse to hold her. "You are not alone, my dear. You have me. It's not much, I admit, but I am here, by your side." Actually she was now in his lap, on the sofa, which did not follow any gentlemanly code of conduct that Rex knew.

Nor was his embrace comforting, obviously, because she kept crying. Damn. Relegating his rising heart rate to the pigsty, Rex stroked her back, he rubbed her shoulders, he said "There, there." Still she kept crying. She had every right to weep and wail. Time was rushing by and he hadn't found the real killer. Now he'd warned her not to run off. He was failing her, and he felt like sobbing himself. "We'll win, I know we will. You'll be free to have a happy life, get a dog if you want."

She sniffled. "With my reputation?"

"Dogs don't care about that rot. Oh, you meant your happy future? With Lady Royce's sponsorship, you'll be a success." He promised the countess's cooperation without hesitation. "The gentlemen will see you shine as bright as those diamonds."

She blew her nose with the handkerchief he held out, Daniel's, as large as a tablecloth. "I suppose I can purchase myself a husband with a necklace or two."

"You will not need to buy a match. The dolts in London cannot be that stupid."

She gave him a watery smile. "Thank you. You are so kind to say that, no matter that it is far from true."

"I do not lie, I told you that. And kindness has nothing to do with it. You are beautiful."

"Now that is stretching the truth, especially today! I must look a fright. Your cousin ran away, didn't he?"

"You look beautiful," Rex insisted, wishing she could see the truth the way he could. Because she could not, and because he had no choice, no more than he could have left her in prison, or left her alone and ill, he tipped her head up. No, there was no choice. He might never have had a choice since his father sent him to London. He was not a firm believer in fate, but having Amanda in his lap, pressed against him, felt ordained, inevitable, and exactly right. He lowered his lips to hers.

She met his lips with a soft moan that reminded him that, written in the stars or written in sand, kissing Miss Carville was still wrong. She was still a vulnerable young female, under his care, under his mother's roof. Rex started to pull back but she had her arm around his neck and would not release him. So he kissed her again, longer, deeper, expressing without words more of his own wants and needs and loneliness. She was so sweet, so soft, so giving; he could feel himself lost in that kiss.

She moaned again.

So did his conscience. Good grief, the woman was his responsibility, his to keep safe. What the hell was he doing, kissing a female who was so beset with woes that she sought solace in the nearest arms? Since when did he let his passions rule his head? He was a gentleman, which meant he did not take advantage of those weaker than him.

He did not seduce maidens. Most of all, he did not believe in marriage for misfits such as he. He did, however, believe that a man who ruined a virgin was duty bound to wed her.

She was willing, though. She was distressed. She was dangerous. His better instincts were at war with his baser ones.

Nanny won the battle, coming to tell them that dinner was almost ready. "There you are, dears."

There they were, suddenly sitting side by side on the sofa like naughty children. Children did not feel their lips on fire.

Rex was furious with himself and the tightening in his groin. He was a rake and a cad. He had no scruples. What must poor Amanda think of him?

Amanda was furious with herself and the quivering of her fingertips. She was a fallen woman and a fool for dreaming. She had no morals. What must the poor viscount think of her?

He thought he owed Miss Carville an apology. "Please excuse us, Nanny. We need to speak a little more about the case."

"Of course you do, lovey. Do hurry though. You would not want the roast overdone or the cock-a-leekie soup to grow cold."

No, but he wished his blood would cool so his brain could work. Rex waited for Nanny to shuffle out of the room before saying he was sorry.

Amanda did not feign misunderstanding. "No, it was my fault, tossing myself at you that way. I was upset. I apologize."

"Your discomposure was natural. I, ah, wished to comfort you."

"I know. Thank you."

He did not feel absolved. "You should have stopped me."

She gathered the jewels back into the silk pouch. "I did not want to."

Her words, in the blue of truth, set his blood to boiling again. He leaned away, to put distance between them.

Amanda stared at her hands in her lap, to keep from reaching for him. "I was forward."

He took her hand. "Never think that. I was a brute. You are a lovely woman and I am only human."

"Thank you. I am human too, and you are a lovely man."

He laughed, but raised her hand to his lips. "What, with scars and a limp and a battered nose?"

"With a good heart and the most beautiful eyes in all of England."

He leaned over and stroked her eyelids. "No, yours are much finer. Like soft brown velvet a man could sink into."

She smiled back at him, relishing the gentle touch. "Mine are common brown eyes. And they are red and swollen, I'd wager."

He lowered his gaze. "No, but your lips are."

Now she blushed. "You really must think me a wanton. I swear I do not kiss every gentleman I meet!"

He stood, thinking of her tender, inexperienced kisses. "I think you are brave and good, and I think I had better take myself off before I forget that I am a gentleman and you are an innocent."

She rose also, but took his hand. "But Nanny and her sister are cooking dinner for you and Daniel. You have to stay."

The invitation to stay was too tempting by half, but he

was staring at her lips again, thinking of their taste, not of the cock-a-leekie soup.

As if his eyes drew her closer, Amanda took a step nearer him, so her breasts almost touched his coat. Almost was not good enough. This must be the animal magnetism she had heard about. She took another step, and his arms came around her.

This time the kiss involved tongues and teeth and lips and sharing breaths and sighs. Her hands moved to his back. His moved to her front, to the sides of her breasts, making her gasp with surprise, then groan with pleasure. Yes, she thought, this was far better than being patted on the head and told to go off to wash, good girl, Amanda.

She was a woman, and he was a man. She could feel his virility through her skirts and his trousers. She was doing that to him. She felt the answering warmth between her thighs, in the pit of her stomach, down to her toes. The heat was nothing to the fires of hell she would burn in for all eternity, and at that moment Amanda did not care.

"More tea, my lord? More— Oh, my!"

They had not heard Dodd come into the room at all. Rex shielded Amanda from the butler's prying eyes, without taking his arms from around her and said, "Miss Carville is upset. The last few days have taken their toll."

"Funny, that's exactly what I said that day you walked in here, all in a huff. My Nell was overset, she was."

Rex pointed toward the door. "Tea, Dodd. And brandy."

Amanda's knees were so weak she would collapse into a puddle if Rex did not hold her, so she clung to him.

His self-discipline was so weak he folded his arms around her. His bad leg could not support them both so they fell forward to the sofa, which was far more comfortable anyway.

"Still overset, is she?" Dodd set the tray down with a clatter.

"Out!"

Dodd paused at the door. "Um, you were not going to mention my Nell to the countess, were you, my lord?" He waggled his eyebrows at what he could see of Miss Carville, half-behind and half-beneath the viscount.

"That's blackmail!"

"That's a narrow sofa."

Amanda giggled, a sound so enchanting that Rex simply had to kiss her again, even knowing Dodd had left the parlor door open behind him.

"He never liked me," she said a few heartbeats—heavy, pounding, rapid heartbeats—later. "Heaven knows what he'll think of me now."

"He will show you the proper respect. He likes his position." So did Rex, with almost all of him touching almost all of Amanda. Lud, what was happening to him? Rex asked himself with the last vestiges of intelligence left to him. All of his self-preservation, all of his precepts, were flown out the window, along with his wits. But his blood, ah, that was rushing from his neck to his nethers, where he was alert and attentive. His body knew she was his, his for the taking, his for the pleasuring. His to wed?

Hell, no! He jumped to his feet, pulling her with him. "This is wrong! I am not a stag in rut, a randy goat. And the door is open. I mean, I do have principles. I have—"

"I have it, a whole bucket full of raspberry ice!" Daniel and Verity raced into the room. "Hurry, you two, before there's nothing left but a puddle of juice. I saw Nanny and she swears we will spoil our suppers, but who cares? Didn't she always say the same, and didn't I always clear my whole plate? I say, Amanda's not still weeping, is she?"

She was giggling again. They both said no.

"Then why are you still holding her?"

Now that was a damned good question.

Chapter Nineteen

Nanny clucked her tongue. She knew Amanda's blond curls weren't all every which way when she'd combed them. And she knew she did not apply any of the countess's face paint to get the young lady's cheeks so rosy or her lips so red. "Lady Royce sent a message that she was on her way," she told Rex as he was leaving. "And not a moment too soon, I'd warrant," she muttered under her breath, making him feel six years old again.

Heaven knew that what he'd done—worse, what he'd almost done—was more than a boyish prank. The problem was, he could not trust his unruly body not to do it again. The only solution was to keep his distance, so he dragged Daniel out to the Grand Hotel.

"I hear they set an excellent table," he told his cousin.

"But I had my heart set on a rare roast!"

Well, Rex had his heart set on a bare breast, and he was not going to get his wish, either. "You were the one who said we had to be seen out and about, on the town, to preserve Miss Carville's reputation. Besides, Lady Royce should be here soon, perhaps as early as tomorrow, so I can move to a hotel. I thought I'd look over the

Grand and see if they will take dogs. It's not as particular as the Clarendon or the Pulteney, I hear. You are welcome to stay with me, unless you prefer that rat's nest you were living in."

"What? Move away from Royce House just when your mother is bringing her cook back with her? That's as cork-brained as the idea they'd take Verity at any decent place. She isn't a dog, she's a four-legged feed bag."

"Then I shall find rooms somewhere until I can return to the country."

"We could always stay with your mother. It'd be all right and tight, with a countess chaperoning the lass."

"No" was all Rex said.

"That bad, eh?"

Rex did not know if Daniel meant living under the same roof as Lady Royce, or keeping his hands off Amanda. "That bad."

They stopped at McCann's Club first. A hunched-over old man in the club's livery and white wig stepped out of the shadows, keeping his eyes deferentially lowered. "A message for Lord Rexford," he said, handing over a sealed note. He bowed and backed away.

"Wait! Tell your master—"

The man was gone, too fast for such a relic. While Daniel went to see who was in the card room—and have a free glass of wine—Rex broke the seal on the letter and unfolded the single sheet. On it were written the same eight initials he had given Major Harrison, the ones from Sir Frederick's journal. Beside each were one to three names, with question marks beside some, addresses under others.

L.B. could be the banker, Lloyd Breverton, the note

indicated, but it could also stand for Lydia Burton, the infamous madam of a high-class bordello.

According to the spymaster, the initials L.C. could stand for a Lysander Cord whom Rex did not know, but he lived at the Albany, so could be assumed a gentleman.

J.J. was Joseph Johnston, with two locations, one near the docks, another in a newly fashionable section of Kensington; or Joshua Jacobs, a jeweler on Bond Street. Rex would bet on Johnston, the wealthy merchant who now supposedly had Sir Frederick's valet in his employ.

G.C. had only one name beside it, George Cuthbert, with a question mark. Rex whistled. Cuthbert was second son to a prominent member of the Cabinet, and a former officer in the navy. No one knew why he'd been shipped home, which silence was unusual in itself, but there had been rumors.

R.V. might be any of three men, only one known to Rex. Roland Vaughan had been a university classmate of his and Rex liked the fellow, despite his idiosyncrasies. Vaughan was decent enough, if one avoided him in dark corners. One of the others had an Esq. after his name, another lawyer; and the last had Fleet Prison as his address.

T.H. was followed by two names, both with minor titles, both of Rex's father's generation.

The single name under A.B. was well known to Rex. Aldritch Bowdecker had been a fellow student at Eton, some years ahead of Rex, who exulted in tormenting the younger boys. The Aide's question mark next to his name meant nothing. Rex thought the man capable of any cruelty, any misdeed.

The last set of initials on the list, N.T., also had one name: Nigel Turlowe, with no question mark.

These were obviously people the Aide's office held in suspicion, but nowhere did the note say suspicion of what. Spying, smuggling . . . hell, they could be white slavers for all Rex knew—and for all Harrison, or Harris, told him. The only directive the man gave was written in an elegant hand at the bottom of the page. *Ask questions.*

Rex knew what was meant was get answers, get the truth.

He just might get the answer to another question at Mrs. Burton's establishment, Rex decided. Or at least a different hunger satisfied.

Daniel insisted on dinner first. "And it won't hurt to be seen about, remember? The more people who notice us, the better."

The wine and food at the Grand Hotel was excellent, the company less so. A group of foxed gentlemen at a table at Rex's back were loud and crude, belittling the waiter and demanding faster service than the poor man could provide. They took offense when Daniel and Rex were served first.

Daniel put his wineglass down and stood to his full, intimidating height, quieting the men for the length of the fish course. Then they started to whisper, none too softly. Rex easily made out the words "Inquisitors," "murderess," and "cripple." He set his own glass aside, stood, and turned.

"Why, speak of the devil," he muttered, spotting Aldritch Bowdecker at the center of the group, food stains spotting his neckcloth, his small eyes sunken and bloodshot. The man looked far older than his years, raddled and wrinkled, and far meaner than he used to be, if possible. Rex did not bother with pleasantries. One did not bow to a boa constrictor. "Did you know Sir Frederick Hawley?" he asked.

Surprised at the blunt question, Bowdecker answered. "Of course I did. We all did." He shifted his beady eyes to his companions.

The others nodded. One raised his glass. "To Sir Frederick, may he rest in peace."

Another guffawed. "Not where he is now, I'd bet."

The fourth man raised his glass in a toast to the wench who'd sent the baronet to his just desserts.

Rex looked directly at Bowdecker. "Miss Carville did not kill him. Did you?"

The man stood up with a roar. "What kind of question is that? I'll murder *you*, you scurvy, scarred dog. Trying to blame me for your whore's crime!" He pushed his table aside, silver and china and food gone flying. "You always were a sneaky little rat. Word is you still were, in the army. No one trusted you, I heard; not the Spanish, the French, or our own troops."

Daniel sighed as Rex took his coat off. "My roast beef."

"My reputation—and Miss Carville's."

"My dining room!" a voice with a French accent called out. No one would have listened except for the seven undercooks in clean white aprons lined up behind the chef, meat cleavers and carving knives in their hands. "Out! I serve only the best. The best food to the best patrons, no? My soup, she is on the floor? Out, or I call the Watch!" He advanced on the man who dared to show his shirtsleeves in the finest restaurant in London. Or in Paris, as it used to be.

Bowdecker's associates were already dragging him away, out of the chef's sight, before a challenge or a punch could be thrown. Bowdecker was known to be a terrible shot, a clumsy fencer, and a coward when it came to facing someone his size, even someone with a limp. They saved his life, for another day.

Rex and Daniel left, apologizing to the gaping diners at other tables on their way out. Daniel lifted a lamb chop off a lady's plate. He shrugged when she screamed. "She was already thinking we were savages. Could you try a little subtlety next time?"

Next time was at Bancroft's, a private men's club that let in anyone with the right price. They were said to serve unwatered wine and well-cooked meals, along with high-stakes games in the back rooms and clean apartments above. Before they could be seated, a gentleman called out to them, inviting them to share their table. Roland Vaughan and a younger man were smiling in welcome. "My dear boy, how happy I am to see you recovering! Such sad news, when you were reported injured. Why, I could not sleep for days, could I, Harold? And your poor face! What a tragedy. I have the perfect concealing cream, don't I, Harold?"

"Um, I don't think I am hungry after all, Rex. I'll just take a peek at the dice tables, shall I?" Daniel looked at the glasses of negus at the men's table, a woman's libation. "And I'll order us a bottle of brandy while I am at it."

"I'll join you in a moment. Roland, did you know Sir Frederick Hawley?"

The young man screwed up his face as if he'd swallowed a lemon. Vaughan answered yes, to his regret.

"Unpleasant chap, don't you know. I always avoided his company."

"Did you kill him?"

Tears sprang to Roland's eyes. "Oh, how could you think such a thing of me? I thought we were friends."

"I take it that is a no?"

"Why, I would not kill a spider in my bathing tub, would I, Harold?"

"But did you kill Sir Frederick, yes or no?"

"No!" The man started sobbing, the nearby patrons frowned at Rex, Harold offered a lace-edged handkerchief, and the manager wanted to know what Rex meant by bothering one of his best customers and favorite residents.

"I meant no harm. My apologies." He tossed a banknote on the table. "Have another drink on me. A pleasure, Mr., ah, Harold."

Daniel was not happy to be leaving so soon.

Rex was not happy to have made a grown man cry. "You drink too much anyway."

"Well, I need some kind of sustenance, don't I? I still haven't had my dinner."

"Let us try Lidell's." That was a place frequented by navy men on leave.

George Cuthbert was there, as Rex had hoped. The former ship captain sat in a corner with a half-empty bottle. No one was near, no one spoke to him. Rex headed in that direction.

Daniel took one look at Rex's target. "Uh oh. I won't bother taking a seat. Or ordering supper."

"I won't be long." He neared Cuthbert's corner, knowing every eye in the place was on him. "Sir, I have a question for you."

Cuthbert looked up, trying to focus his eyes. "Rexford, is it? One of the Aide's boys, eh? And they say I did some dirty deeds. Hah! But you're the one got the commendations, aren't you?"

"Yes, sir, and a bad leg and a scar to go with them. My question is this: Did you kill Sir Frederick Hawley?"

"I wish I did. I wish I did." He threw his bottle across the room, to smash into a window, sending glass flying and officers cursing. "I wish I did!"

"I wish you did, too, sir. Good night."

Silence and disapproval followed Rex as he limped out of the club. Out in the street, he looked around to get his bearings. "We are near Lydia Burton's house of accommodation. What say we go speak to her?"

"I thought we were going to eat first? Do you think she serves supper? If she does, can you try to show a little finesse so we can stay to enjoy it? And the girls, too, of course. Diplomacy, that's the ticket, old man. Mrs. Burton fancies herself a lady."

The building was undistinguished among its prosperous neighbors, the decor was as elegant as Lady Royce's, and the madam was dressed in the height of fashion, except for the depth of her décolletage. She was delighted to see them. Gentlemen with money were always welcome, no matter their reputations. After the pleasantries, Mrs. Burton waved her manicured, beringed hand at a cluster of females sitting on gilt chairs at the side of the room, fanning themselves and giggling like debutantes at Almack's. "May I introduce you to one of my friends?"

The girls were trying to appear young and innocent and ladylike, and failing dismally. Rex turned away. He

did not want a woman who reminded him of Amanda;
the whole point of coming here tonight was to forget
about her, and to let the world know she was not his
mistress. He raised Mrs. Burton's soft white hand to his
lips. "Only the best will do, madame."

She tittered. "The best is *très* expensive, my lord."

He smiled. "And worth every pound, I am sure." He
carefully tucked an extravagant sum between her extraordinary breasts. She signaled for a maid to bring him
a glass of champagne while she informed her assistant.

Daniel walked by and whispered, "Remember, finesse."

"Do you want to ask her?"

"Hell no." Daniel already had a brandy bottle in one
hand and a redhead in the other. "This little lady is more
my type." The little lady was taller than Rex and
broader, and evidently more appetizing than the tiny tea
sandwiches Mrs. Burton was serving.

The madam came back and led Rex to a small chamber decked with flowers and scented candles and mirrors. The room was too warm, La Burton was too
buxom, and Rex was suddenly too bored, tired, uninter-
ested. Damn, had Amanda stolen all of his appetites?
No, the thought of her, her kisses, her soft breasts
pressed against his chest, raised his temperature, and
Lydia Burton's expectations. With her hand on the front
of his trousers, she smiled and whispered, "Oh, my, a
hero indeed," which compliment had a tinge of truth.

The truth? He did not want another woman, only answers to his questions. He stepped back.

The madam frowned, at his distance and the scratching at her door. "I said no interruptions!"

Daniel ignored her and scratched again, louder this time. "Rex, did you ask her yet? I'm done."

"Already?"

"I'm too hungry for seconds. A man needs his strength to perform, don't you know."

Mrs. Burton looked up at him. "What question?"

Her eagerness was gone. So was any notion of diplomacy. "Did you kill Sir Frederick Hawley?"

She slapped him, which was no answer. He held her wrist. "Did you?"

"That man never set foot in my establishment, I'll have you know. I did not kill him! You cannot come here and accuse me of such a thing. You'll ruin my business, you will." She looked at his hand, still on her arm. "Manhandling women? Trading pleasure for secrets? Hah, and they call me the whore. Your brother would be ashamed."

"My brother? I don't even have a brother! Stamfield is my cousin."

She picked up a candlestick and tried to hit him with that.

Daniel was leaning against the opened door, a smile on his face and a bottle tilted toward his lips. "I told you you needed a bit of Town bronze, coz."

She threw the candlestick at Daniel.

Rex grabbed his coat and his cousin and ran into the night.

They stopped to catch their breaths, laughing and sharing the bottle Daniel still had. "I suppose we could try White's," Rex said. "Those two men with T.H. as initials could both be there. Lord Havering never takes supper with his wife, I've heard, and Baron Hove keeps bachelor quarters."

"Lud, if we get thrown out of White's, we might as well go back to the country, so let me handle this one, after I've eaten if you please."

Not terribly hungry, Rex left Daniel with a bottle of wine while he looked into the card rooms. He came back to find his cousin with a second bottle, to wash down the second half of the cow he was eating. Rex reported that both of the men were here tonight, playing at the same corner table with a man who looked familiar, but Rex did not get his name. He was dark-haired, with a small mustache and spectacles, younger than the other whist players, and he had just declared the next to be his last hand. They'd be leaving soon.

Daniel took a long swallow of his wine, belched, and staggered to his feet.

Rex had second thoughts. "Are you sure you want to take over?"

"You haven't fared so well, have you? Watch and see how a professional works."

When they reached the far table, Daniel cleared his throat to get the men's attention. "Ahem. Gentlemen, pardon me. I apologize for interrupting your game." He bowed, but Rex had to hold onto the ends of his tailcoat to keep him from tipping over. "I was merely wondering if you would answer a question for me?"

"You are drunk, sirrah!"

Daniel bowed again. "But I am not a killer. Are you?"

Hove signaled for the waiter. Havering mumbled something uncomplimentary about Daniel's parentage.

"I take it that is a no? Neither of you murdered Sir Frederick Hawley?"

"Of course it is a no, you castaway chawbacon!"

The stranger in the corner was shaking his head in disgust.

"Then I thank you for your—" Daniel groaned, clamped his hand over his mouth and made a dash for the door.

He was not in time.

"Well, you did tell me we ought to make our presence known around town. I'd say we were a success tonight, wouldn't you?"

Chapter Twenty

Soaking his head, and his cousin, in a tub of water did not help. Neither did a full bath when they got back to Royce House. Rex still felt dirty. He'd crossed several suspects off his list, but while doing so had dragged his name, his career, and his best friend through the filth. He was supposed to solve a crime and reform his cousin, not help Daniel drown in spirits and sex. A fine example he'd shown tonight.

What Daniel needed was a nice girl, a solid country-woman who would put up with his rough ways. She'd feed him and f— Well, she'd take care of all his needs, without whining about his poor showing on a dance floor. Daniel was the most loyal companion a man could have. He deserved no less in a woman. Perhaps Amanda knew of a likely candidate. She had been part of the beau monde and knew which debutante was fonder of a good gallop than a tame trot around Hyde Park.

No, he could not bother Amanda with courtship tripe. She had enough on her plate without adding Daniel. Which brought him back to the problem of seeing her exonerated. That did nothing for the problems of seeing her and wanting her, or wanting to see her, but he knew what he had to do, and he knew what he had better not do.

Tomorrow, Rex decided, he'd deal with the gun, not people. Objects did not lie or get insulted. They just existed. Of course, they could not say where they'd been or in whose hands, but proof of ownership should speak for itself. Daniel's latest theory was that a woman had shot Sir Frederick. A man, according to Daniel, admittedly not the cleverest of tacticians, would never leave his gun at the scene of a crime. A pistol was too easy to trace, which was why Rex put the gun on the top of his list. A burglar, especially, wouldn't shoot at a robbery victim. That made his crime doubly dangerous, the punishment far harsher if he were caught.

"But what if Amanda's entrance frightened the man?" Rex conjectured.

"She's a little dab of a chick. He could have hit her with the gun and made his escape. A woman committing a crime of passion wouldn't think like that."

"Known many murderesses, have you?"

Daniel was adamant. "Stands to reason a female would drop the gun and run before Amanda could identify her. They must be acquainted."

Mrs. Burton was the only female on the list, but she was neither a thief nor an acquaintance of Amanda Carville's. Rex wondered why the Aide had included her name, since there must be scores of women with L.B. as initials. But women coldhearted enough to blow away a man's brains? Sir Frederick was not known to keep a mistress, despite the silk stocking in his room, and such affairs were usually common knowledge, no matter how discreetly conducted. Sir Frederick would not have wanted to spend the money, either. His sister and daughter were accounted for. The housekeeper was not a suspect, by her own true words. Besides, Rex still needed a motive for the killing.

He decided to leave that for the morning, too, along with finding a place to stay in London. Tonight he needed a good rest. With his hair still damp from his bath, Rex climbed into his bed with his lists beside him. Then he got out, dragged one of the blankets to the floor, and told Verity to get down. The dog's snoring was as bad as Nanny's. He was not sharing his bed with anyone who chased rabbits in her dreams. His own dreams were plaguesome enough.

Amanda did not hear the cousins come home, she was sleeping so soundly. She did hear Dodd and the single footman grumble about having to haul hot water upstairs at such a late hour, and she heard them carrying coal to warm the rooms for bathing. Then she heard them carrying tubs away, clanking the tin pails as they went. She tried not to imagine Rex in his bath, washing himself with the sandalwood soap whose scent he always carried, lying back to relax until the water cooled. She tried very hard not to picture him climbing onto his bed, dismissing his valet, and blowing out the candle, leaving him limned in the embers of the dying fire.

She tossed off the top blanket on her bed. It was a pretty picture, a masterpiece of a fantasy, even if the details were inexact. After all, she had never seen a man at his bath or asleep in his bed. Or naked. Gracious, how did her room get so very warm?

Was the wound on his leg still raw and painful? Did he sleep on his side or his stomach or his back? She rolled over again.

None of the conjectures were going to help *her* fall back to sleep. Thinking about her own situation was less soothing, and less pleasant to contemplate. How was she supposed to fall back asleep counting days until the trial, instead of sheep?

Maybe his lordship had discovered something helpful tonight. According to Nanny, the cousins were looking for clues, but mostly they were rightfully staying out of the house to protect her reputation, the noddies. She had no reputation since Sir Frederick lied to Charles Ashway. She foresaw no future for herself where a spotless name mattered. What mattered was having any future at all.

Rex could not be asleep yet, and he might know something that would relieve her own mind. Of course going to his room might be the stupidest thing Amanda had done since picking up that gun in Sir Frederick's study. Too bad. She was already lighting a candle.

She ought not. Heavens, no lady would even think of visiting a gentleman's chambers, much less at night, knowing he was abed, whilst in her undress, in secret. Very well, she was a fallen woman just thinking of stepping down the hall. Where were her slippers?

Lady Royce was on her way; such loose behavior was no way for Amanda to repay her hostess. But now, before the countess returned, Amanda could repay what Rex had done for her by showing her . . . friendship. He'd saved her life. She knew she would have died in jail, from hunger or the fevers or despair. She might still die, unless Rex saved her again. Life, especially her life, was too short to worry about propriety and guest manners.

Amanda found her robe. And her honesty. Rex cherished the truth. He kept urging her to speak without guile, so she would, to herself. She wanted his reassurance, yes; she wanted to learn his news, certainly; she wanted to thank him, naturally. And she wanted more of his kisses. Fiercely.

She changed into something more suitable.

Rex was making notations on his list of names and initials when he heard the soft scratching at his door. The butler and footman had left, complaining of the hour, so Murchison must be coming to tell him that Daniel would live through the night.

"Enter."

The door immediately opened, which only proved Murchison could hear as well as speak when he wanted to. Instead of the small, tidy gentleman's gentleman, a vision stood in his doorway, then quickly entered the room and closed the door behind her.

Her? "Good grief, Amanda, what are you doing here?" He pulled the sheet up over his bare chest. "Is something wrong? Where is Nanny? Is she injured?"

"Nanny Brown is with her sister below in the house-keeper's apartment, fast asleep, I have no doubt. The stairs were too much to ask of the dear old soul."

"Then you? Are you ill? Are you having a relapse?"

"Yes."

"The fever?"

"Yes. I feel very warm."

She sure as hell did not look warm in that sheer neg-ligee she wore with nothing over it, nothing under it as far as he could tell by the fire's dying embers, his bed-side lamp, and the candle she still held in trembling hands. He would have jumped out of bed to wrap her in his blankets, but he needed those blankets to preserve his modesty and her innocence. He fumbled at the foot of the bed with one hand, clutching the sheets with the other, to where Verity had insisted on sleeping—on top of his robe. "I'll go fetch Nanny. She'd know which medicine you ought to take, and how much."

"That is not what I need."

His hand paused over the sleeping dog. "Uh, what is it that you do need, then?"

"I . . . I need you to hold me."

Damn. "Here, I'll give you my dog." He pushed Verity to her feet, mumbling about what a poor watchdog she was anyway. "That's what you said you wanted before."

"Is that too much to ask? You did not mind this afternoon."

Mind? What mind? He blinked, as if that would change the image in his head, the scent of her, the feel of her body, the silkiness of her curls, and the warmth of her lips. Oh, lord. "You should not be here, saying such things!"

"Why not? I have nothing to lose, do I? Why should I not take some comfort where I can, while I can? I am not some foolish heroine in a dreadful novel, wanting to experience the marriage act before she succumbs to some mysterious evil. I admit I am somewhat curious, but that is no reason to betray a lifetime's teachings. Nor am I here to show my gratitude, although I am more than indebted to you. I . . . I liked your kisses. I could forget everything else, in your arms."

"You do not understand. A proper lady—"

She held up one slender arm, bare to the shoulder but for one narrow ribbon of a strap. "Do not say it. You and I both know my reputation will never recover. I do not consider myself a lady anymore, and I am glad of the freedom."

"But I am a gentleman, despite the gossip." He tapped his chest. "I am a gentleman here, where it matters." He tapped his head. "And here. I could not accept what I think you are offering without making an honorable offer in return."

She did not deny her intentions, instead making them clear by fingering the diamond necklace at her throat. No woman wore her finest jewels to sleep alone. She looked like a figure from an erotic dream to him, and he could feel his body straining toward her. "It is against all notions of decency."

"Pooh, no one will know."

"I will."

"But if I hang, you will not need to sacrifice your freedom for me."

"You will *not* hang!"

She stared at her toes, which he noticed were bare, tiny pink buds peeking from under the hem of thin white lace. "Would it be so terrible to ask me, then? I would never hold you to an engagement unless there were a child."

A child? Another monster like himself? He took a deep breath, possibly his first since she'd entered the room. Yes, that was why he felt so light-headed—lack of air. "I would be the happiest of men to call you wife, if I had not sworn to remain a bachelor."

"You do not like women?"

"Of course I do. You must have noticed this afternoon." If she looked closely at the sheets, she could see that he liked her very well tonight, too.

She nervously twisted the diamonds at her throat. "Then it must be your mother. Did she disappoint you so much that you will never trust another female?"

"I do not speak of my feelings toward Lady Royce. I have none, in fact. Feelings, that is."

"She will be here soon, I understand."

And not a moment too soon for his comfort and his conscience. But Amanda was going on: "So there is only tonight. I am not asking for your hand or your heart, only one night of joy."

He imagined her in the diamonds and nothing else and was almost ready to hold the blankets up, offering her a place in his bed. Joy? He'd show her heaven, with rainbows and angels dancing. Except the diamonds were a gift from her mother. "Your family would be horrified."

"More so than knowing I was in prison? More than having my name on everyone's lips as a murderess and a soiled dove? I think, I pray, my mother would like knowing I found a bit of pleasure."

A bit? He was not going to be satisfied with a kiss and a cuddle, oh no. His body was warning him that once he took Amanda into his arms, he was never going to let her go. And that was the trouble. "You are asking me to forego my honor."

"You have asked me not to run away, so I could be forfeiting my very life to your honor. Which is more important?" She had set her candle down and now she came closer to his bedside. She stroked the dog, who licked Amanda's hand and closed her eyes.

Rex tried to swallow but his throat was as dry as Verity's bowl after dinner. "Someone might come."

"Who? Your valet?"

"He is very protective. My father sent him to look after me."

"It is the middle of the night. Surely Murchison

knows you are old enough to sleep alone. You have a watchdog."

Who was starting to snore again. "My, my cousin might come."

"I heard him snoring. Louder than Nanny, much louder than Verity."

And Rex knew that Daniel was not likely to wake up for two days, not after tonight.

She touched the sheet, as if to raise it.

He hung on to the top. "I have nothing on under the covers."

"I have nothing on under my nightgown."

"I noticed." Hell, he could barely take his eyes off her, now that she was close enough for him to see the peaks of her breasts, the shadow between her legs. The diamonds glittered in the firelight, sending silver sparks to her brown eyes. The sparks reached his very soul and set it on fire. Only she could douse those flames. He knew that now.

She was his. He'd rescued her; he'd kept her alive. She was not going to become the docile wife of some nameless blighter who married her for the price of her jewels, who'd fill her belly with a dozen sniveling brats.

Children. He pulled the sheets higher, as far as they would reach with Verity's weight on them. "I cannot. I will not father a child."

"You do not like children?" Disappointment resounded in her words. "I always wished for a boy and a girl."

"I like children well enough, I suppose. But not mine."

"Why?"

It was the middle of the night, a nearly naked woman

was tempting him nearly past endurance, and she wanted to dissect his life principles? "It is a private matter."

She huffed. "You asked me not to run away, to trust you with my very life. Yet you cannot explain something so important as not wishing children?"

She was right, and she was sitting on the edge of his bed now, stroking his sleeping dog. Long, strong strokes, back and forth, back and forth. Heaven help him.

Thinking that his silence had to do with some dark secret, she asked, "Who would I tell?"

Verity rolled over to have her stomach rubbed. His tongue went numb. "It's hard"—and it wasn't the only thing that was—"to explain. Just accept that there is an . . . unpleasant trait running through the males of my family."

"Insanity?" She stood up, as if to leap for safety if he turned dangerous. Verity whimpered at the loss of her attention. "I have heard of that occurring in certain bloodlines. Your father is not locked up somewhere, is he? That's not why he and your mother live separately, is it, and he never comes to Town?"

"Lud, no. My father has bad lungs, but his mental facilities are as sharp as ever, thank goodness, although some might consider him eccentric."

"Ah, it is more like weak chins, then? But I see no similarities between you and your cousin, other than your coloring."

"Daniel was not supposed to be affected, coming through the female line, my father's sister, but he is, although not as severely."

Her brows were puckered and her tongue flicked across her lips as she thought. He could tell she was running an inventory list through her mind. Gads, what was she imagining, some hideous deformity? He already had scars and wounds. "It is not exactly visible, like a birth-mark or baldness."

"Ah, then it is a disease that strikes the men in your family at some stage in their lives?"

"Yes . . . that is, no. Please, just believe that I do not wish to bring forth a child who would be so afflicted."

"What of the earldom? I thought that was drummed into a little lordling's head, that his sole job in life was to beget the next peer."

"I cannot do that."

Her eyes narrowed in speculation. "Cannot, or will not?"

Thunderation, now she was imagining him impotent! "I *will* not father a child and that is that!"

She accepted his adamance, for now. "Very well. There are ways, I have heard . . ."

Rex could see the blush start at her chest and rise to her cheeks. She was willing to initiate an affair, the little peagoose, but she could not discuss the earthier aspects. And she thought she was no longer a lady? "I do not have such protection handy. I could withdraw, but that is no guarantee."

She pounded her fist on the mattress, to Verity's dis-pleasure. "Life has no guarantee! Can you not under-stand? I might not live long enough to bear a child! And to conceive in one night? My mother had one child in all her years of marriage. But now I see what it is. You are making excuses, one after the other. You do not want me. Tell me, is it another woman, so I shall merely be morti-fied, not shattered?"

He thought of Lydia Burton. He thought about lying, claiming a prior affection, a previous commitment, even a wife tucked away in the country. He could not lie, though. Zeus, no. "I doubt I have ever wanted a woman as badly as I want you."

She snapped her fingers. "Good dog, Verity. Now get down."

Chapter Twenty-one

She won. And what a prize! He was gleaming like a god in the firelight, all that she could see of him. Broad shoulders, well-muscled arms, the faintest line of hair beginning in the middle of his chest. The blankets covered the rest of him, but not for long, not with him wearing a grin half of resignation, half of expectation.

She was not quite sure what to do with the spoils of victory, but she claimed her ground, climbing up to the high bed. She started to pull the bedcovers aside but he held onto his sheet. He blew out her candle and turned down his lamp. "Not yet."

If she was unsure how to proceed, Rex had strong notions about it. And strong arms, to pull her against him, her head next to his on the pillow, blond hair beside black. A sheet and a spider web of lace was between them, but she did not care, not in his embrace. There it was, that feeling of rightness, of safety and protection. More, of being cherished. His strength was hers, her softness was his. This was why she had been ready to toss her bonnet over the windmill, and toss herself at Rex. This and the kindling kisses he was raining on her eyelids, her ears, her neck. Now she did not have to think of anything but him, and how he made her feel.

Like a princess, like a fairy sprite, like clay for him to form in his knowing hands. Like a lady with her beloved. No fears and doubts loomed ahead, no secrets between them or distrust, only sensation and heat and a craving for more. Closer, warmer, faster. More.

Her gown disappeared. Maybe it burned up, her skin felt so on fire. Somehow she was hotter without it, with his hands on her bare flesh, up and down her back, on her waist, her backside. Now he was touching her breasts, then lowering his head to nip and nuzzle at the tips. The nipples were so taut they were as hard as the part of him pressed against her belly, through the sheet. She reached down, but he stilled her hand.

"Not yet."

"You said that before."

He kissed her to stop the conversation. He used his tongue this time, tickling and tantalizing hers, and she felt they were sharing the dance they had never had, and likely never would. The music of desire raced through her body, leaving her thrumming with the unspoken tempo, the in and out of the universal dance of love. She felt she would burst with the need for something, to reach some unknown plateau, to understand everything, to waltz among the clouds. She met his tongue with hers, and learned how to make him sigh and moan and pull her closer, as if they could become one. Soon, but not yet. Unless she expired first.

His hand stopped its tender exploration. His tongue withdrew and he pulled away, putting distance between them, besides the sheet. "I cannot do it."

"I thought you said you could."

"I can; I won't." His conscience was already raging at him about visiting a brothel; he could not live with himself for deflowering a virgin. On the same night? How could he touch this sweetly giving woman, after being, no matter how briefly or inconclusively, with a practiced whore who sold her favors for money? He could not.

No matter what Amanda said, she was not thinking rationally. Lud knew he wasn't, with her beside him, not even the sheer nightgown covering her exquisite body. And where had the gown gone? he wondered. The dog must have eaten it.

She pressed closer, almost on top of him, her leg over his thigh. He recited the first page of the *Aeneid*. In Latin. *Arma virumque*. Arms and the man. His were reaching for her, despite his good intentions.

"It is my fault. You do not find me attractive. I am too forward. Too thin. I realize you only feel pity for me. I am sorry to have bothered you, yet again."

So he had to kiss her, before the little widgeon fretted herself into another bout of weeping. "I told you, you are beautiful," he whispered between kisses. "I want you. You are just right. See how well you fit in my arms?" He pulled her on top of him.

Which was a mistake. He should not have let any part of her touch any part of him, again. Now they were both on fire. "The Devil knows how much I want you, but this is wrong. Tell me to stop." She did not. Instead she kissed his neck, and touched his sensitive ear with the tip of her tongue. He groaned at his stupidity for teaching her that trick not a moment before. He said it: "Stop," in a voice lacking conviction, possibly lacking sound, for his every breath was gone.

"What if I said I am not a maiden? Would that ease your mind?"

Lud knew nothing but two days in bed with her, maybe three, were going to ease his body. "Say it."

So she did, and she was lying, as red as the virgin's blood that would flow for him and all the world to see, branding him a dastard. "Good try, angel, but I do not believe you. But I am too weak willed to let you go. We can still enjoy each other's company." He would not take her innocence, but he could still give her a woman's pleasure.

She wept anyway, at the revelation of what her body could do, what he could do to her, for her. "I never understood how, how extraordinary the feelings are. But there is more. I know there is more."

"You are not strong enough yet. I am not strong enough."

"But you have not had your pleasure."

"Yes, I have." Listening to her cries of excitement, of ecstasy, of surprise, learning what she liked, were more sensuous than anything he could imagine, and more satisfying. To be entirely truthful, the experience was not quite as satisfying as being inside her would have been, but this way he could worship every inch of her tender skin, adore each curve and crevice, without the weight of guilt on his shoulders. "I am well pleased. Now you must go."

If he had any second thoughts about her leaving, he was too late. She was already asleep. He could have woken her, but he was too busy studying her by the dying firelight, how her eyelashes had one tiny teardrop, how her sweet lips were partly open. Had he ever truly worshiped a woman's body this way? He doubted it.

Rex was content, despite being unfulfilled. That no longer mattered. He fell asleep himself, smiling.

                    *   *   *

He woke up to the noise of the household awakening, dawn's light edging through the drawn curtains. He kissed Amanda awake, and she immediately responded, her hand trailing down his chest where the sheet had become disarranged, on a mission of hesitant exploration. He brought her hand to his lips and kissed each finger. "No, angel. I am not enough of a saint to withstand that. You have to go to bed."

"Hmm," she murmured drowsily, rolling over against him.

"In your own bed," he told her, groaning. "Murchison must not find you here in the morning, or Nanny find you missing. Can you imagine the uproar if you are not where you belong? Come, sweetings, it grows light, the servants will be up."

"I am too weary. You have stolen away the stiffness of my bones."

He knew where it had gone, too.

Rex climbed out of bed, glad she was turned away to hide his injured leg and his all-too-healthy manhood from her sight, and picked up his robe and her gown. He put his on, draped hers over his shoulder, and lifted her into his arms. "I seem to be making a habit of this, don't I?"

She laughed softly, sleepily, sexily. Heaven help him, he wanted to carry her to the rooftop where no one could find them, no could interrupt. He headed for her door. "I must be a saint, after all."

She patted his cheek and kissed him, feeling the new growth of beard. "You are perfect. I think I love you, Lord Rexford."

Luckily they were at her chamber, because he almost dropped her. "No, little goose, you are just in the afterglow of passion. Like Verity adoring Daniel because he feeds her. Not that you are anything like the dog. You smell much better." He kissed behind her ear, where the scent of perfume still lingered.

She shook her head, the blond curls whispering against his shoulder. "No, I would not feel the passion if I did not love you."

She truly, bluely, believed that. "Maybe women are different. But you have not known me long enough for such strong emotion."

"You do not believe in love at first sight?"

"I hardly believe in love at all."

"Well, I do. I shan't ask anything more of you after tonight, however, I swear. Except to find the killer."

"I'll do that, and more." He set her down atop her own bed, amid the tumbled sheets, and backed away quickly, before he was tempted to join her. "Things will be better, I swear. I'll make everything right."

"I trust you will," came from the hallway.

Amanda squeaked and pulled the covers over herself. Rex turned, too fast for his bad leg, and had to catch himself against the wall. He straightened.

"Thank you for taking such excellent care of my goddaughter, Jordan. You may leave her now. I am assuming she took ill in the night. That is correct, Amanda, is it not?"

"Yes, ma'am," she croaked from under the blankets. "Very ill."

Rex thanked heaven not everyone could see the truth. He walked toward the door and shut it behind him, then he took stock of the woman he had not seen since before he left for the army. She looked tired and pale, likely from the hurried journey, but she was still a handsome woman, with a proud, erect bearing. She was staring at him, in turn, which made Rex uncomfortable.

"I shall be moving out shortly," he told her. "I will be staying on in London seeking evidence to prove Miss Carville's innocence."

Lady Royce raised an eyebrow.

"She is untouched."

"Not quite untouched, I would gather." The countess lifted the gossamer nightgown from his shoulder. "We shall speak of this later, when we are both better rested. I shall expect you for luncheon."

Ah, mealtime with Medea. She was the one, Rex recalled, who killed her children and served them up for supper.

He bowed.

Rex left the house early that morning, taking his horse to Hyde Park before anyone was out and about. Daniel would not rise that day—and if he did, he was bound to wish otherwise, with the headache he would suffer and the antidote Murchison would pour down his throat. Maybe that would teach him moderation.

Rex went in by the servants' entrance on his return from the stable mews. Finally, wonderful smells of baking bread, frying bacon, and kippers came from the kitchens. If the cook was not accustomed to gentlemen in her domain, she must have been warned, because she set a plate in front of him without ordering him to the formal dining room. "Happy to feed a hungry man, I am, after all these years of cooking for your lady mother."

Which reminder ruined his appetite.

After eating what he could, so as not to offend the cook for Daniel's sake, he took himself to Bow Street, to offer his services for an hour or two to Inspector Dimm. He found the work satisfying. Lud knew, he needed something in his life that was. Without his cousin, he found a deck of cards and played patience at the desk outside Dimm's office while the inspector interviewed suspects. One tap for the truth, two for a lie.

Dimm came out after twenty minutes, lighting his pipe and apologizing that there was not much work for the viscount today. "We're getting caught up, praises be, and thanks to you, sir." Then Dimm looked over Rex's list of initials and suspects. He nodded. "That Cuthbert chap's had some run-ins with the law. A bootboy in his household a few years ago, iffen I remember right."

"Killed?"

"An accident, they declared it." He knocked his pipe against the desk top in disgust. "With his neck snapped? The swells get away with a lot, and pardon me for saying so, my lord."

"Whoever killed Sir Frederick will not get away with it, no matter his station. I promise you that." One tap.

As the hackney neared Manton's Shooting Gallery, traffic came to a standstill. A dray had overturned, spewing cabbages all over the street. Rex got down and walked, figuring his bad leg could use the exercise anyway. He had not counted on dodging rolling vegetables, the street urchins who were snatching up all they could carry, angry drivers, and curious spectators. He walked toward a side street to avoid the mess, but as soon as he left the main thoroughfare he felt an odd sensation, like a prickling behind his neck. Many of the officers in Spain used to claim they felt some such self-defense instinct, and they always listened to their bodies. Rex had not truly believed them, finding his own brand of magic bad enough. Of course, if he had honed those other instincts he might not have a bad leg and a scar on his cheek. He listened now.

He stopped to look in the window of a print shop, pretending an interest in a display of cartoons lampooning Prinny, as usual, while he studied the glass reflection. The only person nearby was a young clerk carrying a stack of books. So much for instincts. He went on, swinging his cane, knowing full well his scarlet uniform made him easy to track.

Damn, the odd niggling feeling persisted, so he detoured down a different street. A quick glance showed the same clerk still following, more closely. At the next alley, he pretended to stop to check his boot, and came up with a knife in his hand, which was quickly at the young man's throat, as he dragged the clerk into the alley.

"You are following me. Who sent you? And *do not lie*."

"Mr. Harmon."

Blue.

"I do not know any Mr. Harmon."

"Oh, um, Major Harrison. Yes, that must be who. But I mean you no harm, sir. The gentleman sent me to tell you to watch your back. He said you made more enemies than a fox in five henhouses in one night."

Rex pulled the knife away from the man's jugular. "Why not come up to me honestly if you had a message, instead of using stealth?"

"He wanted to see how vulnerable you were."

"As you can tell, I am not. You can tell your superior that I do not need the warning, or a bookish bodyguard." Then he felt the unmistakable pressure of a gun between his ribs. He looked down, and the pistol's barrel was poking between the books in the clerk's arms. He slowly lowered his own knife to his side. "Point taken. Tell your master I have learned his lesson. I shall be more careful in future."

"You might want to mind your manners, too, he said, begging your pardon, Captain. Better for your health, he said." The clerk tipped his hat and disappeared.

The senior salesman at Manton's recognized the gun in Rex's sketch instantly.

"Oh, yes, we made that firearm. One of a pair, it was. And we have an order for another because one was stolen. In fact, I have the widowed one here, to match. Unless you found the missing piece? Mr. Cord would be delighted to have it back without the expense of having another made. They were his father's, I believe."

"Mr. Lysander Cord? Who resides at the Albany?" Rex recited from his list.

"You know the gentleman? Excellent. Then I am sure you can relieve his mind. Sentimental value, don't you know."

Rex did not know the man, but called at his rooms anyway. Sure enough, Cord explained that his prized weapon had been stolen a few weeks ago from his coach while he attended the theater. He spoke the truth.

Cord was also appalled that his missing gun had killed Sir Frederick Hawley, truly. He was not the murderer.

"But you knew him? Did you know what business he was in?"

Cord looked around his lodgings, obviously wishing he—or Rex—were elsewhere. "Sir Frederick was a gentleman. He could not have been in trade."

"Surely even gentlemen make investments, help finance promising endeavors. Do you?"

"Me?" The man's voice rose an octave. "I have money in the Funds."

Which was true, but not complete, Rex felt. "Do you have any enemies?"

"Me?" he squawked again. "Shouldn't you be asking if Sir Frederick had anyone who wished him ill?"

"Everyone wished him ill, it appears. But you? As I read the situation, the killer might have been a random thief, robbing first your carriage, then Sir Frederick's house, but that seems altogether too coincidental. On the other, more devious hand, perhaps someone purposely left your gun at the scene of a crime. After all, the authorities had only your word that the pistol was stolen."

Cord went white.

"I'll see if Bow Street will give your pistol back when they are done."

"Do you know, if it has been used in a murder, I don't think I want it back. Manton's can make me another."

"Good idea. Good day."

It wasn't. It was lunchtime.

Chapter Twenty-two

Daniel refused to get up for the noonday meal, the traitor.

"I might never eat again," he said with a groan, rolling over in bed with the pillow on his head to keep his brains from falling out.

"I consider that pudding-hearted, abandoning me in my hour of need."

"Don't mention food."

"You felt badly enough that I got shot up by the French after you left me in the Peninsula."

"I might shoot you myself if you don't leave me to die in peace."

Miss Carville, Rex was informed by a very superior ladies' maid when he scratched at Amanda's door, was resting after her recent indisposition, on Lady Royce's advice.

Advice? It was more like an order, Rex would wager. So it was to be the two of them alone, *mano y mano*, or man and *madre*, except for the army of servants the countess seemed to employ. He'd faced French cannons and British turncoats, his enemies' fear and fellow officers' disdain. Hell, he'd faced a room full of matchmaking mothers. Surely he could get through one luncheon with the woman who had given him birth.

As loath as he was to make his commanded appearance, he prayed the countess had not made Amanda feel as uncomfortable or unwelcome. Lud knew he had nowhere else to take her. He was the one at fault anyway, since he was older, wiser, not ruled by emotions, and not in fear of his life. He was prepared to acknowledge that much and swear to Amanda's virtue, unless Lady Royce had insulted her. Then he would take Amanda to the first inn he could find and to the devil with the gossip, and to the dustbin with the meal.

They were everything polite in front of the servants in the formal dining room, seated at opposite ends of a long table. Rex forced himself to eat the excellent food in front of him, although he tasted nothing.

The countess turned down most of the dishes. When Rex raised an eyebrow at her nearly empty plate, she said, "I fear a recurrence of stomach disorder I suffered in Bath. I would have left for London as soon as I heard of Amanda's situation otherwise, of course."

Now Rex had the taste of humble pie in his mouth for thinking the countess had selfishly abandoned her goddaughter. "Ah," was all he said, but he did bear more of his share of the conversation after that.

They discussed his father's health, Daniel's sister's planned come-out next Season, and the weather. Oh, and the condition of the roads between Bath and London, as if he gave a damn. Finally the countess indicated that the meal was over. "Will you take tea, or port if you prefer, with me in the drawing room?"

He followed her, and the line of footmen and maids carrying the tray and the decanter and the countess's shawl and her needlework. Drooling, Verity followed closely behind the footman who was bearing a plate of biscuits.

"I did not invite that monstrous, ill-behaved creature into my home," were the first words Lady Royce said when the last servant bowed and shut the door behind him.

"I am sorry. I thought Daniel would be better off here than in the stews where I found him."

She raised her eyebrow, but a glimmer of a smile touched one corner of her mouth. "Your cousin is welcome, of course. And you." She broke off a bit of biscuit for the dog, who sat by her chair, gazing up adoringly. The countess, meanwhile, stared at Rex, then at yet another boyhood portrait hanging on the wall.

Rex said nothing, silently berating the dog for another act of treason.

His silence must have unnerved the countess, he thought, if anything could, for she set her cup down too hard, making a clatter. She cleared her throat, as if wondering where to begin. Start twenty-some years ago, he wanted to shout, but did not.

She looked at the portrait again. "I thought you appeared different the last time I saw you. Your nose . . ."

"A recent misadventure. It will have its own shape in a week, I assume. The scar on my cheek is permanent, but fading."

"And your leg?"

He tucked it back under him, instead of stretched out in front. "Quite well, thank you. Better every day."

She nodded, accepting that he would not share more than impersonal facts. "Thank you for bringing my godchild to me."

"It was my—" He almost said pleasure, but caught

himself. "My honor to be of service." That did not sound right, either, reminding him of a stallion servicing the mares, but he could not retract the words.

The countess inferred no double meaning. "She is a lovely young woman. Wrongly charged, of course."

He gazed at the ruby-colored wine in his goblet, the color of dark lies. "You believe her innocent?"

"Naturally. I have known her since her birth, and her mother was one of my best friends since our own childhood. Amanda could no more shoot a man in cold blood than she could fly to the moon, no matter how deserving of it that man was. More importantly, do you believe she is innocent of the crime?"

She was not asking for his supposition, Rex knew, but his certain knowledge. "Yes."

"Ah, then you should have no trouble proving it."

"How, by telling people that I see blue when she speaks?"

She ignored the anger and frustration in his voice and tapped her lips in thought. "It just might do."

"What might do?" Not his declaration of insanity, surely.

"Why, your marrying her, of course. A handsome young viscount—at least I trust you will be more handsome once your nose is no longer so red and swollen— with a romantic scar and a limp well earned in bravery, to say nothing of a vast fortune, and a beautiful, well-bred young woman. The families have been connected for generations, and wholeheartedly approve. When the *ton* sees how happy I am over the match, they will trust in Amanda's innocence. I am known to be extremely particular in my acquaintances."

"I shall not marry her."

"After spending days—and nights—unchaperoned together? Of course you will. Nanny taught you manners. Your father taught you honor."

"She was ill, and there was no alternative. If *you* had been here to rescue her yourself, there would be no problem."

"I was too ill to travel, to my regret."

Rex could see the truth of that, and not just in her drawn features and pallid complexion. He changed the topic. "Shouldn't Amanda, Miss Carville, be here for this discussion? She knows my views and accepts them."

"She had a tray in her room. Now she is too busy getting ready to go out."

"Go out . . . where?"

"Why, on social calls, a stroll through the park at the fashionable hour, shopping perhaps. She has to be seen, and be seen unconcerned, to quell the gossip."

"She is accused of murder, not of tying her garters in public! You cannot counter such charges with a social sugarcoating."

"That's how much you know of polite society." The countess poured herself another cup of tea. "But you might be right. An engagement announcement would be better."

Rex scowled. "There will be no announcement, no betrothal, no match."

"You used to be such a charming little boy."

And she used to be a loving mother, until she left. Rex helped himself to more wine.

The countess added sugar and stirred her tea. "Do you think you can refute the charges?"

"I am going to try my damnedest."

"But you might fail?"

"I might."

"Then I shall make plans to take Amanda abroad. I know the war has affected travel, but ships leave daily. Surely one goes somewhere livable."

"You would help her escape?"

"I would save her life if you cannot."

"I suppose I should not be surprised. When things are not to your liking, you always run off, do you not?"

She set her cup aside and reached for a handkerchief as her eyes filled with tears. Rex looked away, lest he be swayed by her distress. Nanny had wiped *his* eyes, not this woman sitting across from him.

Lady Royce gathered her composure, tucking the delicate handkerchief away and feeding Verity another biscuit. "I thought you would understand by now."

"I understand that I gave my parole for Amanda's appearance. I pledged my honor, if honor means anything to you."

"Stop this nastiness. You were a child when I left. You are acting like a child now and I will not tolerate it."

He stood.

"Where are you going?"

"We have nothing to say."

"I have a great deal to say. Are you mature enough to listen?"

He stepped toward the door.

"You owe me a hearing, dash you!"

Rex whistled for his dog, who came, looking back regretfully at the biscuits. "I brought your goddaughter to you."

"I gave you life."

Rex could only return to the center of the room. He did

not sit, but stood, Verity at his feet. He stared up at the happy little boy in the portrait over the mantel.

Lady Royce stared at him, as if trying to see that child she once held. Then she took a deep breath and began. "Your father and I married for love, you know. His parents had another young lady in mind for him, but he chose me. I was in alt, over the moon in love with him. We married and then . . . and then, I found him not to be the person I thought he was. He was . . . different."

"He could see the truth, or hear it, in his case."

"Yes. That was disconcerting enough, as you might imagine. What kind of man was this, touched by the gods, or touched in the head?"

"I have wondered myself."

She nodded and went on. "I thought he should have told me before we wed, to be fair. But there were more secrets he left for me to discover on my own. Royce had a mistress before we married." She held up a hand to ward off his interruption. "I know many men do. And yes, he swore he ended the affair when he knew I was the woman he wished to share his life with. Yet he kept seeing her. People were eager to share that tittle-tattle with me."

Rex drew in a quick breath. That did not sound like the man he thought his father to be, either.

"Oh, he said they were merely friends, and he had 'obligations' to her. I tried to be understanding, but he was my husband, soon to be the father of my child! I was young and yes, I was jealous. Horribly, crushingly, corrosively jealous. When I demanded he cease all connection with the woman, he refused. I retaliated."

"By having an affair?"

"By throwing myself into the social whirl of London, flirting with every man I met. I was quite the belle, and your father was furious. Worse, he kept asking who I danced with, why did I go off alone, what buck paid morning calls while Royce was at court, and how long did he stay? I knew I could not lie, of course. And why should I? I had nothing to be ashamed of. Your father insisted I retire in the country, with the excuse of your imminent birth. A Royce should be born in his ancestral home."

"They all have been, as far as I know."

She sipped at her tea, then made a face at the lukewarm beverage. "I thought matters would be better once you were born, with his dark hair and blue eyes, thank goodness. He adored you. Who would not, such a beautiful, cheerful baby? We were happy once more, a real family. Royce's work with the justice system took up much of his time, even in the country, and soon he began to question me about the neighbors, their houseguests, the curate who came to tea. He knew the truth, of all people, yet he was never satisfied. I felt I was on trial, for some future crime I might commit. I . . . feared he was insane, and I began to fear him. I could not bear to see our love turn into a struggle, so I went to London, where I had friends."

"Without me."

"You think I should have taken his heir? His very joy? He would never have hurt you, and I had no legal grounds. And . . . and I did not know how to deal with your questions, your intelligence."

"My knowing the truth from a lie?"

She bit her lip, as if to hold back more tears. "You were different from other children, as he was different from other men. I could not even tell you about the fairies dancing in the meadow, or Father Christmas, not without your looking at me sadly, as if I had broken your trust. Still, I thought he would follow me. He said he loved me, and I believed him, despite the other woman, despite my not having your gift of truth-seeing. I would have welcomed him, for I never stopped loving him or believing we could be happy, if he only learned to trust me. He came to town to press Parliament for legal reform; he did not come for me. We lived in the same house, but we seldom spoke."

"Why did he not bring me with him?"

"I begged him to, but he would not send for you. I think he did not want you in Town to hear gossip of his other connection. Or see that we lived as near strangers. You went away to school soon anyway."

Rex leaned over to rub Verity's ears, not looking at the countess. "Then he was disgraced and you did not stand by him."

She held out a biscuit for the dog, but Verity stayed at Rex's side for once. The countess lowered her hand. "He would not let me. Your father is a stubborn, stubborn man, and I fear you have inherited that trait from him, too. He would not stay on in London and refute the charges, for his defense was nothing anyone could accept. You must understand that, for you said much the same about Amanda's defense. Nor did he want me to share his retreat to the country. He said it would kill him to see me brought so low, that I'd be happier in the city among my friends. He meant my lovers. He'd stopped asking when I made up Lord Wealthy Widower and Sir Handsome Rake. The truth as I saw it, in my heart? He simply did not want me anymore."

"And you did not want me enough to fight him."

"Fight a hurricane? Fight a blizzard? I did swallow my pride and go to Royce Hall. He asked me if I were breeding, accusing me of coming home to plant another man's by-blow in his nest."

Rex swallowed, hard. "What did you tell him?

"I told him to go to hell. I went back to London and never approached him again. I thought that would be easier for you, instead of constant good-byes. I always spoke to my friends of his integrity, his devotion to the law, for what that was worth. I told everyone that there was no more honest man in all of creation. I believed it then, and believe it now, in spite of his behavior toward me, which I told no one. I convinced some people. But not Sir Nigel."

Rex's bad leg was growing weary from standing, but he did not wish to show his weakness by sitting down again. "Ah, Sir Nigel. Did you know he is the one pressing for a speedy trial, and a speedier hanging?"

"Yes, and you can blame me for that, too."

"You?"

"He wished to marry me, you know. No, how could you? He was a promising lawyer then, of good family, and I considered his suit until I met your father. I think that was why he was so vengeful about that minor court case, where your father could not convict an innocent man despite the evidence. Sir Nigel wanted to get even. And then, when I took up residence here, alone, he approached me again."

"You were still married."

The countess raised her chin. "I am married to this very day, and until I die. The barrister had a far less honorable proposal this time. I rejected him again, with a great deal less politeness than before. I tossed my wineglass in his face and barred him from the house. I believe that is why he was delighted to accuse Amanda, knowing of my affection for her."

Rex thought about that, wondering if Sir Nigel hated the Royce family enough to kill Sir Frederick for revenge.

No, he could not know that Amanda would come home to find that gun. "There is more to it than retaliation. I will find out what."

"I have every confidence that you will."

"But if I fail, you will run off with Amanda?"

"I will save her life, yes. I lost you once, I will not lose her. I owe her poor mother that much."

"You leave me no choice but to stay here to watch you, and set guards around the house to keep you here." He did not acknowledge the lift to his heart at the idea of spending more time with Amanda.

The countess sighed. "I suppose you'll follow us around Town, too."

"Around Town?" he echoed.

"I told you I intended to take her about with me. How else to show people that I believe her innocent, to get women talking to their husbands that Lady Royce, that paragon of virtue and wisdom, would not harbor a criminal, a killer? She is not guilty and I will not see her shut away!"

"You'd take her to parties and balls?" Rex could not believe her . . . what? Courage? Foolhardiness? Frivolity in the face of doom?

"I shall take her to every entertainment I can find. I suppose she ought not dance, with Sir Frederick so recently laid in his grave, but no one could expect her to mourn that mawworm."

"But she might be in danger!" Rex insisted, feeling dread wash over him at the notion of Amanda out on the Town, in crowds, among strangers. "Whoever did the killing cannot be at ease until someone else is punished for the crime. If she is dead, the case might be considered closed."

"All the more reason for you to attend us. I depend on you to keep her safe."

"But my presence will lead people to think . . . that is, they will suppose . . ." He could not continue.

"That you are about to restore her good name? I daresay they will. Who would expect Captain Lord Rexford to turn craven?"

From anyone else, Rex would take umbrage. Now he wanted to take to his heels. He suspected the countess had intended to trap him into the parson's mousetrap from the first. "You cannot make such demands of me."

"I realize I cannot influence you, no more than I could change your father's mind. No, you could have come to me all these years to hear my side of the story. You could have responded to my letters beyond a polite thank-you. You could have said farewell when you went to war, over my objections and my tears, you must know. So no, I do not expect any show of filial devotion or obedience. I will put my trust into your own sense of honor, which is far stronger than our ties now. That will suffice. In exchange, do not expect a mother's blind love in return, for I am out of practice. I waited for decades, sending gifts, letters, money, without a token of affection in return. Know this, Jordan, if you harm Amanda, if you leave her with child, if you break that poor girl's heart, I will tell the world that you are a sorcerer, a warlock, an aberration of evil, you and your father both."

She lied. She would never tell.

"No, I will cut out your heart, like you have mine."

"I will not harm her. And she will not get pregnant. The last thing I wish is another boy so horrific even his own mother could not love him."

"Not love you?" She spoke so loud that Verity barked.

"Is that what you think? That I did not love my beautiful, brilliant, unique child? I wanted to shout from the rooftops that he was a marvel, he was a gift from God. Your father convinced me I could not, that you would be in danger if the world knew. But know this, my son. I was never, ever unfaithful to your father. And I missed you every day of my life."

She spoke the truth.

Chapter Twenty-three

Amanda did not know what to say to the countess when the older woman came into her room, followed by a maid bearing a tray with a pot of chocolate and two cups. Fortunately, Amanda did not need to say anything, for her godmother did all the talking as soon as the maid left. There would be no tears, no recriminations, no rebukes, Lady Royce insisted.

And no regrets, Amanda said to herself. Last night was the most beautiful experience of her life. She would not have forgone it for the world. If she were going to repine, it would be because nothing like that would happen again—not with Lady Royce at home, and not with Rex so principled, and so prejudiced against marriage. She had had her moment of joy, however, so could not complain.

The countess patted her hand. "Royce men are simply irresistible. I know." Then she added, proudly, "Jordan is a handsome devil, isn't he? Except for that nose, of course. That must have come from his father's side of the family. Along with his truth—his love of the truth, that is, and his mulishness. Once he understands the consequences, he will do the right thing."

Now Amanda had to speak up. "No, I swore not to

force him to the altar. That would be the wrong thing for him, and thus for me. What happiness could I find, knowing he is miserable? He is not at fault, so why should he suffer? He did not seduce me; I went to his room. You must not blame him."

The countess blamed herself, the tainted meat, and her weak stomach for not arriving sooner. She had her own opinions about the source of her son's aversion to the married state, but she let that topic fall for now, pouring the chocolate into the delicate china cups. "I am only happy he is home, here with us."

"He does not intend to stay in London, so do not expect too much."

Lady Royce smiled over her drink in satisfaction, an expression that would have sent Rex scurrying for the countryside. "Oh, I think I might have found the way to keep him here. We'll just have to convince him to enjoy London while we can. And we will not speak more about last night."

Amanda shook her head. The countess made it sound as if Rex were here on holiday. "You are forgetting about Sir Frederick."

Lady Royce set down her cup. "I cannot forget that awful man and how he treated your mother. I am glad he is dead, glad you are now free to make your home with me."

Amanda's throat closed, choked on tears of gratitude no hot drink could relieve. "I feared I would have no place, if . . . if I have a future at all. You cannot imagine how your kindness relieves me."

"Recall, I said there were to be no tears. There are advantages to being a noblewoman of a certain age and authority. People have to listen to you." She stood and rang for a servant. "Now come, get dressed in your prettiest frock. We are going out so I can show off my godchild. I always wished for a daughter, you know."

"Out?" Amanda dreaded the stares, the whispers behind her back, the actual backs that turned when she approached so the countess's friends did not have to acknowledge her. No matter what Lady Royce declared, not even a countess could force anyone to accept an accused murderess in their midst. From what Amanda knew of the beau monde, they just might accept a killer sooner than a female who had skipped down the primrose path. The ink of scandal might rub off on their own daughters, contaminating them with lax morals or, worse, with minds of their own. The countess might have great standing in London's high society, but Amanda was not willing to put it to the test. She raised a hand to her forehead. "I am not feeling quite well, yet."

"Neither am I, but if you are well enough for midnight trysts, you are well enough for a stroll through Hyde Park."

So much for never mentioning last night again. "But I cannot bear to go out in public. Everyone will stare." If they did not throw stones at her.

Lady Royce was undaunted. "All the more reason to look your best. Too bad you cannot wear some of your mother's jewelry," she said, looking at the finery Amanda had taken out to show her. "But I suppose that would be too brazen, a young woman in mourning wearing colored stones or diamonds, with her relation barely cold in the grave. You do have dark gowns, don't you?"

Lady Royce's efficient dresser had arrived and was already going through Amanda's wardrobe, laying out her more subdued apparel, which meant her older, less fashionable gowns. When Amanda mentioned that, her lady-ship declared that her abigail could make the proper alter-ations in a moment's work. "There is no need for solid black, under the circumstances. There is every need for you to hold your chin high. Remember, you did nothing wrong."

Amanda waited for the servant to take an armful of gowns away with her to the sewing room. "Well, I ought not to have gone to Rex's chamber." If the countess could refer to it, so could Amanda.

"No, I meant, you did not shoot the scoundrel. We shall forget that other business." Again. "My gudgeon of a son seems to have."

A man did not forget one of the most moving, stirring, intense events of his life. The most idiotic thing he had ever done! Hell, he should have jumped out the window and been done with it. Furious with himself for his lack of restraint, the countess for making him feel three years old, and his father for never explaining anything to him, he did what any sensible chap would do. He pounded on his cousin's door and aggravated someone else.

"Get up, you clunch. You have to make sure they don't do a flit. I'll go track down some of the others on the list, but I cannot let the cursed females wander about by them-selves. It isn't safe, for one thing, and they might just get in a coach and not come back, for another. Lady Royce is threatening to take ship for the antipodes if necessary."

Daniel threw his pillow across the room, missing Rex by a yard and hitting the dog, who turned tail and ran, with the tarts Rex had brought his cousin to tempt him from bed. "You do not know a thing about women, do you? Just bribe one of the maids to tell you if they pack. You and that Dodd bloke are already blackmailing each other, so have him notify you if they take a trunk with them. They might say they're donating old clothes to the poor house, but don't believe 'em."

"How do you know so much?"

"I have a sister, don't you know."

"She tried to run off?" Rex knew Daniel's sister was supposed to have her come-out next year, but she was still a child in his mind.

"No, but one of her friends tried to elope when I first came home. Her father asked my help. We caught up with the chit, of course, which seems to have been the would-be groom's plan from the start, because he did not hide his route nor hurry his horses. Seems he wanted to be rich, not married. The girl's father paid him off to keep quiet. Then I beat the stuffing out of him."

"This is different. It's a legal matter. In addition to speaking of booking passage to foreign regions, her lady-ship wants to put Amanda on exhibit first. Taking her to parties and teas, to show the *ton* that she, the countess, is not concerned. She could have her friends or servants gather clothes and such for a journey. So we shall have to keep watch."

"We?"

"If I have to go, so do you. She was speaking of the opera tonight."

"The opera?" Daniel turned green again. Rex left the room in a hurry.

Lady Royce was not plotting an escape for this after-noon, Rex reasoned. She was too busy planning an evening of torture. He set out about his business,

Amanda's business, more determined than ever to clear the charges before the month was over.

On his way to that Bond Street jeweler with J.J. as his initials, Rex kept his ear tuned for following footsteps, and his mind keyed to prickles of intuition. The weather was excellent for once, so a great many people were out and about the street of shops, making it difficult to spot anyone in particular on his trail. His instincts told him nothing except how the upper class spent its afternoons, spending fortunes on items they did not need.

The jeweler told him nothing, either. He'd done some business with Sir Frederick, but that was all. Now that the man was dead, Joshua Jacobs could admit to altering some jewelry for the man, exchanging a few precious stones for glass or paste. Jacobs also purchased the real gems, to be recut and used in other settings.

No, he had no idea what Sir Frederick was doing with the money. The necklace was his first wife's, the baronet had sworn, so the diamonds were his to do with as he wanted.

"Not if they were entailed to his son's wife, they weren't."

It happened all the time, Mr. Jacobs told Rex, when the nobs were under the hatches. Minor titleholders especially, who held heirlooms that were seldom documented or drawn, unlike the more famous pieces of the better families. The toffs Jacobs usually encountered kept the real stones to sell one at a time. Sir Frederick's need for cash must have been urgent.

But why? That was the question. Why had he closed his accounts, stolen Amanda's money, and cashed in as many of his assets as he could get his hands on, and still lived like a pauper?

Jacobs raised his hands. "How should I know? I am nothing but a shopkeeper."

An honest one, Rex judged. He thanked the man and left a gold coin on the counter in appreciation. The jeweler handed it back. "Perhaps something for your lady?"

"I don't have a lady."

"Your mother?"

"I barely have a—" Then he saw a tray full of opera glasses and ornate lorgnettes. If they were going to the opera, Amanda might need a magnifier to see the stage, and to stare down the gawking audience. He selected a delicate lorgnette with various colored stones embedded in the gold handle, to match whichever of her mother's jewelry she chose to wear. He ended up paying far more than he intended for information, but a Town beau was supposed to send flowers to a young lady he had partnered in a dance the night before. Surely what they'd shared deserved a lot more than a nosegay, not that anyone had to know, of course. He told himself a quizzing glass was entirely proper for a friend to give. Just in case, he added silver opera glasses for the countess to his purchase, so his gift to Amanda did not look as particular. He ignored the rings entirely.

His next stop was debtors' prison.

The Fleet was not as noxious as Newgate, and the guards were lax in enforcing the rules, or more greedy.

Roger Vandermere, one of the R.V.s on the Aide's list, had a private cell, with a bed and a chair and table. All the comforts of home, the man explained, which was lucky, since his own house had been claimed by the duns and the constable. He'd be living at the Fleet for some time, unless he managed to pay off his creditors.

Now here was man who ought to be bribable, Rex

thought, estimating how much money he had on him. No transfer of funds was necessary, however, because Vandermere wanted to talk. He was deuced lonely in prison, he said, and bored. His friends did not stop by, afraid he'd ask for a loan. He was not afraid to answer Rex's questions, either. Perhaps word of Rex's reputation had not reached inside the prison walls, or else the man had nothing to fear.

Rex already knew Vandermere couldn't have killed Sir Frederick Hawley, not from his current address. Vandermere laughed when he asked about a hired assassin. "If I could afford to pay the going rate, I wouldn't be here, would I?" He'd be at the baize tables and the horse track, trying to win back his fortune.

He did know the late, unlamented baronet, to his regret. They'd been partners, he gladly told Rex, with a group of other men, investing in a shipping scheme that could not fail. Except it did. The reason the capital was lost, as well as any profits, was that Hawley had not made the final payment on time to ensure the cargo was shipped. Then he claimed the goods were stolen before he could negotiate another deal. No, Vandermere did not know the other investors, only the banker, Breverton. Vandermere suspected the project had something to do with smuggled goods because words like "warehouse" and "Calais" were mentioned, but he never inquired too closely. "Better not to know, eh?"

Hawley had refused to make good on the missing investment, saying he had lost his own fortune and did not have enough of the ready. Instead of tripling his money as the baronet had promised, Vandermere had lost it all, his house, his carriage, his mistress. That last hurt the most, especially when the disloyal wench never came to visit.

Nor did Sir Frederick come. "I guess that was lucky, or I might have been the one to send the dastard to his maker, and then where would I be?"

In a smaller cell.

So Sir Frederick was indeed connected to a shipping venture of some sort, which led Rex to Joseph Johnston, the merchant who had taken on Sir Frederick's valet. Johnston was away from home when Rex called. Brusseau was there. No, he did not kill Sir Frederick. No, he was not in the house at the time. His late master had told him he was not needed. How could he know who killed monsieur when he was not on the premises?

Everything he said was true, to Rex's disappointment. "You have a brother?"

"*Oui.* That is no crime, no?"

"Where is he employed?"

"Why, so you can call at his employer's residence and lay suspicion at his door? No, I have answered enough of your questions. Mademoiselle Carville had cause to wish Monsieur dead. That is enough, no?"

No.

He found Johnston at his offices near the docks, where the air stank of the tidal mud and Johnston's cigars. "I am busy, as you can see." He waved purchase orders, bills of lading, crew rosters, and a few gilt-edged invitations at Rex. "I do not have time for any half-pay officer playing at detective. You can show yourself out." He picked up another document, this one with an official seal on it.

"A moment more, please. I merely wish to know if Sir Frederick had dealings with your company."

"I take on many investors to finance my ships, and I do not keep track. The bank handles that."

"Breverton's Bank?"

"Among others. The contracts are all legal."

"Are they written up by Sir Nigel Turlowe, by any chance?" Rex guessed.

"Among others. Is that what this is about?" Now he put down the papers and took his cigar out of the corner of his mouth, setting it atop a stack of ship's logs. "You want to put some of your blunt on my ships? I'll tell you what I tell all the swells: I cannot guarantee anything. Ships sail, get blown off course, get pirated or shot at. If you can stomach the risk, I'll be happy to have more backing."

Paying for information was one thing, paying to smuggle goods in from France was another. Rex answered the man with another question of his own. "Why did you hire Brusseau, a Frenchman?"

"Why not? The chap was out of work. I must have met Sir Frederick a few times. He always looked bang up to the nines."

"But Brusseau had no references. He might have killed his former employer."

"The girl did it."

Odd, Johnston's statement was a definite red in Rex's mind, an outright lie, with no orange confusion, no yellowish thinking the words might be true.

"I say she did not kill Sir Frederick."

Johnston waved his cigar in Rex's face. "Are you accusing me?"

"He had a lot of money hidden at his house, not all belonging to him."

"That's right, some of it is mine! I'll have my lawyer see about claiming my share. I lost a good deal because of that." He spit out a bit of tobacco leaf. "But I did not kill him, not to get the money back, not to get even."

Bright blue.

Damnation.

Few names were left on his short list, and few hours remained to get ready for—*gads!*—the opera.

Damnation, with divas.

Chapter Twenty-four

The opera was not so bad. Rex got to sit next to Amanda. Lady Royce arranged it so, with them in the front of the private box for the world to see, while she and Daniel sat behind them. That way, she said, no one could notice Daniel's sallow complexion, or the yellow Cossack trousers he insisted were all the crack, or the puce waistcoat embroidered with orange butterflies. If his apparel was not enough to make everyone else bilious, too, she swore, she did not know what would.

As expected, every eye in the huge theater was directed toward their box, one of the best in the opera house. Even without all the current speculation, Rex alone would have stood out in his dress uniform, with its lace and gold braid, his stunning dark looks, his features still handsome despite the scar and a bit of discoloration around his eyes and nose. Nor could they miss Amanda, elegant in brown velvet the color of her eyes, with a black lace fichu at her neckline, and black ribbons under the high waist of her gown. Her pearls were at her neck, making her appear as demure and proper as a woman could look, considering she ought not be in public at all. No one could tell Amanda had butterflies of her own, in her roiling stomach.

Rex thought the careful image of ladylike decorum was destroyed by her headpiece. Instead of the feathers many women stuck in their piled coiffures, Amanda wore a gold tiara atop dashing blond curls. Lady Royce's gift, the tiara made his own offering seem paltry. Worse, the countess might as well have crowned Rex the king and Amanda his queen. Rulers of the gossip columns and the *on dits*, that was more like it. He knew that the audience was watching them instead of the stage, and every tongue was clacking with tidbits of their pasts, and their chancy futures.

Amanda knew they were the center of attention, too. Her head was held as regally high as royalty, but Rex noticed the way she nervously fidgeted with the lorgnette he had given her, which did not match her ensemble at all. The countess had raised her eyebrows at the token, but then she colored and stuttered when he'd handed her a ribbon-tied parcel also, before leaving for the opera. He'd stepped away to take their wraps from the butler, before Lady Royce could think of kissing him in gratitude. He thought Amanda was thinking of it, but they were not alone, curse the countess and her stratagems.

Now, when Rex and Amanda were even less private, he took her hand under cover of her skirts, and whispered to her about anything he could think of to ease her anxiety, and to drown out the whispers from the surrounding boxes. From what he could overhear, the countess was correct: Society was more offended at the lack of proper mourning than the crime Miss Carville was purported to have committed. No one mentioned her supposed lover, not with Lady Royce as her sponsor, and not with Rex glaring at them. Perhaps, he heard one skinny spinster in a turban declare, he was the man Miss Carville had been meeting on the sly. And how romantic that was!

Hell and damnation, he'd not been in Town until days after the murder! Still, if the gossip grapevine wished to wrap its tendrils around a fairy tale instead of a tragedy, and the countess wished to nurture the wayward creeper, he would play his role of gardener for tonight. He raised Amanda's hand to his and kissed her gloved fingers. Hers were trembling, and not from his touch, damn it.

"Stare them down, I say." He took the lorgnette from her and raised it to his eye to ogle the rouged dowager in the adjoining box, the one who had been condemning modern morals in a voice loud enough to drown out the orchestra's tuning. The matron smiled as if she had not been titillating her companions with tales of Rex's hell-raking about Town the past few days. "As for the cousin . . ." died on her lips.

Yes, Rex acknowledged, the countess had been right: Murder was nothing compared to a social blunder.

The opera began at last and most of the audience switched its attention to the stage, at least those not near enough to peer into the darkened private boxes. Rex took advantage of the dimmed chandeliers to hold Amanda's hand more tightly, to drape his other arm around the back of her chair, where his fingers could reach up to caress the back of her neck, the silky curls, the—"Ouch!"

His newly doting mother whacked his fingers again with the opera glasses—the ones he'd bought for the besom! He dropped his hand back to his own side of the chairs and watched as Amanda lost herself in the story and the music, the ones on the stage, not the drama playing through his imagination.

At the intermission, Rex woke Daniel before the jack-anapes could fall out of his seat, and announced he was going for refreshments. Lud knew his throat was dry after sitting next to Amanda without touching her, inhaling her scent without nuzzling behind her ear. What the devil was he doing, besides torturing himself?

"Keep everyone out," he ordered his cousin. "I do not want Amanda besieged by curiosity seekers."

He did not want any other man thinking she was unprotected and available, either, although the countess's presence would keep rakes and roués away. That lady, he understood, had dropped hints all afternoon to a few of her closest friends—thirty, at least—that Miss Carville possessed a fortune in gems and was about to have her dowry restored, although Rex had told her the decision was up to Amanda's stepbrother. She had also informed her friends, with unmistakable pride, according to Amanda, that dear Jordan was going to see to it that Amanda was vindicated shortly.

Hell, when had he become an object of pride for that female? It was bad enough that Amanda had her hopes pinned on him; she merely had a murder to disprove. He had years of rancor against the countess to overcome, as well as misinformation and bitter hurt. He'd concentrate on the murder.

At least now he had a motive, as he explained again to Amanda when he got back with the champagne. Sir Frederick had obviously embezzled the funds of a doomed investment group, whether at his own conniving or under orders from another. He'd made a lot of enemies, costing men their fortunes, and had no friends left. He was apparently planning on fleeing the country—Rex cast a glance at the countess, who was listening intently, along with Daniel, as he imparted this—which explained why he had the money at home, why he had stolen or usurped every farthing he could accumulate, and why he had pawned his family treasures and beggared his estate.

"But why didn't he leave as soon as the money was discovered missing?" Daniel asked, still disappointed the valet had proven innocent of the murder.

"Perhaps he was waiting for his own daughter to be married," the countess suggested. "He was bringing her out in style, albeit not lavishly."

Amanda did not think he was worried about Elaine. "Sir Frederick did not have enough fatherly devotion to care one whit about her happiness. He was intent on wedding her to a titled gentleman with money, no matter his age or her affections. He always seemed obsessed with titles."

Rex nodded. "Most likely so he could demand another fortune in marriage settlements. Or so he could use his new connections to avoid pursuit. Either way, I think one of his victims, his fellow investor in whatever scheme they were hatching, killed him, then tried to frame another of them for the murder by leaving his gun behind."

"Which I picked up, like a peagoose."

Rex touched her arm above her gloves, where it was bare. "But such a pretty peagoose."

The countess cleared her throat. Daniel groaned.

At the second intermission, Lady Royce demanded Daniel's escort for a breath of fresh air.

"I fear your mother is playing matchmaker," Amanda said, concerned lest Rex think she was manipulating him, too. "But please ignore her efforts. I may not understand your principles, but I respect them. And I know I have said it many times, but it bears repeating: You are helping me, and I did not expect that much. I shall never expect more."

He was holding her hand, and now he leaned closer so

no one overheard. Interested observers might suppose he was whispering tender love words in her ear. He did not care. "I may have begun your rescue as a favor to the countess. I might have continued in the interests of justice, and out of curiosity about what Sir Nigel was up to. But now I will not rest until you are a free woman, and that is for your sake, no one else's. You have every right to expect that, for what we shared."

She blushed like a schoolgirl, and he was reminded that she was still young, no matter how many years she had been forced to deal with life on her own. He wished he could take her in his arms right there, and to the devil with his vows of bachelorhood and childlessness. Jupiter, the woman was like a potent wine, stealing his inhibitions, his balance, his good sense. He sat back, as far from her as he could get, so he could think straight. "What we shared must not happen again."

"No," she agreed. "That would make me want forever."

Rex was saved from falling to his knees and promising just that by a sound coming from behind them.

"Why, look at the lovebirds," a low voice said, ending on a hiss. Sir Nigel, his hair pomaded in place and his neckcloth tied up to his ears, stepped into the countess's box, uninvited. "The new symbol of a travesty of justice. You will not get away with this, Rexford. Your father could not rewrite the legal system to include witchery, and you shall not, either, I swear."

"Good evening, Turlowe." Lady Royce sailed into the box like a man-of-war, all cannons firing. "I see you are still pursuing lost causes. My goddaughter is innocent. Now go away."

Sir Nigel did not leave. Instead he raised his voice for listeners in the surrounding boxes to hear. "I say she is guilty, and I intend to move the trial forward before this . . . this savage you call son makes a laughing stock out of the justice system."

The countess stood between the viscount and the barrister, like a lioness protecting her cub. She folded her arms across her impressive bust and said, "If you are half the man my son is, or my husband, you would know the truth instead of following the path that leads to your own advancement. I say that if you are in charge of our justice system, it is already a failure." She raised her own voice, with a growl in it. "You, sir, are no gentleman."

Sir Nigel turned purple with rage, his fists opening and closing, as if wishing he had the countess's throat between his hands.

Half-amused at Lady Royce's defense, and half-furious that Amanda was cowering in her seat, Rex thought about tossing the man over the balcony railing, but that might upset those beneath. No one wanted to be struck by falling night soil. "I will thank you to leave my mother alone," he settled on. "She obviously no longer wishes your presence. I never did."

Daniel was about to escort Sir Nigel from the box, by the knot in his neckcloth if necessary, but the countess cried out, "You called me mother!"

It had slipped out. Rex hurriedly redirected everyone's attention to Sir Nigel. "Furthermore, I wonder at your connection to the dead man. Had you been one of his fellow investors, those he choused out of a bundle? Your name was in his personal ledger book," he said, exaggerating on a pair of initials.

"What, you are suggesting I killed the man now? I did not!"

True.

"I had nothing to do with him."

False.

"No financial dealings?"

With so many people looking on, Sir Nigel could not slink away, nor bluster a refutation. Yet he feared a false-hood would strike him dead, like lightning. He knew Rex, like his father before him, was threateningly, terrifyingly different, although Sir Nigel did not understand how.

Rex capitalized on the man's hesitation. "You know I can recognize the truth. I can smell the fear on you. I can see your eyes looking for a hidey-hole. I can hear your breaths coming ragged and raspy. Tell me, in front of these people: Did you invest with Sir Frederick Hawley?"

Sir Nigel had no choice but to bluff. "Since when has a man's private business become public knowledge? I was at Almack's the night Sir Frederick was killed. I danced with Lady Bottswick." He gestured toward a many-chinned matron across the theater. "I saw your paramour leave the assembly. Everyone did. She is the guilty party, no one else. You are contemptible to cast doubts on hon-est citizens."

"And you, sir, are evasive. Honest? We shall see. I will find the answers, you can wager on it."

Daniel had one large hand on the barrister's shoulder, making Sir Nigel's knees buckle. He stumbled out, but called back, "I'll see you in court, or in hell."

Amanda expressed her concern when they were settled in the coach on the ride home. "Did Sir Nigel threaten you personally? That is what it sounded like to me."

Rex shrugged it off. "That man's posturing is of no ac-count. He is a lawyer, trained in dramatics. Why, he is a better actor than any of those on the stage tonight."

"Be careful," Lady Royce urged. "I never liked him, and trust him less."

"Don't worry, Aunt Margaret, I am at Rex's back," Daniel said, promptly falling asleep against the cushions.

They shook him awake when they reached Royce House, enough for him to stumble toward the stairs. "Didn't sleep a wink last night, you know. Good night, all. Lovely evening. Uh, what opera did we see?"

Dodd brought a tray into the parlor, but the countess was tapping her foot after a single cup of tea. "I think Amanda needs her rest, also. Tomorrow we have tea at Princess Lieven's, then a reception for the Ziftsweig delegation at the Austrian embassy."

Rex rose when Lady Royce did, but stayed Amanda with a smile. "Amanda and I need to speak of our progress."

"Surely you can speak in the morning. I think you have made quite enough progress with her."

Rex's cheeks grew warm. "I meant her case."

The countess raised her eyebrows.

Rather than let the two strong-willed Royces battle over her, Amanda stood and curtsied. "I am a bit weary. I, ah, hardly slept last night, either. I will bid you farewell, my lord. My lady."

The countess waited for Amanda to leave the room before turning to her son. "As for you, Jordan, you need to know that you cannot have your cake and eat it, too."

He could not have any, for Verity had eaten the last one on the tray while his attention had been on Amanda, and how her gown hugged her curves on the way out. He swallowed. "Meaning?"

"Meaning if you do not intend to marry the girl, you cannot dally with her. You can keep your bachelorhood, or you can warm yourself at the fire I see burning between you. Not both. I told you, I will not let Amanda's heart get broken, or her virtue given to anyone but her rightful husband."

She was right, Rex knew, but he could not help feeling insulted. "Would that you had stood up for me that way, just once in my life."

"I stood up for you all your life. I hired Nanny Brown and I selected your tutors. I fought to keep you from the army, then insisted you were put on the Aide's staff when I lost the battle. I—"

Rex interrupted. "You know him, the man they call the Aide?"

"Do not underestimate me, you silly boy. I know a great deal. I know your grades at school and your accomplishments in the military. I have spent my time, and my influence, with the authorities and their wives, defending your reputation, demanding you and your cousin be rewarded with advancements for your contributions. I did not cross you off my list like an unwanted guest at a dinner party. I will fight with every fiber of my body to keep you safe, but not at Amanda's expense. I will not let you be a heartless fool like your father. Do you understand?"

He bowed. "Good night, madam."

She stared back at him. "You called me mother."

"You called me a heartless fool."

He acted like one, too. He stayed awake for hours, thinking of the countess's words, yet still wanting what he could not have. He wrestled with his conscience, but lost the battle. He pulled on his robe, but not his slippers, to make less noise. Then he slowly opened his door, thanking the countess's efficient household that the hinges did not squeak.

*   *   *

Amanda knew she was a fool without anyone telling her so. She'd had all the happiness she'd asked for in one night; more, she expected, than many women experienced in a lifetime.

It was not enough. She knew Rex did not love her, although she believed he did care for her. He was definitely attracted to her, but that was not enough, either. His mother might demand an offer of marriage out of him, but that was ridiculous to contemplate for a woman in Amanda's position. No matter what the countess said, no matter how many jewels she found in her coffers, no one married a murderess.

She could not force Rex to love her, Amanda admitted, but she, sure as Eve talked to the snake, could make him make love to her. Tonight she wore a different silky nightgown, one trimmed with sweet little forget-me-nots she had embroidered on the bodice herself. She smiled. The night rail looked anything but sweet when paired with her mother's sapphire necklace. Amanda tiptoed to her door and peered out into the hall.

Lady Royce was *not* a fool. She had a footman stationed in the corridor.

Chapter Twenty-five

Lady Royce's plan—one of her plans, anyway—appeared to be working. Soon invitations to the countess included ones for Miss Amanda Carville, and their escorts, of course. All but the highest sticklers welcomed the party from Royce House, and one or two of those who refused to countenance the countess's questionable guests actually canceled their evening plans altogether, rather than offend Lady Royce. She was on too many charitable committees, behind too many worthy foundations, too big a contributor to political causes. Besides, as her son was quickly learning, too many people actually liked his . . . mother.

As for the others, what a coup it was for a hostess to have the latest scandal broth brewing right on her doorstep. The ladies vied to have their invitations accepted, sending round notes and reminders. They stopped inviting Sir Nigel after the countess declared she would not attend any function where the barrister was present. No one wanted to be excluded from her ladyship's elegant dinners; no one wanted to be in her black books. An official of the high court was nothing to a peeress of the highest social standing.

The beau monde was happy enough to have the dangerous cousins and the killer among them. Then, too, if Lady
Royce claimed Miss Carville was innocent and not bachelor fare as they'd heard, they would believe it, also. The
countess was known to be the most upright of matrons,
with nary a whisper of wrongdoing in all the years apart
from her peculiar husband. Loyal to a fault, she would
never hear a word against Lord Royce, either, the *ton* had
soon learned. What, believe that scurvy, scrimping Sir
Frederick instead of one of their own? Never.

Amanda was treated with courtesy, if not warmth. She
sat beside the countess and made pleasant conversations
without being pushing. She did not encourage the gentlemen, would not dance or go off alone, and she wore
somber colors. The polite world agreed that she was a
prettily behaved miss. But they had always thought so,
they told each other and the countess.

Everyone watched to see Rex's behavior toward the
young lady. He felt as if he were a canary in a flimsy cage
surrounded by hungry cats, all of whom were sharpening
their claws. He could not dance with Amanda, take her out
to the balconies, or find hidden paths through darkened
gardens. He could not sit beside her all night, keeping her
safe from the tabbies and the gossips. He could not stare
at her, admiring her poise, her charm, her luminous
beauty. He could not even tuck an errant blond curl back
under her bonnet, not without having the banns called.

So he took a page from Daniel's book and disappeared
as soon as he saw the ladies seated at whatever affair the
countess decreed they attend. That is, Rex tried to escape
the scrutiny and the speculation. Instead, he found himself
swamped with gushing misses, all wanting to declare they
had not killed Sir Frederick, just so they could be thrilled

and chilled by looking into his startling eyes. Young men wanted to know what he called the knot in his neckcloth. He called it a knot. They dubbed it the Rexford Knight Fall, in honor of his quest to rescue the lady.

Older men pressed him to join their political parties, their committees to reform this or to bolster that. He nodded politely without committing himself. Older women met the same fate: no promises, no encouragement. They bored him to tears, every one. Worse, he was wasting time, Amanda's time. The men on his list of suspects or conspirators did not attend the same gatherings as the countess. Lydia Burton certainly did not.

Daniel went where the countess directed, but was better at finding the card room or the refreshments table or an empty library with comfortable sofas for a nap. He had no title, no fortune, so had no metaphorical bull's-eye painted on his back. Every time a female spoke to him, he found a new itch to scratch.

"Why the devil can't they tell the truth?"

"What, they should say your neckcloth is a shambles, your dotted waistcoat is dotty, your conversation is dull, and dancing with you is a torture that their poor feet will never recover from? Be happy they lie and say it was a pleasure."

After a few days of this, both cousins rebelled. The countess allowed them to attend the theater instead of a rout party, where Daniel enjoyed the farce, and Rex enjoyed watching Amanda laugh as if she had no cares in the world. And he got to hold her hand where no one could see. They also went to view the Egyptian Exhibit and the new waxworks, where no one told lies. Of course, no one was alive, but Daniel and Rex found that a relief. On pleasant afternoons the cousins dutifully accompanied the ladies' carriage to the park, but both gentlemen rode off as soon as Lady Royce's friends gathered around, halting the flow of traffic behind them.

Rex's elusiveness seemed to add to his appeal as a man of mystery, a dashing soldier with a doubtful reputation. His pursuit by matchmaking mamas and their desperate daughters was merciless, which amused Daniel as much as the mummies had. Showing as much sympathy as his cousin, Lady Royce reminded Rex that a betrothal announcement in the newspapers would end the chase immediately.

Amanda decided she had been seen enough. She'd rather stay at home with a book, one with a happy ending.

Almost every morning Rex had a real gallop in the park, before the fog lifted, and before the paths were clogged with the dandy set showing off their ensembles, or Corinthians showing off their highbred horses.

After his ride Rex often went to assist Inspector Dimm. Daniel disliked going to Bow Street, saying he had rashes for hours afterward, but Rex found the work interesting, the criminal mind a fascinating study. As for Dimm, the Runner was thinking of taking a holiday, his first in dog years, because the crime rate was so low. He was winning commendations and collecting rewards for all the convictions, plus making the streets of London safer. If he could only figure out how Rex could tell the guilty from the innocent, he said, he'd be a happy man.

No news came from the Aide, or Major Harrison, or whatever name the man was using that week. No messengers accosted the viscount; no messages awaited him at McCann's. All Rex could do was go over his list and call on the last remaining names, with little success.

Robert Vincent, Esquire, was indeed another lawyer, a

solicitor who freely admitted drawing up some papers for Sir Frederick Hawley's prospective investors, but he did not recall the names or the amounts. His clerk had handled the petty details. No, the clerk was no longer in the lawyer's employ. He had emigrated to Canada. And no, Mr. Vincent did not have a copy. Lord Rexford could show all the warrants he wanted, his large cousin could glower until the cows came home, but a recent fire in the office had destroyed all of the files. Yes, he had invested some of his own money to finance a sailing venture.

"For what? Surely you must have asked what the ship was fetching?"

"I believe it was gold. Stolen gold. Gold from a sunken pirate ship that was recently discovered."

"You gave your gold to find gold?" Daniel was incredulous, but he was not itching.

"Hawley had the charts and records of the sightings, official ones, from the navy. It was all a hum, of course. No one knows where the *Black Speculator* went down."

With the name of the ship, Rex and Daniel could return to some of the people they had questioned before. Lydia Burton's door was closed to them, of course, but White's was not, and Lords Havering and Hove were both still dining there nightly.

Havering admitted he'd invested. Hove slapped his knee and laughed. He'd turned down the opportunity to bring back doubloons and bullion that existed only in a madman's pipe dream.

George Cuthbert had met with a hunting accident and was being sent to recuperate at his family's plantation in Jamaica. Now that Rex knew the right questions to ask, he discovered that Cuthbert was suspected of stealing maps and charts, old ones at that, from the Admiralty offices.

Joseph Johnston of the shipping business would not see them. He left by the back door of his office when they went in the front. He took refuge in his house, with six dock-workers guarding every entrance. No matter, one of his captains enjoyed the rum the cousins bought for him. What else was a sea dog like him to do, stuck in harbor? Yes, rumor had it they were to sail on some secret mission, but he was never ordered to outfit the ship for a journey, so here he sat, growing barnacles instead of rich. The *Black Speculator*? He laughed so hard he almost spilled his drink. Who would believe that old legend?

The banker, Breverton, had gone on a sudden vacation in Scotland, and Lysander Cord had moved out of the Albany, without a forwarding address. At least Roger Vandermere was still in Fleet Prison, but had no more information to add.

Bowdecker, the belligerent drunk, had been struck by a coach last week and was not expected to recover. Added to Cuthbert's injury and the fire at the law offices, Bowdecker's accident was looking highly suspicious.

By now Rex was having a hard time deciding which were the pigeons being taken, and which were the hawks doing the plucking. He could not tell the honest investors, if there was anything honest about the shady transaction, from those who had helped concoct the scheme. All he knew was that they were all left with nothing by Sir Frederick.

Then Murchison related a bit of information he had unearthed in the emigré community. Sir Frederick's former valet, Brusseau, not only had a brother, but the brother was known to travel to France, by the light of the full moon.

"I knew it! I knew they were involved with smuggling,"

Daniel swore when Rex told him at breakfast the next day, forgetting all of his other theories. "With all that money and havey-cavey treasure hunts, there was bound to be a French connection."

Rex knew Daniel would blame the constant rain on the French if he could. "But how can we prove it, and prove Sir Nigel and the others were part of it?"

"I say we find the brother and beat the tar out of him."

"You are forgetting that we are gentlemen now."

Daniel swallowed the rest of the kippers and looked around to make sure the countess and Amanda were busy at their own breakfasts, discussing the day's plans. "Um, coz, no offense intended, but I don't think gentlemen go around creeping into ladies' rooms in the dead of night."

"I did not go into her room. I was merely checking on Miss Carville's whereabouts, lest she escape out the window or something."

Daniel scratched his nose, and grinned. "Um-hum."

"And how did you find out I was in the hall anyway? You were fast asleep. I heard your snores."

"Dodd had it from the footman stationed in the hall. I gave both of them a coin to keep mum."

"So did I. The servants here will all be wealthy by the time we leave."

"When will that be, do you think? I love your mother and all, stands to reason, she's my aunt, but I have to tell you, I ain't much for the opera and the art gallery, and less for dance parties." He leaned closer to Rex. "And she's talking about taking Amanda to Almack's."

Rex fed Verity his suddenly unappetizing breakfast. "Hell. We better get to the bottom of this mess soon, and not just because that court date is looming. Too bad

Murchison's sources had no idea where the brother can be found."

"Then what if we find the valet and choke the information out of him? Oh, I forgot, we are gentlemen."

"Not by half, not when the alternative is Almack's. We'll try for him soon. He's bound to leave Johnston's place sooner or later." He posted watchmen outside the house, who watched the guards, who were watching for Rex. He also sent another note to McCann's Club, relating his latest findings.

Brusseau never showed his face, to Amanda's disappointment. She did not know what the cousins intended, thank goodness, but she knew they were running out of suspects, and out of time.

Rex tried to reassure her, not liking how her eyes had shadows under them and how she barely tasted the food set in front of her. They were getting closer, he swore. Soon they would unravel all the loose ends and find what Sir Frederick was truly doing with the money. Perhaps they would find he'd cheated others with his far-fetched tale of a lost pirate ship filled with gold waiting to be hauled up from the ocean floor. One of those men had to have killed him.

What kept coming back to haunt Rex was the notation N.T. Nigel Turlowe was the only name the Aide had supplied for those initials, and the only likely one among everyone Rex encountered at the men's clubs and the social gatherings. He and Daniel even scoured banks for officials with those initials, and looked over rosters at the Admiralty.

Sir Nigel, unsurprisingly, refused to speak with them, which was telling in its own way.

Rex had a worse problem. Charles Ashway came to

call. Amanda's former beau brought a huge bouquet of flowers, an abject apology, and his sister to prove he did not think Amanda a bad influence. A gentleman never introduced his kin to a ladybird, did he?

Rex glared, refusing to leave the room to give the jackass privacy to renew his suit.

As managing as always, Lady Royce demanded Rex show the sister the portrait gallery, while she consulted with her cook.

"This one died in battle. That one died of the plague. Great-great-grandfather choked on a cherry pit. Your brother must be ready to go home."

He was, rather than face Rex's obvious hostility. As soon as the door was shut behind Ashway and his sister, but before the countess could return to chaperon, Rex tugged Amanda out the rear door, to the gardens. "I don't care if it's too cold. I have not had you to myself in years, it seems."

Amanda laughed and grabbed her cape from its hook on the way out. Rex found a bench sheltered from the wind, and out of sight of the windows. He sat beside Amanda on the bench and put his arm around her, in case her cloak was not warm enough, he told himself. She sighed and leaned against his shoulder. Soon they were both warm enough to melt the stone bench.

"I take it you did not accept his offer? He was too quick to leave for a newly betrothed suitor."

She sighed again when he kissed the top of her head, then her ear. "He asked if he could pay his addresses once the legalities were disposed of. I told him I would speak to him then. He is a very nice man."

"He is a clod." He kissed her neck, touching the back of it with his tongue.

"His family is pleasant." She rubbed her hand over his chest.

"The sister had no conversation." He stroked her back, through the cloak.

Her hand found its way beneath his coat and waistcoat to his thin shirt, where she could feel his heart beating. "He offers security, a home, a family of my own."

Rex withdrew his hand. "Do you love him?"

"No, I never did."

He put his hand back, only this time under the front opening of the cape, to touch her heart, and her breast. "He did not believe in you at first, so he is not worthy of your affection." Rex thought about how his father never trusted his mother. "You will not be as secure as you might hope, because he will always have doubts."

"I know. But I will always doubt him, too, for being so ready to believe the worst. I had not expected love, but hoped for loyalty."

He started to unfasten the ties at the back of her gown. "You deserve both. Did he at least profess his love for you?"

She gasped when his hand touched her bare skin. "He never used that word, but he never used the word 'homicide,' either. He did mention diamonds and how there are none in his family. And that his sisters will be needing presentations at court, perhaps under Lady Royce's aegis."

"Mushroom."

"That is the way marriage is done these days." She was loosening his neckcloth.

He paused. "Will it be done? Will you accept him?"

Amanda stopped her hands too, to look into Rex's eyes. "I cannot imagine making love to him. How could I let him touch me the way you did? Kiss me as you do?"

Which deserved more than a touch, a kiss that was more than a meeting of lips. When Rex could breathe again he said, "Good. I'd have to kill the man if he tried. But . . ."

She pulled out of his arms and pulled her cape closer around her to ward off the sudden chill. "But I know, you will not offer for me."

Rex jumped up and started pacing in front of her. "Gads, what a cad I am. My mother is right." He supposed he was getting used to calling her that. "I am truly the dog in the manger, wanting to keep others from you, while I cannot have you for myself. I cannot force myself to keep away, though. I tried. I know right from wrong. I know we should not be doing this!"

"I know it, too. And I know we should not be alone together because the same thing will keep happening despite our good intentions." She stood, holding her wrap tight against her with one hand in case her gown was loosened. She raised the other hand to his lips. "I just wish you would tell me why you will not marry."

Rex touched the collar of her blue cape, the one so easily identified in the park at night. "I wish I knew who you met when you went out."

Neither spoke again as they returned to the drawing room.

Amanda went upstairs to cry. Rex left the house, knowing he would find no peace within its walls. He decided to go check on the watchmen he'd hired to be on the lookout for Brusseau at the shipping magnate's house. Daniel was at a prizefight at the outskirts of town, so Rex took Verity along, to the disgust of Lady Royce's fussy driver. Rex dismissed the carriage some blocks from Johnston's town house, and got out and walked, or limped, the better to gather his thoughts, to find a way out of the conundrum of his conscience. He wasn't really paying attention, this far from his goal, or listening for footsteps or clamoring instincts. Verity was, fortunately. The fur on the back of her neck stood up, while her head went down. She growled, low in her throat.

Rex slipped the blade from his sword stick. "What is it, girl?"

The better question was what good a flimsy sword was going to be against a man throwing bricks at Rex's head.

The answer was: not much.

Chapter Twenty-six

Rex woke up dead, looking down at his body. Twice. That is, there were two of him watching. He shook his head, which was a mistake. Satan's blacksmith started hammering, with Rex's skull as his anvil. Rex raised his hand to his temple, another mistake. A huge bandage covered most of his head, with a huge pain under it. Then another hand raised a glass to his lips.

"Here, drink. It might help."

Now there was one of himself hovering over the bed. "Am I dead?"

"Not yet. Badly concussed, though."

The voice was familiar, but not his. The hand holding the cup was not his, either. Rex tried to focus his eyes for a better look. This was his bedroom at Royce House, all right. The stranger had his own black hair, the same black-rimmed blue eyes, but no uniform. His clothes were well tailored, his boots highly polished. He was older, a bit heavier, but he was enough like Rex to be his—

"Bloody hell, you are the 'obligation' my father had all those years."

The man bowed slightly and frowned. "I generally prefer 'connection' to 'obligation.' Lord Royce owed me nothing, but has been generous beyond measure. Few men in his position would have been as openhanded, or as kind. You are lucky to have him."

Rex had to concentrate to keep the "connection" from splitting into two. Damn, one of his father's bastards was bad enough. "But who? How?"

"You can call me Harry."

"Like the Devil after all."

Harry laughed. "Others have noted the similarity."

If Rex's head hadn't been spinning, it was caught in a tornado now. Then something else occurred to him. "Great gods! You are here, in my mother's house! If this does not upset her digestion again, nothing will."

"I admit it is an awkward situation."

Hell, being at Royce House was awkward for Rex, and the countess was his own mother. If his wits had not been scrambled he might make sense of things, or at least know what questions to ask first. The first one of forty that popped into his addled brain was: "Yours?"

The stranger sat back down in the chair by Rex's bedside, as if he had been there a while and intended to stay. "My mother passed on long ago. She was a dancer, a beauty, they say, and nothing but a young man's fancy. An unmarried man, I must add. When she died, your father, my father, took responsibility and found a wonderful family to raise me. I've had a fine education, entree to places no opera dancer's son could expect, and exceptional career opportunities, all thanks to Lord Royce."

"Can you . . . ? That is, do you . . . ? Botheration. I do not believe you are my father's son."

Harry made a face as if he had tasted something rancid, which should have answered Rex's unspoken question. "You know I spoke truly, but I suppose you wish to test my skills. Yes, I can taste the truth. It is uncomfortable at dinner parties, but I cherish the gift as part of my heritage, another gift from my sire."

Rex's head was aching, and he knew he had more important facts to gather, but he had to know: "Then you do not find it a burden?"

"A burden, when I can help save civilization, or some such rubbish? I know I can make my little corner of it a better place. What could be more gratifying? I'll admit I find the necessary secrecy a strain, but then again, I also hide my true birth. Strange, is it not, a family so tied to the truth, hiding it from the rest of the world?"

Rex could not think straight enough to untangle that knot. He stayed on the topic that had gnawed at him for all of his life. "You do not resent being different from everyone else?"

"I feel I am repaying my debts for the chances I have been given. I can accomplish much that is worthwhile, things few others can do. I know you were invaluable to the army. Don't you find that gratifying?"

Rex recalled his military career, sifting through information to find the real facts so the generals could plan their strategies, saving soldiers' lives. Then he thought of his work with Inspector Dimm, preventing crime by ridding London of so many guilty criminals. "Yes, I suppose some good can come of it. Do you mind the other?"

"Hiding the true tale of my birth? That is the way of the world, I regret to say. By-blows are outcasts in our society, so, no, I do not repine on what I had no hand in. Or do you mean do I mind not being in line for the earldom? Not having to attend Parliament, not being responsible for legions of dependents, not supposed to produce the heir? Hell, no. Besides, I never expected to be the earl's heir.

You were born Rexford, in the bed where generations of Royce heirs saw their first dawn. I was born in a boarding-house, on the wrong side of the blanket."

"Then you always knew? Your adopted family told you?"

"They did not need to. I was four when I came to them. Recall, I could tell when I heard the truth or a lie. Tasting sour lemons every time your new father called you 'son' was a bitter lesson, soon learned. And the earl was a frequent visitor. Our appearance was too similar to be accidental." Harry stood up again and brought the glass back to Rex's lips, changing the subject. "Here, they said you need to keep drinking."

Rex sipped carefully, trying not to move his head, which was more painful than thinking.

A bastard, a brother. Blazes!

Rex could not begin to absorb all he'd heard, not with the din in his skull. Which reminded him of his own circumstances. "How did I get here? I don't recall anything of what happened after seeing someone hurl a brick at me."

"Your dog started howling like all the hounds of hell, thank goodness. Half the residents of the neighborhood closed their shutters and hid at the noise, but others came running, some of them the men you hired. They found a hackney and got you here, just in time, the surgeon said."

"Verity, she is all right?" Rex did not dare raise his head to look for the mastiff.

"Fine, except for a stitch or two. The surgeon who attended you was not willing to do the sewing at first, but your mother quickly set him straight."

Rex could imagine. It would take a brave man indeed to disobey the countess's orders.

"The hero of the day is in the kitchen right now, being pampered and fussed over and fed the dinner you won't feel like eating. The dog, of course, not the surgeon."

The very mention of eating made Rex's stomach clench, and also reminded him of his cousin. He had to tell Daniel to be extra alert. "My cousin?"

"Mr. Daniel Stamfield, if that is who you mean, is out bashing heads. He was furious that you'd gone out without him, and feeling guilty that you'd been accosted, so he decided to revenge himself on the denizens of the neighborhood where you were attacked. Your friend Dimm is with him, at least, so I suppose he will not be arrested. I believe Stamfield's mayhem is masquerading as a search for your assailant."

"Daniel takes his guard dog role too seriously." Rex knew he'd shoot anyone who harmed Daniel, so he could not fault his cousin for going off in a berserker rage, except that it was a vain effort. "He'll never find the man, and I could not help identify him, either. I did not get a good look at him, and he wore a wide-brimmed hat that hid his face."

"Ah, but he should be easy enough to find if Daniel and Dimm are quick enough. A trail of blood led away from where you were found, not the pool of red you were lying in. We assume the dog went after the brick thrower. That's how she came to be hurt. How many men are out there with tooth marks on them? Someone will know who needed stitches or who wears a bandage."

That made sense, and Daniel would find the man if anyone could. Rex hoped Dimm kept him from killing the dastard long enough to discover who had hired the attack. Other than worrying about the name of his enemy, Rex could not wait to tell Daniel about their new relation.

"I say, can I mention you to my cousin? He'd never bandy your birth about, you know. I trust him with my life."

"He already knows. He'd heard rumors, you see, in Town. It's my eyes, I suppose. I try to keep out of the public sight, but what's a man to do? One look was enough to bring the pieces of the puzzle together for him."

"And he never told me the rumors? That rotter." Rex thought he would not have been so shocked if he'd been warned. A brother, damn, and a gentleman, it appeared. He still was not used to the idea. "What about you? Where did you come in?"

"Your mother sent for me. No, don't try to shake your head in disbelief. You are supposed to stay still. Lady Royce got the notion that someone tried to kill you in particular, that it was not a random robbery. You still had your money and your watch. Of course the dog might have frightened a cutpurse off before he could grab anything. On the other hand, the animal could have gone for an assassin's throat when he tried to finish you off."

Rex was certain it was a murder attempt. "I'd been warned." And he'd ignored the warnings, damn it. "But what can you do?"

Harry smiled. "Remember, I am not a gentleman. I can speak to people who will never talk to you. I know my way around London's underside, and have connections in all walks of life. Furthermore, your mother called for me because time is running out."

"I thought you said I wasn't dying."

"No, you are not, and you are regaining your wits nicely, too. The surgeon held out no guarantee that you would, you understand, after such a blow to the head."

Rex did not want to think of the possibilities. He was

alive and somewhat coherent, unless he was imagining this whole bit about his father's butter stamp. The pain in his head was proof enough that he was not dreaming. "You said time was passing?"

"You have been in a coma for two days. Turlowe heard of your, ah, injury and he is trying to move Miss Carville's court date closer."

Rex tried to jump out of bed, and almost lost consciousness from the dizziness and the agony. Now he had two brothers looking at him again, this time in concern.

"Steady on, lad. They cannot give you laudanum for the pain, not with a head wound. You'll do better lying still."

Rex couldn't do anything else. He hoped his new relative did not see the dampness in his eyes. "Lud, I am helpless. What am I going to do?"

"Well, none of us think there is much you can do, right now, or for the next few days at least. So Lady Royce sent for the earl. He is on his way."

Rex stared at the ceiling, trying to make the room stop spinning. "Now I am certain I am dead and hell has frozen over."

Harry laughed. "Not quite. And I am here to help meanwhile. The countess even let me sit with you while she slept. Your old nursemaid had to be put to bed herself, from the shock of seeing you carried into the house."

Rex tried to think. He did not know this man, could not rely on him, a stranger with the same blood running through his veins, but a stranger for all that. "If you would, please send word to a man called the Aide. Have you heard of him?"

The man's mouth quirked up in a smile. "Everyone has."

"He is a smoky fellow, but he can help. The man has his fingers on the pulse of civilization, it seems."

The smile grew broader. "He will get the message, I swear."

Rex believed him, as he saw a wash of blue through the veil of pain. He tried to lift his hand to shake his new relation's, then let his drop to the mattress when he could not get it past his shoulder.

"I owe you."

Harry tucked the blankets up. "Not at all. I always wanted a brother."

"Did you know I existed?"

"Almost from the day you were born. The earl was so happy, so proud. And he did not want me to hear the news through the grapevine."

"But he did not care if I did?" Then Rex grew more upset. "Why did you not come find me? I wanted a brother, too, someone who could answer questions."

"You were an infant, my boy. Later, our father was convinced that you would be embarrassed. I think he did not want to admit to a youthful indiscretion. Your mother, well, she did not want to acknowledge me at all."

"They were wrong."

"I think so, too. We'll make up for the lost years as soon as you are well."

"And you will look after Amanda for me now?"

"Of course."

He spoke too readily for Rex's comfort. "I say, are you married?"

"No, I have not found the right woman yet. You know, one who will understand our, ah, idiosyncracies."

Both of them thought of their father and his wife. Rex

said, "You wouldn't want to live with a woman who did not accept what you are."

"No, but it appears you have found a treasure who just might do. Judging from her tears, she's fond enough of you to accept anything."

Rex was not going to discuss his feelings toward Amanda and marriage, not with a man he had met twenty minutes ago. "I am not sure yet."

"Well, I better be going in case you decide, to make sure you can have the bride you want, if you want." He headed toward the door.

Rex stopped him. "Harry?"

"Yes?"

"Thank you. Truly."

Harry smiled. "What are brothers for?"

Chapter Twenty-seven

Amanda took the first chance she could to nip into Rex's room. The newcomer had gone, Lady Royce was resting after her night's vigil, Daniel was again out combing the streets for the would-be killer, Nanny was in a laudanum-induced sleep, and Murchison was furiously scrubbing his lordship's uniform to get the bloodstains off it. They all knew the viscount could purchase another and was resigning his commission shortly anyway, but Murchison needed something to do.

So did Amanda. She was tired of fretting outside Rex's door waiting for news of his welfare or of Daniel's hunt. Daniel had laughed when she pleaded to accompany him, blood in her eyes. She was already accused of one killing, he'd said. That was enough. Amanda was so mad she felt another murder would not matter. Besides, ridding the world of the rat who had thrown the brick at Rex was not murder; it was extermination.

Amanda dismissed the footman who was assigned to watch the viscount until Lady Royce or Murchison arrived. The man protested that he had his orders to stay, but Amanda took a page from her godmother's book, raised her eyebrows, tapped her foot, and crossed her arms. The servant left.

Amanda walked softly toward the bed. Rex was lying so still, his eyes closed, that she feared her worst nightmare had turned true, but no, someone would have told her. She could breathe again.

They had him dressed in a white nightshirt that was far too big. He slept naked—Amanda blushed to think of how she came to know that—so they must have borrowed the bed gown from Daniel. The cuffs were folded back, his hands atop the covers with billows of fabric at the sleeves, like a buccaneer pirate's shirt. The overlarge neck opening gaped far enough for her to see the start of that faint line of soft, dark hair down his chest, the well-formed muscles. She clenched her fists to keep herself from reaching out to touch him, to make sure his heart was beating. Closer now, she could see that his chest was rising and falling in even measure, not labored or strained. She took another breath.

Between the white nightshirt, the white sheets, and the white bandage on his head, Rex could have been a ghost, or one of those Egyptian mummies they'd seen. His face had almost as little color, but he was alive and not in the troubling coma any longer.

She was as quiet as she could be, intending to sit in the chair and watch, or will him to recover, but a sigh of relief must have escaped her. His blue, blue eyes opened. He blinked a few times as if trying to remember where he was, who she was.

"It is I, Amanda."

The viscount tried to smile without moving anything that might hurt. "Yes, I know. I was just making certain you weren't a dream. For a minute I thought I had died and gone to heaven."

She pulled the nearby chair closer to his bed and sat down. "Silly. You are *not* going to die."

"No matter how much I feel as if I am ready for the grave, or so Harry told me. Did you know I had a brother?"

"I heard. And I met the gentleman earlier. He did not disturb your rest, did he?"

"Other than shaking the foundations of my life's history and my confidence in my parents' wisdom, no."

"He is rather formidable, don't you think?"

"Formidable? Did you find him so? By George, he was not insulting toward you, was he?"

"Oh, no. He just seemed confident and commanding, somewhat like how you appeared to me at first."

"Arrogant, you mean?"

"Not at all. You were a soldier, an officer, every inch a gentleman. And he is . . ." She did not quite know what Harry was. "A self-made man, I suppose, yet a gentleman."

"Indeed, and I admire him for that. I found him to be a fine fellow, one I would like to know better. Handsome, too," he added.

Amanda laughed. "What, are you fishing for compliments? You must know he could be your twin, except he is older and does not have the distinguished scar on his cheek. But you are far better looking."

"I am? How do you figure that, if we are so alike?"

"His nose is perfectly straight. It has no character."

"Do not make me laugh, my skull hurts too much." He raised his hand an inch or two off the mattress. She took it and carried it to her cheek. "Oh, Rex, I was so worried."

"Don't you know I have the hardest head in the kingdom? Except for my father, perhaps."

"But you could have died!" She brushed away the tear that had fallen from her cheek onto his hand. "And it was all my fault."

"Hush, angel. You were not to blame. How could you be? I was the bacon-brained idiot who went off alone with nothing but a dog and a flimsy sword stick. That was almost as foolish as walking into the French patrol."

She swiped at her eyes with the sleeve of her gown. "You rushed off without thinking because you were upset with me. You would not have gone near Mr. Johnston's house in the first place except on my behalf. I daresay you would never have encountered the man at all, because you would not have been in London if not for my difficulties. I have brought you nothing but trouble. And now this." She turned her face away, knowing tears upset him.

He squeezed her hand, not with any degree of force, but enough to make her look at him. "You have brought me awake."

She pulled her hand away, ready to leave. "I am so sorry. They said you should not sleep constantly, but if you are weary . . ."

"No, I mean awake to life. I was half-dead back in the country, with no ambition and no goals or desires, nothing but clouds on the horizon. I am still not certain about what to do with myself, but now I have seen the rainbows and the stars, thanks to you. I would trade that for any number of broken heads."

Amanda found her handkerchief and blotted at new tears caused by his words, not her guilt. "You will do something fine, I know. You will help your father, and you will help your Inspector Dimm. You will learn to be as

good an earl as your own sire." That was her fondest hope
and most fervent prayer, that he would realize his duty to
beget the next heir, no matter what mutton-headed vow
he'd sworn to himself.

He reached for her hand again. "Thank you for your
confidence in me, that I will be a worthy successor to the
title."

"You believed in me, remember?"

"Ah, but I had proof."

"You did? Then we can disprove the charges against
me?" In a perverse way Amanda was disappointed. She
was thrilled not to be awaiting the gallows, of course, but
once exonerated of the charges, she'd have no excuse to
reside with Lady Royce. Lord Rexford would have no further need to stay on in London. "Did you find evidence at
Johnston's house?"

"Um, not quite. My proof is not exactly submissible to
the court."

"I do not understand."

"I want to explain, truly I do. Perhaps I will be able to
make you see someday." He made a feeble attempt at an
excuse: "When I am feeling better."

"I will try to be patient." She leaned over to kiss his
cheek. "I hear footsteps. That is either the footman with
the beef broth I sent him to fetch or Murchison with your
uniform. Murchison is to sit with you this afternoon."

"You'll come back?"

His wanting her company meant Amanda would move
heaven and her godmother to visit him again. "As often as
your mother permits me. She thinks we must behave with
discretion, especially with our increased notoriety after
your incident."

The footsteps she heard were more a scrabbling of hurrying claws on the bare wooden floor, through the door Amanda had left open for propriety's sake. "Oh no!"

She threw herself in front of the viscount just as Verity launched her heavy body to rejoin her master on the bed.

The dog's weight knocked her over, right atop Rex.

The dog sat wagging her tail, licking Rex's face, then Amanda's as she tried to disentangle herself from Rex.

"Ahem."

Murchison was at the door, with a tureen and a ladle and a towel, to serve Rex his soup.

"The dog jumped," Amanda blurted out. "I was protecting Lord Rexford. I fell, I swear."

"Um-hum."

"Nothing indecent about this at all," she said, scrambling off the bed, pulling down her skirts and pulling up her neckline, scrubbing at her cheek where the dog had slobbered in joy at being united with her master.

"Hmm."

"You can ask Lord Rexford."

Murchison could ask, if he felt like speaking, but he'd get no answer. Rex had passed out from the pain. The dog, the woman— How many bricks had he been hit with?

He was unconscious again.

The French were firing, pulling Rex from the sweetest dream of Amanda in his arms. No, those were not rifles, he realized, they were loud voices, angry voices, fired across his bed.

"I shall sit with him."

"No, I shall."

"He is my son!"

"He is my son, too."

Good grief, his parents were in the same room, his

room, and they were arguing over him as if he were the last tart on the platter. Rex decided to keep his eyes closed until they figured it out.

"You look too feeble to watch over a flea," the usually polite and poised countess hurled at the earl.

"Well, you don't look like any spring rosebud yourself," the ever-calm and even-tempered earl fired back.

"I haven't lived like a hermit, if that's what you mean, hiding myself away and eating heaven knows what."

"Well, I have not been trotting about town to every gad-fly entertainment."

"No, you have been nursing your grievances in solitude for decades."

"While you have forgotten you were ever married."

"Oh, no, you don't, my fine lord. You dare not accuse me of infidelity, not ever again, not once! I have honored my wedding vows—you know I am speaking the truth—and that is the last time I shall defend myself against your charges for all of eternity. I remember my promises every day, and I remember how you stole my son from me."

"You left us!"

"You forced me to leave!"

"You could have come back."

"You told me not to."

"And so you did not come for the son you now profess to love with a mother's devotion. Bah! Leave us alone again, and go to a play or a party or a masked ball. You'll like that."

"I am sure you'd like me to leave my house, and my son, so you can claim them again. I will not go!"

"They *are* mine, madam! This is Royce House, he is Jordan Royce, and I am Lord Royce."

"I am Lady Royce, you wretched old man, and have every right to be here."

"You sent for me."

"I would not have, if I thought you were as cantankerous as always. But now that you are here, do something useful. Go to your friends at the high court and stop Sir Nigel Turlowe from calling Amanda's trial for next week."

Next week? Rex struggled to sit up, ignoring the pain. Amanda's trial was next week and he was still abed? Damn it! And damn his parents for caring more about past arguments than Amanda's future. Then he felt a hand on his chest, pushing him back. He looked up to see Amanda's face, pinched with concern. She was not looking at him, but at his parents, at either side of his bed.

"My lord, my lady, can you not see you are causing Lord Rexford pain and agitation, which the surgeon said was bad for his recovery? *I* shall sit with him."

The countess recalled her manners. "I am sorry we aired our dirty linen in front of you, Amanda, but you can go now. The earl and I can act like adults and resolve the matter amicably."

"Quite right, my dear Miss Carville, and I also apologize that you had to hear our little contretemps. My wife and I shall take over the sickroom duties now."

Little contretemps? Rex thought. He'd swear the entire household heard them, if not the neighborhood. He was about to speak, but again Amanda stopped him.

"I am sorry to disoblige you, sir, but I will not leave Rex until I am certain you will not shout and carry on, or do each other injury."

The countess smiled. "If we have not torn each other to shreds by now, we shall survive our son's recuperation. Furthermore, you know how improper your presence in his bedroom is. We have been at pains to correct any un-fortunate impression your own illness created."

The earl nodded. "Highly irregular, miss. You'd best go along before you start still more tittle-tattle. I have already sent messages to anyone with influence at the magistrate's office. The trial will not be held until your defense"—he looked down at his son, who looked away—"is quite ready."

"I care nothing for the gossip, my lord. I do care for Lord Rexford. He was injured on my behalf, so I feel re-sponsible. I thank you for your assistance, and I regret that you had to travel all this way, but I will not leave now." She took a deep breath and looked at both of Rex's rela-tives in turn. "You have caused him enough pain. I do not know your differences, and have no right to interfere, but I beg you to consider the harm you have caused the son you swear you love. You have kept him from his own brother, and from having two caring parents. Please, go settle your differences elsewhere, without tearing him apart between you two."

The earl and the countess looked at each other, then at Amanda. Finally they looked at Rex. He smiled, and held out a hand to Amanda. "My angel."

"She is right, you know," the countess told her hus-band, leading him from the room. "And you need a good meal. I'll have Cook fix your favorites. Do you still prefer lamb over beef?"

The earl glanced back once, then followed his wife. "I like that gal. She has a good head on her shoulders, and good bottom, too."

"Of course. She is my godchild."

Chapter Twenty-eight

Too bad Rex could not enjoy the company he wanted, now that he had Amanda in private. The door was left open for convention's sake, but they were alone for however long it took his parents to eviscerate each other. Just him and both of her. Damn.

She laid a cool cloth across his eyes and told him to rest. Rest? That was all he had been doing, and the sands of time were cascading through the hourglass. Still, Amanda's touch was soothing. When Murchison applied a cold towel to Rex's head, it felt like a sack of wet sand pressing his brains against the sides of his skull as if to hold off a flood. When Amanda did it, he felt butterfly kisses, the lightness of a spring day. He sighed in pleasure. Not as much pleasure as he wanted to feel, even in his debilitated state. He wasn't dead, after all.

He sighed again, because he might as well be. "I suppose they think it's safe to leave us alone, knowing I am too weak to ravish you."

He could not see with the cloth over his eyes, but he could hear the smile in Amanda's voice when she asked if he wanted to ravish her.

"Take you against your will? Never. You must know I

would never hurt you. But want you? I have wanted you since the first time I picked you up and you fit so well in my arms. I despised myself, because you were helpless, needing care and protection. But then I had to bathe you and I was lost. I might be despicable, but your body is like a magnet to me, a lodestar with a siren's song. Then, knowing you, hearing you, seeing your courage and virtue, I found more to admire, more to desire. I suppose it is fortunate I am too befuddled to do any ravishing."

"But I am not." Her hand stroked his cheek, where Murchison had shaved him that morning. "Recall, I was the one who came to your room. I wanted you ever since I woke up in your arms, knowing I was safe. Everything about you befuddles me, and I have no broken head for an excuse."

He pulled the cloth off his eyes so he could see her— one of her, thank goodness—and note the rosy color that stained her cheeks at the admission of unladylike impulses. He blessed those impulses. "Gads, you are so beautiful I could weep for not being able to hold you again. No matter how wrong I know it might be."

She placed a feathery kiss on his lips. "But would it be so wrong? You almost died. I might still face the hangman."

"It would be very wrong," he insisted, the edges of his vision starting to blur from the effort to keep her steady and single in his sight. "But for the life of me I cannot remember why."

"Because I would only love you more, and you would feel duty bound to offer for me. That would be far worse."

He heard her distress, that he should speak of wanting, while she spoke of love. He tried to soften her disappointment. "I feel far more than wanting, angel. Truly I do."

She smiled. "I know that, silly. Do not fret. I shall not take advantage of your weakened state. Should I leave?"

Leave, when he felt a hundred times better, simply by having her near? "Please stay. Your touch is like . . . Your voice is like . . . Hell, I am no poet. I just like having you here. Please stay, talk to me."

Amanda sat beside his bed with the chair pulled close, but she kept her hand atop his. At first they spoke of his parents, but Amanda did not know all of the stumbling blocks between the older couple, and Rex was not ready to explain about the truth-seeing. She would only suppose his brain was severely damaged by the brick. Worse, what if she ran off, thinking her protectors, Daniel, the earl, Harry, and himself, were all demented or all deviants? He was not ready to put her understanding to the test.

He felt disloyal, but to her or his family, he could not say. He decided to ask about her parents instead. Had they been happily married, her mother and father? How had they met? Had they wished for other children? He had few enough examples of good matches, love matches, to consider.

Marriage was not a good topic at all, he realized when Amanda started gnawing on her lower lip. Her parents were dead, and her last beau, Ashway, wanted her for material gain, not affection. As for himself, well . . .

"They are getting closer to the valet's trail," he quickly said.

She leaned forward and squeezed his hand, as eager to drop the subject of marriage as she was for more news. "Do you truly think they will find Brusseau soon? Nearly three days have gone by."

"If it is at all possible, Daniel will find him. Dimm is helping, and half of Bow Street is after the reward we've

posted. Harry says he knows the demimonde, the underworld, and he'll be paying for information there. The valet
cannot have gone far, not with the men we stationed at the
docks and the posting houses and tollbooths asking for an
injured Frenchman."

"But what if he was not the one who threw the brick?
You said you already believe he did not kill Sir Frederick."
She did not ask why he believed the valet. Perhaps Brus-
seau had an alibi.

"If he did not commit the murder, he knows who did. I
think he is the one who attacked me because his height
and weight fit the man in the alley, and no one else has
reason. Besides, if Brusseau is not guilty of assault, or
lying wounded by Verity, why did he go to ground? He
knows we are looking for him, and we know he is not at
Johnston's any longer." He took her hand in his and let his
thumb rub against her wrist. "They'll find him. We'll have
answers. Then we can think about those other questions."

Before Amanda could ask about the other questions,
Rex fell asleep. When he awoke, Amanda's hand felt
cooler and stiffer in his. "Have I kept you sitting here too
long, sweetheart?"

"Not at all, darling," Lady Royce said dryly, patting his
fingers.

He grabbed his hand back and tucked it under the covers. His mother brought a cup of lemonade to his mouth
and then dabbed at his lips when he was finished drinking,
almost as if she knew what she was doing. "Thank you,"
he said. "Where is Amanda?"

"Where she belongs, which is anywhere but your bedroom. If you were not so ill I would give you a piece of
my mind for what you are doing to that poor child.
Doesn't she have enough to worry about?"

How could he tell her godmother that Amanda felt her virtue entirely dispensable? "As you can see, I am not up to hell-raking today. Perhaps tomorrow."

"Sarcasm is uncalled for, and I do not refer to Amanda's innocence. I am thinking of her heart, you lummox. I warned you I would not tolerate your trifling with her tender feelings."

Rex tried not to squirm like a child with his pockets full of pilfered cookies. "Speaking of tender feelings, have you and my father finished tearing strips off each other? Is he on his way back to the Hall?"

The countess fussed with the pitcher of lemonade and glasses on the bedside table rather than face Rex. "Royce and I have agreed to cry peace. We did not so much as toss the turtle soup at each other at dinner. Of course, I insisted Amanda join us for the meal to maintain the pretense of politeness, but we managed quite well. Your father was charmed, as I knew he would be. He has agreed to stay in Town to help clear Amanda's name."

"I am relieved that she will have his expertise in legal matters, especially when I cannot count on riding to her rescue."

"No one knows more about the law than your father. He is resting now. I do not know what that man was thinking, to let himself get so frail."

Rex supposed heartbreak and disappointment had much to do with the earl's condition. "Do you care?"

"I do." When she knew that Rex understood she spoke the truth, she came back to his side and straightened the covers around him. "Would it bother you to see me and your father reconciled?"

Rex remembered the argument he'd overheard. "Is that possible, after all these years?"

"I pray so. I have always loved him, you know. Now we are older, and hopefully wiser, and have seen the cost both to you and to us in all the wasted years. I am not afraid of him any longer, or you, seeing what a fine man you are and how much good you have done. His other son has turned out to be an excellent gentleman also, with no assistance from me, to my shame. Royce swears he trusts me, and will never doubt me again. More, we have both realized that pride is a sorry companion. We have enough regrets. Maybe we have a chance to find happiness."

"Nothing would please me more," Rex said, wishing she could recognize the truth when she heard it. Both of his parents seemed incomplete and alone. They needed each other, while he had his own life to make. "Try." He tapped his bandaged head. "We Royce men have thick skulls, you know. But we can change. We can learn."

"I hope so, for my sake, and for Amanda's sake."

She left Rex alone to think, but his mind shied in so many different directions he could barely catch an idea to harness. He was concussed, he told himself, not half-crazed with trying to tell himself lies about murder and marriage and Amanda. He fell asleep again, wishing she were beside him. Forever.

"Impossible," he muttered when he woke up.

"I agree," Murchison said in French. The usually silent valet was frenzied, trying to care for three gentlemen at once, one wounded, one weary from his journey, and one wearing circus costumes.

"News, man, what news?" Rex did not even know what day it was, or how much time had passed.

Murchison gave a Gallic shrug. How did he have time to find a killer? Then he gave a piercing whistle that knifed through Rex's poor head, but brought a footman running with a clean nightshirt. They crammed the vis-count into it, leaving him damp and seeing double again. Damn, he had to get better before they killed him! And where was Amanda?

Later—at least he thought it was later, because the room appeared darker—he thought he saw her in the corner with some sewing. "Angel?"

"Why, the angels have not come for you yet, Master Jordan," Nanny Brown whispered, looking over her shoulder. Her eyes were all swollen with weeping, and her fingers were trembling so hard that he felt it necessary to take the cup of tea she brought him before she spilled it on his chest. Rex was not up to having his nightshirt changed again. But he was better, he was relieved to see. He could even bring the cup up to his lips without bumping his nose, and there was only one of his old nursemaid.

"Do not worry yourself into a decline, Nanny. I'll be fine. Why don't you find your own bed?"

"Oh, I could not leave you alone!"

Since his bladder was full from all the water, tea, lemonade, barley water, and soup they'd been pouring down him, she'd better leave, or embarrass both of them. Nanny scurried out when he made his need for the chamber pot known, and Rex was pleased to see he could do something else for himself finally. He'd be up and about his business—Amanda's business—before the surgeon could say permanent damage.

His next caller was not Amanda, either, but he was happier to see his cousin than he expected. "Have you any news?"

"No, but I have raspberry tarts fresh from the oven. Best eat them quickly before that starchy cook of my aunt's comes with a carving knife. Don't know what the woman was saving them for, if not family."

"I cannot feel like eating."

"Even better," Daniel said, splitting the first one in half to share with Verity. "I thought you'd be starving, after all that infant food they serve in the sickroom."

He'd come back from the search, he said between bites, to see if Rex remembered anything more about his assailant. They both knew he'd come back to check on Rex's progress. "Happy to see you looking more the thing." He took another bite, then studied the remaining tart. "Word is you've been looking at Amanda like she's as sweet a morsel as this. Your mother doesn't trust you with the gal."

"Interfering autocrat," Rex muttered.

Daniel smiled and wiped crumbs off his mouth. "When are you going to admit you love her?"

"The countess?"

His cousin laughed. "Miss Carville. Your ears are turning red just thinking about her. Bet your heart is racing, too."

"Lust and love are not the same thing."

"Have you ever wanted a woman more?"

Rex did not bother trying to lie to his cousin. "No."

"And aren't you half killing yourself trying to free her from suspicion?"

"I suppose," Rex murmured. "But there's more to it than that, like solving the crime and finding Sir Nigel's role in the embezzlement scheme."

Daniel snorted, sending crumbs flying. "Could you live without her?"

"How should I know? Just make sure I won't have to, damn it." Rex changed the subject. "I suppose you've heard about Harry?"

"You can never have enough relatives, eh?"

"What do you think of him?"

"He's great guns. We went back to Lydia Burton's place last night for dinner, and to see if any of the girls heard anything."

Daniel was not known for asking questions around willing women, or needing an excuse to visit a bordello. "I cannot believe Mrs. Burton let you in."

"She and old Harry have been friends for ages, it seems. See how useful kin can be? The ladies didn't know anything, but we had a grand time seeing who could tell the biggest clankers."

"Whatever for?"

Daniel started on the second tart. Verity whined until he shared. "Testing our skills, I suppose."

"A pissing contest, more like it. Who won?"

"Well, I'll have a rash for another week"—Daniel adjusted his privates—"but old Harry cast up his accounts on Lydia's new rug. I guess we won't be going back there soon." He and Verity both sighed, the dog because the food was gone. "We're to go to some of the other brothels tonight."

Rex decided to talk to Harry about leading Daniel astray, or following him. For now, he said, "Be careful, old chap. Even you are no match for an assassin's bullet or a thrown knife. And I don't fancy losing my new brother so soon, either. Look after him, will you?"

Daniel was laughing as he left.

Rex did not see the humor of his two kin out facing danger while he was stuck in bed, alone, so he decided to test his own strength by getting up.

Amanda found him on the floor, his disordered night-shirt leaving little to her imagination. "No, I am not hurt.

No, I do not need a blasted footman to help me back into the bed, and no, you do not need to hide your giggles behind your hand. I missed that sound."

Once he was back under the covers, Amanda stayed and read to him from he knew not what volume. He enjoyed hearing her voice, smelling the light floral scent she wore, watching her chest rise and fall, with the ruby pendant between her breasts. She did not wear her mother's jewelry in public, naturally, she said, but she seldom left the house now, and then only to pick flowers in the garden or take Verity for a run in the park across the street. A footman attended her, she told him when she saw him frown. His father also did once, keeping to a slower pace, but looking at least ten years younger than when he had first arrived. "London, or the countess, appears to agree with him. He is a wonderful, gentle man. I can see why you both admire him so much."

Rex did not admire the earl at all when he interrupted their conversation an hour later, the book long forgotten. He had come to take his turn sitting with his son, he said. Besides, Miss Carville had callers.

Rex told her to stay, especially if the callers were Ashway and his sister again. Amanda was undecided about going until the earl said, "We will manage, my dear. You can leave without worrying about either of us. You cannot keep a Royce down forever, you know."

The earl watched her blush, and frowned at Rex. "Seems that's not all you can't keep down, eh?"

Amanda fled with her book and Rex's dog. The earl watched her leave, then smiled at his son. "I like that girl. I'd be happy to call her daughter."

Rex did not reply, showing a stony face at the overly

personal comment. Besides, he had more than a few bones to pick with his sire.

Lord Royce pulled up the chair where Amanda had been sitting and settled into it. He sighed once, then said, "I suppose you are wishing I called Harry son."

Then he tried to explain why he could not.

Other gentlemen accepted their illegitimate offspring into their homes, he said, but they were always considered less than family, less than acceptable in polite society. That was no way for a boy to grow up, knowing he was not good enough, that his little brother was the chosen one. "But Harry was my son, and I did love him. I would have had him closer, but your mother hated the idea. She was jealous of his mother at first, then jealous of him, thinking I might love him more than you. Her jealousy planted seeds of doubt in my own mind."

Rex sat up against the pillows, pushing away the earl's helping hands. He folded his arms across his chest and declared, "My mother is an honest woman."

"Yes, but she was afraid of me, afraid of you. She loved you, I know, but she did not understand. She said she did not wish any more strange children. That was what she called you, strange. But you were beautiful, a joy, so I took her words to mean she did not want me in her bed. That was when I decided she must prefer some other man. Here I had this wondrous gift for the truth. How could I not use it by asking her?"

"You were a fool."

The earl's head sank to his chest. "I know. And your mother was rightfully insulted past bearing."

"She was more honest than you, keeping my brother from me to hide your own past sins, even after she left us."

"No, it was more than that, I swear. I thought I was acting for Harry's best interests, too, protecting him from the cruelty of his bastardy."

Rex knew that for the truth, although misguided. Who was he to say what was right, what he would have done under the circumstances? He listened as his father went on, desperately trying to make him understand.

"Harry had to make his way in the world. I would have paid for him to live abroad, in India or the colonies. I offered him an allowance, or an estate somewhere, but he would not have it. He had our gift too, of course, and he wanted to use it for the good of the country. The same as you did when you reached manhood," he reminded Rex, calling up memories of arguments about Rex joining the army.

"Harry chose to work in London, where he had been raised. My presence, or yours, would have ruined his chances and embarrassed your mother, dredging up old scandals and new gossip. Harry was doing brilliantly in his chosen career, on his own except for some inquiries and introductions I made for him. Your acknowledging him, coupled with my blighted reputation, could have destroyed the new identity he had, and after the Harrisons did such a fine job of rearing him."

"Harrison? Harris? Major Harrison?" Rex got out of bed and did not fall down this time, his anger strong enough to keep him standing and the room from spinning. He gripped both sides of his father's chair to make sure of his balance, and shouted, "My brother is the Aide? He knew who I was all these years? He put on those ridiculous disguises so I would not recognize him? I'll kill him."

The earl shook his head as if to rid himself of the discordant notes he heard. "That is a lie. You would do no such thing. And Harry constantly goes about incognito; he has too many enemies to do otherwise. Besides, he thought it a great joke. Now get back in bed or I shall call for your mother."

Rex went back, but he was still fuming.

"You must know that Harry has been invaluable to the country. He has also assisted with my work on the coast, putting a stop to the smuggling of state secrets, keeping spies and English gold from traveling between us and France."

"You?"

"And Marceau, of course. You know him as Murchison."

"What, is he a relative, too?"

"No, but his entire family was wiped out by Napoleon and his supporters. We have broken up at least six smuggling rings in the past few years and captured many more spies. What did you think we were doing so close to the coast, if not aiding the war effort?"

Rex had thought his father was moping, in fact, withering into old age. "And you did not tell me? Let me help?"

"You were at university and too young to let you get involved with such dangerous activities. Then you were in the army. Lately I was waiting for you to recover from your wounds, and from your malaise. I was hoping to retire from the spy business, let you and Harry keep England safe."

"He is still a bastard."

That was the truth. By both definitions.

Chapter Twenty-nine

After the earl left, Rex thought about trying to get up again, so he'd be ready to wrestle with his half brother. Maybe tomorrow, he decided when his head started to pound again. No, that was Amanda, tapping softly on his door.

Her cheeks were pale and her lower lip was between her teeth again, not good signs, Rex decided. She asked if she might bring her company to speak with Rex.

Not if it was Ashway, Rex thought. Did that nodcock come to ask his permission to pay his addresses to Amanda? Rex was her guardian, more or less, but he'd be damned before he gave her hand or any part of her to another man, especially one who did not appreciate what a gem she was in herself.

She stayed in the doorway. "My stepbrother and stepsister have come to London to see you. Will you meet them? Are you well enough?"

"Of course." He felt almost well enough to boot Ashway down the stairs. Surely he could see what Sir Frederick's progeny were made of, and whether they intended to do right by their stepsister. They would, by

George, if they wanted that gold from the globe without a fight.

They were young, dressed in deep mourning, and nervous. The sister, Miss Elaine Hawley, squeaked in fear at the sight of Verity, who only wished to make friends, not drool on the chit's skirts, which upset the female worse. She was no beauty, although she was pretty enough in the current fashion, with her blond tresses falling from a topknot to frame a round face, a porcelain complexion, and blue eyes. The girl made a hurried curtsy, then cowered behind Amanda like a frightened fawn, or a seventeen-year-old orphan. Amanda pushed Verity out the door, then pushed Elaine into a chair, the farthest from Rex's bed. The new baronet, Sir Edwin Hawley, a few years older than his sister, showed some mettle, choosing to stand in his countrified tailoring where Rex could see him. After Rex's polite offer of condolences, and the pair's equally stiff inquiries into the state of Rex's health, Amanda said that her relations had things to tell him. She stared from one to the other. "Don't you?"

After a silence that lasted too long, Edwin cleared his throat. "I received notice from the London solicitor about the account you established. Thank you for finding the money and placing it in safekeeping. And for rescuing our sister, of course. I mean to restore what we can to her, once I see where we stand with Father's debts and bills. I know she is not to blame for anything, not the murder." He looked toward his real sister. "Nor the rumors. Tell him."

Elaine was mangling a handkerchief. Amanda took her hand and said, "Just tell him the truth. He will not shout or grow angry, at least not at you." She glared at Rex to make sure he did not frighten the girl more than she already was.

Elaine stammered and turned red, as if she were about to cry. Rex tried to ease the situation by fingering the bandage wrapped around his head. "As you can see, I am rendered harmless. Moreover, I am certain you have done nothing to be ashamed of."

"But I have. I . . . I borrowed Amanda's cape."

Thunderation, he wished he weren't a gentleman, or that Amanda weren't watching. "You . . . you were the one who went out at night to meet a lover?"

"No! That is, yes, I went out, but I met my brother, no one else."

Edwin stepped forward again, ready to defend his sibling. "I came to Town because Elaine wrote how terrible our father was behaving. I naturally knew he was beggaring his estate—he'd tossed me out when we argued about that—but I had no idea he was not letting Amanda wed, or that he was stealing her dowry and her inheritance."

"Worst of all," Elaine piped up, "he was going to arrange a marriage for me, to Lord Thibidoux."

"Thibidoux? What is his given name?"

"Navarre, but why?"

Because N.T. was on Sir Frederick's list and the illustrious Aide had missed that name. And because if Monsieur Thibidoux was a conspirator, Nigel Turlowe was not. Damn.

Amanda hurried to say that the marquess was fifty and fat, lest Rex wonder why an arranged match was worse than stealing one's own stepdaughter's future.

Elaine obviously thought so. "He is French! He already buried two wives in England, and no one knows how many in France. He spoke of his lands there, and how he would recover them soon. I did not want to live in

France!" She looked toward Amanda. "We are still at war with them, aren't we?"

Rex held up a hand to stop the chit's babbling. First things first. "You, Sir Edwin, were in Town when your father was shot?"

Edwin spoke as if he knew what was coming. Of course he did. Everyone knew his father had wiped his hands of Edwin, and was determined to squander Edwin's patrimony. "No, I left three days earlier. I had to consult my own man of business to see what I could do under the conditions of the entail and Amanda's mother's marriage settlements. And no, I did not kill him or pay anyone to do so. I might have wished him to the Devil, but he was my father."

The lad went on to prove his claim, with mention of post chaise schedules, an appointment with his solicitor in Hampshire, a horse fair he visited on his return to the family estate.

All of that was unnecessary, of course. Rex believed him from the first "No." The youth seemed sincere and decent. The sister appeared to be a peagoose. "What about you, Miss Hawley? You wrote for help, and yet you sneaked out of your home, wearing Amanda, Miss Carville's, cloak?"

"My father would be furious if he saw Edwin in the house."

"Yes, I understand why you felt you had to meet elsewhere, but you must have had a cape of your own."

"But Amanda's was warmer."

And far more noticeable. "You did not wish to be recognized as making assignations after dark, I think."

She had the grace to blush and stare at her shoes, the handkerchief in shreds. "I could not let my reputation be ruined. I hoped to marry Martin, you see, then have Amanda come live with us. Martin's parents would not have approved."

"Ah, you were thinking of your stepsister all along?"

Elaine nodded eagerly, missing the sarcasm in his question. "That's right, I was."

Which statement was as red as the girl's cheeks. "What of Amanda's chances for a good marriage?"

The silly twit started weeping.

Exasperated, Rex turned to Amanda. "And you did not protest?"

She handed Elaine a fresh handkerchief before saying, "I thought she was meeting the young man she was enamored of. He returned her affection, but Sir Frederick would never permit them to wed because he was a mere second son."

"But Martin loves me. We were going to elope, if Edwin was willing to help."

Rex held onto his temper by a thread. "And none of you thought the rejected suitor might have been the killer? You did not tell me, Amanda, in order to protect some fool not brave enough to face the girl's father or intelligent enough to plan his own elopement?"

Elaine squealed and hid her face in her hands.

Amanda looked at Rex crossly, as if to blame him for the ninny's tears. "He did not kill Sir Frederick. He was still at Almack's when I left that night, waiting for his one dance with Elaine. There was no need to bring his name, or Elaine's, into this."

Edwin put his arm around his sister to muffle her sobs. "Elaine knows she was wrong. I told her then, but it was too late when I realized the blue cape was not her own. We mean to make it up to Amanda. We'll take her home with us today."

Or carry her to Gretna Green with the young lovers and hide her in Scotland, or put her on a ship somewhere out of reach of Rex. That is, he amended in his own mind, out of reach of British justice. "No, she is bonded into my care. She stays here."

Edwin puffed out his chest, trying to look older, larger, stronger. He looked like a ruffled cockerel instead. "Amanda is my sister. I am head of the household now and I do not think it at all proper for her to be living elsewhere."

"But you thought it seemly for your real sister, who is far younger, to meet you in secret?"

The young man was stymied at that. "But you . . . that is, your reputation . . ."

"Have you heard a single rumor about my mother? Did no one tell you that she is the Countess of Royce, held to be one of the most upstanding ladies in society? She is in residence, as is my father, the earl. Do you actually think either of them would permit anything untoward under their roof? Or that I, as a gentleman, would betray your stepsister's trust in me?"

Elaine must have kicked him, for Edwin bowed. "No offense intended on your esteemed parents, sir, or your honor. But Amanda belongs with us."

"It is too dangerous." Rex touched the bandage on his head. "There are people who do not wish to see her exonerated. They will go to desperate lengths to see your father's murder become a closed case."

"So she said. I cannot like it."

Rex glared at the halfling who wanted to take Amanda

away. "Do you think I enjoy having bricks tossed at me? Your sister is safe here, and respectably chaperoned."

Edwin knew he'd been outgunned. He bowed again. "If you send me a reckoning, I shall pay her way, of course."

"Do not be more of a fool than you have been. Your sister lacks nothing her own godmother cannot supply. You cannot take umbrage at that, can you?"

Edwin swallowed, his pride as well. "Very well, I shall speak to the solicitor about transferring what funds I can to her account, with your permission. My sister's dowry is intact, but she will not be needing it this year while we are in mourning."

Amanda stepped forward, outraged. "I will not take Elaine's dowry!"

Edwin stood firm. "She is too young to wed, and our father stole yours."

Rex respected the young man, although the sister was a twit, and still crying. For the loss of her dowry or the postponement of her elopement, Rex neither knew nor cared. He was only happy the chit was not his responsibility. "I will be happy to sign whatever documents are required to release the funds. I know you will do your best with them."

Amanda silently thanked him with her smile. Then she said, "There is more to tell you."

Damn, Rex was hoping the pair would leave so he could have Amanda to himself again. "Yes?"

The sister stopped acting like a watering pot now that no one was blaming her for anything. "Aunt Hermione went insane after Father's death. She wanted to tear up the carpets and the molding the night before we left for the country. The surgeon had to come and give her laudanum."

Rex started to nod until he remembered his sore head. "She was looking for the money. So she knew her bother had stashed it somewhere."

"But I did not, or I never would have agreed to leave," the girl said. "Except for all the gossip, you know."

She knew Amanda was in prison, and the brat was worried about gossip! Rex glared at the female to go on.

"When . . . when we buried my father, Aunt Hermione started raving at his grave. All the neighbors heard her, and the servants. We thought she was grief stricken, but Amanda thinks it might have something to do with the . . . the crime."

"Continue."

"She raged at our father for not taking her with him as he'd promised. We thought she meant to the grave, which was queer enough, but then she carried on about how he was going to buy a title and take her to court."

"He was going to pay off Prinny's debts in exchange for a barony or some such? His ambition must have known no bounds if his own baronetcy was not good enough."

"Aunt Hermione said he was going to be a count."

"A *comte*," Edwin corrected. "A French noble. We all thought she was turning into a bedlamite, out of shock and sorrow. Father was her only kin, you know."

"But she was not dicked in the nob, was she? Your father told her they were going to France, with his new son-in-law, I suppose. Deuce take it, my cousin was right all along. Hawley was sending money to Napoleon, from the poor fools who thought they could get rich on sunken pirate's loot. He never intended to finance any treasure-hunting expedition, only his own advancement on foreign soil."

Edwin said he thought Rex's assumption sounded correct. "He also wrung what he could from the estate, and stole more from Amanda's inheritance. According to Aunt Hermione, Father was going to have Elaine wed next month by special license. Napoleon was going to win the war, he believed, and the emperor was going to build a new court around himself, full of his loyal supporters. Those who contributed the most money, I suppose."

"We told the neighbors Aunt Hermione was too overwrought to know what she was saying," Elaine told Rex. "Didn't the French try to do away with all the aristocracy?"

"Napoleon is restoring some titles," Rex explained, thinking aloud, "in exchange for loyalty. And money."

Edwin handed his sister yet another handkerchief. "We are hoping you will not spread this around. I'd rather people think Father died during a robbery or whatever, rather than as a traitor."

Rex could not promise silence. "Too many people were involved in his scheming. The Frenchman, his investors, whoever pulled the trigger. But I have a . . . connection who can be very discreet. He'll want to speak with your aunt. Did she come to London with you?"

"Yes, we feared she would do herself harm in the country. Or convince the neighbors that we were all French sympathizers. I do have a servant watching to see if she uncovers more of the missing money."

The lad had a good head on his shoulders. "Good. Make sure she does not leave your house until I can get men there to follow her. Who knows but she might lead us to more of the plotters. In fact, I'll need both of you to promise to stay handy until Amanda is cleared, because we might need your testimony."

"Of course." Edwin shook Rex's hand. "On my honor."

"And your promise, too, Miss Hawley. No elopements. No running off with your young man."

"Oh, I wouldn't do that. Edwin promised I can have a lovely wedding next spring. With flowers and ribbons and—"

Amanda saw Rex's eyes start to cross so she rescued him by hurrying her relatives out to watch Aunt Hermione.

When she came back into the room after seeing them to the door, Rex was making notes on the papers he kept at his bedside. She stepped in quietly, taking the time to study him. The bandage on his head made him look as exotic as a turbaned sheikh, needing only a ruby or an emerald pinned to the front to complete the image of wealth, power, and pride. His nose was nearly straight now, and the day's growth of beard lent a shadowy, raffish look to his strong jaw. He looked up at her with those incredible blue eyes just then and Amanda sighed. Had there ever been a more handsome gentlemen?

He misinterpreted her sigh of appreciation for one of distress. "I am sorry that your relatives' behavior cannot be swept under the carpet." He tore a page from his notebook. "I'll have to send a message about the aunt to Harry, you know."

"I know. Elaine will recover. After all, Aunt Hermione can be considered batty. What is a lunatic to a murderess in the family, or an embezzler, or a traitor, for that matter? And if her Martin loves her, a closet full of skeletons will not deter him."

Rex set his papers and pencil aside and patted the place next to him on the bed.

Amanda looked at the open door, then at Rex smiling

at her. Gracious, could she really be that wanton? His smile widened, showing a dimple on the side of his face that wasn't scarred. She could be. She handed Rex's note to the footman in the hall, telling him to see it was delivered immediately. Then she shut the door, kicked her slippers off, and climbed up to the tall bed. Rex tucked her against his side, where she fit perfectly. She could smell his scented soap, and marveled at his long dark eyelashes. No, there had never been a more handsome gentleman, and she was determined to enjoy his company, and his kisses, while she could. She sighed again, this time in satisfaction and expectation.

This time he ignored her sigh altogether, but did give her shoulders a shake. "You are as much a peagoose as that rattlepate stepsister of yours. I suppose you would not name the chit out of loyalty."

"Not entirely. There was simply no reason to bring her name into your investigation. I told you I knew young Martin could not have killed Sir Frederick."

"But you could have cleared your name of fast behavior, at the least."

Amanda shrugged, rubbing against his chest not quite by accident. "Those who wished to think ill of me were going to, anyway. Elaine could not have weathered the gossip, while I always had your mother's support."

He was still angry. "And that is why you did not go to her years ago, when you realized what that bounder Hawley was doing?"

"Elaine was too young," was all she said.

"You were too good, too loyal, too unselfish. And too closemouthed, dash it. You could have trusted me."

Amanda pulled away a bit. Now a hair could fit between them, if it lay sideways. "That was not my tale to tell, especially not without your trust in return."

It was Rex's turn to sigh. "Yes, it is past time I told you about my family curse. At least the Royces have never produced a ninnyhammer like Elaine."

"She is not a blood relation."

"Thank goodness." He pulled her back, across his lap, in fact, so he could wrap both arms around her. "Remember what I said about the weak chin occurring through generations in certain families?"

She touched his chin, stroking the soft bristle there. "Yours is wondrously fine, square and manly, but with that tiny indentation in the center." She kissed his chin, then used her tongue to measure the size of the cleft. He had to kiss her chin in return, then her eyelids and the tip of her nose, then her lips. Then her lips again, and still.

"Are you well enough for such strenuous activity?" Amanda asked when they paused to breathe.

"Seeing as how I will likely expire soon if I do not make love to you, I am fine." He kissed her once more, long and deep, their tongues taking turns. "As long as I do not move too fast."

"I am not in a hurry." Pleasure like this was far too delicious to rush.

Rex smiled, changing the kiss from sensuous to silly. Amanda found she liked that, too, especially when he said how much he had missed her.

"Me, too. But is this a ploy, Lord Rexford, to keep from telling me your deep, dark secret?"

"No, it is to keep you here, in my arms."

"In that case, it is working, on both scores. I am not leaving, and your entire family might turn into werewolves once a month. I do not care."

"It's the truth."

She let her hand drift down his chest over his nightshirt, then lower. "What, that you howl at the moon?"

Rex was already ready to howl, but he did not stop her hand. He bent his head to lick at the soft skin that rose above the low neckline of her gown, while his own hand crept under her skirt to her ankle, her calf, her thigh, her hidden curls. "Do you believe in magic?"

"I do now."

Chapter Thirty

"We've got him, Rex!" Daniel shouted up the stairs from the front entry. "We've got him!"

Rex did not care if his cousin had Bonaparte by the ballocks right then, but Amanda quickly leaped off the bed and tried to find her shoes. She should have been trying to fasten the back of her gown, Rex thought as his cousin burst into the room, Verity leaping beside him in matching exuberance. Rex stood to shield Amanda from Daniel's view.

"We've got Brusseau!" Daniel skidded to a halt, tripping over the dog. "I say, sorry for not knocking. Um, Rex, had you ought to be doing what you are?"

"Getting out of bed? I am nearly recovered." He wasn't. His head ached, and so did the seat of his unsatisfied desire.

"That ain't what I meant."

Doing up Amanda's gown? Rex did not think that was what Daniel meant, either. He did not wish to discuss the matter. "How did you find Brusseau?"

"He was boarding one of Johnston's ships with the crewmen, carrying a trunk, making a getaway. He didn't walk like any sailor, though, or talk like one. Remember that captain we talked to about going after that sunken pirate gold? It was his ship Brusseau was boarding, and the captain said he never saw the bloke before."

"Where is he?"

"Downstairs in the butler's pantry, trussed like a Christmas goose. Dimm and his nephew are keeping watch. I thought we ought to wait for Harry. I promised to let him know when we had the villain in chains." He looked toward Amanda, gauging if she could be trusted. "National security, don't you know."

"I sent for him an hour ago." Rex told Daniel about Amanda's relatives' visit and what they had learned. "He should be on his way. Bring them all up when he gets here."

"Up here?"

"I doubt my mother would welcome the interview in her drawing room. Besides, I don't think I am ready for the stairs."

Daniel muttered, "You didn't think you were ready for leg shackles, either."

Rex shot a dark look at his cousin, but smiled for Amanda as he finished with the bothersome buttons and ties. "You better leave, my dear. This could get ugly."

"You are not going to . . . ? That is, you wouldn't . . . ?" She looked from Daniel to Rex.

"Beat the truth out of the valet? Is that what you still think of the Inquisitors? No, we will not harm him—"

"Unless he tries to escape," Daniel interrupted, grinning wickedly.

"He is tied up. But we might have to strip off his clothes to see if Verity left bite marks. You would be embarrassed."

"Oh, of course. But you do not think he is the killer, do you?"

"No, we already asked that."

"You believed what he told you? The man was trying to leave the country!"

Both cousins shrugged.

Harry arrived, apologizing for not putting Thibidoux's name on the initials list. "We were aware of his presence, of course, but we thought he was a Royalist, waiting for the Corsican's defeat to claim his ancestral lands. Instead, it seems, he was trying to buy them back from Napoleon. I am not perfect, as you must know by now. "

If that was an apology for the disguises and deceptions, Rex was not accepting. "We will discuss your lack of perfection in a few weeks, brother, at Gentleman Jackson's Boxing Parlor. Perhaps you might tell me, meanwhile, how Lydia Burton's name *did* get on your list."

Harry laughed. "She's an old friend who wanted to meet you, that's all. I couldn't resist."

"Maybe you prefer pistols to fisticuffs?"

Daniel was trying to figure which brother to place his money on when Lord Royce entered the room. They all knew the case was far beyond a murder investigation by now and the earl wanted to hear what went forward, too. The safety of the kingdom might be at stake, to say nothing of his wife's godchild. The dear girl could be more if his sap-skulled son could be brought up to scratch, the gudgeon. Heaven knew the countess was practically throwing them together these days, hoping nature and youth would get the job done. If Amanda's tousled look when she hurried past him in the hall were any indication, his wife was right and he'd hear wedding bells soon. He just did not want to hear the patter of little feet first. Lud knew there was enough scandal in the family already. But a grandson, ah, that was enough to warm an old man's heart, if his wife's welcome hadn't already. The earl's joy would be complete if they could not only free Amanda of suspicion, but connect Nigel Turlowe to the crime.

Inspector Dimm and his grandnephew Clarence dragged Brusseau into the room. Clarence left and Dimm went to stand by the window, observing the Royce males, thinking what a rare tale he'd have to tell his own grandsons.

There were so many truth-seers in one place a lie could not have gone unnoticed if it hid under the carpet.

"Wait," Rex told them. "Get Amanda to identify the man as her stepfather's valet first."

"But both of us questioned him before," Daniel complained.

"This has to be a thorough interview, following proper procedure. Don't you agree, Mr. Dimm?"

The Runner scratched his head. He'd never heard of conducting a murder investigation in a swell's bedroom, surrounded by that same nob's relatives, while the gent wore a robe, a bandage with a flower stuck in it, and no shoes. "Seems all right to me."

They sent for Amanda, who nodded. "That is Brusseau," she said. Then they ushered her from the room again.

Brusseau was shaking, looking from one to the other. "My name is Brusseau. I did not kill Monsieur Hawley. I did not throw a brick at Monsieur Rexford."

Damn.

Rex saw blue. His father heard a clear chime. Daniel felt no itch, and Harry tasted his own disappointment.

"Do you know who did?" Harry asked.

"My name is Brusseau. I did not kill Monsieur Hawley. I did not throw a brick at Monsieur Rexford." This time the valet said it in French. It was still true.

Lord Royce asked, "Do you know Sir Nigel Turlowe?"

Brusseau repeated his rote statement.

Daniel flexed his knuckles. Harry cleaned his fingernails with a wicked-looking knife that had been up his sleeve. Dimm cleared his throat until they both stepped away from the prisoner.

Damn.

Dimm suggested they strip him.

There was no need, but they did it anyway. The man had no bites, no bruises, and not a lot to be modest about.

Rex cursed again. "He didn't throw the brick, the dog didn't take a chunk out of him. He's not guilty, as far as I can see."

"But he was trying to escape," Daniel said. He must be guilty of something."

No one noticed Murchison in the corner until he made a snorting sound in disgust. "His name. Ask him that."

"We know he is Brusseau."

"His first name." Murchison turned his back and started to tidy the room.

Brusseau would not answer that question.

Dimm pulled the man's papers from his own pocket, the ones they'd taken along with knives, pistols, and a sack of coins from Brusseau's trunk. The Bow Street Runner adjusted his spectacles.

"Is your name Claude?"

No answer.

Four voices almost shouted: "Yes or no, damn it." Four angry men advanced on one naked Frenchman.

"Yes."

That was the truth, they all agreed, and Dimm nodded, handing the Frenchman his clothes. That was the name on the papers.

Rex consulted his own notes. "But the valet's name is Jean!"

Murchison wore a smug smile. "Twins." Then he left, taking Amanda's lace garter with him.

Rex and Amanda were taking up where they'd left off, this time with the door locked. And they were in the stuffed chair instead of the bed, making their tryst a sliver more respectable. A thin sliver.

Amanda was trying to understand their conclusions, while Rex was trying to unfasten her gown again.

She batted his hand away. "So the twin took the valet's place, and told the truth when you asked him? That means we are no closer to finding the real killer."

"Much closer." Rex pulled her back against him, much closer. "Claude admitted that he and Jean exchanged identities regularly, so they were familiar with each other's households. Now we have reason to hold him for further questioning."

"But the real valet, Jean, is gone. Claude would not say where?"

"We'll find him."

"Not if he has gone back to France." She touched his cheek. "Rex, let me go."

He took his arms from around her, reluctantly.

"No, I mean let me leave England. Let me flee. You might never find the real valet, never be able to clear my name. They will demand the trial be held sooner or later, no matter how many debts your father calls in, and I cannot prove my innocence. Even if no one can prove my guilt, I cannot stay on with your parents. Have you noticed they are smelling of orange blossoms? They need their privacy after so many years apart. Nor can I go back to live with my stepfamily. Why, to plan Elaine's wedding? There would always be a taint to my name, no matter what."

He held onto her arms. "No!"

"But I need to go. You must see that. You do not need to help or even know the details. In fact you can say I overpowered you. I'll hit you over the head again to make it look real, although that would hurt me, too. Let me go, Rex!"

"I cannot."

"Your honor is satisfied if you are unconscious. And mine is also, for I never gave my word not to go. You have tried your best, I know, and I am grateful. Now do not make me wait for a trial, to become a headline in the scandal sheets again, to be placed on view as an accused murderess. Sir Nigel will not accept the word of a sneaky French valet. Or of you or your cousin. We have no proof!"

"We'll find Jean."

"We might not!" She stared at the window, her lip trembling.

Rex had to concede the possibility. Thibidoux had already left London, for who knew where, before they knew to question him. Dimm's men were looking, Harry's, too, but another servant in a nondescript coach, another guard sitting with the driver, meant there were too many chances for Jean to slip through the web. Rex gently tugged on one of Amanda's curls so she would turn to face him again. "A few more days, my dear, and then we will leave together."

"Together? You would flee England to live elsewhere?"

"I don't think I can live anywhere you are not, my love."

"But what about your honor, your given word?"

"You asked me once which I valued more, my good name or your life. I choose you."

Tears welled in Amanda's eyes as she threw herself back against the viscount's chest. "Oh, Rex. I do love you."

After an earthshaking, chair-rocking kiss, Rex told her, "There can be no more lies between us. I love you. And who knows how much good our sons can do in the world, even if not in England?"

"Our sons? You intend to have children?"

"I intend to make love to my wife, constantly and with great enthusiasm. Children are the usual result."

"You would marry me?"

"We sure as Hades do not need any more bastards on the Royce family tree."

"But all of your oaths, all of your vows to remain unwed and—"

He silenced her with another kiss while he tugged down her bodice. "One more week. If we cannot find the valet in a week, we'll leave. But we will find him, or information about him. We think we know where to look. Only one man outside the family could have briefed the valet to speak the truth and nothing else."

"I do not understand."

"And you will not, not ever. No one can, not even us." He took a deep breath. "The Royce men, and Daniel, through his mother somehow, can tell truth from lies."

"No, that is impossible."

"And that was a red falsehood, my dear. Try again."

Her brows knit in concentration as she tried to comprehend what he was saying, while ignoring what his hands were doing. "I love you."

He smiled. "True-blue. Try again."

"Very well, I do not love you."

"That would break my heart if it were true. Luckily for me, it is a lie, a cherry-red falsehood. And do not even try to say you do not like my lovemaking, for your own body tells the truth. Here." He bent his head to kiss her taut nipple, already pressing toward him. "And here." He put his hand between her thighs, where she was wet and warm with wanting him.

"This does not lie, either," she said, wrapping her hand around the hard length of him.

"Aah. Never. Try again."

"You are the best lover in the world?"

"Hm. That one is a rainbow, which means you hope it's true, and that's all that matters. Of course I intend to be your only lover."

"Of course," she echoed, then asked, "You really can tell truth from falsehood? And your father and your half brother, and Daniel?"

"All of us. Our sons will be able to also, in varied forms, with all the trouble it can cause. Daniel gets rashes, which is why he is not welcome at Almack's. All the lies people tell have him scratching furiously until people think he has lice or something."

Amanda laughed. "The dowagers and doyennes of polite society do not lie."

"No?" Rex raised his voice in a chirping falsetto. " 'I am so happy you came tonight, my dear.' That is a lie. The matron wishes you to perdition because you are prettier than her own daughter. 'You are looking lovely.' A lie. This patroness thinks your gown is too revealing." He smiled. "I myself adore it."

Amanda was giggling at his imitation of the *ton*'s affectations. "Stop. I can see where poor Daniel would be uncomfortable."

"My father used to work with the courts, for justice. Harry, well, Harry helps at the War Office. I suppose he helped Daniel and me develop our evil reputations, instead of letting the family affliction become known. We pretended to be ruthless interrogators, rather than have people believe we were sorcerers or some such. I have been helping Inspector Dimm, telling him which alibi is honest, which claim of innocence is a falsehood. It never fails. Now that you know the truth, will you still have me?"

"True love never fails, either."

Then he explained about his parents, about his father's jealousies, his mother's fears.

"I could never be afraid of you."

Which deserved another kiss, and another explanation of how the family gift tore apart the family, and why the unearthly trait had to be hidden.

"But your parents always loved each other, didn't

they? They are so joyous in their reunion that they forget to chaperon us altogether."

"Excellent parents, don't you think?"

She agreed by wriggling on his lap until he groaned.

"I . . . I don't know where I'd be without them."

"You would not be half as special, or half as dear to me."

Chapter Thirty-one

Amanda was packing. She wondered who could help sell some of her jewelry without becoming implicated in her escape.

Rex was pacing, going over lists of every place searched, every suspect questioned.

Harry and Dimm and Daniel were pursuing every lead or hint or purchased bit of information.

Lord and Lady Royce were planning their futures, together.

One day went by. Two.

Rex was feeling better, enough that he set himself up as a target in the park at dusk. No one bothered him, except Daniel, who was forced to stay behind, since such a large man did not skulk well. Harry did, of course, disguised as the old man again.

Three.

Amanda was in a panic. Would Rex really go with her? How would she live alone, without him?

Rex was in a quandary. How could he leave England, never to return, giving up his new work with Dimm, his family, his estate? He did care about the earldom after all, it seemed, now that he might lose it. And where could he go to keep Amanda safe?

His parents were in the conservatory, with the door locked.

Four days.

Rex decided to take Amanda to the theater, with her relations, Sir Edwin and his sister. Daniel refused the invitation, as did the Hawleys' aunt Hermione. The earl and the countess attend as chaperons, and simply their presence together diverted some of the attention from Amanda, but not much, not with the way she was dressed. She did wear a gray gown, the color of which was suitable for mourning, but in watered silk that shimmered—what there was of it. She decided to wear her mother's diamonds, proper or not, to fill in part of the low décolletage. She no longer cared what anyone in the audience thought, and she might have to sell the glittering necklace and matching bracelet tomorrow. Besides, the matching sparkle in Rex's eyes was worth the raised brows and clucking tongues.

Her stepsister wore severe black, with no jewelry. She complained throughout the first act of looking like a crow, especially next to Amanda. Then her beau Martin arrived at the intermission. He thought she looked beautiful.

"He really does, you know. He's not simply being polite," Rex whispered in Amanda's ear, ruffling the black feather that curled down her cheek from a black velvet headband, tickling her skin. Or was that his warm breath that had her tingling, or simply his nearness? Amanda touched the necklace and turned away, knowing both the diamonds and her happiness were to be sacrificed soon.

Five days.

*   *   *

"You're free, darling!" He swung her up in his arms and around in a circle, laughing.

"You can put her down now, Harry," Rex said dryly, but he was grinning, too.

"I am free? You found Brusseau?"

Daniel stooped over and kissed her cheek. "It is true! Not the way we planned, but true."

Daniel and Harry took turns explaining the recent events, interrupting each other constantly. As near as Amanda could understand, Sir Frederick's deranged sister, Miss Hermione Hawley, never left the house, watched so carefully by her niece and nephew. So Rex took it upon himself to see what she would do if given free rein. What she did, sure enough, was creep out of the house while they were all at the theater, telling the servants, who were now on Rex's payroll, besides young Edwin Hawley's, that she was taking a donation to the nearest orphanage.

"I told you, didn't I?" Daniel crowed. "That friend of my sister's who eloped did the same thing. Charity, my arse, and especially at night. Sorry, my dear. If you see a trunk full of clothes being loaded on a hackney, worry."

Amanda's satchels were already hidden, one by one, behind the garden shed. At least she was not claiming to be giving her wardrobe away.

Rex was furious. "Why did no one send for me?"

Daniel looked at Harry, who looked back. "The sawbones said you shouldn't do anything strenuous for another week."

Amanda said, "I did not know that!" then blushed.

Rex said what he thought of the surgeon's edict, in one short word that made her blush deepen. "You should have sent for me!" he insisted.

Harry shrugged. "The family hope, don't you know."

"Do not protect me, not ever again, either one of you, do you hear?"

Amanda liked that the others watched out for Rex. "Do you want to argue or do you want to know what happened next?"

Rex conceded. "Go on."

"Our men followed the hackney and sent messages back," Harry continued the story. "Your guess was a good one, Rex," he added to appease the viscount. "And paying the Hawley servants was a downy notion, too. Some of them took off after the hackney, also."

"She did not go to any orphanage, did she?" Amanda wanted to know.

"Of course not," Daniel said with a snort.

Rex guessed she went to Sir Nigel's house.

"Exactly." Daniel admitted he was all for barging into the barrister's residence, but Harry said no, Miss Hawley and Sir Nigel were not doing anything wrong that anyone knew. Perhaps they were lovers, having a tryst.

Daniel made another rude noise. "Harry never met the aunt."

Then both of them got in the same hackney, with one of Sir Nigel's servants.

"Brusseau?" Amanda asked. "The other brother, Jean, the real valet?"

"Exactly!"

"Did you arrest them then?"

"No, we decided to see where they went." Daniel told how he and Harry followed behind on horses, with a coach full of Bow Street Runners coming after the Hawley servants' coach. They all went to Grave's End, where Sir Nigel anchored his private yacht, which was under watch by the Royal Navy and the Revenuers, again at Rex's urging.

"You arrested them before they boarded the yacht, didn't you?"

"Not exactly."

"Explain."

Neither Harry nor Daniel wanted to relate the next part. Finally Harry spoke up while Daniel poured them all glasses of wine. Inspector Dimm, it seemed, as the officer in charge of the murder investigation, ordered the suspects to halt as soon as they left the coach at the dock area. They did not. Sir Nigel and Brusseau ran for a rowboat that could take them to the yacht, with Hermione Hawley screeching behind them. Daniel and Harry and some of the Bow Street Runners ran after them. So did the Hawley servants who were promised part of the reward.

Sir Nigel leaped for the boat. Daniel leaped for Brusseau, who could not go as fast because of a bandaged leg, and dragged him back to the dock. He had his hands on Brusseau's neck. "Say it." He did not have to spell out what he wanted; he did tighten his grip on the valet's throat.

"I . . . I killed Sir Frederick."

"And Lord Rexford?"

"I hit him with the brick. If the cursed *chien* hadn't been hanging on my leg, I'd have killed him, too, and we could have gotten away."

Everyone heard him, right before they heard Sir Nigel shoot him from the rowboat. The barrister threw his empty gun aside and leaped into the water. Harry was stuck holding Hermione Hawley from leaping after. He pushed her into the arms of some of her former servants and jumped into the boat.

The crew of Sir Nigel's yacht sent a boat out to haul their master aboard. One of the Revenue officers sent out a skiff. They started shooting at each other. Then another ship, a merchantman in the distance, weighed anchor, set sail, and surprised them all by sending a broadside at the navy cutter. The merchantman, they later learned, was one of Johnston's traders. He'd been hiding out, ready to make his getaway too, as soon as Sir Nigel paid him his share. The harbor was all smoke and sails and shouts and small boats colliding, oarsmen falling overboard, servants screaming. The cutter tried to come about to stop the merchantman before it reached open waters. No one got to Sir Nigel in time.

"He got away?"

"He drowned. We fished him out. The navy boarded Johnston's ship and found Breverton—with the money from the bank! And Thibidoux, too. We got them all! Neither turncoat nor tuppence got to France to finance Bonaparte and his plan to conquer England and the world. All the ships were confiscated, the crews arrested, several fortunes rescued. The War Office is delighted, the navy and the Excise officers are fighting over the prizes, and we are all heroes!"

Amanda was happy for them, of course, but still worried about her own future. "But if Brusseau is dead, how will I prove my innocence? The others were traitors who sought to buy titles and lands at the expense of their own country, but the charges against me are not a matter of the nation's welfare."

Daniel and Harry reassured her. Scores of people heard Jean's confession, and his twin brother confirmed everything when he realized he was an accomplice to a huge failed plot. Claude confessed his part, and his brother's, in

front of Dimm and his superiors. There was no hint of co-
ercion, no chance of a lie.

As Rex and his parents expected, Sir Nigel was behind
it all. Sir Frederick never had the wit to think up the false
investment scheme, only lofty ambitions and greed. He
followed Sir Nigel's plan, but then he was going to cut Sir
Nigel out of the profits, to use Thibidoux and Johnston to
get to France. He'd been a problem from the first, scrimping on his payments, which cut down on Sir Nigel's influence with the French, and leaving too many trails back to
the barrister. He had to be eliminated. Jean Brusseau carried out Sir Nigel's orders while Claude was seen in a pub,
then switched places with his twin. Claude could deny
everything without perjury. Jean left the gun to point the
blame toward one of the investors, all of whom had good
motives.

Harry concluded: "Amanda's appearance merely
stirred up Sir Nigel's ill will toward Lord Royce and gave
him a way to revenge himself on the countess and further
discredit the family. He had his own obsessions, beyond
money and foreign titles."

Daniel finished: "Everything is neatly tied, with no
loose ends. Unlike Rex's neckcloth."

While Rex hastily repaired his cravat, Harry told
Amanda, "You are free to go, free to stay. Free to live the
rest of your life any way you want."

Daniel handed them each a glass and raised his in a
toast. "To Amanda and her future."

Amanda kissed him. Then she kissed Harry.

"What about me?" Rex asked. "It was my idea that
Miss Hawley would lead us to Sir Nigel, and I was the one
who ordered a watch on his yacht."

So Amanda kissed him, too.

Daniel and Harry left—Amanda and Rex did not notice—and went to inform the earl and the countess, who kissed them both, too, then each other. With Sir Nigel not only dead but a proven traitor, no one would doubt the earl. They had another toast to a better future.

Daniel and Harry went to Lydia Burton's bordello to celebrate the present, and their new partnership in saving the country.

Amanda and Rex chose a more private celebration.

Amanda put her hand over Rex's heart so she could feel it beating. "What do you think will happen to Aunt Hermione?"

Rex pulled a blanket over them both, then lay back against the pillows. "I suppose she might be released to her nephew's care. After all, everyone thought she was insane to start with. He might have to swear to lock her up, but Dimm can ask for clemency. I don't know that she actually did anything wrong."

"And what about the money? The government took all of it, even what you took from Sir Frederick for Edwin and me."

"And the Crown hates to part with a shilling, but they'll have to. It will take a Solomon to figure out who gets what, the bank customers, the swindled investors, the relatives, and the men who made the arrests."

"Your father could distribute it justly."

He kissed the top of her head. "Excellent idea. I will get Harry working on that. He can see it done. Father will see that you get your fair share. You deserve it for the treatment they gave you." He kissed her again, then turned to look into her brown eyes, tenderly cradling her cheek in his palm. "But will you still marry me, angel, when you get the gold? You can do whatever you wish now—stay with my mother or help your stepbrother plan his sister's wedding. You can travel, you can set up your own establishment with a paid companion. You can marry Ashway."

She placed two fingers over his mouth. "You can be quiet now. I know what I can do, and what I want to do. I told you I love you. But what about you? You are done with me and my woes, so what do you want?"

He kissed her fingers, then took them into his mouth. "I want to be doing what we are doing right now."

"No, after that."

"Oh, I thought we could do it again. I will never be done."

"Rex, I am serious. You can go back to the army, or work with Bow Street. Your father might take up his career as a justice, so you could help him. Or you could mind the family estates while he is in Town. You could have any female in London. Or every one, while you are free."

"Every female in London? My, you do think a lot of my stamina. But I want only one woman for the rest of my life, one who will help me decide what to do, where to live. This one, the one I love."

"What color do you see?"

"True-blue, my love, true-blue."

Epilogue

A few months later, Amanda was again in Rex's arms, in the bed they shared at Royce House in London. The earl and the countess were traveling, and Daniel had taken up bachelor quarters with Harry. "Have I told you lately that I love you, Lord Rexford?"

"Not lately enough, Lady Rexford. Lud, I cannot believe you are really my wife, or how happy one man can be."

"I hope you will be even happier at my news. I am going to have a baby."

Rex's brow puckered. "I am sorry, angel, but you are not."

"But the physician said I am breeding."

He shook his head. "The color does not lie."

She started to weep, there in his arms. "I wanted this child so badly, to raise with pride in his gifts, pride in his father and grandfather, his Uncle Harry, and Daniel. I must be going to lose the infant."

He was confused, but certain of what he saw. "No. That is not true, either."

She shoved away his arms. "Well, which is it? Either I am going to have a baby or I am not."

He thought for a minute. "You said *his* gifts. Are you carrying a son?"

"How should I know?"

"Guess."

"Your father wants an heir, so yes. I am carrying a son."

"That's true."

"How can that be?"

"Are you having a daughter?"

She smiled, beginning to see. "Your mother always wanted a little girl to pamper. Yes, I am having a daughter!"

"Twins, my love. You are not having *a* baby! You are having two! *We* are having two! Now I am doubly happy."

"And I love you twice as much, Lord Rexford."

"Truly, my lady?"

"Would I lie to you?"

BARBARA METZGER
The Hourglass

Coryn, Earl of Ardeth, has spent an eternity in Hell. Fed up, he gambles with the Devil and wins a second chance: if he can find his heart, his soul, and his hourglass in six months, he can return to life. Then he meets Genie, a disgraced water-girl at the Battle of Waterloo. Now, her only hope is this crazy stranger—and she's half-terrified of and half-in-love with the eccentric Earl. Together they have to find his humanity, her social acceptance, and overcome someone bent on destroying their lives.

Available wherever books are sold or at penguin.com

BARBARA METZGER

Ace of Hearts

Book One of the *House of Cards* trilogy

Never did Alexander "Ace" Endicott,
the Earl of Carde, imagine himself to be
thrice-betrothed against his will by the doings of
three desperate debutantes. So he escapes
London for his property in the country, where
he follows through with his father's last wish—
to find his long-lost step-sister.
But the search takes a detour, leading him to
Nell, and forcing him to wonder if two
mismatched lovers can make a royal pair.

**ALSO AVAILABLE
in the *House of Cards* trilogy**

*JACK OF CLUBS
QUEEN OF DIAMONDS*

Available wherever books are sold or at
penguin.com